FEEDERS

FEEDERS

A Novel

MATT SERAFINI

G

GALLERY BOOKS

*New York   Amsterdam/Antwerp   London
Toronto   Sydney/Melbourne   New Delhi*

G

Gallery Books
An Imprint of Simon & Schuster, LLC
1230 Avenue of the Americas
New York, NY 10020

This book is a work of fiction. Any references to historical events, real people, or real places are used fictitiously. Other names, characters, places, and events are products of the author's imagination, and any resemblance to actual events or places or persons, living or dead, is entirely coincidental.

First Gallery Books trade paperback edition May 2025

GALLERY BOOKS and colophon are registered trademarks of Simon & Schuster, LLC

Simon & Schuster strongly believes in freedom of expression and stands against censorship in all its forms. For more information, visit BooksBelong.com.

For information about special discounts for bulk purchases, please contact Simon & Schuster Special Sales at 1-866-506-1949 or business@simonandschuster.com.

The Simon & Schuster Speakers Bureau can bring authors to your live event. For more information or to book an event, contact the Simon & Schuster Speakers Bureau at 1-866-248-3049 or visit our website at www.simonspeakers.com.

Interior design by Hope Herr-Cardillo

Manufactured in the United States of America

10   9   8   7   6   5   4   3   2   1

Library of Congress Cataloging-in-Publication Data

ISBN 978-1-6680-6097-1
ISBN 978-1-6680-6098-8 (ebook)

For Michelle

He was a God who observed without intervening in this hell he created.

—David Morrell, *Creepers*

PART I

Hazy Shade of Influencer

Annabeth Dies at the End

Kylie Bennington watches her dad pull from the driveway. He gives a limp "see you" wave through the half-cracked window as his taillights disappear into the night. Then she's alone in the dark. As usual.

Instagram glows hot in her palm, lighting the way as she moves to the front porch, sidestepping the yard equipment that Mom has neglected to pick up for going on two months now. Her phone dings as she nears the door.

Erin:

Home yet?

Kylie's thumb smashes the green FaceTime button before her device can get a ring off, and then she's looking into Erin's bedroom, a scrawl of summer clothes strewn across woolly pink carpet.

"Did I lend you my linen skirt?" Erin asks.

"Funny."

"The one from the beach. Short. Kinda see-through when the sun hits it just right?"

"When do you lend me anything?"

"That's what's bothering me."

"Why don't you just message the label? Have them send you another?"

"Because I think I actually bought this one."

"Ah, the rare designer that isn't comping your wardrobe."

"Never pay if you can help it."

"Yes, well, some of us plebs have no choice."

"You'll get there," Erin says. "You're my long-term project. Gonna prove the Erin Palmer Method is bulletproof. They'll pay me to speak at conferences and shit."

Kylie finds her way by cell phone light through the darkened house. A note on the kitchen table says there's a bowl of spinach salad in the fridge and is signed, "Love, Mom."

She takes it out, sets it aside.

"Off-white," Erin's saying. "More like cream, I guess?"

But Kylie's distracted, barely listening as she pulls open every cabinet.

"Assume I find it," Erin continues. "It's appropriate to wear. Right?"

"Um, sure?" Kylie's rummaging through the refrigerator for the tuna steak she'd asked Mom to buy.

"Yeah," Erin states. "I think it's appropriate. It says, '*I'm grieving, but not at the expense of comfort.*'"

"You're not grieving because nobody's dead."

Erin flips the phone around and stares. The remnants of a clay mask at her hairline. "Kylie. She's been missing since April."

"*Missing*," Kylie emphasizes. "Annabeth is missing."

"And her parents sold the house and left town."

"She was a friend and—"

"In the fourth grade." Erin brushes a couple of stacks of fall wear off the edge of her bed, done with this conversation. "Another outfit, I suppose. But what, though?" The camera slips down and she's topless.

"God, Erin, put something on. I know your tan lines better than my own."

"Speaking of which, we should totally get back indoors. I'm over the sun. Look at this—see these freckles above my boobs?"

Kylie minimizes the screen instead and toggles to a recipe for mustard-seared tuna. It's a lap around the kitchen to gather the ingredients.

This is where it gets hard:

It isn't enough to cook the tuna steak to taste. It needs to *look* good.

She pulls a frying pan from the storage cabinet and places it on the stove. Then she fills a mixing bowl with maple syrup, Dijon mustard, lemon juice, oil, and crushed red pepper and whisks it all together into a texture that's heavy but smooth.

"Why does your evening sound more interesting than mine?" Erin asks.

Kylie sets aside four teaspoons of syrup mixture and drops the tuna steak inside the bowl, coating it on all sides. "It's not."

A smidge of oil hits the pan, and she waits for the heat while Erin starts talking about her date with Cameron. How he'd been the perfect gentleman tonight and how that was . . . really pretty boring.

"I mean, he barely made a move." Erin says this with genuine disbelief and a dash of offense. "How many TikTok boys would kill for this opportunity?"

Kylie's no longer listening, too focused on the task at hand: getting a Gordon Ramsay sear on this tuna. Ninety seconds of heat on each side. Done. The smell is sweet and savory, and it's time to think about plating.

Now Erin's going off on Cameron's arms and how she's addicted to the feel of his bulges on her fingertips.

And Kylie's setting the tuna down on a dish, carving it into careful slices. The inside is noticeably redder. Good. Perfect for contrast.

She plates it alongside some leftover potatoes and green beans, grateful that no one would really be able to tell they're not freshly made, then drizzles the remaining syrup over everything. The smell is vaguely tempting.

Next, Kylie sights the dish through her phone's camera, pacing the kitchen, searching out the best vantage. She takes a snap. Then another. One more. Yeah. Any of these will work.

"Now that you've heard the argument, Your Honor, let me ask: Do I see him again?"

"Yes," Kylie says, hoping she hasn't spaced on any traumatizing details.

"Good. I mean, I was gonna do it anyway, but it's nice for us to be on the same page."

Kylie carries the plate through the house, to the living room doors that open into the backyard. She places it down on the brick patio there and calls out, "Sporto!"

An excited huff spins up in response, bushes rustling, the floodlight kicking on, catching the graying snout of the neighbor's collie as he pushes through the shrubs.

"Good boy," Kylie coos and closes the door. She takes a can of flavored seltzer from the fridge and carries the spinach salad upstairs.

"Hello?" Erin's extra annoyed by this radio silence.

"I'm listening. I'm here."

"You sure?"

"Whatever. I don't want you watching me eat anyway. Text."

"Ugh, such a prude. I've got a shirt on now."

"Even so." Kylie ends the call before Erin can respond. She enters her room, kicking the door closed, dropping onto the bed beneath the Katy Perry poster she's had pinned there since kindergarten. She runs the tuna photo through Lightroom, toggling her preferred filters until one makes the syrup pop just right.

She captions it, **Hungry?** and adds the hashtags: **#Instagood**, **#yum**, **#homemade**, **#eeeeeats**, and **#foodie** before blasting it off into social space.

Twenty hearts come back in the blink of an eye.

With her social life fed, Kylie starts in on Mom's spinach salad as a stream of notifications fills her phone. Not bad for a modest four thousand followers. Nothing compared to Erin's sixty thou, but not bad.

Someone called @JordanGentleman comments in all caps: **SHE EVEN COOKS! PERFECT WOMAN.** Kylie taps his name to get a better look. His face is hidden and his shirtless dad bod might be okay if not for the disgusting Brillo curls covering it.

He looks like the type of guy who sends dick pics for a living, but Kylie doesn't block him.

Erin:

watcha eating?

Kylie:

spinach

knew it . . . lying bitch lol

Erin understands that performance is all that matters. Her audience is composed entirely of men like @JordanGentleman who follow a thousand girls just like her, and whose comments are always on the edge of inappropriateness.

Sometimes Kylie wonders why she and Erin cater to cretins, and Erin's always quick to remind her that it doesn't matter. Let them be perverts, so long as they're perverts who follow and like.

Erin's enough of an influencer to get an annual VidCon invitation. She's paid to attend club openings all over New England, despite being two years under the drinking age, and comes home to daily packages of product and clothing. Most recently, it was a pair of Amina Muaddi Belgian satin slingback pumps, pointed toes with crystal embellishments, that forced Kylie to suffer an existential crisis. Genuine fears of, *It's never going to happen for me.*

Kylie works hard to catch Erin without ever coming close, always five steps behind, like she's come in at the tail end of a good thing, like when there's no more room at the table.

She wedges AirPods into her ears as she eats the salad, streaming Katy Perry's *Witness*—an underrated album the critics simply did not get. *Spin* wrote that it was "a spectacular failure," *Rolling Stone* dismissed it as "art pop soup," and everyone failed to recognize its purpose: depicting a world where the barriers between celebrities and normies has come all the way down, leaving everyone to grapple with the same problems, relationships, self-censorship, and relevancy in a distracted world.

Kylie scrolls the 'gram, giving out hearts like Halloween candy.

Until Erin's post stops her cold.

A topless photo that's cut off right above Erin's breasts so that only the rounds of her Cs—and those sun freckles—are visible. Her hair's soaking wet and draped over her forehead. The smile on her face, suggestive and naughty. The caption: **Ready for bed.** 😛

Nine. Thousand. Hearts.

"You couldn't let me win, could you?" Kylie's voice cracks, nostrils flaring. It's how it is when a friendship is fundamentally made up of a bundle of raw nerves.

Kylie's dinner post is performing fine—fifty-two hearts and counting. But the victory's tainted.

Her stomach rumbles and she wishes she'd eaten the goddamn tuna as she refreshes her post, about to cross one hundred. Waiting for a certain someone to be among the hearts.

Shit. She promised herself she wasn't going to do this but can't help it. Brady's off at Williamson University, sure, but he has notifications for Kylie's content. So why hasn't he liked it yet?

She goes to his feed and checks to see if she'd somehow missed any of his posts. Impossible, given her own settings. The two of them are so entwined that the algorithm would never be able to untangle them.

He hasn't posted anything since noon. **Late lunch with the new roomie.** The two of them slumped into the same side of some restaurant booth, clanging pizza slices together like beer bottles.

Lame, but cute.

Erin's back in her texts, asking if she should lock Cameron down for the year. With their freshman orientation coming up tomorrow, she can't risk him meeting someone else.

Kylie loves Erin. Sometimes, though, she hates her. It just can't be helped. The way she talks, talks, talks and how it's always her, her, her until that brief moment of self-awareness kicks in and reminds her to be a human being. To ask about someone else's life for a change.

"Come on, Brady," Kylie whines. She rolls over onto her stomach, face buried in her pillow while Katy is breathing on her brain. Empowering words that usually help. The song is "Roulette," a real bop about running into an ex-lover and having a spontaneous evening with them, and it would've made this album a massive hit had it been released as a single, but it's making everything worse tonight, because maybe Brady has spun that wheel and is currently going round and round with another girl.

Kylie feels sick. Every word Erin sends enrages her, because of course there's no room for Kylie's troubles in them. Somehow, she's been made to feel like a bit player in her own life.

Brady's update appears, as if on cue. As if Kylie has willed it into existence through sheer desperation.

Ding, ding, ding. Erin keeps on texting. Kylie doesn't read them. She's too busy wiping her eyes, staring at Brady's post. At her fucking life going to pieces.

The photo is of @BradyStyle with some new friends.

Ding, ding, ding. Notifications vying for Kylie's attention. But she just can't. Because every girl on campus seems to be in this picture. Brady and his roommate, front and center, surrounded by an avalanche of Williamson U Greek Life, hands reaching out, touching their shoulders and arms. Smiles on their faces because look at this new hotness . . .

Ding, ding, ding. Erin, determined to be heard. Now FaceTime's a-calling and Kylie's breath is short. Her heart pounds and her soul burns and the fire spreads through her body, eating her oxygen and squeezing from her the will to live.

She doesn't answer the call and then her phone goes back to *ding, ding, ding*ing. It won't stop, never stops.

Kylie wonders how much lorazepam she needs to swallow right now in order to die.

Only she's too cowardly for that and so she finally opens Erin's messages, knowing that all she needs is to feed the thread some kind of response in order for it to slow down. Make it stop for thirty seconds so she can think this all through.

Erin:

this is so fucked but you gotta see it

it's not real right?

This burst of panic catches Kylie off guard. Draws her focus. She opens the text thread in full, where, three messages up, Erin had sent a video.

Kylie recognizes the face in that thumbnail right off. Annabeth Wilson?! Fourth-grade recess buddy. The girl who sat behind her in two classes last year. The girl who has been missing since April.

Kylie taps the play arrow.

On-screen, Annabeth comes into a darkened room and flips a switch on the wall, revealing the kitchen. She yelps into the camera that she very clearly hasn't expected to find there.

Now Annabeth is staring straight into the lens, eyes seeming to lock with Kylie's for a moment as her mind slots in an unspoken puzzle piece.

"*Nothing else works, Little Lamb,*" a voice hisses from off camera.

Annabeth spins around to face the speaker.

What she sees, what Kylie is seeing, is a yellow emoji mask bleeding out of the shadows there. An oversized and circular head that's two blushing dots beneath thin, angled eye sockets, a lopsided grin that finds humor in Annabeth's startled shrieks. The mask sits atop a petite frame, a T-shirt that ends at bronzed and smooth thighs.

Then the emoji hoists something overhead.

A flash of steel. A barbecue slicer knife swinging down, seeming to carve through Annabeth. She goes spinning toward the camera, spurting blood like a sprinkler.

The emoji winds its arm back and the slicer blade falls again, smashing through Annabeth's head with a thunderstorm crack. She drops onto the gray tile like a slab of beef and the video cuts off, cuts to black, leaving Kylie to process what she just watched.

Erin's still feeding messages into the thread as questions race through Kylie's mind. Who recorded this? Why?

And yet, Kylie's so dazed that she's incapable of feeling anything in this moment. On video, the murder feels far removed from reality. A scene from a movie. Easily dismissed as a trick. Special effects.

Except in her heart, Kylie knows it isn't fake. Annabeth is missing. That was her in the vid. Occam's razor. Or in this case, Occam's barbecue slicer.

It isn't something she's supposed to see. Which makes it exciting.

So she does the first thing that comes naturally.

She clicks play and watches it again.

Like Mourning

Erin's BMW is idling in Kylie's driveway just before seven. Erin's *thing* is that she doesn't honk. Doesn't get out of the car. She just sits.

Sometimes Kylie lets Erin wait. Like today, standing in the foyer with the Annabeth video on repeat, unsure of how many times she's watched it now, kind of numb to it, but still utterly fascinated.

How many people see somebody they know die this way? Kylie pauses right after the emoji makes its first cut, Annabeth whirling back around, her eyes popped wide with shock, crimson splatter pocking her face. The way she crashes against the floor, dropping out of sight.

These images engrave themselves on Kylie's mind and suddenly she's had enough, stepping out into the morning light, rushing toward Erin's ride, spinning up her enthusiasm as she slides into shotgun. "You found the linen."

"But do I pull it off?" Erin asks, knowing full well that she does, adjusting the skirt to cover more of her thigh.

"Not sure how grief-stricken you look."

"Oh, well, it's not like we had a mass shooting."

"Thank God," Kylie says, wondering how that would go over for her. It worked out pretty well for those Parkland kids.

"It, uh, was Melissa on that video, right?" Erin asks. "Doing the deed?"

"It can't be," Kylie says, then wonders why she thinks that, given that both Annabeth Wilson and Melissa Crigan have been missing for five months. Now one of them is dead and the other—

"I'd recognize those legs anywhere," Erin says, backing onto Kylie's street, stomping the gas. "She's got that stupid-ass mask on, and it's just like, why bother? It's way easier to identify Melissa from her body. Swimmer's thighs. Used to be so jealous of that sculpt."

"Are you sure?"

"One way to brand yourself," Erin says, almost admiringly. "Psychos aren't usually hot, so there's a market there." She glances over, notices Kylie is struggling this morning, makes a face like she really hates to change the subject. "All right, talk to me."

"You already know."

"Hate to say it, but—"

"Not helping."

"Well, what am I supposed to say, Ky? If you took my advice, you'd be so much happier."

"Your advice is to have fun. What does that even mean?"

"It means . . . forget Brady."

"So I can make out with two guys at once? Like you did after the prom?"

"Oh, that was just a few kisses . . . no biggie. It was in the moment."

"So, you're not talking about that kind of fun? Just so I'm clear?"

"More like . . . find a Cameron of your own."

"He's not even *your Cameron* yet."

Erin grins. Without taking her eyes off the road, she unlocks her phone and swipes through the screens in an impressive display of muscle memory, then drops her device into Kylie's lap.

It's the source photo from Erin's late-night Insta selfie, unedited, her boobs in frame.

"Maybe Cameron got that in a DM. And if you scroll over one, you'll see"—she clears her throat—"his hardened response."

Like most women on the internet, Kylie lives in constant fear of unwanted dick pics, though maybe there is some morbid curiosity this time because she knows Cameron. But the topic of boys has her feeling lemon-sour today and she doesn't want to look.

She locks the phone and places it on the seat between them. "I'm good."

"But no fun."

Summerfield Community College's parking lot is nearly full, one open spot. A dented Volkswagen comes puttering in from the other end, a bit closer. Erin blasts her horn, rattling the other car into braking. She takes that opportunity to gun it, stealing the space and flipping the driver off through the rearview.

"Eat me, you total geek!"

Behind the wheel of the Volkswagen, Ben Austin looks like he's about to cry.

"Be *ni*-ice," Kylie says, her voice filled with singsongy insincerity.

"Oh God. You know him?"

"Um, he was our Bio partner. Maybe you just weren't paying attention."

Erin shakes that thought away, refusing to waste another on Ben Austin.

On the quad, everyone's taking selfies, showing off their best mourning faces. Nobody's grieving, exactly. Annabeth wasn't popular enough for that. This is mutually beneficial acknowledgment.

A sign hangs over the school's entrance. WELCOME FRESHMEN TO SCC! Then, in smaller letters, *You Can Still Find Your Future Here!* A flyer taped to the door reads, WE REMEMBER ANNABETH. It's hastily made, which is understandable, given that she hadn't been "confirmed" dead until about twelve hours ago. But the video is really making the rounds. There're already two subreddits dedicated to solving the mystery, and some news stations have begun reporting on it, adding fuel to the "Did Missy do it?" speculation.

"Chessie King followed me last night," Erin announces as she spins around and lifts her phone in one fluid motion, snapping a selfie—the Annabeth pamphlet visible in full just over her shoulder.

"Um. I don't know who that is."

"Only one of the best travel-and-fitness influencers out there." Erin's response isn't quite disgust, but disappointment. Her star pupil has much to learn.

They walk the rest of the way in silence, Erin's thumbs tap-tapping her screen while uploading her pic, slapping it behind her own filter and adding a few hashtags. All before they're in the building, a social virtuoso.

Cameron Sullivan is waiting for them in the hall. He slides his wavy brown bangs behind his ears and drapes a familiar arm around Erin. "Looking good, ladies," he says. "Yo, is that dress see-through?"

Erin bites her lip to stifle her smile, but keeps walking.

"Does she . . . know about the pic?" Cameron asks, eye-checking Kylie with a grin out the side of his mouth.

"If you're wondering if my best friend has seen your dick," Erin says, deadpan, "she declined to look."

Cameron seems deflated by this, and Kylie feels a twinge of satisfaction over having burst his balloon.

They follow the flow of freshman students through nondescript halls, community college feeling like high school on steroids. Sporadic signs marked ORIENTATION point the way.

"Think they'll mention any of this?" Cameron wonders. "Melissa?"

"Who cares? We know what happened." Erin gives an empty shrug because that's just life in the Current Year.

"Makes you think," Cameron says.

"And what are you thinking about?" Erin asks.

"That you never know who might want to kill you. Melissa and Annabeth were best friends."

"And are we sure that Melissa killed Annabeth?" Kylie asks. "I feel like nobody knows what the hell they're talking about."

"Poor Kylie," Erin says. "So naïve."

Cameron pulls them into a huddle, words becoming whispers. "It's true, guys . . . my dad says—"

"You dad's a patrolman," Erin groans.

"Yeah, well, he knows things," Cameron snaps, eyes narrowing as he watches a few stragglers pass by. "Supposedly, Melissa livestreamed the killing."

"Oh, come on. Melissa's been radio silent since April," Kylie says.

"Not everyone understands the game," Erin adds, as if the necessity of daily content was Kylie's point.

"Radio silent on TikTok," Cameron clarifies. "The video we're talking about came from somewhere else."

"From where?" Kylie asks. "Reels?"

"No. It started getting shared around, though. Nobody wants to take credit but—" He looks as though he knows he shouldn't continue.

"Oh my God!" Erin exclaims, loud enough to draw eyes. "Chessie King just liked my post!"

Kylie snaps her fingers in Cameron's face to keep him on task. "Hello? But . . . what?"

"I think it came from Duc."

"Makes sense," Kylie says. "If there's something awful on the internet, Duc would know about it."

They had a Chemistry Slack channel last year. A place for the lab groups to compare notes. Duc's only contributions were to spam it with links to disgusting videos disguised as "study guides."

Two girls, one *something* . . .

"I showed him this morning," Cameron says. "You know, in case he hadn't seen it, and he got super hostile. '*Get that shit out of my face!*'"

"Do you think Chessie wants to collab?" Erin's asking no one in particular.

"This isn't just some anonymous internet vid, though," Kylie says. "We know Annabeth. *Knew* her."

"Let's go, peoples." Mr. Davies comes around the corner, fanning his arms, corralling them through the open auditorium doors.

"Peoples?" Cameron asks.

"I don't assume gender, Cameron. Now let's get a move on." Mr. Davies, with his thinning hair and sparse goatee, wearing an off-white button-down, had given the Summerfield High seniors a campus tour last year, and he remained their faculty contact for all academic questions throughout the spring and summer. Kylie's stunned that he seems to remember their names. And was that a little smile just for her?

"God, he needs to log off," Erin whispers and Kylie giggles.

They break formation and head inside as questions about Annabeth and Melissa swirl. Best friends. One victim. One killer. Why?

Kylie's unable to think about anything else.

Ice Cream Secrets

Orientation lasts an hour. It's mostly a sounding board for various services and clubs offered on campus. Counseling. Tutoring. A handful of intramural sports for those who can't let it go. Cameron winces at these mentions, still traumatized by the torn ACL that ended his athletic career last Thanksgiving in the big game against Westvale.

He leans into Erin's ear and whispers, *"Maybe I'll try cross country,"* though she doesn't acknowledge this, never takes her eyes off her phone. Just scrolls for the entirety of the assembly.

Kylie's first class that day is Ancient and World History. She's not in her seat ten minutes before zoning out, Mr. Beauregard's "Welcome to College" lecture drier than toast. Not even his surprising segue into cannibalism is enough to bring her back, daydreaming of Katy's "Bon Appetit" video instead. The one where she's half-naked and tossed around in a vat of flour the size of a swimming pool. Katy covered in fresh vegetables, soaking in steaming broth, about to be devoured by the ravenous men cooking her.

Thinking about that gives her "Hummingbird Heartbeat."

Brady hates that video. Says Katy was past her prime and trying to be edgy, clinging to relevancy. And suddenly Kylie's on the verge of tears because fuck you, you never disrespect the Queen, not ever, and because Brady still hasn't texted.

The entire morning is like this, little bites of Brady depression interrupted only by the overwhelming mystery of Annabeth and Melissa. A distraction she's grateful to have.

On the way to lunch, Kylie spots Erin sneaking off campus with Veronica Gomez. Veronica flashes an aqua-tinted Juul in a leather charging case, Kylie's invitation to come with. "This is us coping with tragedy."

So gauche, Kylie thinks. Why don't they realize Juuls are out and Puff Bars are in? "You guys aren't going to lunch?"

"In this dress?" Erin brushes her fingers down the length of her prized linen. "It'll stain if I fart. I'm fasting until school's out."

"Come vape," Veronica offers.

"Can't." Kylie starts to move past them. "I'm looking for someone."

That someone is Duc. Kylie finally finds him in the cafeteria, sitting at a table of indistinguishable skinny jeans and printed tees. He stands out among his pack in Gucci stripes and linen chinos. Has a gold band around his wrist and his hair is perfect. She heard him bragging once that he gets it done in Boston every three weeks and spends a buck-twenty per cut, and she admires this utter dedication to image.

Kylie pulls a chair from the empty table nearby. The chatter stops cold as she wedges herself in.

"You looking to rip woods?" one of the burnouts snickers. "I sold through my stash before breakfast. Guess murder makes everyone anxious. Real good for business." He high-fives the guy sitting next to him whose eyelids are all the way closed, and whose laugh is a low, maddening, atonal stutter.

Kylie's locked on to Duc. "Can I talk to you for a second?"

"Still mad about Slack?"

"God, stop it."

"You came to me."

"This isn't about that. I've moved on," Kylie says. It wasn't even the prank that had angered her, but Duc's effort to record her reaction to it. He used to have a YouTube prank show called *DucTales*, three hundred and fifty thousand subs before the high school administration tired of his constant interruptions and threatened to suspend him if he didn't stop.

Duc did, walking away from all those subscribers. That monetization. Kylie never understood it. Would've let the school toss her out on her ass.

"All right," Duc says, unwrapping an ice cream sandwich and licking the cream around the perimeter. "Talk."

A hall of burnout faces stare at Kylie. She glares back, annoyed that these losers are trying to intimidate her. All except Duc, who enjoys being the alpha to his pack of betas.

"Somewhere else, please," she says.

Duc cleaves off a hunk of ice cream sandwich like a snapping turtle. "Anything you have to say—"

"Okay, fine—let's talk about Melissa Crigan."

The confidence immediately falls off Duc's face and he pushes away from the table, stands up. "Over there."

The small courtyard off the cafeteria is surrounded on all sides by floor-to-ceiling glass. The ground is decorative rock and sporadic flower beds. Two girls sit on the concrete there, giggling over TikToks.

"Melissa," Kylie whispers as the door to the cafeteria clicks shut behind them.

"What about her?" Duc asks, mouth full of ice cream.

"Cameron told me you—"

"Cameron's mouth is bigger than his brain."

"Anyone else watches that video and gets spooked off it, I believe it. You? LiveLeak used to be your homepage."

"LiveLeak," Duc sighs. "Press *F*." He twists his mouth as if he's trying to lock the rest of his words away. "I shouldn't say anything els—"

"Yeah, you should."

He glances around. The nearby girls aren't remotely curious about their conversation, and his boys are watching through the glass as if their leader's life is in mortal danger.

Kylie waves, hoping it might antagonize them. "Remember when you and Matt used to swap porn DVDs?" she asks. "That day you dropped your bag on the bus and a couple of them spilled out across my feet?" She claps her hands together, laughing.

"Wasn't funny."

"I used to call you guys the Bang Brothers. Still the first thing that pops into my head when I see you goons together. Point is, Duc, I harbored that. Kept it our little secret."

"That's supposed to make me want to trust you?"

"No, but it's proof that you *can*."

Duc leans in so close that, for a second, Kylie thinks he's about to kiss her. She recoils a little and he scoffs at her skittishness. "Ever consider that I'm trying to protect your dumb ass?"

"Thanks, Dad. I'll worry about myself."

"Fine, Jesus. There's this app, all right? A goddamn app."

"Which app?"

"One you don't have."

"Tell me which one and I'll—"

He takes out his phone and shows the screen. Among the familiar social media icons is a strange yellow one Kylie doesn't recognize. An abstract logo. One dark diagonal slash and a half circle underneath, almost like a closed eye. She squints to read the fine print of the app name.

"MonoLife . . . ?"

"Shit's secret," Duc says. "You have a better chance of seeing aliens than getting this on your phone."

"I can't download it?"

"Nope."

"Did Melissa have it? Annabeth?"

Duc pushes a finger into the notch above his lip.

Kylie takes her voice down to a whisper. "That's where the video was posted? Cameron said—"

"Cameron's going to get you all killed."

Kylie gives a reflexive laugh. Dramatic much? But Duc's stone face stops her cold. She's known him since grade school. Jesus, he wasn't this serious when his mother died. "Okay . . . what does that mean?"

His voice drops so low it's almost gone. "It'll know if I show you."

"Uh." Kylie glances back at Duc's table again, thinking this has to be another dumb prank. The boys are still watching, looking every bit as dumbfounded as she feels.

"Is this another one of your bullshit jokes? 'Cause I swear—"

"No. *No*. No joke here. It's made to stay hidden. Like, way, way, way hidden."

"How'd you get it, then?"

"Nope."

"Duc, I'm not going to rat you out."

"*No.*"

"Trust issues? Okay. Let's see . . . Um, freshman year, I caught the Bang Brothers peeping on Stacy Corliss. Right in her backyard, you goblins. I mean, okay, who walks around their house naked after a shower? But that's beside the point. I could've ratted you out. Could've told Stacy to lower her shades—I didn't even do that. Because I saw you pervs both looking so desperate and pathetic, puppy-dog eyes and everything and . . . I had mercy."

"I owe you? For *that*?"

Kylie lifts an eyebrow that asks, *Don't you?*

Duc paces back and forth, screws sufficiently turned. He takes a deep breath, and there's a ridiculously long pause before exhaling. "Phone kiosk at the mall. Ask Deacon to give you the life."

"What—"

Duc spits and starts back into the cafeteria. "That's it. You heard what I said. And whatever happens next, keep me out of it. I mean that."

"We're all a little messed up, Duc. If you need to talk about what happen—"

"I didn't know Annabeth at all."

"You knew Melissa."

"Missy and I only . . ." He stops in the doorjamb, reconsidering his words. Whatever he's thinking disappears with another headshake. "Forget it."

"I won't."

"Then don't. Fuck do I care? You've heard everything I've got to tell you. Seriously, Kylie, fuck off." He rushes back to the lunch table, his boys whooping at the sight of Kylie being put in her place.

Her heart thunders. Even the girls are staring now. It doesn't matter. What Kylie wants are answers.

Why had Melissa gone dark on Instagram five months ago, while remaining ExtremelyOnline™ enough to do what, exactly? Stream a murder?

Why does Duc know her well enough to call her *Missy*?

And what about this MonoLife has him so scared?

App Store

They go to Erin's house after school.

Kylie doesn't drive, so she's always on Erin's schedule. What she's affectionately come to call ErinTime. It's not so bad, because Erin's always in a hurry to get where she's going.

Only problem is that ErinTime serves Erin's followers and no one else.

"Time to feed the beast," she'll say. And that means doing things like pulling over to grab a selfie in front of a food truck called OH MISO HUNGRY.

It's those instincts, always on point, that brings them straight to Erin's house. Cameron's along for the ride because he's costarring in this afternoon's 'gram. A shot across the bow to every other SCC student who looked at him today and thought, *Maybe this is my year* . . .

It's not. It's Erin's. And she's about to illustrate that shit.

"You know what to do," Erin says as she turns into the driveway and stops. Cameron ducks across the back seat as Kylie hops out, jogging up to the front steps and blotting the Ring doorbell's field of vision.

Only then does Cameron slither out, going around the house to the pool gate as Erin rolls the BMW all the way down the pavement. She joins Kylie on the front steps, where she punches in the unlock code.

"When does Cameron get to meet the family?" Kylie whispers this into her hand just in case Mr. Palmer is watching the Ring video feed from work.

"Never, ever, ever, ever." The door swings open and they enter. "Dad doesn't want me seeing anyone, thinks I need to focus on my studies to escape this 'community college ghetto.' That's what he calls it. Like we're supposed to go into Ivy League debt for lives we don't even want." They walk through the house to the rear porch, then down to the pool area, unlocking the tall iron gate where Cameron waits.

"I missed you," he says, pushing in on Erin for a peck.

"Down, boy." She shoves him off, tugging his T-shirt up to flash his abs. "Take this off and go for a swim while I change."

"I didn't bring a suit," Cameron says, slipping the shirt off anyway and watching Erin strut toward the pool house.

"No cameras back here, Ace. You can strip."

"But please don't," Kylie adds, dropping into one of the oversized chairs at the shallow end.

Cameron isn't listening. He unbuckles his belt and pushes down his jeans. "Don't worry, I wear boxers."

Kylie has her phone, thank God. She opens Instagram, where for some reason the algorithm thinks she'd love to see Erin's mourning selfie.

Two hundred comments, each one of them **Sorry for your loss**, as if Erin's actually lost anything.

She continues to scroll, but can't get it out of her head. All those hearts. People genuinely care about Erin. What does that feel like? What does Kylie have to do in order to know what that feels like?

People who don't matter say digital love is transactional. Parasocial. Something imagined that cannot be felt or understood beyond the confines of a user agreement. To Kylie, it's preferable to an empty home and a boyfriend who is almost certainly gearing up to ghost her.

The pool house doors swing open, jostling Kylie from that thought.

Cameron, slumped face down on the diving board with one arm dangling into the water, perks up. "Wow."

Wow is right. Erin catwalks out, her porcelain skin contrasting with the black bikini that's thinner than a string of yarn and sparkling beneath the sun. Kylie doesn't hate any body more than that body.

Cameron's on his knees now, practically clapping like a seal. Erin bends over his face, dangling the bottle of tanning butter like a sardine, sloshing it around with a dirty grin. "You do me and I'll do you."

Kylie retreats back into her feed, creeping on Brady, who hasn't posted a thing since yesterday's sorority sister sandwich.

Their last text was Friday. Three nights ago. Brady had signed off with a heart emoji followed by a finger pointing up at it. Then . . . nothing. Once a relationship reached this point, it was probably over. Might as well accept the situation.

Kylie brushes one stupid tear from her eye, listening to Cameron and Erin giggle while lathering each other up. She thinks, *Screw it*, starts typing.

Kylie:

Hey . . . How's college life?

An ellipsis immediately appears at the bottom of the screen.

Brady:

Hey! Life's great. 😊

Then a second ellipsis.

Erin slides her bathing suit straps down, play-shrieking as Cameron sweeps "cold" tanning butter across her shoulder blades.

The ellipsis disappears, Brady deciding not to elaborate.

Kylie's mouth pops into an O. That's it?

He doesn't ask about her first day back? About the murder of a classmate he knew and has probably already forgotten? Kylie stares at the screen. That *can't* be all.

Seconds of disbelief tick upward.

Okay, that's *really* it. Fuck him. She tosses her phone onto the side table and shifts, the plastic seat groaning beneath her.

Erin and Cameron are fully lathered now, tanned bodies glistening beneath the late summer sun. Their curves are Grecian, statues out of her Ancient and World History book, both of them good enough to eat.

Bon appetit.

Kylie looks pretty good in a bikini now too. Motivation spurred by past experiences. Stupid exes who had trouble understanding why people IRL didn't measure up to the girls they jerked off to on TikTok.

"Take a few pictures, babe?" Erin asks, though it's really more of a command.

Kylie gets up, feeling overdressed as she approaches the half-naked bodies, arranging her subjects into poses on the diving board, taking a number of photos.

Then Cameron and Erin huddle over her for review. They settle on a shot of their faces because the light hits them just right and Erin thinks they look "sexy but conflicted," which is appropriate for today.

"Can we hit the mall now?" Kylie asks, the same way she used to ask Mom and Dad for an ice cream on the way home from the beach.

"Couple more minutes, sweetie," Erin says, picking up the same vibe. She takes Cameron by the hand and tugs him toward the pool house. He goes willingly, grinning like a dope.

Kylie opens Brady's texts, fingers tapping the keyboard so fast she barely has time to process the message she's sending.

Kylie:

> I'M FINE, THANKS

Her eyes narrow, daring that fucking ellipsis bubble to show itself. She wants the fight. The raging fire inside her feels so righteous. Anger being preferable to loneliness because there's a fifty-fifty chance the fault isn't yours.

From inside the pool house comes the sound of plumbing turning on. Erin and Cameron showering while Kylie seethes. Erin emerges a few minutes later, wearing jeans and a tee, smiling like there's a story to tell. And Cameron comes stumbling out behind her, struggling to shut the door.

Kylie crosses her arms. "Now can we?"

"I'm tagging along," Cameron says. "Erin said I could."

Kylie throws her a look.

Cameron goes to collect the rest of his clothes poolside. "Hey, you wouldn't know anything without me."

"Can't believe we're even listening to Duc," Erin says. "Secret app. *Psh.*"

Kylie continues to glare at Cameron, incensed by his intrusion on ErinTime. "You're riding in the back."

Cameron looks to Erin for confirmation. She nods without hesitation. "Know your place, boy toy." A playful wink softens the blow.

He slumps across the back seat like a contented animal. Goes quiet while fidgeting with his phone.

"Did you?" Kylie opens her mouth like she's trying to swallow air.

Erin giggles. Now they're both laughing.

Erin's diving board post has 209 hearts already.

"Jeez," Kylie says, unable to mask her jealousy. "I'm in the presence of royalty."

Erin sees her checking on the post. "Might be doing a couple adds. Maybelline's been in touch. Revlon . . ."

I was joking, Kylie thinks, irritated as she again wonders, *Why you and not me? Why does every single break in life go to you?*

The mall parking lot is so vacant it has to be closed. Kylie doesn't remember the last time she came here.

The doors slide open to reveal the ruins of an ancient civilization. The vacant, wide-open space that at one time anticipated the accommodation of many. Stale air neither cool nor warm. Shop lights flicker as if begging for attention.

According to the directory, the phone kiosk is just an escalator ride to the second floor. The guy slumped over the counter there, nose to laptop, has to be Deacon. Probably only a few years older than Kylie, maybe twenty-three, with natural curls and heavy brown eyes. He might've been cute once, before the all-carb diet.

"It's your thing." Erin gives Kylie a gentle nudge. "Go for it."

Kylie clears her throat on approach and the clerk eyes her.

"Deacon?"

"Guilty as charged."

"Um . . . I was told you could give me the life?" Kylie drops her phone down on the counter and nudges it closer.

"We fix cracked screens." He taps the sign on the counter with the tip of a chewed-up pen, a rundown of all the models they repair. "Yours seems fine."

"Yeah," Kylie says, unsure of how far to push this. "That's . . . not why I'm here."

A moment of silence, Deacon gnawing the pen as he chews on Kylie, trying to decide what she knows. He spots Erin and Cameron a couple of feet back and really clenches his jaw. "You drop your phone on the sidewalk, I'll be here. Otherwise . . ." He swivels around on his stool and returns to his laptop.

Kylie clears her throat. "I said, I want you to show me the life."

Deacon's head does one of those funny twitches, as if reacting to something Kylie doesn't hear. He turns back over the shoulder. "And I don't know what you mean."

"MonoLife," Kylie says, Erin and Cameron edging closer.

"Sounds like a disease."

"MonoLife," Erin repeats, voice high enough for the food court to hear, which would be a real problem if anyone was there.

"Stop it," Deacon snaps.

"Thought you didn't know what she meant?" Erin folds her arms. Checkmate.

"We heard you're the guy," Kylie says.

"And we're not gonna talk about those things," Deacon hisses.

"Well, we're not going anywhere." Erin lifts her phone. "I'll go live right now and broadcast your face to the world. Tell my sixty thousand followers all about MonoLife." She flashes Deacon her profile to prove those numbers.

"No, no, no," Deacon says. "There's no need for that."

"Then give me the life," Kylie says.

"Okay. You want it?" The clerk is visibly irritated. His voice drops low even though there's one person passing by but nowhere within earshot. "All three of you, right?"

They nod, the oldest end-user agreement. "I'll need to load it on. It'll take about an hour. Hundred bucks each. That's the fee. Nonnegotiable."

"I don't want my phone jailbroken," Erin says.

"It won't be." Deacon sounds beyond pissed.

Erin's forehead becomes a nest of wrinkles. "Then . . . how's it work?"

"Don't worry about that, you either want it or—"

"Do it." Kylie steps aside so the others can drop their phones.

"Seems steep, guy," Cameron has to say.

"That's three hundred in cash," Deacon clarifies.

"How do we know anyone will even see us on there?" Erin places a hand on her hip, tilts her head. "Like . . . is this another off-brand platform? 'Cause let me tell you, the last thing anyone needs is another Rumble or Bluesky."

Deacon has already gone to work, placing each of the phones side by side on an old wooden board. "It's a risk you'll have to take."

"Well, then," Erin sighs. "I gotta hit the ATM. Be right back."

As she and Cameron walk off, Deacon signals for Kylie to stay behind. "Something else to go over."

"All right."

"I don't know anything about . . . the life. Nothing. You hear? Once it's on your phone, we're done. You ever *do* crack your screen, you go someplace else."

"Fine."

"And understand this: Once it's on your phone, you gotta use it twice a day. Two log-ins every twenty-four hours or the app deletes itself. And once it's gone, you don't get it back. Not even if you switch devices or providers. I don't know why. I don't know how. That's just what it does. You get me?"

"Sure."

"I didn't make the app. I don't know who did. All I do is put it on your phone. And the guy who asked if I wanted to make some extra cash by installing it . . . never saw him again either."

"I understand."

"Really? 'Cause lemme tell you—you don't look like you understand."

Kylie shrugs. "Use it twice a day or else. Sure. I mean, I check Facebook twice a day." She wonders if this cardinal rule is how the app harvests its data. Guarantee its users are always logging on, or the party's over. If that's the case, well, whatever. She assumes the CCP already knows all there is to know about Kylie because of her TikTok days, and Zuck and Musk aren't far behind. Privacy's always been an illusion.

Deacon gives an unfriendly laugh, spots Erin and Cameron on their return walk. "Tell your friends what's up. I don't repeat myself."

Erin approaches and counts out the necessary amount of twenties, laying crisp bills down on top of their phones. "You guys are paying me back for this. I'm not a charity."

"Come back in one hour," Deacon tells them.

"Yeah, I'm not leaving my phone with you," Erin says.

"You think I'm gonna steal your fucking nudes, kid? Drain your daddy's bank account? Don't flatter yourself. Look . . ." He lifts each of their phones and squeezes the power buttons until they're shut down. "There. These can be off while I work. I don't need your passcodes."

Kylie wonders how he's able to do that. She looks over at Erin, who doesn't seem so thrilled but stays quiet.

"Once you start using," Deacon tells them, "I mean . . . *really* using, you're in. Just so you know."

"I get it," Kylie says.

Erin looks from Kylie to Deacon, completely lost.

"Give you the details in a sec," Kylie tells her.

Cameron tugs Erin away from the counter. "We should—"

"Scout this place," Erin says. "Try and get some content out of it." ErinTime. All the time.

They start off and Kylie follows at a distance, unable to shake whatever odd sensations are beginning to move through her. The excitement of exclusivity. She's always wanted to be an early adopter, the thrill of using technology others can't . . . even if Erin and Cameron have to tag along.

Life is never perfect. But maybe it can be.

User Agreement

They stop for tacos on the drive home. A place called Birria Basket that Erin mostly likes because their presentation is top-class and allows for an aesthetic nighttime post with minimal effort.

Asher and Brandi are there finishing up their burritos. Cameron heads right over and makes camp at their table.

Kylie joins them. Her freshly jailbroken phone sits inside her pocket. MonoLife out of reach, digital withdrawals as everyone forces mundane conversation.

"You'll never get a transfer scholarship that way," Brandi is saying. "One year to bring your grades up is all you need to get us out of this town. And you're about to throw it all away for a couple of swollen knuckles."

"Don't I know it?" Asher sighs. "Black dude kicks the shit out of some pervert and he's the problem. No way in hell I'm putting myself through that."

"Who's the pervert?" Cameron asks. "Maybe I'll knock him around." He takes a seat beside Asher. The two of them in matching letterman jackets, though Asher's tee is tighter, hardened abs stretching the fabric.

"Mr. Sykes," Brandi says. Her shorts are maybe an inch long from waist to thigh, and she wears a belly shirt that's almost as tiny.

Kylie catches Erin sneering at Brandi just a little.

"The weirdo janitor?" Cameron asks.

"More like the pedo," Erin says, correctively. "He literally got busted with my underwear in his desk last year . . . Kylie's too."

Everyone at Summerfield High had assumed "Sykes the Sleaze" was perennially up to no good, but it was Mrs. Keogh who spotted him hovering around the girls' locker room during gym class and decided it was sus. Checked his workstation and found a few soiled panties stuffed away inside an old toolbox.

Sykes copped to it, and to doing a whole bunch more over the years, pleading for help because he was, in his own words, "sick."

"He's working nights at an office park in Westford," Brandi tells them. "And he hasn't been cured."

"There ain't no cure for that." Cameron laughs, mocking the sentiment.

"How would you know?" Erin is still low-key sneering at Brandi, incensed that someone other than her is catching most of the attention in here, with every other table unable to stop side-eying the girl's barely there attire.

"Anyone want to split nachos?" Cameron asks.

"I don't think I'm hungry," Kylie says.

Brandi taps a finger on the table. "So listen—Sykes the Sleaze got himself doxxed on Messenger. Trying to lure Cassie Langen's little sister over to his place."

"Messenger?" Erin wrinkles her nose in disbelief over the idea that someone would use that app.

Cameron leans across the table. "Someone better nail his pedo ass. Yo, Asher, nachos?"

"You said you wanted tacos." Erin sighs. "You don't need both. Nobody's metabolism is that good. And if the word's out on Sykes, how come they haven't arrested him?"

"Cassie told her dad," Brandi says. "He's hoping the neighborhood takes care of it."

"Someone should nail his pedo ass." Asher and Cameron nod in agreement.

Brandi clucks her tongue. "Absolutely not."

"Fine," Asher says, adding, "Well, maybe. I mean, if everyone else is too chickenshit, then I might . . ."

"Why can't I get nachos?" Cameron's looking at Erin now.

Brandi stretches a foot out beneath the table, settling into Asher's lap. "Let it go, baby."

"I'm starving," Cameron moans. "Specials all around, cool?"

"Only if you're paying," Kylie tells him. She really isn't hungry. Can't stop thinking about MonoLife. How badly she wants to get home and dive in. The thrill of something new and unknown.

"Of course he's paying," Erin adds.

"Just think somebody should do something," Asher says.

"That is messed up," Kylie agrees. Brandi shoots her a defensive look that reads, *He's mine, bitch,* but Asher flashes a cute smirk of appreciation that negates her hostility.

"Baby," Brandi says. "I'll give you something else to spend that energy on." She reaches across the table and takes Asher by the hand, pulling him from the group, leading him toward the exit, slamming her hips back and forth as she goes. Asher's laughing the whole way, turning back with a shrug before he's dragged outside.

"So territorial." Kylie finds she admires Brandi's theatricality. "She gonna jump him in the parking lot?"

The server drops off three plastic baskets of "the special," and Erin insists on taking a photo of everyone's dinner once the foils are removed and the sauces applied. Says she wants to rub the calories in everyone's face. That they can eat like this, still look like this.

Kylie's too miserable to eat. She was a fifth wheel at this table. Now she's a third. Her thoughts trapped in a cycle of Brady. On that ellipsis that began typing a couple of hours ago but never followed through.

Erin giggles at Cameron staring at his phone, second-guessing his decision to load the app onto it after Kylie explained the rules. What he probably felt was too much responsibility. "Just do it," she urges.

"Maybe it won't be so bad," he says, accidentally spraying taco puree on Kylie from across the table. "If it doesn't have all that woke crap that's infected every other app. Oof—sorry, Kylie."

Kylie reaches for the basket of napkins between them. "Woke crap? Your dad's a cop, Cameron, but that doesn't mean you get to turn a blind eye to the world."

"What's going on out there, Kylie? In the world? Tell me how you know about it from your little safe-ass suburban street."

"Can you all just focus?" Erin says. Then Cameron's back to looking at his phone. At the new app icon he's too afraid to open.

Kylie wipes her face and pushes her plate aside. "Duc has it on his phone, right? And he's fine."

"You said he was super skittish," Erin says.

"Well, yeah. But there can't be any danger in just downloading it." Now Kylie's eyeing her phone with suspicion too.

"Ten. Thousand. Likes." Erin waves Instagram around so the whole restaurant can see. "In three hours. And you want to throw that away on nachos."

"My abs aren't even in that photo."

"Not the point. We have to build on this momentum. Your abs may be the star of the show next time."

Cameron pushes his phone a little farther away, happy to avoid opening MonoLife. "Maximize the 'like' equity. Smart."

"It all comes down to tricking the algorithm into believing we have things that others want." A naughty laugh as she flips through this afternoon's camera roll. Two dozen shots of her bikini body. "I'd say we do."

The soullessness of this exchange makes Kylie feel hopeless, like an imposter pretending at being a peer.

This world is exhausting. Why does she covet Erin's stardom at all? Like, really. How can she ever catch up?

Kylie's slumped against the BMW's window on the drive home. Downtown trudges past. Details fading, becoming shadows in real time as the moon rises. Her house is a silhouette by the time Erin gets them there.

"Hey," Erin says, reaching across the seat, a supportive hand closing around Kylie's forearm. "Forget him. Okay? God, he completely sucks."

"Sure." Kylie stares out at her lawn. It's overrun with patches of crabgrass. "I will."

"Look, I'll come over after school tomorrow. We'll collab. Make Brady remember what he's missing." She pulls Kylie's collar away from her chest like she's trying to see down her shirt.

"Only if I get to watch," Cameron adds from the back seat.

Kylie tears from Erin's grip with a giggle and pops the door. "You guys are so weird."

"But you love me."

"I do," Kylie admits as she climbs out. She'd feel better if she could air some of this angst, all this bad Brady mojo, but someone out in digital space would surely take issue with her issue:

› How dare you give a man that kind of power.
› Why do some girls let men define their happiness?
› This post doesn't pass the Bechdel Test.

Kylie's no symbol. Or example. She's a person. She's in love. Yes, she'll admit that to herself now. And the fact that love is killing her.

The idea of pushing out content tonight is burdensome. Everything feels played out. But if Kylie maintains social media silence, then Erin will be back in her driveway at dawn, lecturing her on the importance of brand-building. And Kylie would rather rupture her eardrums than catch that spiel again.

The house is empty. Abnormally cold for late summer. Mom is almost never home this time of night, taking as much overtime as her customer service job allows. The moon spies on Kylie through each window, throwing oversized shadows across the floor and walls, making her feel small and insignificant.

In her bedroom, she falls atop the sheets right beneath Katy and is suddenly aware of the phone in her hand. It feels like a dumbbell. Does too much technology make you sick? She can't be bothered to google that.

She stares at the poster across the room, the Los Angeles skyline at sunset, purple and gauzy, and there's maybe one moment of silence, a solid thirty seconds, when pure exhaustion pushes everything from her brain. When she exists in whatever passes for contentment as she imagines herself there, standing on some balcony in the hills, a warm breeze rolling in off the Pacific with whispers of a golden future.

Katy warns of the isolation that comes with transplanting oneself there, and her song "Lost" is a haunting and brooding reminder of how lonely life in the City of Angels can be. So lonely that she and Orlando almost moved to Kentucky to escape it, but thankfully reconsidered.

A draft comes gusting through the house and kills the daydream with a couple of shivers. Kylie is well aware that MonoLife is right here. Ready.

"Okay." She takes a deep breath and drops the phone against her propped-up thighs. Taps the yellow and black icon. Here we go.

The loading screen is a block of cool yellow, that squinted eye logo again. The screen reads in clean dark letters:

MonoLife.

Under that, in a smaller font, sits the tagline:

In. Here.

And then Kylie is in here, sort of, looking at the terms of service:

THESE TERMS OF SERVICE ARE A LIVING DOCUMENT, AND LIMITS MONOLIFE'S LIABILITY. READ IT CAREFULLY.

ANYONE CAN USE MONOLIFE, IF YOU CAN FIND IT. YOUR
CONTENT IS YOURS, AND IT IS ALSO OURS. YOU PERMIT US
TO FEATURE IT IN THE APP AS NECESSARY. WE WILL NEVER
SCREEN OR MONITOR YOUR CONTENT OR MESSAGES FOR
ANY REASON, EVEN IF YOU ASK US TO. RESPECT THE RIGHTS
OF FELLOW MONOLIFE USERS (HENCEFORTH KNOWN AS
"LIFERS") AND THEY WILL RESPECT YOURS. WE ARE NOT HERE
TO KEEP YOU SAFE, BUT SEEK TO GIVE YOU A PLATFORM
ON WHICH TO FREELY EXPRESS YOURSELF. NOW AGREE TO
THESE TERMS AND YOU ARE READY TO BEGIN THE FUN. DO
NOT EVER SHOW THE APP TO THOSE WHO DO NOT HAVE IT
ALREADY INSTALLED ON THEIR OWN DEVICE. WE WILL FIND
OUT IF YOU DO.

And that's it. No other twisty-turny legalese.

Kylie taps AGREE. There is no option for DECLINE.

The next screen asks for a username. She's not going to use @KylieAtNight for this, and after a moment of serious contemplation, more thought given than to any college curriculum, she decides on the handle @CrystalShips—close enough to an old song Dad would sing around the house, by the Doors, maybe? It's a warm memory, and a name that might help make a few more of those.

MonoLife has no verification process and, from what Kylie sees, no way for the app to scan her phone's contacts in order to find other people she knows.

"Who the hell am I supposed to follow?"

Usernames and posts appear on the screen, unbidden. Who are these people? Some account called @JaspersBrain is wondering where all the tits are.

An account with the handle @CrockerDiamonds asks why he needs to log in every day, then makes a second post asking if that's even true.

This content has zero likes. Zero engagement. People shouting into a hurricane, too boomer to realize it.

MonoLife's interface isn't as clean as Instagram's or TikTok's. Isn't as evasively casual as Snapchat's either.

The logo sits in the upper-left corner, an otherwise blank strip of yellow stretching across the entire top, as if the app has failed to load completely.

You can scroll, seems like the only thing you can do, and the content is sequential.

You post by tapping the little icon at the bottom of the screen. A floating button that resembles a squinted eye. It conjures an overlay where you choose between text and video.

You can't see who your fellow "Lifers" are following, can't look back through their old posts, and definitely cannot DM-slide.

A super-limiting experience.

Kylie continues scrolling. There *has* to be something because so far there's nothing.

Vanilla content teetering on spam. Generic thoughts posted from accounts with usernames like @Kris2489759843734590.

They share stories about pets and promote URLs you'd have to be a grandmother to click. One headline reads YOU DON'T BELIEVE HOW THIS CAT EATS DINNER.

"Nice try, Putin," Kylie mumbles while scrolling past, seeing that story reposted again and again. You *don't* believe? The English is wrong. Which doesn't make it bad, but if you're ExtremelyOnline™, it sets your scam senses tingling.

She scrolls and finds another story being spammed in much the same way. This one about a bombing in Syria. A school bus filled with children turned into collateral damage via drone strike.

She keeps scrolling. Passes surveillance videos of people getting "rekd." Passes recipes for decadent cake with pretty pastel frosting. Kylie's mouth waters. She lifts her shirt and rubs the flat of her tummy to stave off any unwanted urges.

Honestly, this app is exhausting. Worse than Threads, which she opened once two summers ago and never looked back at. Kylie would've logged off already had she not dropped a hundred of Erin's bucks on it. But there's nothing here. A ghost town so lame Mom wouldn't scroll through it.

She tosses her phone to the foot of the bed and reaches for the bottle of lorazepam on her end table. Pops a pill, crosses her arms, and pouts at her device as if waiting for it to apologize.

"This is stupid," she says. "*You're* stupid." She crawls to the edge of her mattress and recovers it, closing out MonoLife. Probably for good. "See, problem solved."

If she skips Instagram tonight, everyone tomorrow will be talking about those who did not. Part of being a content creator means producing the content that people talk about. Digital silence isn't an option when you're trying to climb the ladder.

Only, she doesn't want to see Erin's Instagram. The hearts on that diving board post will be insane by now. She can't stomach that. Her and Cameron, rubbing their relationship in her Bradyless face.

She gasps at the amount of unread notifications on her phone: Eight missed calls. Twenty-nine texts. All these came through while she was on MonoLife. Never got a single alert.

"Oh God, Brady." A trembling thumb slides into her messages, finding nothing but Erin.

Kylie:

> hey, looks like stupid MonoLife doesn't show your messages while you're using it . . . sry

Erin:

> u were using it for that long???

> yep

> how????????

How? What kind of question was that? Before Kylie can answer, the ellipsis appears. Erin in rapid-fire mode.

> any luck figuring out how to use it?

> not rly

> will kill Deacon

> seems like a scam?

> def

Kylie brings her phone into the bathroom and streams "Ocean Drive" by Duke Dumont as she showers. A soothing escape as the lorazepam loosens her nerves and the warm water opens her pores, inviting electronica daydreams.

She's refreshed by the time she steps out and towels off, looking herself over in the mirror, clucking with disappointment: one breast appears larger than the other. Kylie strikes a dozen different poses looking for a position in which it does not appear that way.

She's got stretch marks on her inner thighs, like hot white scratches running vertically toward her hips. Swimsuit season's a bitch with these and Kylie presses her fingers against them, pulling her flesh to make them disappear. It's no use. Never has been.

Finally, there's her toes. The second one is taller than the big toe on both feet. Royal toe, they call it. Kylie avoids looking down whenever she's barefoot, otherwise she fixates.

It's no wonder Brady has ghosted her.

She slips an old *Friends* tee over her head, last year's Christmas gift from Mom because bingeing the show was the only thing she remembers them doing together, and can't even recall when that was. And now that she's clean and covered, she's thinking about content creation again.

Something innocent but . . . not.

She snaps a few pictures, settling on one where her nipples poke against the fabric. Her sweet-yet-seductive smile is catnip to the creepers, but whatevs. Erin says living online inevitably means being immortalized in someone's fap folder.

"This one," Kylie says. The longer she stares at the photo, the better she looks. Better than Erin, honestly. Wet red hair darker than cherries, lighting that makes her crystal blues pop, and all her hideous imperfections out of frame, out of mind.

Good enough to go #nofilter, except people who use #nofilter are always bragging about how good they look. And if you have that attitude, then you're inviting people to meme you into oblivion.

The internet hates arrogance. The trick is hiding yours behind humility.

So, nah. Kylie applies a filter. A light one, taken from her usual set so her brand remains consistent—the first rule of Instagramming: ensure all your photos are of a piece.

She captions it **All Clean**, adds a winking emoji and a few hashtags. The likes find her in record time, most from people who don't follow.

Her notification bell goes off instantly.

Erin:

> nice tits, slut ;)

She doesn't like the post, though.

In a world where people bend over backward to lie to your face, nothing cuts to the truth like someone's refusal to like your post.

This "friendly competition" is doomed to go on forever, unacknowledged. Because the truth is uncomfortable. Kylie knows where she stands. And that's right in Erin's shadow. Exactly where Erin wants her.

But that's how Kylie knows her content is really good. When Erin ignores it.

She hops into bed and rolls onto her side. The TV sits against the far wall. A little Disney+ before passing out. *Hannah Montana*. Pure, unfettered nostalgia that takes her back to simpler times.

Kylie's phone barks. A metallic screech that stiffens the hairs on her arm, makes her jaw vibrate. A sound she's never heard before.

She reaches for the device. That weird logo with its squinted eye stares up at her.

MonoLife, wanting to be heard.

The lock screen notification says: **You've used us. Now join us!**

Kylie sits up. Huh. *This* is interesting. She swipes the lock screen and MonoLife loads.

Want to see more?

Post a profile picture to get people talking.

Navigation dots at the bottom indicate a few more screens to swipe through.

The second one is a static shot of a MonoLife feed, only these posts have engagement, a comment counter and fist bumps, which seems to be this app's version of a "like."

Swipe.

The third screen says, **Tell your story, live your life with others**. It encourages you to make a post in order to get on your way.

Maybe that's the trick. Find something to post about. Funny how she wasn't given this guidance earlier. She puts the phone back down and stretches, realizing she doesn't have any sense of what MonoLife is beyond a bunch of garbage content with zero engagement.

Outside, an animal's yelp shakes her back to reality. Then a second, more wounded cry passes through the air.

A whimpering animal.

Now Kylie's sitting up.

And then someone outside begins to scream.

Neighborhood Watchers

Kylie stands in the open doorway, looking at a lump of shadows on the front lawn. The porch lights don't reach that far into the dark.

A whimpering voice shouts, *"Sporto! What did they do?"*

Kylie is startled but curious and takes a step down, clicking on her phone light. A few more steps and the shadows melt off Mrs. Elrond, her next-door neighbor, kneeling in the grass, nightgown mud-caked and torn from having pushed through the shrubs that divide their yards.

Her collie, Sporto, is plopped onto his side by her knees, wheezing. What looks like a small arrow shaft is jutting up from his stomach.

"They killed him!" Mrs. Elrond shrieks. The word *killed* reverberates down the street as porch lights click on in weirdly perfect succession.

The dog's fluffy golden mane has been repainted red. He lifts a lazy paw, trying to crawl farther into the lap of his owner because it's safe there.

"Call an ambulance!" Mrs. Elrond screams.

Kylie lifts her phone, starts to say, "I'm not sure you can do that for—" then glimpses Mrs. Elrond in the residual light, snarling and panting like an animal herself, and decides to call 911 anyway.

She explains the situation to a frustrated agent. Yes, she knows this isn't for pets, but someone's dog has been shot and could you please just send someone?

Mrs. Elrond's ambient hysteria convinces the operator to dispatch a patrol car.

"That you, Cathy?!" someone calls out. Other neighbors are beginning to take watch on their porches, curious silhouettes looking to ensure the disturbance is contained because the reality of life in the burbs is *This better not become my problem.*

And it definitely better not fuck up my lawn.

Kylie toggles to her phone's camera, circling the collie. Sporto's wheezes are the sound of a snow shovel on pavement. She films the dog from all angles and then decides that broken old Mrs. Elrond is a more interesting subject.

She zooms in on streaking tears, fascinated by the grief. By Mrs. Elrond's guttural sobs, her far-gone eyes possessed of shimmering madness. If this is what it's like to love someone, it's just too much pressure.

"Put the goddamn phone down, will ya?" an approaching neighbor shouts. The vitriol in that voice is so strong that Kylie actually does.

Poor Sporto. This trusting dog would drop his long gray snout into Kylie's lap whenever she sat outside texting Brady. He barely ever barked. Never shat in anyone's yard. If he was outside, he would follow the youngest kids to the school bus in the morning and greet them again at day's end.

Kylie gets on her knees and runs her hand through a clean patch of fur by the dog's head. Sporto shifts to see who's touching him and Mrs. Elrond swats Kylie's hand away, screaming, "That's too much energy! He'll die!"

"Hey, it's me, buddy," Kylie whispers. "Take it easy, okay? Help's coming."

The dog gives a miserable whine and another small geyser of blood blasts out from around the bolt, as if rejecting her assurances.

"Where are they?" Mrs. Elrond shrieks.

Kylie brings her head closer to the grass, right up against Sporto's snout so he can see her. So that she can see him.

Despite her taking vids, Kylie doesn't enjoy this. It's not looking good for Sporto. She'll miss her old pal, though her curiosity is genuine: What does it look like when the lights go out?

Mrs. Elrond screams into the dirt, rubbing her face around like she's trying to stick her head underground. In the moment, she looks ridiculous.

Kylie has no poker face for this sort of thing. Has to bite her cheek to keep from laughing. But that's when she realizes something else: she doesn't care.

Doesn't care Sporto is dying. Doesn't care that someone has murdered him. And *definitely* doesn't feel the need to console Mrs. Elrond.

"Who did this?" Kylie asks, because that's the most interesting question in the world right now.

In the distance, police sirens grow closer.

"I saw it," Mrs. Elrond says at barely a whisper.

"Saw what?"

Mrs. Elrond points to the unkempt bushes wrapping around the side of Kylie's house. Her finger pegging a spot directly beneath Kylie's bedroom window. "They had a . . ."

People are rushing toward them, flashlight beams dancing across the lawn.

"What?" Kylie asks.

A police car bounces up onto the curb, lights flashing, but lacking the screeching siren wail that would sell this as an emergency.

"Mrs. Elrond?" Kylie says.

Her neighbor looks up, face smeared with dirt, blood, and streaking tears, everything swirling together into a nightmarish watercolor. "They shot him with a crossbow" is all she can manage.

Kylie bites the inside of her lip again, drawing blood, desperate to prevent the inappropriate smile this revelation brings: there's an actual psychopath in the neighborhood.

Melissa again? Is there an emoji-masked psycho girl creeping through backyards and shrubbery here in Summerfield?

This revelation should terrify her—Kylie's alone in the house way more than she isn't. For some reason, though, it barely bothers her.

She's still chewing on her cheek, still fighting that smile that's desperate to be revealed, truly grateful for some excitement in her life, finally.

First Tries

The boy Kylie's hoping to find is in the college theater, center stage in an otherwise empty auditorium, surrounded by an armory of Styrofoam swords.

"Hi, Ben," she calls out from the back.

Ben Austin, on hands and knees, turns around. He's using a detailing brush to touch up flaking paint on the props. "Hi!" he exclaims, taking his glasses off and wiping them with the bottom of his Nintendo shirt. He's maybe the only person left on earth who wears Coke-bottle lenses.

Last year, Kylie had stressed to him the importance of shampoo and is happy to see he's taken that lesson to heart. No more flakes on his head and shoulders.

She climbs the stage and nudges him with her hip. She's wearing red flowy shorts, mostly all thigh, and that prompts him to flinch. "Why are you working so hard? It's only like day two of the semester."

Ben twists his face, can't seem to understand why he wouldn't be. "We're doing Shakespeare this year and these things look more like kids toys than theater props."

"How boring. Shakespeare, I mean. Not your efforts to glow these up."

"You transferring into theater? That why you're here?"

"Pretty sure my stage days are over."

And if they weren't before, they would be now. Shakespeare is for cowards. The Bard gets a continued pass because nobody actually understands what he's talking about. Audiences fool themselves into believing it's culture while their only real thrill comes from watching teenagers spout sexual innuendos, those they can recognize anyway.

"So, you're, what?" Kylie asks. "Getting a head start on all this?"

Ben runs a hand over the tip of a foam sword. A clear tube of Lexel is beside it. "Coating each blade with elastic sealant, giving them a nice, shiny texture. Paint them cherry red after and they'll look nice and gory beneath the theater lights once people start getting stabbed."

"Out to trigger the soccer moms?"

"Standards and practices are boring." Ben looks away. "I haven't talked to you in like forever."

"I know. I miss Bio. Was actually sort of hoping you'd do your old lab partner one more favor?"

"Sure," Ben says. No hesitation. "Right now?"

Kylie wants to tell him to not be so eager, but that lesson can wait.

His yellow Volkswagen is well-kept, not so much as a straw wrapper on the floor. They putter over to Kylie's place and she keeps him waiting in the driveway while she grabs supplies. He's eyeing her backpack when she returns, tossing it onto the floor between her legs.

"This isn't going to get me beaten up or anything . . . right?" he asks.

"And if I said yes?"

"I mean . . . I'd still do it."

They drive to Sundae Hill Plaza on the edge of town and park on the far side of Target.

"Okay," Kylie says, clamping her phone to a gimble and then attaching a tripod. "I'll set up over there." She gestures to a spot between two pickup trucks, then reaches into her bag and removes a pair of leggings, dropping them in Ben's lap.

"These?" He looks like a mischievous child as he turns the reality of what's being asked of him over in his mind. Kylie hops out and then the car's bumping around as Ben slides off his jeans and shimmies into the supplied tights.

When he emerges, he's thin, kind of gangly, but doesn't look terrible in leggings. Nobody does, so long as their body has any kind of curve. That's the beauty of them.

Kylie arranges the scene, popping the Volkswagen's hood, bending Ben over like he's having engine trouble. "Like this," she says, pulling his hips back a bit so his rear stretches tight over the fabric, making it a little transparent. Making his ass really pop. She's seen this prank a million times on Reels and it never misses.

"Hold it there." Kylie frames his butt in the shot, stepping back across the pavement until she's nestled anonymously into her alcove.

"How do I look?" Ben asks, finding the nerve to twerk without the slightest hint of rhythm.

"Like a juicy apple," Kylie giggles. "You clear on what we're doing?"

Ben gives a thumbs-up and stays bent in position.

A guy comes out of the sporting goods shop across the way, AirPods in, sunglasses on. Ben spots him and sticks his ass way out, broadcasting.

Sporting Goods Bro picks right up on the signal, neck craning as he passes, mouthing, "Damn." That's when Ben brings his pasty head up, Coke-bottle lenses reflecting the afternoon sun.

"Whatcha staring at?" Ben asks, confrontational. His confidence in this moment, rather surprising.

"Oh, hey, man," Sporting Goods Bro says. "My bad."

"Don't stop looking. You were into it."

Kylie's laughing so hard her stomach is doing crunches as she fights to maintain silence.

"I'm straight, bro."

"You sure?" Ben says. "It's no big thing these days."

Sporting Goods Bro takes off, breaking into a nervous jog, but a couple of girls are coming up the same row now and Ben has spotted them, already back in position. Their conversation dips as they near him, spotting that ass.

Ben pokes his head up again. "What do you say, ladies?"

They erupt into peals of laughter.

"Were you checking out my butt?"

More giggles.

"You're not jealous, are you?" he asks. "This sculpt?"

"Oh my God. You need help!"

Ben starts bouncing for them and it's a bridge too far for the girls, who rush off, shrieking, in the same direction as Sporting Goods Bro.

Kylie and Ben capture half a dozen unsuspecting victims like this. It's all very liberating for Kylie, showing men what the unending leer of goblin eyes can feel like.

A few of Erin's friends and former cheer teammates—Samara and Brandi—are coming up the hill, boyfriends Asher and Shaun beside them. Neither boy is shy about turning their head as they pass.

"Hey." Ben springs up like a striking cobra, and everyone sort of lunges away from him. "What's up, guys?"

Samara and Brandi scoff, but kind of chuckle too.

"Why you looking at my butt?" Ben asks.

"No one is—you got problems, man," Asher says, laughing.

"*I* do? You're the ones looking."

Shaun spins around, gets in Ben's face, shoving him, puffing out his chest.

"Hey," Asher says. "Cool down—you're probably being pranked or some shit." It's possible that he's spotted Kylie across the way, but Asher keeps his poker face, and Kylie both notes and appreciates this confidentiality.

"You'd better not be here when I get back," Shaun growls.

"Or what? You'll stare at my ass again?" Ben tugs the fabric so his bum is even more transparent. "Can't say I blame you."

"Fuck off, weirdo," Shaun barks, but doesn't escalate things any further than that.

Once they're gone, Kylie rushes across the lot and throws her arms around Ben. "You did amazing!" His hands hover against her back, too timid to connect.

"Th-thanks," he says, looking down at his leggings. "Want these back?"

"Um, no. They're yours now. A souvenir."

"They are pretty comfortable."

"Everyone loves yoga pants."

Ben brings her back home and they're sitting in the driveway, a moment of silence passing between them. Kylie lets it hang, rooting to see a little more confidence out of him, curious if he's anything but one of those soft boys Katy writes songs about.

Ben shifts his gaze to the driver-side window. "I had fun."

"Me too."

"Promise you won't be a stranger?"

"Yeah," Kylie promises. All she wants is to get inside and start cutting this footage. She hops out and on her way to the door throws Ben a flirty grin over her shoulder.

He smiles the whole way down the driveway and probably for a lot longer after that too.

Kylie AirDrops the footage onto her MacBook—last year's Christmas gift, and only a slight upgrade over the previous year's model that she begged for anyway because of its improved FaceTime experience. An entirely new image signal processor that enhances detail in normal lighting scenarios but, more importantly, makes her look great in trickier low-light moments.

She scrolls MonoLife while the data transfers. The content in her main feed is somehow worse than last night, a few racist jokes mixed in alongside an author attempting to promote her "existential apocalypse novel" while berating her imaginary audience for constantly labeling her a "genre writer."

Kylie minimizes the window, goes to Google, and types in: *Mono-Life*. Some European band has the same name, and the app seems to have zero web presence.

How is that even possible? Kylie clicks through seven pages of results. There's exactly one relevant entry, from the 4chan archive of all places:

Believe me anons, you may think MonoLife is everything you want, but the more you use it the harder it is to put down. It's digital crack, guaranteed to kill you. Curb your curiosity, before it's too late. Already is for me.

Zero replies. Even the darkest corner of the internet is afraid to touch this. It's ominous, unsettling, and a flicker of apprehension settles inside Kylie's stomach as her footage finishes transferring to the laptop. The discomfort passes quickly, before she spends any real amount of time considering it.

She streams an album, Katy's *One of the Boys*, because she needs that vibe to create something fun here and that record is loaded with good memories. She was only two when it came out, and inherited her initial appreciation from Mom, who would spin it on CD over and over.

Kylie remembers how Dad would film these cute little videos of her prancing and singing the title track at the top of her lungs. How he'd laugh hysterically because the playful coming-of-age message was over her head—Katy singing about taping down her D-cups, shaving her legs, loving *Evita*—Kylie still doesn't know what that is, some old movie from the nineties, last she googled.

Whatever. Katy helps her find the necessary headspace to work, and the video's first edit is four minutes. She cuts it down, then even more mercilessly. Now it's one minute, fifty-eight seconds.

Kylie's flirty intro is her face from the mouth down, a fresh mint smile to get people's attention. The rest is all money shots. Ben doing his thing.

She finds some zany public-domain song to layer beneath the action and it's ready to go.

She logs on to MonoLife and fills out the rest of @CrystalShip's profile so that her bio reads "Floating in the night," which makes her sound way deeper and more contemplative than she is.

"Here goes," she says, heart pounding. Her mind flashes ahead, imagining thousands of followers off this.

Kylie hits the little eye icon at the bottom of her screen and clicks UPLOAD VIDEO. Her thumb hovers. One deep breath before pressing.

Click.

The content is MonoLife's now. Kylie feels accomplished. And exhausted.

It's a quick shower and a bowl of oatmeal before bed. She catches up on Insta. Erin's post is a bunch of abs, Cameron and three others, their shirts pulled up. The caption reads, **One for the ladies.**

"Four thousand likes?!" Kylie sighs. She double-taps the screen, giving it a begrudging endorsement.

Erin immediately texts:

FaceTime comes calling. Erin, lying in bed beneath pink sheets. "Why are you still up?"

"Late dinner." Kylie dips the phone down to the oatmeal.

"Mmmmmm, gruel. Yum."

"How was your night?"

"I think I pulled a muscle working out. My left ass cheek hurts."

"Ask Cameron to rub it."

"He tried. Felt like aliens at a petting zoo."

Kylie laughs.

"Oh, hey . . . how was your date with Ben Austin?" Erin tries to suppress her laughter and it becomes a throaty snort, like clearing phlegm. Of course Asher and Brandi had noticed Kylie outside Target. "That's . . . a major step down, hun."

"It wasn't a date."

"Well, I hate to tell you this, but everyone's talking about your new boyfriend."

"He's not . . ." Kylie doesn't finish the sentence. Disconnects instead. "Asshole."

A high-pitched wail ignites through the phone speaker, grinding metal she can't stand to hear. It's so severe she cups her hands over her ears and grunts, "What the hell?" Head-splitting noise that gets her eardrums pulsing, refusing to recede, even as she ticks the volume all the way down to mute. An on-screen badge slides across the display: *People are noticing you! Log in to see.*

She opens MonoLife, annoyed but craving validation even more. Something to show Erin in the morning so she can watch that smug face drop. Prove to her that Kylie's someone.

Four replies. Eight fist bumps.

Kylie feels like she's stepped outside herself. This can't be right. There's no way. She clicks COMMENTS to open them.

@DirtNap10: Fuck off back to TikTok.

@AdeleDazeem: Show your pussy or gtfo

The others are in foreign languages and MonoLife lacks a translation feature.

She refreshes the feed, thinking her Wi-Fi's just slow, or this app is on a delay or . . . something.

But no. She shot her shot and sank like a stone. All that effort and MonoLife has rejected her.

Kylie tosses and turns all night, never once finding sleep.

Where You See Yourself

Kylie's sitting in her academic advisor's office for what's supposed to be a meet and greet, but he's already grilling her about schools she should be looking at transferring to next year. That's because Kylie told him she doesn't want to bother with her associate's, and he's taken that to mean she's looking for a four-year school. And now she simply doesn't feel like correcting him, letting him scroll a couple of university websites, describing their strengths and weaknesses as her eyes glaze over.

"What about Williamson U?" he says.

"I heard that's a bad school. Like, really shitty."

"Depends on what you want to study."

Fame and fortune is what she wants to say—the only answer for someone who wishes to be professionally hot for a living—but knows how it'll sound. She just shrugs instead.

"They have a social media class." He says this like he's humoring a child. "That should be interesting. So—I'll email you this link, you can check it out." He forces a smile that looks like he's staring at the sun.

Kylie leaves his office without thanking him. Finds Erin in the hall, waiting. Eyes wider than umbrellas.

"What are you doing here?"

"Some new energy drink wants to fly Cameron and me to Los Angeles!" Erin squeals. "Shoot a couple promos at a launch event. All expenses paid and a few extra days to make a vacation out of it!" Kylie hates getting this news in person. So much more difficult to fake enthusiasm face-to-face. The good thing is Erin barely notices this sourness. "So who knows? I mean, Mom will be fine with me going because life is more than classes, ya know?"

"My advisor doesn't think so."

"Dad won't understand," Erin says. "I mean what else is new, right? But that's what mothers are for . . . running interference."

"Yay for you." It's a sulking response. The best Kylie can do.

"Going to be awesome." Erin drives right over it. "And once a few other companies see us doing it . . ."

Kylie tunes it out, haunted by the psychic violence of five simple, cutting words from a complete stranger who thought @DirtNap10 was the best handle out there: *Fuck off back to TikTok.* How could she have misread MonoLife so badly? She wanted to be funny. That video *was* funny. And cute and kind of mischievous. The perfect brand. But maybe not?

"Gotta get to class, but had to tell you," Erin says, rushing off.

Kylie remains there and opens MonoLife, thinking maybe her post has gained some traction somewhere between this morning's Nutri-Grain bar and now.

The eight fist bumps hang there, a screaming indictment of her failure. In a way, it would've been better if it had gone completely ignored. She could blame the algorithm. But no. People watched her video and hated it so much they crawled out of digital dark space to tell her.

Failure follows her everywhere. To class, where lectures and lessons are distractions. To a lunch break, where Erin isn't done talking about her good fortunes and Kylie's expected to sit there and feign excitement while her life is in tatters. Erin making a few more snickering comments about Ben Austin that Kylie has no desire to address.

She's just so . . . defeated.

Mom texts after the last class of the day to say she hasn't had a chance to go grocery shopping, so here's thirty bucks in your Uber Eats, but Kylie can't even think about food right now. She wanders the halls, nose to phone, contemplating a Lyft ride across the state when a hand clamps on to her shoulder. Kylie yelps. Heads turn, everyone looking.

Ben Austin's there, smirking. Tall and gangly and his hair cemented into place from too much gel, probably because nobody has ever told him that you're supposed to rub it in once your head's *dry*. Another lesson she'll have to impart.

"Sorry, Kylie."

"Nah, it's fine."

"Was just wondering, uh, if you need any more help?"

"With?"

"Anything?"

"Go paint your swords, Ben."

That strikes him like a crossbow bolt to the heart, and he looks about as pathetic as Mrs. Elrond's dying dog. A couple of turned heads snicker. Text messages already flying. More grist for the rumor mill.

Kylie hurries off, thinking about Williamson University. How it's two hours from here and the ride's eighty bucks. One way.

She checks train schedules. There's one that goes straight to the center of that college town, and the university runs shuttles until eleven.

The next train leaves the station at five. Commuter time.

"Okay," Kylie says, and a few minutes later has a purchased ticket on her phone.

She needs Brady. More than she's ever needed anyone.

She reaches Williamson U around seven.

The campus quad is roughly three times the size of Summerfield Community College. Half-naked trees sway in fresh swirling air and students lounge in tiny pockets beneath them. Their laughter and friendship are sickening.

The boy at Residential Services won't let her upstairs to see Brady because Kylie isn't on his guest list.

And he's not in his room.

"Can I just wait, then?" she asks. The student barely nods.

Kylie drops into one of the oversized lobby chairs, no idea how she's getting home. If this isn't somehow the dumbest thing she's done in a week jam-packed with dumb things . . .

"Hi . . . you're Brady's girl?" A guy who's just come in is asking this, hovering a couple of feet away. He wears a criminal justice polo branded in the university's colors, and his weight shifts between left and right feet as if he's standing on hot coals.

"Yeah. I'm Kylie," she says pointedly.

"No, I didn't mean to imply you're property. Shit. I need to be mindful of that." This annoys Kylie even more. She isn't some live wire to be hot-stepped around. "I just mean . . . I recognize you from Brady's profile pic."

"Oh." Now she's fighting a smile that keeps trying to form because it is nice to be recognized. Even nicer to be remembered. "Is he here?"

"Nope."

"But you just walked in. Do you . . . know where he is?"

"Nope." He's very fast to get that out.

"Then how do you know he isn't here?"

The color flushes from his face. No chill.

"Sorry, what's your name again?" she asks.

"Andrew."

"Andrew . . . okay. I get it. You don't want to betray your bro. But here's where I'm at . . . it took me a *long* time to get here tonight and now I'm kind of stranded. I have no choice but to hang around. And if I don't see Brady, I'll just have to tell his parents there's no sign of him up here. And if you know his parents—well, that'll make things worse. A *lot* worse."

Andrew's whiter than milk now. "Yeah, okay. Yeah. I, uh . . . I guess I can take you to him."

He goes back out the door. Doesn't bother holding it for her.

They're headed down a side street off campus and Kylie asks, "Who lives around here?"

Andrew quickens his pace so that Kylie's a few steps behind.

"*Andrew.* Who?"

"Uh, upperclassmen. Most of them live off campus." He stops at the foot of three stone steps that lead to a tilted porch. The muted Cardi B bass line barely hides the moans coming from beyond the window there.

Kylie's heart flops into the pit of her stomach. Turn around and go, just go and forget, she knows. The path of least resistance preferable on most days.

Her fist buzzes.

Erin:

> need to tell you about this call I just had

It's hard to know what incenses Kylie more in this moment. Brady being balls-deep in some girl, or Erin with yet another golden opportunity. And it almost doesn't matter, because life is passing Kylie by either way.

She climbs onto the porch. Sneakers bending the wooden planks as she passes the jutting bay windows, a headboard smashing to the rhythm.

The round of her fist hammers the door, demanding entry.

Behind her, Andrew sulks off, practically melting into the shadows.

Approaching footsteps. A blur crosses the peephole. Muffled words Kylie hears anyway: "I don't know. Some girl."

A chain clacks from the other side. Then the door opens an inch and there's a woman's face beneath golden bangs.

"Is Brady here?" Kylie's voice is small but determined.

"Um, I don't know who that is."

The moans coming through the wall speak on Kylie's behalf.

The blonde's mouth tightens. A wincing look. A hard swallow. "Your boyfriend . . . ?"

Kylie nods.

"I'll get him."

The door slams and Kylie goes to pieces, wiping tears from her eyes. The sound of sex going on pause. Silhouettes pass in front of drawn curtains, shadows looking out. Then, in a second, they become rushing footsteps.

The door creaks open again and here's Brady in the jamb. Shirtless. Sweaty. He glares out like Kylie's a stray cat that followed him home. "What?"

"That's all you have to say to me? '*What?*'"

"How about '*What the fuck?*'" Surprisingly cruel eyes stare back at her. This person looks a lot like Brady, except she's never seen him so cold and detached. "Why are you here?!" He's shouting now.

"I missed you isn't enough of a reason?"

"Take a hint, okay?!"

"Hint! Hint? We dated for a year and a half—I'm entitled to more than a hint!"

"Because you say so?"

"Because it's the decent thing to do, asshole!"

"Well, news flash: turns out there's a whole world out there, and I have a whole world of needs. More than you could ever give. How's that for decent?"

This open hostility makes Kylie lightheaded. Knowing that his partner's probably in earshot just beyond the door makes it all the more humiliating. "Why didn't you just talk—"

"Oh, I shouldn't have to spell it out, Kylie!" he roars. "Piss off back to kindergarten!"

The door rushes toward Kylie's face. She leaps back and yelps. That unexpected rending of emotion breaks her. Tears flood down her cheeks as she stands in the gloom, utterly stunned. She didn't come here expecting to have to defend her celibacy. For as often as Brady begged for it, Kylie had assumed she had more time. Time to find her confidence, time to make it good and right.

At nineteen, Kylie has accepted that many people her age had grown up with an overarching awkwardness. For a while, their world had been one of perpetual Zooms, intimacies exchanged via FaceTime as a substitute for everything else. Lives vacuum-sealed inside inescapable digital realities. In truth, Kylie has always preferred that world to the harshness out here, the pressure of having to know what others are thinking while adhering to unspoken expectations. Always worrying whether you're good enough.

You're not.

She collapses on stone steps, crying as her phone continues to ding. Erin has written a novella and Kylie can't stand to read it right now. She ignores it all, typing:

Kylie:

I saw him. It's over.

Immediate ellipsis.

Erin:

wat? who???

Brady

u went there? To Will U??

yeah caught him screwing someone else

oh god. how r you getting back?

idk

A long ellipsis, then:

I'll be there in 40 minutes. Go to the library and wait

It might as well be forty years, as Kylie can't move. She's anchored to these steps. She wishes she was stronger, but has always been a weakling. Always been stupid. And ugly.

God, she's devastated. And she really fucking hates that she is.

The last thing she wants is to stagger into the library with a tear-streaked face, wet puffy eyes, red nose. Make a fool of herself in front of a bunch of strangers. No, the shadows are better. Anonymous. She puts her head in her hands and cries.

She sits there for so long the music comes back. Some Young Thug song. The moans are slow to follow, but they come too. Little grace notes punctuating her ears with additional torment.

Then the headboard's knocking again.

Kylie sees sidewalk cracks through her trembling fingers, eyes beginning to blaze. Everything's falling apart.

Piss off back to kindergarten, he said.

Fuck off back to TikTok.

She rises. Crosses the porch, instinct and emotion riding her. She glances down—her phone's tight in her fist, MonoLife open. She doesn't remember doing that.

A few quick taps and she's looking at herself in the glass, a mess of smeared mascara and frayed hair. A real Taylor Swift in "Blank Space" vibe.

One more tap and the camera is back to looking out on the world. She smashes RECORD as her leg goes sailing through the front door, breaking the jamb into splintered wood. The sound of scrambling bodies moving in panic.

"If you can hear that," Kylie growls, "it's the sound of my boyfriend screwing somebody else on his fourth day of college."

In the kitchen, the girl who had met her at the door stands with her phone in hand, filming.

"Don't bother!" Kylie shouts, banking a right and kicking through the flimsy interior door.

Brady and some other blonde in bed, writhing in almost perfect rhythm. Their bodies glistening beneath the lava lamp mood light.

Kylie goes straight for it, tearing it from its wall socket, hurling it across the room.

"Hi, Brady," she says as the bodies scramble apart, struggling to cover their modesty beneath bedsheets.

"Get out, you crazy bitch!" the blonde screams.

Kylie's circling to Brady's side of the bed. She sits down, patting him over the thin sheet. "Want to tell my followers why you're cheating on me?"

"Out of my house!" Blonde #2 screams. Kylie lifts the phone, giving MonoLife a glimpse of her pasty ass as she scurries out of frame, rushing for the exit with clothes in her fists.

"That leaves just us," Kylie says, bringing MonoLife back to Brady, who's placed an empty pillowcase over his face. "Oh, stop that—you're not a ghost."

"I have nothing to say!"

"That's fine." Kylie yanks the bedsheet away and Brady cups his hands over his shriveled modesty.

"Kylie, Jesus!"

"This is Brady McKenna, ladies and gentlemen. A freshman at Williamson U. He's handsome and eligible. And if you're thinking about dating him, just know the kind of guy you're getting. Pond scum."

He rolls onto his side, gets caught in his own tangled legs, and tumbles off the bed, flashing his most unflattering angle.

And he's whimpering now, but mercy is a lost cause where Kylie's concerned. He crawls toward the door as Kylie's phone roves his body. "Not much of a man, is he?"

"Total psycho," someone from the next room is saying.

This sends her. Kylie plucks a field hockey stick from its leaned position against the wall, holds it like a club. She slams it down across

Brady's naked back, smashing him again and again, making him cry out in pain as he drops to his side.

"See, Brady thinks I should've given him my virginity. We never discussed it, of course. He just thinks I should've been glad to do it. Want to know what really hurts? I was *planning* to. Didn't think there was a clock I had to beat, though. I mean, you couldn't go four days. A well-behaved dog lasts longer."

Brady scurries to his feet as he reaches the kitchen linoleum. Kylie follows. The other suitemates are gathered around the table, one of them on the phone to campus security, the others hot-stepping to keep their distance.

This fear emboldens her, filming naked Brady as he cowers behind Blonde #2, who's now cinching a bathrobe.

It's immediately exciting, uncharted territory for Kylie.

She flinches forward and they hop backward. Something about this makes her laugh. "You could've talked to me, Brady." Kylie opens the fridge, pulling an egg from the tray. "You could've told me you were getting impatient."

"You pretend to be so naïve," Brady says. "How about you step up and make something happen for once."

"I am."

"Just go, bitch!" one of the women screams.

"What you don't get to do is treat me like the last year and a half never happened." Kylie winds back. Blonde #2, sensing what's coming, ducks as Kylie throws. The egg catches Brady square in the face, breaking across his mouth.

The girl on the end—the one who originally opened the door and seemed to give Kylie a little sympathy—laughs and Kylie decides that she kind of likes her. Collectively, these people have given her this power and she's fucking high on it. A rush like nothing she's ever experienced.

"Enjoy him," Kylie snarls, taking one last look at the domestic carnage she's caused. The fear manifesting on each of their faces, except Brady, who's actually crying now. Sufficiently broken.

Then Kylie's marching back through the ruined front door and to the street in confidence, feeling like a new woman.

She's close to the library—the large glass structure at the end of the street is like a beacon, warm and glowing. She speed-walks while her phone screams out, ears rattling to the sound she can't seem to silence. Mono-Life's refusal to be ignored. She has to slide the device into her pocket.

Across the street, a shadow moves silently over a tiny patch of lawn, sidestepping all streetlights.

Kylie walks harder. Behind her, the shadow glides onto the sidewalk, clopping along, keeping pace with her. Footfalls that are closer in sound to that of an animal. *Clip clop clip clop.*

She's walking faster, the library light stretching across the horizon like a band. She isn't going to run. Some stupid abstraction inside her that favors dignity over preservation.

This creeper won't have the satisfaction. He doesn't get to rain on tonight's parade. Not when for the first time ever, Kylie feels powerful. In control.

Clip clop clip clop. The shadow in her peripheral.

Now she's on the last block before the library. Close enough to see students in the glass there, slumped in lounge chairs, heads to laptops.

And the shadow keeps perfect pace on the sidewalk across the street, matching not only her speed, but her motions too.

Up ahead, a few kids in off-campus housing are laughing hysterically at something that's probably funny only to them. Their presence offering something close enough to safety. Kylie looks over and—

—the shadow has stopped.

Because so has Kylie.

The shadow is taller than any man she's ever seen. Lopsided and lanky. It rocks nervously on the balls of its feet, just like her. She thinks it's a man? The darkness keeps its face a secret, though its motion seems determined to catch her attention.

One arm that's too long for its body drifts up to the front of where its face would be.

Kylie squints, catches it waving.

"Whatever," she sighs. "So lame." She rushes toward the laughing students. Toward the library light beyond them. Glances back over her shoulder and the shape is still there.

Still waving.

A pain ignites against the small of her back—a stitch of discomfort, like a massive bug bite—and then is gone in an instant.

The library's closer. Kylie rushing faster. Another glance over her shoulder where the shadow continues to wave, but is done following.

"How come you didn't ask me to come with?" Erin asks. But the question is just a springboard to other topics. She doesn't even wait for Kylie's answer before segueing, winds up talking the entire ride home. Mostly about potential sponsorships and what a big shot she's become. Kylie only listens. Sort of.

Her phone is in her lap. Somehow MonoLife has stopped shouting, has switched over to vibrating notifications without any modifications in Settings. It feels like a fluttering heartbeat against her thigh.

Erin's rambling about some upcoming collab with Lululemon. People whose names Kylie doesn't know. In this moment of personal triumph, though, Kylie realizes she feels genuine happiness for her friend, and is somewhat relieved to discover it isn't resentment that haunts her, but insecurity. Pure FOMO. The fright of being left behind.

Terror comes from having life goals one may never meet. Not everyone gets what they want, and what if it's Kylie who has to settle for second place? Or nothing at all?

No. That's not going to happen.

She looks at her phone every couple of minutes. And each time, her MonoLife view count is higher. Too many comments to read. She scrolls through anyway. Most of them are encouraging. A few laughing at the size of Brady's manhood. Those are okay too. Her favorite is, **u dodged a bullet, girl.**

One comment tells her to **Bobbitt the prick.** She has no idea what that means.

"You're sure you're okay?" Erin finally asks.

"Don't I look it?"

"Yeah. That's the thing. You *do* look it."

"I just needed to know. And now I do."

That's how things sit until they're in Kylie's driveway. "Hey," Erin says. "I would've been happy to come."

"Kind of a private thing. I, uh, actually thought I'd be spending the night."

"I thought there were no secrets between us."

"There aren't," Kylie says, thinking, *Except for all the bottomless, seething resentment I thought I had for you.* "I needed to do this myself. I probably need to do this more."

Erin's smile is sad. "You mean without me?"

"Well . . . we're getting older, right? You won't always be here."

Erin clicks her tongue disapprovingly. "I'm proud of you." She has more to say but leaves it at that.

"Thanks."

Erin sits idling as Kylie walks to the front door and unlocks it. And even when Kylie goes inside and closes it, Erin doesn't leave. Not for a moment or two.

Video

Kylie watches the video from the sanctuary of her bedroom, where it suddenly feels in poor taste, on the verge of going too far.

"Oh God," she mumbles, barely recognizing her on-screen actions, never once imagining she'd be capable of this.

But then comes the egg toss, the way it cracks oh so satisfying across Brady's stupid mouth. He flinches like he's been shot, his body reacting in a spastic, jerky rhythm. And there's the way one of the girls present reacts to this, a roaring hyena laugh from off camera. It becomes the lighthearted punchline, slightly softening Kylie's fire and fury. It's sort of why the whole thing works. One great big happy accident.

There's a chance she would be suspended if this were any other social media platform, but MonoLife loves it.

MonoLife loves @CrystalShips.

The view counter is at forty thousand. Nine hundred and ninety-eight fist bumps—

Make that nine hundred and ninety-*nine* fist bumps.

It's taken Kylie six years to find a fraction of this love on Instagram. And forget TikTok. Too much work to be like everybody else. "*Hey guys . . .*" All it took for MonoLife was one drastic bout of self-care.

Her first video, the leggings prank, is catching a bit of residual goodwill. Mostly from thirsty men commenting on how much they want to see Kylie in front of the camera for future videos. Maybe catch a glimpse of *her* ass in those leggings.

She's mulling over that request when tonight's video hits one thousand fist bumps and MonoLife's screen flickers in her hand, displaying a full-screen pop-up that reads, "THEY LIKE YOU! WELCOME TO USER."

She presses the OK button directly underneath the pop-up and suddenly the app seems . . . different. There's been no indication that it was updating—it all just blinked into existence. The MonoLife logo at the top of the screen is gone, replaced by a collapsible menu that currently offers two options: PROFILE and INBOX.

She taps PROFILE and that section now shows a follower/following count. She follows zero "Lifers" because this feature is brand-new to her, but she can finally begin to customize her experience with accounts that interest her. And she's followed by 2,003 people? Holy shit.

"I'm home." Kylie laughs, absolved in this moment of every care in the world. She brings MonoLife close to her face, basking in these mentions. She glances up at Katy, flashes the crinkled glossy poster a quick glimpse of her phone like they're suddenly peers.

No. *She* is Katy tonight. Somewhere on the road between the albums *Katy Hudson*—where the singer began her career under her birth name as a quirky Christian rocker—and *One of the Boys*, the moment she ascended to pop deity under the name Katy Perry, unleashing the masterpiece "I Kissed a Girl" on a now-permanent sexually fluid public. Coincidence?

It's Kylie's turn to emerge from her digital cocoon as a candy-colored influencer.

The comments under the video are adoring, mostly terrible pickup lines, but that's fine. She reads them all.

Twenty-five hundred followers and climbing.

Does she tell Erin?

No. Absolutely not.

It isn't enough of a head start. Maybe once Kylie's foothold here is so great that there's no reasonable way for anyone to catch up, then Erin can know.

This is all Kylie wants. Her own place in the world. A kingdom to call her own.

She hops from bed and moves into the bathroom, dropping her palms atop the cold ceramic sink, squinting at herself through the streaky mirror glass.

"You're not a bad person," she tells herself, wondering only now if anyone inside that dingy, off-campus apartment has called the police. She laughs at her empty self-assurance. Good people don't sit around waiting for the cops to come knocking.

Brady the cheater has blocked her across all social media. That doesn't bother her. He's been humiliated for all the world to see, for all of MonoLife to see, at least. He'll want it to go away. Fast. If Kylie's arrested for her actions, it'll just linger.

Nearly three thousand followers now. More messages than she can read.

Aaaand here come the DMs.

She gets comfortable in bed, stretching out, taking a deep breath. A smile, because why not see what the *men* of MonoLife are packing.

Her teeth are pressed against her lower lip in a bracing gesture as she smashes INBOX. The first message shows some tiny thing, a turtle head surrounded by a ring of foreskin hiding inside a forest of wire brush.

A deep belly laugh spills from Kylie. "Ugh. Gross." And instantly blocked.

A couple more, some bigger. More kempt, at least. *Why don't men understand how aesthetically challenged they are?* she wonders, deleting them all, feeling more playful as she goes, deciding against blocking the nicest ones.

Next up, a video message. Kylie plays it. A woman on her knees, head buried in her sofa. A panting German shepherd climbs onto her back, nibbling her shoulder as she laugh-screams, "*Oh God, honey, he's actually doing it—!*"

"Eww!" Kylie can't press BLOCK fast enough.

Another message lands as she's cleaning the rest of them out.

@BlueFerox: ever eat good?

Instead of the ellipsis that comes with text messages, the italics at the bottom of MonoLife's DMs reads *@BlueFerox is currently typing . . .*

A video drops into their conversation. Kylie braces, wondering whether to watch, realizing this is exactly what she needs. To be someone people want to talk to. She presses play.

The camera's pushing in on a small kitchen table, moving over warped linoleum past appliances older than Kylie. On the circular table sits an empty, foil-wrapped pan. "Hola, *Crystal,*" a woman says off camera. Her slender forearm reaches into frame and lifts a thick glove off the chair, sheathing long, brown fingers inside. They wiggle around in adjustment. "*Welcome to the party, baby girl.*"

The gloved hand reaches out of frame, voice straining as she lifts something onto the table, into the foil pan. The meatiest rack of ribs Kylie's ever seen.

"*They want us to wait in bread lines, you know.*" The woman's hand is dabbing the ribs with a paper towel, soaking up excess blood. "*Police are around to keep order, not to help.*"

Then the gloved hand squirts a bottle of mustard out over the ribs, fingers massaging the surface area with yellow condiment.

"*This one gets a chance to serve his community rather than his govern-ment.*" Once the ribs are coated in yellow, she gives the meat a playful slap. "*A binding agent, Crystal. It gives some flavor, sure, but what it really does is hold your rub in place.*"

Now the hand shakes a small bottle over the mustard-covered ribs until they're fully coated in seasoning. And the camera moves across the kitchen to a small patio that overlooks a city skyline. A small grill sits smoking there.

"*Slow and low for the next six hours.*" She carries the pan to the patio and uses a large pair of tongs to get the ribs onto the grill. "*Indirect heat, of course.*"

At last @BlueFerox turns the camera around, showing herself. She's older, mid-twenties, probably. And gorgeous. Raven-dark hair frames her face, highlighting sparkling green eyes, large lips, perfectly tweezed eyebrows.

Kylie is in awe of @BlueFerox, of Blue, and immediately decides she hates the sight of her.

"*We do what we must to keep going*," Blue says. "*That is life. And I am very interested in seeing more of yours, my lovely little piece of Crystal.*" Blue smiles, gives a casual wink as the video cuts to black. The end.

"Sure," Kylie says to her phone. "Whatever the hell that means."

The video has to be fake, right? That's her first thought, though if she were to believe the prevailing theory that Melissa had posted the murder of Annabeth to this app, then there truly were no limits here.

Why wouldn't there be a cannibal cooking channel?

Kylie's fingers wobble as she prepares a response to @BlueFerox, figuring it's the polite thing to do.

@CrystalShips: I want to see how those ribs come out. Make my mouth water. 😊😊😊

And that's enough inbox for now. Tomorrow she'll check the settings and find a way to prevent the weirdos from leaving dick pics. For now . . . oh wow, for now she can't get enough of her adoring public.

Every compliment validates tonight's rage.

Kylie wishes she could tell someone. Anyone. Even if she had to keep it vague so as not to spoil the MonoLife secret, there are no serious options. Mom, were she to be here, would simply shake her head. And Dad was even less plugged into the digital world. He would say he's "proud" while glancing at his watch and waiting until he could excuse himself from the conversation, get back to his new life.

Strangers on social media would have to do. In some ways, it's better. She feels closest to them now. Dancing for shadows is far less pressure.

Eventually she puts the phone down and stretches out beneath the sheets, trying to get comfortable. Her brain too wired for sleep.

There's that discomfort in her lower back again. She reaches around. "Ah!" Stunned by the sharp intake of pain. Her fingertips, stained with crusted blood. What the hell . . . ? Then she's back in the bathroom, twisted around, shirt up, looking at a small discoloration at the base of her spine.

She maneuvers some bacitracin on it and goes back to bed, the realities of tomorrow looming.

Suddenly, a bigger problem is on the horizon. Kylie's stomach wiggles as she considers it.

What exactly is she going to do for an encore?

The Love Interest Has Logged On

"Come on!" Erin barks. "The weekend's going to be over by the time we get our order."

"You're not gonna start honking, are you?" Kylie says out the side of her mouth, her MonoLife notifications stacking on the lock screen. Somehow the app is intuitively silent while in the presence of others, though every one of its *thump thump*s creates enough vibration to raise Erin's eyebrows.

"I might." If Erin is still using MonoLife, Kylie hasn't found her content there, doesn't want to ask for fear of opening a can of worms. Hopefully she forgot to log on twice a day at some point, is too embarrassed to admit it.

The Starbucks line stretches to the street. Smarter people go to Morning Bean down the road, in and out in less than five, only Morning Bean doesn't have drive-thru and that's an absolute deal-breaker for Erin.

"You and Cameron going to Jacob's Halloween party?" Kylie asks, trying to get her thoughts off MonoLife.

"I think so," Erin sighs. "God, how are we talking about this already? I haven't been able to focus."

"You should figure it out soon, Err—it's only two weeks away."

September was gone like that. Annabeth Wilson seemingly passed into memory like last week's content, memorialized on a patch of empty concrete wall in the SCC art wing. Her legacy? A tragic anecdote. The girl who got butchered senior year.

The press isn't talking about her murder anymore since there's nothing new under the sun and the only police statement is that they don't comment on open investigations. And nobody's talking about Melissa these days either. Everyone just assumes she did it, then disappeared. Living on some beach in Mexico, free from extradition, as if that makes any sense whatsoever.

Kylie's phone thumps again and while she's trying to keep a poker face, her heart hammers at the sight of this particular notification, her body reacting to the chemical surge, betraying her otherwise casual demeanor.

Erin rolls up on the bumper ahead of them. "Who's texting?"

"Ben," Kylie lies. It's really a MonoLife DM from the one user who hasn't tried forcing his junk into her inbox.

@EndlessNights: Yo, I'll say it again, you're fast becoming the one reason to check this site. Respect.

Kylie's in her messages now, casually angled away from Erin.

@CrystalShips: 😃
@EndlessNights: Ever gonna show your face in full?
@CrystalShips: what's the rush? 😌

Kylie has given glimpses of her face. Just never enough to dox herself. Her rampage at Will U could've been recorded/posted by anyone in that house, turned Kylie into a more vanilla viral sensation, though it was through sheer luck it hadn't happened.

Another *thump thump* against her thigh. This time, no notification to go with it.

She's tempted to ask @EndlessNights if he knows anything about Annabeth. He's clearly used the app a bit longer. Maybe he used to follow her? Maybe, maybe, maybe. She bites her digital tongue, doesn't want to scare him away by coming off like some wacko blood freak.

It's a vibe and it could just be an affectation, but he seems nice and normal. Kylie doesn't exactly trust normal post-Brady, but maybe she'll get back there one of these days.

@EndlessNights's account appears to be mainly car pranks: provoking unsuspecting people into red-light drag racing, highway stunts like breaking the speed limit backward. And it's always sprinkled with enough eye candy to keep him evergreen, appealing to anyone who appreciates the finer things. Strong arms, mostly. Those veins.

@EndlessNights: No rush. I'm very patient. ☺

He started following @CrystalShips in the wake of Brady's humiliation, even though that video was Kylie's way of announcing that the crazy ex-girlfriend had logged on. But he's clearly interested. And his comment makes Kylie smile. It's cute. A bit forward, but hey. She sends back two wink emojis, then decides that's enough flirting, closes the app.

Erin's looking at her. "You're not skipping the party, are you?"

"I might. Ehh, I don't know."

"Oh, no way. You're coming. There's no excuse on earth to bail, unless . . . you're texting some mystery man over there? In which case you best spill—"

"I'm not."

"Look, you're going to be celibate forever if I don't intervene in your love life. And that's what I'm going to do."

"I'm good. Really."

"You're wilting, babe. *Wilting*."

"I'm nineteen."

"In medieval times, you'd be on your third child by now."

"Good thing we're not in medieval times, then."

"You just seem . . . out of it. That's all."

That's completely fair. Kylie has been distracted. Experimenting with MonoLife while the leaves changed from green to orange to brown.

She posts thirst traps in between her videos: a booty shot in her sexiest thong, her exposed midriff, and one night while feeling incredibly adventurous, her nude body in silhouette.

It isn't for her audience, even though the way in which they respond is humbling (each new post summoning a barrage of dick pics she's gotta block).

She posts them because she wants to feel good about herself. And once the fist bumps roll in and the comments come, there's simply nothing else like it. The anonymity of MonoLife is liberating. She doesn't have to be some girl from Summerfield, Massachusetts.

She gets to be herself as she always imagined. Larger than life.

Video content takes more time. She produces them in secret, getting off on the idea of mastering something that Erin cannot. In this case, MonoLife. Erin doesn't need to master it, of course. The public already adores her.

Kylie considers letting her other social media platforms slip away. MonoLife is hers. Its landscape, stranger, more dangerous. More honest. Those who use it are exactly like Kylie—in search of a space where you can completely be yourself.

And it isn't hard to guess the reason behind Annabeth's and Melissa's Instagram blackouts in the months leading up to Annabeth's murder. They very likely and easily got sucked into this app too.

There is, however, no explanation for why Melissa, Annabeth's presumed murderer, has dropped off the face of the earth. Her social media accounts gone, deleted.

Sometimes Kylie scrolls through MonoLife, hoping to find her. If Deacon's words of wisdom were to be believed, Annabeth's profile would've been nuked as soon as she failed to log in twice a day. That probably happened to Melissa too, just for a different reason.

"I'm not guilting you," Erin's saying. "But . . . as your friend, you should know that your content? It's lacking. And that's whatever, you know, but I know you want more out of it and so—"

"I'm okay, really. Just . . . reassessing things."

By September's end, Kylie had amassed nearly a hundred thousand MonoLife followers. Right now, she's close to a hundred thousand more.

"That's why you need Jacob's party. A little fun in your life."

"You and Cameron go. I'll save some money."

"You don't have to spend money when you look the way we do. Let's go as sexy mummies or something."

"I'll think about it." Kylie figures she can probably get a really good post out of it if she dresses right.

"If you come, I won't make you pay me back." Erin looks at Kylie as she says this.

"For what?"

"For that stupid app . . . waste of money."

"You gave up on it?"

A beat. Erin trying to decide if she wants to answer. "Less than a little. Enough to keep it from self-deleting. But I might bail soon."

Kylie refuses to believe Erin isn't interested. Problem is, even at Kylie's user level, the app has no way of searching for other accounts. In navigating the MonoLife waters, Kylie found out very quickly that it's designed to make you connect with total strangers, force you to break from your social circles.

It's frustrating, but she's never felt more accomplished at anything, ever.

That first video, Ben in leggings, amazingly continues to grow in popularity. Users crushing on @CrystalShips, leaving comments wishing she'd **do something cute like this again**. Boys basking in naïveté, pretending she's a "nice girl" at heart. Projecting her as girlfriend material ("I can fix her"), rationalizing that the Brady video was a bad day, a one-off that could happen to anyone.

Brady remains her greatest hit. The video she made right after that was a stumble. Another prank that lacked any serious edge. Ben again, the two of them sneaking into that upscale vegan restaurant downtown with a bucket of ribs, smearing their chins with barbecue sauce and moaning with increased orgasmic intensity as they chowed down . . . until getting thrown out. **Your sophomore slump,** someone had posted immediately. Sucked to see, but yeah, probably true.

That didn't stop her from responding, **My sophomore video was my biggest hit, dipshit.**

Sophomore slump, huh? Those words had forced Kylie into jean cutoffs and a tight black halter top that accented her body in a way she'd never once had the confidence to try.

Ben went behind the camera for vid number four. They drove to Alewife and took the T into Faneuil Hall, where Kylie slipped a wind mask over her mouth for a bit of anonymity, strolling up and down the brick-lain streets, slapping drinks from people's hands.

It was cheap and desperate. But there was undeniable comedy in watching burly men drop their coffees and leap away from their spills like a hand grenade had gone off, only to really humiliate themselves by chasing a girl half their size.

It was maybe the bare minimum Kylie needed in order to appease the masses, pandemonium that wasn't as personal or severe, but still destructive.

Comments found it an odd follow-up to something as raw and humiliating as the Brady video, stating that's what they really wanted out of @CrystalShips before giving her a reluctant fist bump anyway. A warning: fly right, or crash and burn.

She finally found her footing with the only remaining weapon in her video arsenal: Mrs. Elrond's breakdown over Sporto the dog's slaughter.

She posted it two nights ago out of desperation. Pressure that came with the need to feed her fans and having nothing to fall back on.

Some people laughed. Some didn't. There were plenty of "poor pooch" replies, and just as many mocking the old woman for dispropor-tionate grief. A few weirdos posted that the dog got off easy—whatever that meant.

That's when Kylie came to understand her brand. Chaos. Reality. People in moments of vulnerability, herself or others, didn't matter.

And at the same time, Kylie started to notice the looks.

Duc in the cafeteria today, squinting hard as she passed. Nothing to say, just cold judgment because she hadn't listened to his warning.

Then there was that weird kid Jerry from English Lit who never said a word but suddenly talked her ear off about pranks like he was trying to win her heart.

It's odd to realize at least a few of her classmates have seen her in various stages of undress. But it's kind of exhilarating in ways Kylie cannot fully articulate. Like she's already evolving beyond the tiny eco-system of Summerfield.

Kylie's back to thinking about @EndlessNights, trying to figure out how to get some possible information out of him about Annabeth without blowing it.

Meanwhile, Erin finally pulls up to the drive-thru window, fumbling to reload her Starbucks app as Kylie's phone buzzes.

@EndlessNights: If you ever want to collab with me, let me know.

Kylie fights a smile. The mystery man has game.

@CrystalShips: u could be anywhere in the world
@EndlessNights: And yet, I think we're kind of neighbors? 😁

"Ten bucks for these things," Erin's saying, passing a grande cold brew into Kylie's hand. "And the line gets slower every day. You'd think I'm a soccer mom for as long as I'm willing to wait."

The barista shrugs, gives a look of resignation.

"Erin, stop," Kylie says, but her tone is distracted and without conviction. Is @EndlessNights really from the area? Now that meeting up is on the table, she's reluctant to respond. IRL is a whole different kind of pressure.

Mom texts to say she's flying to Baltimore for the weekend to oversee a quick call center training for Corporate. It's last-minute but she can't resist all the overtime and then adds that a change in scenery will do her some good, and Kylie isn't even sure what that last part means.

"You staying over tonight?" Erin asks.

"I don't know . . ."

"Come on, we'll go live, paint our nails, take questions from the creeps. Maybe that'll rekindle your passion for influencing."

Kylie looks down at her MonoLife inbox and decides to leave @EndlessNights on the hook for a while, spontaneously grinning at the thought.

"What do you say?"

Kylie takes a sip of salted cold cream, says, "Sure."

Ghost in the Glass

Kylie and Erin are between a spread of sushi rolls and Cameron's perched on a stool at the end of the table, eyes bloodshot from too much wasabi.

"Have some water, you goon," Erin says.

"I like it like this," he insists as tears slide down his cheeks.

Tonight is almost fun. Almost old times. Cameron's actually a good listener. He laughs at Kylie and Erin's old antics, interrupts to ask questions, as if he can't know enough about Erin and finds actual joy in hearing about her years of friendship with Kylie.

And Kylie's starting to like him—actual respect as opposed to that uneasy tolerance one gives to most bestie relationships.

Cameron takes a few gulps of water to clear his eyes, says to Erin, "I think it'd actually be perfect."

Then Erin hisses "shhhhhh" across the table and Kylie adjusts herself in the high-backed wooden seat.

"What?" she asks, eyes clocking between them.

Cameron's mouth hangs open, unsure of what to say next. Clearly, he's already said too much. And Erin pops a shred of ginger into her mouth, chewing softly while glaring through him. "Asher and Brandi called it quits last week."

"Whoa. I didn't know that."

"'Cause you've been distracted, weirdo."

"What I mean is . . . you didn't think to tell me."

"Yeah, it's bad. It was Asher who did the deed. Brandi's now completely obsessed, driving past his house at night to see if he's home. His parents actually had to call the police to get her to stop."

Cameron's picking sesame seeds out of his teeth. "Asher, on the other hand, is looking to move on and—"

"Oh," Kylie says. "I see. No. No no no. I'm all set."

"What's wrong with Asher?" Cameron notes, suddenly indignant about the shade being thrown on his pal.

"Nothing," Kylie replies. "He's hot and really nice but . . . I don't want anything like that right now."

"You don't want anything hot and really nice right now." Erin smirks. "Told you she's celibate."

"I'm literally just enjoying my life."

"By doing what?"

"Nothing, okay? I don't know. Living? Some of us enjoy the peace and quiet."

"Look, Ky, this isn't an easy thing to ask, but I have to, okay?"

"Oh God. What?"

The question hangs off Erin's lips. It's kind of refreshing to see her looking uncomfortable for once, drawing patterns in the soy sauce on her plate with a toothpick. "Are you, like . . . secretly dating Ben Austin?"

"I'm not answering that."

"I knew it!" Erin cups a palm over her mouth. "I'm right."

"No. You're an idiot."

"I'm not the one dating Ben Austin."

"I am *not*—" Kylie stops because Erin's doubled over, laughing. The exact reaction she wanted. Erin Palmer, the only person with Kylie's nuclear codes.

"You . . . you're being nice to that . . . geek," Erin manages to get out, trying to catch her breath. "I get it. But . . . people are talking and—"

"And what?" Kylie shoots back. "Ben isn't on the state-approved list of eligible bachelors?"

"What's he got that Asher doesn't?" Cameron wonders.

"Nothing. I'm fine being friends with him too. Oh my God, you guys make it sound like I'm trading down when I'm not even—"

"Women *should* trade down," Erin says. "If you date a guy as hot as you, you're always wondering when, not *if*, he's cheating."

"Hey, yo." Cameron is vaguely aware there's an insult for him in there.

Erin talks right over him. "On the other hand, if Kylie Bennington lowers her standards to, say, Ben Austin, well . . . he'll treat her like a goddess forever."

"So, your advice is to date Ben Austin? Is there a chart so I can keep all this straight?"

Erin pats Kylie's forearm. "You and I are addicted to the finer things, Ky. Brady was slime. Very good-looking slime, but slime nonetheless. Oh come on, I'm not telling you to date Ben—I know you too well for that. I'm only saying that you *should*."

"Erin, this is sending me."

"Fine."

The conversation then segues into something far worse. Collabs. Suddenly Erin and Cameron are brainstorming something to shoot and post tonight. *Can't stop, won't stop* being Erin's unofficial motto.

They move into the living room, where Cameron works on getting a fire going. "Whatever we shoot has to go on Kylie's profile," Erin says. "She's getting lazy. Needs to remember to keep her eyes on the prize."

"Yeah," Cameron says absently, stacking wood around a small blaze.

"Can't we just, I don't know? Talk instead?" Kylie asks.

Erin circles the living room, chewing the inside of her cheek. Pondering things.

Once the fire's crackling, Cameron falls onto the couch. Erin sizes up the room, her silence unbearably dramatic, stepping down to the recessed living space and dropping into Cameron's lap.

"Yeah," she says, fireplace shadows sharpening her features, giving them sinister edges. "Sure. Let's talk, Ky. About what you've been up to. Running around the state with some theater geek, ducking me on weekends . . ."

"Just messing with MonoLife. Whatever." Kylie shrugs, though the gravity of the room makes this admission sound like she's copping to a drug problem.

"Cool," Erin says, high and mighty, sitting on Cameron like he's a human throne. "But I can't find you there, can't find anyone I know."

"Me either," Kylie says.

"So let's see. What you've been messing with."

"There's nothing to show."

Silence percolates off that. Erin's thoughts locked tight behind a stoic glare, and Kylie's matching that expression now. A psychic stare-down.

"Fine." Erin's allotted moment for confession passes and she slides from Cameron's lap. "If we're not going to talk . . ."

Cameron allows himself to be pulled upright, toward the stairs.

". . . then we'll catch you in the morning."

"Um, okay," Kylie says, watching them slink off. This night has turned on a dime. And for what? Because Kylie has maintained her privacy and Erin feels entitled to even that?

I see you, Kylie thinks, then settles onto the couch, finding immediate relief in MonoLife's familiar yellow start-up screen. Like an old friend who never judges.

Overhead, the ceiling starts thumping with the loudest, most per-formative sex imaginable. Erin's passive-aggressiveness a true art form.

Kylie barely cares. MonoLife's metallic cry ignites, telling her some-one has sent a DM. She rushes to that notification.

@BlueFerox: collab???

@CrystalShips: why are people asking me to do that all of a sudden?

@BlueFerox: because you are a star, young Crystal

@CrystalShips: idk about that

@BlueFerox: come to Venezuela

@CrystalShips: ummm . . . I can't

@BlueFerox: see if my latest video changes your mind
@CrystalShips: not that I don't want to . . . just can't
@BlueFerox: come and see

Kylie toggles to Blue's feed, to the video just posted. It's titled "Sashimi" and it opens on a close-up of what looks like raw liver plopped onto a ceramic plate. A perfectly manicured hand brings a knife into the shot, slices off a hunk of meat. Another hand plucks it, turns the camera around to show an open mouth, lip gloss shimmering in ambient light. Katy's "International Smile" comes to mind, somewhat contemptuously, as Blue drops the meat into her mouth, pearly whites grinding it to mush, soft chews bringing waves of ASMR relief—if Kylie's being honest—even as her stomach turns.

"Ew, no." Blue has turned cannibalism into an art form, sure. One Kylie is happy to observe from afar.

She decides to reread @EndlessNights's DMs to relax. A couple of awkward interactions at the beginning, casual flirtations he wasn't initially good at but is getting better at all the time. She reaches the last thing he typed to her and goes a little lightheaded:

I think we're kind of neighbors?

She warms to the idea of meeting him IRL, scrolling his profile while Erin has a verbose religious experience on the other side of the ceiling plaster.

Kylie clears her throat. The energy swirling through her is in desperate need of expulsion. She's worked up, considers getting off to the sound of Erin getting off, then glimpses a wicked smile in the reflection of her cell phone screen.

A ghost in the glass.

Kylie's transfixed. Loves the way she looks there: eyebrows playfully arched, lips twisted up to one side, cheekbones chiseled . . . hot enough to go live.

So she does, with the simple smash of a button.

"Crystal here," she whispers, broadcasting Erin's popping fireplace, pausing so the swirling cries overhead have a chance to resonate with her viewers. "Who wants to peep something we're not supposed to see?"

Kylie goes slinking up carpeted stairs toward moans that show no sign of slowing. *Go Cameron*, she thinks.

Only the sex isn't happening in Erin's room. It's the master bedroom's door slightly off jamb. The sound of rustling bodies beyond it. Erin's doing it in her parents' bed?

Ew.

Kylie's fingers feel numb as she pushes it open, her phone aimed straight on.

Erin's on the bed, facing Kylie, propped on all fours, her flesh glistening. Cameron's behind her, his hands on her hips, thrusting hard.

Shock ripples through their features as they notice Kylie, but it's gone in a flash because Cameron isn't stopping, and their agonized ecstasy returns in full.

Kylie's phone fixates on the thumping bed, second thoughts preventing her from lifting it past the tufts of bedspread in Erin's gnarled hands. In that same moment, Kylie is also distracted by the tripod beside them, a phone mounted and recording.

"Kylie!" Erin snarls. "What the he—"

This unexpected declaration of her name jolts Kylie into killing the feed. She's just been doxed in front of her viewers. *Fuck*.

"Nice," Cameron huffs. "She wants to join in." He's still pushing into Erin, staring at Kylie with a creepy grin—all that goodwill earned over dinner dissipating in a flash.

"Asshole!" Erin screams, disengaging and wrapping a bedsheet around her body.

"You guys are making a sex tape?" Kylie can't tear her eyes away from their setup. A cold shiver moves through her. Erin taking things to the next level, always so efficient in making Kylie feel ten steps behind.

"*Out!*" Erin charges, bedsheet flowing behind her, spinning Kylie toward the hall, shoving her. The door slamming so hard it nearly smacks her ass.

Beyond it, Cameron whines about not finishing while Erin responds full-throatedly: "I don't care!"

Kylie slinks back downstairs, dragging heaps of guilt behind her. What was this, exactly? A violation of her friend's trust, certainly. For what? Clout? A hundred thousand likes?

Well, she thinks. *How am I going to get that now?*

Now she's wondering something else: Had Erin and Cameron been trying to lure her into bed? Priming her with all that talk of collabs? For whom were they shooting? If not for MonoLife, had Erin started an OnlyFans? Time to pour all her Insta simps into that sales funnel?

Smart.

Be smarter.

She's wrestling with this as she drops back onto the couch with MonoLife. A DM notification unfurls across the bottom of the screen. A user she doesn't know:

@SolidusRush: Kylie Watch This.

Oh God, Erin said her name and the people watching definitely heard. Doxed for sure.

She clicks into the conversation, where there's a video embedded beneath.

@SolidusRush: Thought you might like to see the prequel.

"Prequel to what?" Kylie asks her screen, hitting play.

Grainy handheld footage. A forearm reaching into the shot, brushing aside skeletal branches to reveal a two-story house in the distance. It's pitch dark, save for one corner of the second floor.

Kylie's bedroom.

The point-of-view camera hovers over crabgrass, deep breaths are steady, slightly anticipatory, making them kind of deranged.

Kylie catches another glimpse of herself in the cell phone's glass. Her half smirk twists her face in a way she barely recognizes, and she's only now aware of her blazing heartbeat.

On the video, her stalker slides between the two overgrown shrubs her dad was always threatening to remove because they block the oil pipe he had to shovel a path to each time it snowed.

There're pins and needles in the puffs of Kylie's cheeks as she watches this psycho lift a crossbow into the frame, then whistle.

Complete silence for a moment, and then comes the distant sound of an animal's collar bell. A huffing dog on approach.

The crossbow takes aim. A silver-tipped point glistens in the moonlight. Sporto comes trotting across the lawn, collie nose lifted to the sky, sniffing with curiosity.

The shooter fires. The bolt nails Sporto in the chest, blowing the dog back across the grass with a whimper.

A scream ignites as the shooter retreats, Mrs. Elrond's fated cries receding as the killer hits the trees.

Hard cut to black.

Kylie feels weightless as she clicks @SolidusRush's profile. His avatar's some anime girl with green hair and huge boobs and there's a red X stamped beside his name—MonoLife's version of verification?

"There's a level beyond 'user'?" Kylie wonders aloud.

His content is bleak. Lots of animal deaths. Frogs with firecrackers down their throats. Moles burned alive inside metal buckets. A deer trapped inside a deadfall.

Dad used to say every neighborhood had one of these freak show kids. A serial killer waiting in the wings.

One thumbnail though stops her cold: a blonde girl facing the camera, balayage hair, familiar blue eyes. Kylie had complimented them once for resembling little pools of the Atlantic.

It's Melissa Crigan. She goes by @MissyMiss here, standing beside fresh-plowed snow, swimmer's physique nearly spilling out of her string bikini.

"I'm MissyMiss and welcome to my first MonoLife collab!" It's strange to hear her voice again. She bends down, giving a healthy glimpse of her cleavage. Her face is scrunched in anticipation.

Whatever she's waiting for growls off camera, a sonic wall ramping up. A dented white Hyundai speeds into frame, driving up the side of the snowbank, jumping over Melissa's hunched back, barely, smashing to the ground with sparks and scrapes as Melissa screams and laughs.

Kylie stares at it, feeling again like she's stepped outside herself. Everything's beginning to make sense. Because she knows Melissa and also recognizes that car. It belongs to Duc. @SolidusRush IRL.

Witching Hour

They're in Erin's backyard on the patio swing overlooking the tree line, hinges squeaking.

"What the hell was that about?" Erin finally asks, staring straight ahead.

Kylie wants to answer but there's no justification. Just shakes her head over and over.

"Were you, like . . . ?"

"Curious?" Kylie asks.

Erin turns at that, looks her through.

"I don't know," Kylie says. "You guys were being loud and—"

"Ky, you came in with your camera running."

"I deleted it. I swear—"

"Well, thank you for *that*, but—"

"I know. You don't trust me."

"Yeah, that was sus. And you've been distant. Like you're hiding stuff from me."

"I'm sorry . . ."

"Can I see?" Erin asks, studying every twitch on Kylie's face.

"See . . . see what?"

"MonoLife." Erin says this in a rising tone that suggests frustration.

Kylie's tempted to hand her phone over, doesn't want to be out of Erin's good graces, but catches herself. Remembers the user agreement.

Duc had refused to show Kylie his phone any further than the home screen that day in the cafeteria. And the burnout at the mall, Deacon, had spelled it right out. You don't show MonoLife to anyone.

Kylie's been pondering the logic, and it seems to go like this: there's a reason the app doesn't want people to easily find their friends—you have to work so hard to establish yourself that you'll take MonoLife to your grave, rather than risk losing it.

Kylie stuffs her phone into her pocket, as if the app might be listening to Erin's request. "You know I can't."

Erin's expression hovers somewhere between innocence and ignorance. No, she doesn't seem to know that.

"When Brady told me it was over, I lost it. Went live and fought back. The app loved that. I like, I don't know . . . started finding my confidence there, posting pics—"

"Naked pics?"

"Artsy pics."

Tired laughter. "Right."

"Posted that video of my neighbor crying over her dying dog. Wouldn't you believe that went over well too."

Erin looks up at the moon. "Shit, Ky, this is all kinds of wrong."

"Oh please—"

"You're posting a video of your neighbor in tears? Terrorizing people in public? Are you like stupid or desperate?"

"Desperate? You used to cast spells on our classmates."

"Oh, don't even. I grew out of that."

"Really. You tried putting a curse on Brandi last Halloween." Kylie's giggling because it sounds so absurd to say it out loud.

"A year ago. That's, like, two decades in high school time."

"We had to go all the way to Salem to buy a special rock." Kylie's laughing even harder now. "That carnelian stone?"

"Shut up."

"Twenty-six bucks down the drain at that crazy person store, Witch Slap. The currrrse of Errrrin—I shall make Brandi gain *thir-rrrty pounds*!"

None of this is especially funny to Erin, whose cheeks are so flush they're glowing beneath the moonlight reflecting off the swimming pool. "Fuck you, Kylie. You're trying to absolve yourself of any responsibility here. I'm not going to let you. You have a problem, you know that?"

It's that judgment, that hypocrisy, that burns Kylie. "Ohhh, you're not going to *let* me? How about, I have more followers on MonoLife after a month and a half than you've got everywhere. *That's* what you're pissed about."

Erin's so indignant she actually touches a hand to her collar. "*Excuse me?* How can I be pissed about something I didn't even know?"

Kylie's now getting furious in increments, can't stop herself. "You're just mad because it's my time to shine."

"Ky—I'm trying to help you here."

"How? You've been throwing me scraps all this time. Little crumbs of advice long after you've moved on."

"Scraps . . . ?" Erin's never looked more hurt. It's possible she's never *been* more hurt. "Okay. I couldn't care less about your followers. I'm worried about *you* because you're acting like a freak. You were creeping on us before, trying to film us having sex. Why? To give to your followers? Do you know how messed up that is?"

As Erin wipes sudden tears away with the back of her hand, Kylie realizes that right now would be the time to reach out. Find common ground. Lower this temperature. But no. She doesn't. She can't. Whatever mechanism exists inside a human being that fosters the need for such comfort—what one would call empathy—has never really existed inside her.

She hasn't realized that until this very moment.

"Let's just go," Erin growls. "I'm taking you home."

"What?"

"I'd make Cameron do it, but you'll probably try and suck his dick on the way. Anything for a few extra likes, huh?"

"Okay, fine—whatever you want. Beats walking, I guess."

Then they're in the BMW and there's even more silence. Erin looking over in utter disbelief that Kylie can just sit there, kind of unbothered. And once those glares don't do the trick, little sniffles begin punctuating the silence, lasting all the way to Kylie's driveway.

Kylie cracks the door to get out without addressing her friend, and Erin finally snaps: "Find a new ride to school too. Bitch."

Kylie ignores that too and slams the passenger door shut a little too hard on purpose. And then the BMW accelerates out of the driveway and is gone, Kylie watching red taillights stain the night like vapor trails, the angry engine racing off, accelerating growls forever echoing.

It isn't until Erin has entirely faded from earshot that Kylie starts for the front door, peeling her clothes off as she climbs toward her bedroom, where she finds herself getting off to the video of Erin and Cameron, even though it's dark and mostly audio, turned on by access to this private moment, moaning along with them until she's breathless and exhausted and honestly kind of jazzed by the prospect of content possibilities she hasn't fully considered.

Then she's back to MonoLife before even realizing that she's opened it. Back to Sporto-killer @SolidusRush's feed.

In her inbox, @EndlessNights and @BlueFerox have sent messages, but they can wait.

Because @SolidusRush is verified, Kylie can't seem to follow him. She scrolls down to Sporto's assassination video, typing:

@CrystalShips: stay out of my yard you fucking creeper.

A DM response dings back almost instantly.

@SolidusRush: no real names here, cool?
@CrystalShips: too late for me
@SolidusRush: why you commenting on my shit? I sent a DM so
   we could chat.

@CrystalShips: DMs are private . . . I figured I might pick up a few new followers if I started a public feud, ya know?

@SolidusRush: wow . . . you're fitting right in here

@CrystalShips: I have questions

@SolidusRush: no shit

@CrystalShips: come over

@SolidusRush: can't

@CrystalShips: you're literally ten houses away

@SolidusRush: ain't there . . . going to be at the game tomorrow?

@CrystalShips: no b/c I'm not in high school anymore

@SolidusRush: come on . . . show a little regional pride

Oh God. The game. Anything but the game. Kylie doesn't need another reminder of how quickly life changes. A year ago, Erin would've been cheering. Cameron would've been playing. Simpler times. Kylie wipes more tears off her cheeks, wondering how she could've let Erin walk out of her life like that.

@CrystalShips: yeah . . . ok

@SolidusRush: see you tomorrow

Kylie still has Erin on the brain. She opens their text conversation and types: **I fucked up. I'm so sorry.**

The lack of an immediate ellipsis is devastating. Maybe Erin isn't home yet? Though she never lets something like driving get in the way of checking her messages. Siri would be reading that shit aloud.

No. Kylie's officially been ghosted. And rightfully so.

Back to MonoLife, then.

Kylie visits @MissyMiss's profile and clicks FOLLOW. The most recent video, titled "Dusk Swim," is a slow striptease for the camera, followed by Missy bouncing on a diving board and jumping into a pool, swimming the length of it before climbing out and slinking back to the camera, her naked body shimmering beneath the moonglow.

There's no Annabeth murder video anywhere on this account, though. Maybe she removed it?

Then Kylie realizes something else. @MissyMiss's account is still active. Hasn't been deleted.

Wherever she is, she's still checking it twice a day.

The Rules of Attraction

Ben Austin's there to pick Kylie up on Saturday morning. He's wearing a faded polo tucked into khakis—a little too short at the ankles, flashing a band of pasty, hairy shin in the space between the hem and his off-brand sneakers he probably got off Temu. His hair's combed, but still messy somehow, and the overabundance of Old Spice burns so badly that Kylie has to crack the window.

After a long stretch of silence in his Volkswagen, he clears his throat to ask, "Any more video ideas?"

"No." She's thinking about a vid though where she catches Ben by surprise by pulling a gun and shooting him in the knee, humor derived from the inflated terror ballooning across his face before he collapses in roaring pain. A delightful concept. She has to bite the inside of her cheek to stop from laughing.

"I do," he says. "So many we could go on forever."

Kylie feigns a smile, the idea of being shackled to him too depressing to contemplate.

"How about this," he says. "You go to the library with your laptop and watch porn at full volume, only your earbuds are unplugged and everyone hears it."

"I've seen those," she says. "Not my speed." MonoLife has made it very clear what's expected of her. She stifles another laugh over the recurring thought of blasting Ben's kneecap—*surprise!*—just to see his reaction.

He sort of slouches over the steering wheel, deflated.

"But thanks for the offer, Ben."

"There's other stuff we could—"

"Ben. I appreciate your help. And the ride. But I've got everything under control for now."

He waits until they reach the field, then asks, "What are you doing with all those videos anyway?"

"Special project." That ought to buy her a few months.

He drives up the path to the ticket booth and shifts into park. "Can I ask you something?"

Kylie says "Sure" in the driest tone possible.

"I've been crushing on you since Bio." He's so nervous his words are mostly breath. "This past month has been the best time of my life."

"That's very sweet."

"So . . . If I were to ask you out—"

His face scrunches as if to shield himself from the inevitable answer.

Kylie's already shaking her head slow and sad. "Oh, Ben. You're a good friend to me."

"A friend who . . . who wants to be more." His words are steadier now, finding the fight.

"And I . . . don't. I'm really sorry."

"You won't even try?"

"It's . . . the feeling, yeah, it just isn't there. You're a nice guy. And you're going to find someone." She takes a long, hard look at him while considering Erin's advice: *If Kylie Bennington lowers her standards to, say, Ben Austin, well . . . he'll treat her like a goddess forever.*

I'm not telling you to date Ben . . . I'm only saying that you should.

But the rules of attraction cannot be defined or explained. It's simple chemistry. Ben would throw rose petals at her feet, bring her breakfast in bed, and even drink her bathwater on command. All that disgusts her. She sees weakness when she looks at him. A nauseating simp. He can't do anything to change that.

"I don't want to crowd you," he says. "So . . . go do your thing. And if you need a ride back, text me."

"Ben . . ."

"It's okay. Really. I'll be around."

"I'm so sorry." She gets out and closes the door and within seconds he's already speeding off, just like Erin. A coward's temper tantrum.

Past the turnstiles, Veronica Gomez stands at the BeanieGang table, selling headwear that benefits cancer research. She's got a gray cap pulled down over her ears, which makes the black lipstick and dark eyeliner around her eyes stand out. Normally, Kylie would avoid her, because she and Erin stay in touch, but Veronica is in Kylie's Fundamentals of Marketing class this year and they're sort of partners.

"Two hundred orders today," Veronica notes sarcastically. "No thanks to my marketing director, who refused to give us any kind of social push this week. And who no longer answers her messages at all."

"I'm sorry. I've been distracted."

"I know you want the extra credit for class but you shouldn't have volunteered to help if you didn't want—"

"I *do* want," Kylie says. "I do. Really. How about I do some stuff now, encouraging people to come over at halftime?"

Veronica's unmoved but receptive. "Okay. Sure."

Kylie welcomes it too. One more day she doesn't have to brainstorm content for the 'gram. She snaps a quick picture of the table, a row of Styrofoam heads modeling the trendiest beanies, then hammers out a quick post and a few minutes later holds it in front of Veronica's face. "See? More likes than the SCC Business Administration account could ever get."

Veronica's eyes soften as she shivers in the fall breeze.

"I really am sorry." Kylie points to the refreshment table across the way. "How about something to warm you up?"

"Wow, you are sorry."

Kylie walks over and snaps up two paper cups, fills them with hot chocolate, and tops both with an excessive sprinkle of mini marshmallows. They're completely melted into goo by the time she gets back to Veronica, who takes one of the steaming cups, grinning.

"Gonna rub my back too?"

"Give me a ride home after this, and I'll do your feet."

"Now it makes sense. Erin said you two were on the outs."

"Ah. Word travels fast."

"It does." Veronica's eyes flick down Kylie's length. "Fine. You got yourself a ride. Now let me work, bitch."

Veronica may not be a friend, her function being more utilitarian, a socially acceptable body to be seen around school with now that Erin has rejected her, but Kylie feels better knowing she hasn't alienated everyone in her life.

She wanders the field, ignoring the game, spotting Duc up on the hill behind the end zone, Puff Bar between his lips. He gives her a double take as she approaches. "You're killing it there, Crystal Ships."

"Just trying to figure things out."

"And what've you figured out?"

"Not as much as you."

Duc stares, slack-jawed. "Huh. If you only knew." Like that day in the cafeteria, he has a lot more to say but keeps it to himself.

"I know you're a complete psycho."

"It takes one to know one, doesn't it? Never would've thought to record that old bitch crumpled over her dog like that." He tucks his hand over his stomach, bows. "A masterstroke."

"Whatever wins you a following."

"You feel like you've won?"

"Um, kind of?"

Duc takes a few more puffs. The smell of roasted coconut tickles Kylie's nostrils. "You haven't won anything," he says.

"How'd you get the red X? What's it do?"

"Ah, ah—not supposed to talk about it. You'll figure it out . . . just like I did."

"C'mon, Duc. Light the way."

"Nah. It ain't supposed to be easy."

"You gotta kill a dog? That when they stamped you?"

"You thinking of going out and clipping someone's pet, Kylie?"

She hasn't considered that, how far she's willing to go. She's already lost friends to MonoLife. No turning back.

"The dog came later," Duc says.

"Your collab with Missy? Did that bring you over the line?"

His smile inches closer to *Getting warmer*.

"Did Missy kill Annabeth?"

"You already know."

Kylie taps her phone. "No. The video's not here."

Duc waves to a few faces moving through the crowd. "That's the fucked-up part," he says. "Missy uploaded it to Annabeth's account. So, technically, Annabeth posted her own murder."

"Why?"

"Missy's style was to push boundaries."

"Annabeth's account would've been zapped, though, right? Like, a long time ago? So who took the video off the app and floated it around last month?"

Duc takes another puff. Holds the bar to his mouth as if he's afraid of answering that question.

"This is getting annoying," she says. "*You're* getting annoying."

Vapor seeps out of Duc's closed mouth. "Missy's in hiding. Don't know where, but . . . she's messaging me."

"These last six months?"

Duc turns his hand outward, phone clenched in his fingers.

Kylie stuffs her face into the crook of her elbow to shield her eyes. "Hey—"

"Relax," Duc says sharply. "I'm not showing you anything you can't see." On his screen, the note app is open. The heading reads: *Chat history with @MissyMiss*. "Transcribed this shit just for you."

@MissyMiss: you will not be saved by your friends or your parents or the police

@MissyMiss: or by Buddha your god

@MissyMiss: YOU WILL ABANDON ALL HOPE
@MissyMiss: The Profile are patient
@MissyMiss: best of luck tho 😀

Kylie looks up. "The hell is this?"

Duc's grin resembles a blinking sign, blinding at first but then cold and black. "You've got the same look."

"As?"

"Missy. A rat that will do anything for that bite of cheese."

"Wow. Thanks, Duc."

"I'm telling you this app does things to your head and it's, like, barely your fault."

"I'll tell you what I see. A child. Trying to prove he isn't scared. Except your hand trembles each time you stuff that Puff Bar into your mouth. And it's cold out, but not that cold. So, what are you afraid of, Duc?"

His silence confirms she's over target. "You don't get it."

"So help me to."

"She wants to kill me."

Kylie's first instinct is to laugh, but Duc's not even projecting that fake smile anymore. He looks tired. Helpless.

"Just . . . help me find her," he says so quietly it's nearly a whisper. "Please. Do that and I'll write you out a primer for this whole shitty app. How does that sound?"

"I bring you Melissa, and you help me go all the way?"

"Yeah."

"Fine. Great. Where do I start?"

"Right there in your pocket," he says, and then goes rushing off toward the crowd.

Kylie is in Veronica's car after the game. The girl is stoked by the amount of beanies sold today. It means she gets to donate their earnings to *two* charities, and in her world, this is such a wonderful turn of events.

She keeps looking over at Kylie, baffled as to why she doesn't reciprocate the excitement. "You have to admit this is great news."

"I guess," Kylie says, can't mask her disinterest.

"Did you just roll your eyes?"

"What? No. Look, you kicked ass today."

"At least say it like you mean it."

"It's a *me* thing, all right? I just don't see the point. No one knows you're doing this . . . unless you tell them. So why bother?"

Veronica laughs. This has to be a bit. But the smile falls off her face one feature at a time until she's wearing a stone-serious mask. "Because it helps people. We could all try and be a little more—"

"Could we make a quick stop?"

"Um. Where?"

"Lampkin Lane."

"That's nowhere near you."

"Yeah, but I'm enjoying this conversation."

"You are?"

"Sure. It's interesting."

"So are you, Kylie."

There are times when Kylie tries to understand what makes others tick. Her natural bias assumes that everyone is just like her, fighting for their small sliver of social space. Whenever she meets someone for whom that goal is incidental, it's akin to communicating with an extraterrestrial.

"So let me get this straight," Veronica notes after a moment. "You think I'm wasting my time . . . being equitable?"

"I don't know," Kylie says. "This was for class, so I guess you had to."

"How about, I wanted to. You think that makes me . . . *weird* or something?"

"No, I'm glad you're busy with other pursuits."

They swing onto Lampkin Lane. It isn't a street so much as a suburban postcard. Kylie has been to Annabeth Wilson's place only once for a study group freshman year, and the only way she can still find it is from the chipped white fence in the front yard.

"Here—stop here."

"Uh, why?"

"This was Annabeth's house."

"What are we doing?"

"Just keep the car running? I need, like, five minutes."

Veronica looks at the house and around the street, then at Kylie. "No chance. You're not leaving me alone." She kills the engine.

They both climb out and hurry across the front lawn, past matching Kias in the driveway. The iron pool fence is too high to climb. Kylie walks to it and lifts onto her toes, looking over the shrubs past the bars.

In the palm of Kylie's hand, MonoLife is tuned to @MissyMiss's profile. To her "Dusk Swim" video, playing and replaying on mute.

Sure enough, there's the same pool shed tucked into the back of the yard between two pine trees. The matching sandstone around the pool, the same scattered patio furniture.

"This is it," Kylie whispers, a tremendous sense of accomplishment lifting her spirits. Missy had skinny-dipped right here at Annabeth's house. Just before the two of them vanished.

So where the hell was Annabeth murdered?

"Are you, like, playing detective?" Veronica asks.

Kylie dodges the question, starts back to the car. "Ready?"

"How about we chill this afternoon? Let me try and convince you that it's okay to help others."

Part of Kylie would like to say yes. Part of her would find it interesting to hear what an NPC expects out of life. But it's admittedly only a very small part.

The rest of her is thinking about MonoLife, eager to get home and disappear inside it.

Pranks

Missy's profile is the same level as Kylie's. Both users, with Duc as @SolidusRush being one step ahead of them. Only Missy doesn't allow direct messages from nonfollowers. And since Missy isn't following @CrystalShips, Kylie has no way of initiating a conversation. Best she can do is comment on the "Dusk Swim" vid and see if Missy takes the bait.

> **@CrystalShips:** Wow . . . Nice bod. ☺

MonoLife dings, and it's @BlueFerox checking in from Venezuela. Blue is also a user, and even though she's been around a bit longer, she's less popular than Kylie. Probably because her entire brand is hello, cannibalism, and that's a real niche.

> **@BlueFerox:** find a partner yet?

Kylie figures everyone's eager to team up because Duc implied that was how you reached the next level. She doesn't think she'll ever be hungry enough to take Blue up on her offer, though.

> **@CrystalShips:** nah . . . you're my only friend 😩
> **@BlueFerox:** hah you will have no problems
> **@CrystalShips:** see, a true friend . . . how are you?

@BlueFerox: really want to know?

@CrystalShips: wouldn't have asked otherwise

@BlueFerox: you ghosted me last time 😩

@CrystalShips: you were inviting me to eat raw liver . . . but that's your thing

@BlueFerox: for me it's all survival . . . and vengeance

@CrystalShips: Show me? Pls?

Kylie reaches up to her Katy poster, fingers rubbing the slightly crinkled paper as her tongue traces her lips, eagerly braced for whatever's coming. More of this taboo, both mysterious and exciting. Her heart is pumping the kind of energy that gets your body crackling, reminds you you're alive.

The screen reads, *@BlueFerox is currently typing . . .*

A video appears, then:

@BlueFerox: a preview . . . just for you 🖤

Kylie takes a deep breath, presses play.

Fade in on warped linoleum. Zipping along fake tiled floor toward the sound of labored breaths. Desperate gurgles.

"*This* pendejo—" Blue's voice ramps up over each vowel, so by the time she pronounces *ejo* it's a rumble. Off camera there's a smack. And a whimper.

"*Stealing purification kits to make a quick buck on reseller markets while we drink polluted water.*"

Now the camera's on twitching legs, then a torso undulating against the blood-streaked floor. Adrenaline shoots through Kylie, the same sensation she felt watching Annabeth get torn open by a meat slicer. Only this is even easier to take. A wretched person meeting a wretched end.

A bearded mouth. Puckered fish lips kissing air. Lifeless eyes staring up into the beyond. A swivel blade wobbling out one side of his neck.

Hard cut to black. Kylie sits up, jarred. Feeling cheated. Wanting more. Blue, over there ingesting her enemies, absorbing their power. Becoming a goddess.

> @CrystalShips: oh you tease
> @BlueFerox: feeds my entire building for a weekend
> @CrystalShips: tastes good?
> @BlueFerox: best meat you'll ever have
> @CrystalShips: srsly???
> @BlueFerox: someday I'll cook for you 😊

Bon appetit, Kylie thinks, looking up at Katy, that seductive grin encouraging her to live deliciously.

> @CrystalShips: I'm super interested
> @BlueFerox: ttyl . . . and another video soon, pls 😎

Blue is a total contradiction, murderous and cannibalistic, though otherwise . . . normal? For the last month they've touched base a few times a week, and their conversations are generally ordinary. Talk of workouts, skin care, music. The only strike against her is that she's not a Katy fan, arguing that Dua Lipa is the true reigning queen of pop, an argument Kylie refuses to even consider.

Kylie warms to the idea of collaborating but isn't going to risk her life like Melissa, allowing Duc to jump her with his shitty Hyundai. And with Blue being in another country, there's only one person she trusts IRL. And it's hardly trust. That simply does not exist on MonoLife. It's just that @EndlessNights does normal well enough.

"Him, right?" Kylie asks, still looking at Katy, whose piercing and smoky eyes seem to agree.

There's always Erin, she supposes. Though she remains radio silent. Kylie could reach out, apologize again, and, as a gesture of goodwill, offer collaboration.

But no. She won't hand that to Erin. Last thing Erin needs is another fucking opportunity. Petty, sure, but it's also life. Kylie has to win at something. Once.

She opens Instagram and needs to key in only the first letter of Erin's username for her profile to autopopulate in the search window.

Today's Reel is a low angle on Cameron, first one to sprint across the finish line of an intramural cross-country meet. And good for him; that torn ACL has kept him from being as active as he'd like. The crowd around him erupts—Erin included, congratulating him—the love of her life—on today's surprise win.

A hundred and fifty thousand views.

Kylie sighs.

In MonoLife, Duc has posted a video called "Uber Strangers"— whatever he'd been out of town shooting last night. He's in some shopping plaza Kylie doesn't recognize. With each cut, a new car rolls up to the curb and Duc approaches, pulling open the door.

Each driver shouts a variation of "What the hell are you doing in my car?" and somehow Duc keeps it together, flashing his phone and insisting they're his Uber. Funny, but nothing you can't find on YouTube.

Until Duc slips into the back seat of an elderly man's sedan, a guy wearing a mesh ball cap with some kind of veteran insignia on it. "Can you stomp the gas?" Duc says. But the old man's too startled, too shocked. He reaches for the door, pawing the lock like a helpless animal.

"Oh shit, call for help!" Duc's laughing in hysterics as he climbs out, hopping up and down excitedly, shouting at the nearby gawkers to call an ambulance.

The old man suddenly spills onto the pavement, writhing as Duc runs toward the camera, cackling, "Cut it, cut it, cut it. Let's get the fu—"

Hard cut. The end.

In a way, so much worse than Blue's content. Yeah, you could argue zero distinction between the two, but this is the closest MonoLife has come to disgusting her.

She minimizes the app and finds a couple of texts from Ben.

Ben:

> I feel terrible about today

> Can we chat?

Kylie has a better idea. Orders an Uber and waits twenty-five minutes for it to arrive. Only when she hops into the back does she reply to him.

She chooses a few dirty selfies from her Photos folder and feeds them into the thread one at a time, saving the last for when she reaches his street.

She gets out and presses send as the Uber drives off. Ben's getting a nude: Kylie sitting on her bed, angled to hide her lopsided breasts. Her body in full—more than she's ever shown anyone, even Brady.

Never even had the guts to give this to MonoLife.

She approaches Ben's house in shadow. His bedroom window isn't hard to guess—it's the only one glowing from cool computer light. Kylie's broadcasting to the world before she gets there.

"Hey guys," she whispers. "Crystal here. Paying one of my biggest fans a surprise visit."

She peers through the window and Ben's hunched over the computer screen, Kylie's photos splayed across his monitor, arm moving up and down in his lap with true coomer fury.

"Oh God," she snorts, nearly dropping her phone.

Ben slides a porno clip onto his second monitor, jerking off to Kylie's photos as, behind him, Kylie captures every horny detail in grainy low light.

His body's already tensing, a silent spasm quakes through him from head to toe. Then he falls back, contented, gasping as his stomach rises and falls in the monitor's glow.

It's never easy to know when you've got "the post," but sometimes you feel the energy. That which springs from the humiliation of others, making every loser on earth feel better about themselves. This isn't as good as blasting Ben's kneecap but . . .

Kylie walks down the street and orders a Lyft this time. Ironically, the same car comes back to get her. The driver turned around to watch her climb in, most of his face obscured by the shadows beneath the brim of his Red Sox cap. "No luck?"

"The opposite," Kylie says, watching the fist bumps pile up. Her follower count is expanding by the hundreds.

Ben's gone viral by the time she's home and there's a recurring pattern in the comments: **Holy crap, you're famous now!** and **Wow, she likes your stuff!**

"Who likes my stuff?" Kylie wonders, scrolling through an hour of comments until one stands out.

@PurpleLipGloss: Sooooo funny . . . and hot

An account that doesn't even have a red X, so who cares? Why are people going nuclear over it?

> **You got a shout from the top!**
> **You're blowing up huge, bitch.**
> **OMG lucky**

"Who are you?" Kylie clicks the username and @PurpleLipGloss's profile page blurs beneath a pop-up overlay.

You are unable to view this content . . . yet.
But please keep posting in order to prove your life's work.

She is able to follow Duc with his red X, no problem, but this @PurpleLipGloss is off the menu?

"Holy shit," she says. That must mean the red X isn't even the final stop.

On MonoLife, you can climb even higher than that.

Useful Idiots

B en pleasuring himself gets Kylie one million views and a follower count that's closing in on five hundred thousand.

Can MonoLife really have this many users?

She wants to think that it does, so she can reach the top, like Katy, who was at one time the most popular celebrity on Twitter, and the first to reach ninety million followers.

People love writing articles about how there're way more people in the world than on social media, and how it's important to remember that none of *this stuff* matters. *This stuff* is "not the real world."

Boomer mindset. Every person who lives in the *real world* is one less person competing with Kylie. And she's grateful for that.

She's having a lazy morning in bed when her phone dings.

@EndlessNights: LOL that video.
@CrystalShips: u like?
@EndlessNights: Very mean.
@CrystalShips: going soft on me?
@EndlessNights: Naw. Not on you lol. See my latest?

As Kylie is clicking over to his profile, he adds:

@EndlessNights: I hope not, cos you didn't like it. ☺
@CrystalShips: k mr. needy, give me a minute

@EndlessNights: 😊

He's recently changed his avatar, doubling down on the fact that his dad bod's harder than math.

A tease. Just like Kylie. Game recognizing game.

His recent video's called "ZombieShop" and features him in decaying makeup, shambling through a grocery store, drooling over the meat case to a bunch of mortified expressions.

Normie crap. Basic and lame. Come on.

@CrystalShips: cute

It's not getting a fist bump, though.

@EndlessNights: I'll take it.
@CrystalShips: where are u?
@EndlessNights: Somewhere near the water.
@CrystalShips: narrows it down
@EndlessNights: You're in Central MA, right?

She hesitates to answer, fingers absolutely trembling. Is this going to get real?

@EndlessNights: I recognize the Target in your first video . . . used to drive a delivery truck.

There's a "Hummingbird Heartbeat" in Kylie's chest because there is a point in every online relationship where you either take a leap of faith and dox yourself or decide to keep anonymity forever.

@CrystalShips: let's meet, maybe collab?
@EndlessNights: How about now? Lunch? Near Target?
@CrystalShips: lunch is good . . . someplace neutral tho . . .

@EndlessNights: Bolton? Panini place across from the office park that that used to be an old mill.

@CrystalShips: k . . . 1 pm?

@EndlessNights: Works! See you then.

It's Mom's one day off and she's out running errands, all the things she doesn't have time to get to during the workweek. They have tentative plans to grab an early dinner at Birria Basket, but Kylie sends a text letting her know something has come up. Gets back one word:

Fine.

Kylie showers until her skin is lobster red. Spends extra time painting herself up because she wants @EndlessNights's jaw to be on the floor.

She applies a base of black eye shadow to her whole eyelid, adding a silver shade to the creases, starting at the outer corner. She uses her MAC supply, twenty bucks a tray, reserved for special occasions. Bubble-gum-pink lipstick, also by MAC, to complement her wavy red hair.

She slides into blue plaid Lycra leggings because her butt looks spectacular in them, so good Erin had once accused her of wearing Spanx, then sits on the bed in front of an open closet looking for the right top. Something a little more confident than she's used to.

Her phone buzzes and she picks it up.

@MissyMiss followed you back.

The notification stops her cold. Kylie takes it straight into her DMs, breaths becoming scrapes as the screen reads: *@MissyMiss is currently typing* . . .

@MissyMiss: i knew you

Kylie's hyperventilating. Speaking with another murderer, this one a lot closer than Venezuela.

It takes a minute for her to locate the correct response. Be too thirsty and Melissa goes scampering off into digital dark space forever. Wrong question might even prompt an unfollow.

> **@CrystalShips:** civics freshmen year of high school
> **@MissyMiss:** can't remember much . . . everything fades . . .
>   help me
> **@CrystalShips:** ok. how?

She stares at the screen for a long time, heart in her throat, antic-ipating what might come next. But nothing does. Melissa's gone. At least for now. Though Kylie has established contact and that's enough of a victory for today.

Wherever she's hiding, it's only a matter of time now.

Interview

Ben's Volkswagen is idling and Kylie strides out looking like a piece of candy: black midriff crop top, a little band of golden baked belly showing. Red hair tied up in a messy ponytail with face-framing strands that dangle down.

It dawns on her—she looks more like a pop star than a college freshman. More @CrystalShips and less Kylie Bennington, after the lighting has been adjusted and the filter applied, flaws exorcised in Photoshop, of course.

Here's the person she can be.

Ben's mouth pops into an O as soon as she slides in.

"My own personal rideshare."

"Is that, uh, why you sent those pictures?"

"Boobs for rides, sure," she laughs. "I was just joking around with you, Ben."

He's quiet a second. Clears his throat. "I guess I don't understand." And then he's driving. "Where am I taking you anyway?"

"Bolton." She senses the tension. "We're friends, right? I'd like to be able to run things by you."

"I told you, I want to be more than—"

"That takes two, Ben."

"So does friendship."

Kylie draws back, touching her collarbone—a real Erin gesture. "Really, Ben? You don't want to be friends?"

He looks her up and down, jaw tightening because he's in the mood for some candy. "I just . . ."

"What?"

"I feel like you're torturing me."

Kylie has to fight the giggles off. This little loser who thinks the way to a woman's heart is weakness, never realizing that's a door to desperation. She doesn't even bother responding.

"You send me those pics because you're 'joking around' on the day I tell you that I love you."

"You never said '*love*.'"

"Well . . ."

"You didn't enjoy them? The pics?"

"No," he snaps. "I mean, I liked them. Look at you. But I didn't . . ."

Kylie drops into MonoLife while he's fumbling for words, her phone angled away so he can't see that she's watching him jack off on mute. A hundred thousand fist bumps and climbing.

"I guess I felt a little bad," Kylie says. "About the way we left things. I wanted to make it up to you."

"By showing me what I can't have?"

"You'll find someone, Ben. Soon."

"I don't want anyone else."

"That's 'cause you don't know anybody else. I'm really not someone you should be interested in."

"Who are you meeting?"

"You're sweet to worry."

"Tell me who you're meeting so I can stop." Ben's staring daggers now. It isn't worry in his eyes, but jealousy.

"Eyes on the road. If I call you tonight will that be enough?"

"Enough? You make it sound like a requirement."

"I just want you to stop giving me grief."

"You really don't care about me at all, do you?"

"As. Friends. That's it—nothing more."

Ben speeds through an intersection as the light flicks red, ignoring the blaring horns. He's breathing heavy, starting to sniffle, and Kylie's just embarrassed for him. "Why can't you give me a chance?"

"This isn't fair, Ben. For either of us. Just pull over and I'll walk."

"No."

"*No . . . ?* Pull over—*now*. I'll walk."

The Volkswagen cuts across two lanes, Ben risking another accident to bolster his tantrum. Kylie hops out and slams the door, shouting, "Have a nice afternoon!"

Then she's speed-walking past some apple orchard with signs for HARD CIDER PIE in the window.

Ben the loser idles in place behind her, his shitty car grumbling on his behalf. What a headache today is.

She walks a lonely stretch of road until reaching the old mill that @EndlessNights had suggested. Lo and behold, there is indeed a panini place in the makeshift strip mall there.

An actual bell goes off as she walks in and she turns back toward the glass to make sure Ben hasn't followed her. He's too chicken for that, and she's proven right.

"You in trouble or just early?" The person who has to be @Endless-Nights is sitting by the hallway to the bathrooms. A sleeveless vest over a tight black tee. He stands to greet her and the fabric tightens on his arms, showing impressive sculpt. Captain America with a slightly tragic fashion sense.

"Just eager to get started."

"Go-getter, I like that. I'm Simon," he says. Short blond hair cropped tight, a day's stubble for added sex appeal. Smile whiter than snow.

"Kylie." She sits down. He's older, three or four years over Brady. Boyishly handsome without the schoolboy baggage. "It's really nice to—"

"Same," he says in rushed staccato that reveals he's just as nervous. "I kind of assume everyone on there is some sort of bridge troll."

"Except you?"

"Yeah." Simon laughs. "I thought I was the god among lepers."

"What if it's all beautiful people?"

"Hey, we're two toward your hypothesis."

Yeah, except Kylie has an inbox full of unsolicited dick pics to prove his thesis wrong, but it's too nice a day to go there.

Simon admires her as she takes her coat off and slings it over the seat.

"You live around here?" she asks.

"We exchanging secrets now?"

"That's a secret?"

Simon gives a smirk that's kind of arrogant. It twists his features to resemble somebody trying to fart, an actual tragedy, though it's obvious he's never thought of himself that way. "Everything we *do* is secret. I mean . . . that's why it took you a month to agree to lunch. You weren't sure you wanted your worlds to collide."

"Are you so eager to tell the world who you are?"

"The world? No. I don't mind telling you, though."

Damn, Kylie thinks. *That's good.*

He gestures with his chin over Kylie's shoulder. "Everyone is trying to figure out where they know you from. And that means they're wondering who I am. Kind of cool."

You really want to be somebody, Kylie thinks. *He's either the perfect man or a pain in the ass. Probably a little of both.* "Who cares what they think?"

"Fuck 'em if they can't give a fist bump, right?"

"That's why I'm here."

"Ah. The collab."

"You've been asking." Kylie looks over her shoulder and a few eyes flick away. "So have plenty of others."

"I'm honored." He looks at her straight on as he says this.

"You seem pretty normal, thank God. And successful."

"Wish I felt that way. I don't even know what *successful* means on MonoLife. I've seen your views. Mine aren't anywhere close to that." He says that last part a bit quieter, then adds, "How can we go higher?"

Kylie's low-talking too. "I know one of the red Xs. And I know the video that got him the stamp."

"Can you show me?"

Kylie hesitates. There're rules about this sort of thing.

Simon senses this trepidation. "It's fine. We're Lifers. The house rule only applies if you're letting others in on the secret."

Kylie realizes she already kind of knows this. That it wasn't the "house rule" that prevented her from showing Erin her phone the other night on the swing. The reality was she hadn't wanted Erin to see. "You're . . . sure about that?"

"Trust me," he says. "Tried and tested."

Kylie calls up Duc's MonoLife profile, thinking about how not even Duc would show his phone the other day at the game. How he's straight-up terrified of this app. *So why aren't I?* she wonders as she slides her device across the table.

Simon glances down. "Ohhh. I follow this guy. He's a real fucker."

"You don't know the half of it. Though I wouldn't be here without him."

"I should thank him, then."

Kylie smiles, even if that's wayyyyy too presumptuous.

"They stamped his ass? Not much of a celebrity. Think there's any bona fide stars on here? Is Kim Kardashian a lurker?"

"That's gross."

"We must have different definitions of that word."

Kylie isn't going there. Instead, she wants to see how much of himself Simon is willing to divulge.

He's twenty-four, lives at home, and takes care of his mother. She has stomach cancer and isn't expected to make it much further than next year. He works some boring nine-to-five as a sales rep but is also a day trader with a large portfolio, and just recently he's started getting into crypto. All this makes Kylie's eyes glaze over.

It's not hard to understand why he's into MonoLife—a way to blow off some steam. Wage slaves are always trying to figure out the meaning of life because theirs didn't turn out how they thought, and they're still desperate to know they matter.

Kylie orders an iced chai latte and Simon's face drips with disappointment. She tells him to go ahead, order whatever. She wants to see him eat. You can tell a lot about a person by the way they stuff their face. And if she hears so much as a single burp, it's over.

"So, are we going to do it?" he asks.

"If we do, then what do you propose?"

"Why do I feel like this is a job interview?"

Kylie lets that question sit. No reason to soft-pedal this.

"Okay, well," Simon continues. "The reckless stuff doesn't work. We did some *Fast and Furious* shit with a statie. Chased us down 128 into Danvers, life flashing before my eyes the entire way."

He drops his phone onto the table, slides it over. The video's cued. Kylie clicks and watches Simon in the driver's seat of a speeding car. A galloping-horse Mustang logo on the steering wheel. This is posted to his collab partner's account, someone called @RazorBladeOrangatun. Whoever that is sits in the passenger seat, panning between Simon, scenery zipping past his window in a blur, and the rear window, where a Massachusetts state trooper's grim and determined face rides their bumper, siren blaring.

"We're about to lose this pig at the intersection!" @RazorBladeOrangatun hollers, punching the roof.

The camera glides back to Simon, then out the front windshield, capturing the dangling red traffic light. Simon smashes the horn, screaming something unintelligible. Cars zip through the intersection ahead. It seems certain they're about to nail one.

Simon cuts the wheel and skates around them, skidding through to a freak-out chorus of horns.

The trooper slides off target, his cruiser crumpling as it crashes into a telephone pole. Glass explodes into tiny fragments. The pursuit's finished in a second, the Mustang speeding toward freedom to the sound of laughing jackals.

"We're, uh . . . lucky nobody was hurt, I guess," Simon tells her.

Kylie chews the inside of her lip so not to betray her thoughts as she slides the phone back. "Kinda cool."

"Ehh. Not cool enough to move the needle. Barely got a follower bump. And I had to change my license plate."

"Got to be meaner," Kylie says. "That's what works for me."

"But not your friend, though, right?" Simon pauses, looking at his phone. "I mean, @SolidusRush doing *Jackass* as some girl shows off her bikini body ain't exactly cruel, so I'd say the whole thing's a pretty big mystery."

"You think it goes by the number of followers, then?"

"I've got twenty thousand of them. Give or take. So, no. What else you got? What's your brand?"

"I guess I . . . I guess I hurt people."

"I don't."

"I hurt people who deserve it." She adds this as a qualifier, thinking briefly of Brady's beatdown, but in no way really believes it. What had Mrs. Elrond ever done to her?

"The bikini girl?" Simon asks. "Did you know her?"

"A little."

"Well, on here she was all about sex and drugs. The good life."

"Yeah," Kylie says. "Skinny dips, public flashing . . . That's what MonoLife knows her for. That's what she brought to the collaboration." Her eyes widen as everything comes together. "Duc, as you said, is kind of a fucker. The kind of person who risks a girl's life by trying to jump over her."

Simon isn't following.

"Maybe MonoLife wants you to stay in your lane?"

"I look at MonoLife as the ultimate democracy," Simon adds. "That's how I see it. How do you get the algorithm to notice you? Your followers tell it you're worthwhile. And that doesn't sound any different than the other apps, but it is. See, I think you're right. You have to play to their interests. Which are *your* interests. The reason they follow you."

"That . . . honestly makes sense," Kylie says. "It wants authenticity."

"MonoLife loves it when people get hurt."

"But that's just life. People want to watch you lose."

People like Erin. Kylie has spent her entire social media life wanting to watch Erin fall from grace. And each time Erin posts something, Kylie has to shove it out of her mind because it's another reminder that she isn't at such a level yet and all her life has become is a series of constant, soul-crushing reminders of that.

But then Kylie realizes it's *@CrystalShips* who's here now. Crystal dressed up like a candy-colored dream. Crystal who turned every head in this place, including the soccer moms who *tsk* and likely think, *What a whore*, while deep down wishing they still looked like her. If they ever did.

There's more than one way to lose, though. If Kylie stops now, closes her MonoLife account, and returns to normal, she kills Crystal, and that's that. Life is full of losers. Of middle managers and wage slaves, throngs of homeless dregs living in cities beneath bridges and on sidewalks—Kylie will *not* exist among any of them. She guesses Simon doesn't want to either. He risked lives in a high-speed police chase because he's so afraid of losing.

"I don't think we have to go out and slaughter a kitten," she remarks. "Although the sick fucks on there would probably love it."

Simon stares down at the floor, reliving some memory he's unwilling to share. He clenches his jaw. "Don't take this the wrong way."

"What?"

"You're not taking this seriously."

"Everyone's always telling me that."

"Everyone's right. It hasn't become real for you yet."

"Excuse me?"

"I don't mean it like that. I just think—"

"You can handle this, but *I* can't?"

"You're a beautiful woman and your whole life's ahead of you. College. Marriage . . ."

"Didn't think you lived in Sexist City, Simon."

"I didn't mean it like th—"

"You already said that. Yet here we are."

Simon stops. Collects himself with a deep breath and then another. "I live in Gloucester," he says finally, through an apologetic smile. "And now that I'm getting to know you, well, you're no longer just a name to me. I mention this because I don't want to see you get hurt."

"You don't get a say in what I do." She taps her phone screen. "What's there is mine. Maybe we're not meant to collab."

"Oh, I think we are." He lifts his hands in surrender. "And I crossed a line. I'm really sorry. You're right."

The prospect of starting this search from scratch doesn't entice her. She's here because there's exactly one person on that app she can imagine collaborating with. "I do have one thing in mind," she says.

"I'm all ears. Please."

"Something I think will get us to where we need to be."

Simon forces an attentive grin the rest of his face tries to reject. "What've you got?"

And she tells him.

Sykes the Sleaze

Kylie woke up excited, bagging class today to see Simon again.

She had gone to sleep last night embracing her body pillow, wondering what it would feel like to be draped beneath one of his arms, the faint smell of Dove Men in her nostrils. Total "Hummingbird Heartbeat."

Simon wanted to pick her up today, but it's still too early for that. She takes a shower and then orders a rideshare, dresses in a navy blue Raquel Allegra printed track suit that she got on The RealReal for two hundred dollars, a buck-sixty off retail, then leaves the hoodie unzipped to show her scoop-neck sleeveless top by Vince underneath. A casual high-maintenance look so Simon doesn't think he's an automatic shoo-in.

He's already at Morning Bean when she gets there, sitting at a table near the door with two cold brews. He's in jeans and an off-white crew tee and throws a smirk that bruises her rib cage. "Trusting me to come a little closer to home, huh?"

"Maybe a little."

"You look good."

"Thanks. You . . . called out of your job?"

"You call out of first grade?" He laughs out loud at his own jokes. Kind of annoying. "We should go." He then leads her to his classic blue Mustang and then they're heading out of town, Simon eyeing her as he drives. "Which of us gets to do it?"

"Do what?"

"Host the stream. We'll both get credit, I think. One of us is going to get a little more."

"Oh, we're totally doing it from mine." She can tell Simon would like to say something about that, but it's Kylie's idea and she has all the followers, so there's no serious leg to stand on.

Mr. Sykes lives on the edge of town. One of those long, winding connector streets that aren't much of a neighborhood. Just a loose string of houses stretching from one town line to another.

They pass his place on the left and turn onto a narrow fire road, driving far enough down to get the Mustang out of sight. Simon kills the engine. "What'd this guy do, exactly?"

"Stole panties out of the gym locker room." Kylie does a full-body spasm, as if that's the only way to exorcise those disgusting thoughts.

"One of those," Simon says, suddenly a lot darker.

Kylie pops the door. "Let's go."

They move between trees, approaching Mr. Sykes's backyard. He's got a day job as an office maintainer at some business park, and it's only a little past ten, so there's no need to rush. They cross patches of crabgrass, crushing dead dandelions. One side of his property has a tilting picket fence that's missing most of its slats.

If you didn't know who lived here, you'd still have a strong sense of the type of person who lived here.

Simon goes for the back door, kneeling in front of the bolt, snapping rubber gloves against his wrist. "Keep watch."

Only there's nothing to watch. The house is far off the street and traffic zips along like a gust of wind. No curious neighbors in sight. Mr. Sykes is probably pretty certain he's off the grid here. Guard down.

Simon slips a bobby pin from his pocket, jiggles it around inside the keyhole until the lock clicks and he looks back. "You got any?"

Kylie answers him with a blank stare.

"See, this is what I was talking about when I said you're not taking this seriously. You need to be prepared." He's got another pair of rubber gloves in his hands then, tosses them over. She slips her fingers through. "Don't worry," he says. "I'm going to teach you everything."

Kylie isn't worried. She edges past him, bumping his shoulder as she pushes inside.

The house isn't the hoarder's nest she expected. Unwashed plates in the sink, an overflowing trash bucket stuffed with microwave dinner cartons, but otherwise fine.

She films their exploration. Soon they're moving into the finished basement, where the air is sour, a swirl of bleach and sweat.

They pull shirt collars to their noses and move between swaying chains that dangle off a drop ceiling. Across the wide-open floor is a sprawl of sex dolls and ladies' underwear.

Kylie shoots every inch of it like it's police evidence. "You've got kinks, Mr. Sykes."

Celebrity photos are printed on glossy paper, mostly women under the age of eighteen, pages warped by stains. Kylie finds a few of Katy Perry's most infamous pics among the detritus, the same ones that perverts are always posting to r/katyperry while looking to jerk off with others of their ilk.

"Bastard," Kylie says, taking more offense to this than to the time Sykes had stolen her underwear.

"Oh, it gets better." Simon isn't as repulsed, his voice a lot closer to amusement.

In the center of the room, a real doll lies on an old couch, tiny, and modeled after a prepubescent child.

"Where do you even order this?" Kylie asks.

"What a gold mine."

They search the rest of the house once they've overturned every nasty surprise in the cellar, but it's clear the dungeon is where Sykes does all his unwinding.

Kylie takes a seat at the kitchen table, scrolling MonoLife with her gloved fingers. "What are you doing?" Simon asks.

"Waiting."

"For?"

But she's already lost in a digital daydream, doesn't answer.

"I'll take your silence to mean, *For him.* As in, you think we should actually wait for him to come home."

Kylie gives @BlueFerox a fist bump for her latest video, a recipe for human flesh grilled and served on a pindo palm.

"Nope. I can't," he says. "I get busted and my mom's on her own. She doesn't have much longer, Kylie . . ."

"Nothing's going to go wrong." She taps her phone. "This world is a secret because it's the only place you get to be yourself."

"We're tearing this guy apart because he *is* being himself."

"You're defending him?"

"Of course not, I just . . ." His words trail off as he walks circles in the living room. "We live out *here.*" He stomps his foot to emphasize reality. "And there're laws out here. We still have to avoid being caught."

"Don't worry. We're just going to put the fear of God into him. Nothing else."

Simon takes a couple of breaths. When he's flustered, his mouth somehow tips upside down and becomes a Muppet frown.

Kylie rises and crosses the room, takes his hand. He's jumpy and yanks it back because he's lost his chill.

"Hey," she says and takes it again because who the fuck is he to resist *her*? "Think past all this, to when we've got a bulletproof video and followers that won't quit. Red exes, right? Eyes on the prize. Who's taking this more seriously now?"

Simon pulls his hand out of hers again with an incredulous laugh. "Shit, man, you can talk the pants off a kangaroo."

"Whatever. Sit. Relax."

Instead he stands. Paces. Moves through the halls, doing circles around the throw rug. He keeps sighing so Kylie knows he doesn't like this plan. It's the most annoying sound she's ever heard.

She's debating how to calm his nerves when an old Lincoln pulls down the driveway.

Simon's hands shoot up to his mouth to cover his gasp. "Whoa whoa whoa . . . is that him?"

Kylie shakes her head, doesn't know. Time stands still as she zones out Simon's frantic whispers. He watches her with silent pleading, eyes begging her to slip out the way they'd come in. No chance of that. This is a gift.

"He's home early," she says from behind a smile to the sound of a slamming car door.

In a second, Mr. Sykes moves across the living room window, a gaunt man with stringy sick hair and a soft limp. Kylie waits in place at the dining room table while Simon curses under his breath. The doorknob jiggles, then clicks.

The door opens and Sykes freezes in the jamb.

"Hi, Mr. Sykes," Kylie says as if greeting an old pal. "Remember me? You took a thong out of my gym locker last fall?"

Sykes says nothing, his attention drifting to the table, where Simon has placed some of the basement paraphernalia—the real doll, a mound of underage underwear, stacked like a colorful pyramid, and a couple of stained photos, including Katy in green latex with a palm tree pattern— this at Kylie's insistence.

Justice is coming, Katy.

"Come inside, bro, sit down." Simon's voice wavers as he says this. "We need to talk."

Sykes closes his eyes, his expression rinsing away, turning blank. He closes the door and shambles into the living room, dropping into the reclining chair with an arm draped over his forehead.

He says nothing. Barely moves.

Kylie has her phone out, pinches the screen to zoom closer, keeping the camera on him.

The old janitor has traveled elsewhere behind his thousand-yard stare. He's like that for so long, Kylie begins to worry about her phone battery. And once life returns to those coal bean eyes, he reaches down into the recliner's magazine pouch and produces a handgun.

Simon and Kylie jump back, but Sykes still doesn't acknowledge them. He simply pushes the gun barrel against his temple, one side of his mouth twisting upward in a detached smirk as his finger curls the trigger.

The *bang* is softer than expected. The custodian's head flings back, whatever were his final thoughts flying through the crack in his skull, splattering against the wall.

"Holy *shit*!" Simon's screaming. "Let's *go*! We need to get out of here—*now*!"

Kylie is still shooting, pushing in on the body, watching Sykes's head dangle to one side as more brain matter falls through the jagged exit wound above his ear, plopping to the floor like mashed potatoes.

She zooms in on that mess. "There it is," she says, performatively. Her voice remarkably unshaken. "All the secrets he took with him."

Simon's in the doorway, exaggeratedly waving his arm so she'll follow.

But Kylie's focused on the dying fire inside the janitor's eyes. A bullet through the brain isn't an off switch. There's still some light there, and eyes go dark the same way a dying flashlight does. Gradually. She stays with Sykes, filming until his eyes go all the way out. Until they look like two black marbles stuffed inside empty eye sockets.

Only then does Kylie calmly exit the house. Simon's hunched at the tree line, breathing heavy and saying something, his words like echoes from the end of a distant hallway.

They drive back to Summerfield, not speaking, Kylie wondering whether to post this, deciding pretty fast that it's not a serious question. Her only reason for such concern is getting caught.

And Kylie knows that she won't. She trusts MonoLife implicitly, more than she's ever trusted anyone.

"Where am I dropping you off?" Simon asks flatly.

If he'd asked to bring her home, she would've declined. Nice try, not so fast. But he didn't. The guy may be a bit too taken with himself, but he's got character where it counts. And the last thing Kylie wants right now is to be alone, because those dying eyes are dying all over again and again each time she closes her eyes.

She gives Simon her address and he takes her there, both of them gradually coming back to ease as they roll through the safety of her quiet suburban street, maybe beginning to feel as if they'd outrun the severity of their deed.

Simon purrs with approval, studying the expanse of wide homes and big yards around them. "Nice," he says, "your folks got money."

"Maybe we used to but they're separated now."

"That must be tough."

"My mom's always whining about how hard it is, how she can barely keep us afloat."

"I meant tough on you."

"Yeah. Whatever. Park in the driveway."

They go to her room, where Simon stands with his hands on his hips. "The inner sanctum," he says triumphantly, a bit too much self-congratulation stuffed into those words. "Looks a lot smaller in person."

Kylie ignores this, goes to work on the video, editing the footage, cutting it down to ninety seconds and then titling it, "Check Your Neighbors."

It begins with Simon picking the lock, a quick exploration of empty rooms, then thirty seconds in the basement from hell. Sykes gets the final fifty seconds, including the aftermath of his broken brains plopping out of his head like pumpkin guts.

Kylie AirDrops it back to her phone and they stand looking at each other like they're about to input nuclear launch codes.

"You ready?" she asks.

Simon nods. "Rubicon."

Kylie selects the video, adds "Collab with @EndlessNights" as the subject, and stands with her thumb hovering over the button. "Push it for me," she giggles.

Simon steps close. Looks straight into her eyes. She's certain he's going to kiss her. He only stands there, flashing a cocky grin that she sort of hates, but also kind of loves. He cups her phone hand in his palm and presses down on her thumb.

The life and death of Martin Sykes goes online.

They watch each other as the resounding silence of MonoLife taunts them. A minute that takes forever to pass. Then their phones are vibrating in unison. Distinctly different heartbeat patterns.

Notifications hit so hard their batteries get zapped in real time, dwindling down to the red.

Music to Kylie's ears. She lifts onto her haunches and goes for a celebratory kiss.

Simon presses a hand to her mouth as he takes a step back. "No. Not yet."

"You've got to be joking."

"Call me old-fashioned." He sidesteps her and goes to exit the room, turns back. "If our night's going to end with a kiss, it's because I've taken you out proper. On a date."

"What was this?"

"Work. Or maybe the biggest mistake of what will be our relatively short lives. I don't know which, but I'll message you tomorrow."

"How about you call me instead?"

"Yeah?"

Kylie shrugs. Or don't. She isn't about to repeat the ask.

Simon ambles back over and gives Kylie his phone so she can input her number. Once she's finished, he takes it back and his cocky smirk suggests she's just played into his hands.

And then he leaves without another word. Kylie watches from the upstairs window as he walks to his car and climbs in without once looking back.

"That man," she hisses, somewhat perplexed and annoyed, as her phone goes from silent thumps to the shrill metallic scream she feels in her fillings whenever it's just the two of them alone—she and MonoLife. Her phone choosing to psychotically trill now in notification songs.

PART II

X Marks the Spot

Mister Strangles

Mister Strangles followed you

is the first thing Kylie sees on waking up.

She's on her stomach. First time ever sleeping that way. Her head feels like it's piled high with bricks. Can barely lift it off her pillow, which is covered in phlegm. Tiny beads of yellow mucus glow like radioactive waste.

"What the hell . . . ?" she asks in grog, trying to rearrange herself and yelping at her body's resistance to motion.

The small of her back hurts again. That dime-sized bug bite. Pain that comes and goes.

Fingers brush the spot and return blood-caked. She's remembering last night's dream: lying on her stomach, a stranger's mouth pressing against the base of her spine. Soft lips. Warm kisses. Her defenses down, never questioning who. It's too hot to wonder who. Then, a hard bite, quick and searing pain, wet and greedy slurps. Who's got the kink? Who's doing this? She can't see them—

Dreams crisscross with reality. Kylie's subconscious in a blender. It's painful to sit upright, but she forces herself to, hoping the change in posture will get her brain working again. Sort out what's real. What isn't.

She wipes crusted phlegm off her mouth with an old shirt, wondering why she's being notified of a new follower when she turned those notifications off long ago. Without knowing who anyone is on this weirdo platform, she doesn't exactly care *who* follows her. Only that they do.

What makes Mister Strangles so special that he gets a notification in spite of her wishes?

She's ready to click into MonoLife and peep him out when a couple of texts from Simon win her attention.

Simon:

> Close but no cigar, huh? We tried.
> And should try again. 😎

"What? No." She's shaking now, full-body tremors while opening MonoLife, tears threatening to spill when—

The interface has changed. Again.

The top of her screen has even more options. A collapsible menu that had once been a notification indicator and a mailbox icon. Again, no push notification that the app had updated on its own. She taps open the new list and reads what's available:

LIVING NOW—a way to scroll trending topics

BEST LIFE—a tab for "Influencers" showcasing recent content from MonoLife's biggest users

And the usual options are there as well: **MESSAGES, NOTIFICATIONS,** and **SETTINGS**.

She's crossed over. So what's Simon talking about?

She's ready to text him back when a notification ribbon unfurls across the bottom of her screen: **MisterStrangles messaged you.**

"Going to show me your dick too, *Mister* Strangles?"

His avatar is an unnaturally narrow head beneath a full-faced swimming mask. Not a diving mask, but a vintage stretch cap from what looks like a hundred years ago that's somehow strained to cover its entire face. Skin-colored latex. Painted-on lips showing disproportionately drawn rows of teeth. Tiny little cuts for eyeholes and baked-bean orbs staring out of them.

This profile has zero public content. No option to block. Or follow.

@MisterStrangles: This is what you want, this is what you get

Mister Strangles drops a video beneath his gibberish. The thumbnail's blank. A sudden vibe crawls over Kylie like a spider, every bit of common sense she possesses instantly begging her to back out. Delete this thread. Forget all about Mister Strangles.

But his words are curious. *This is what you want, this is what you get.* How does he know what she wants?

She taps play and the silent, colorless footage is spinning up. The camera's point of view lifting off pavement, focusing, finding a footbridge arched over two land beds. A woman leans against a rail there, watching placid water pass gently beneath her.

The camera inches closer to her shoes, traveling up her ankles, legs disappearing beneath a silk-blended crepe dress that's cinched at the waist. She turns, a bit shyly, uncomfortable with what was probably brand-new technology in whenever time period this is.

The woman's facing the camera now. Her dress has a wide-open flat collar buoyed by a puffy bow tie. She's so cloistered beneath all those layers, and it's difficult for Kylie to imagine wearing anything like that.

The stranger's smile tightens in close-up. Flirty eyes give the lens the attention it craves.

Whoever's shooting this is transfixed by her beauty. And when she starts walking, the camera follows, almost desperately.

A cut and we're on a busy city sidewalk, weaving in and out of shops, surrounded by old brick buildings, a newsboy silently shouting headlines on the street corner as the camera pans to a horse-drawn carriage, then settles back on the subject of this video as she emerges from the nearest storefront with a small collection of department store bags swaying on her arm. People break around her with fleeting, almost superstitious, glances at the camera.

Next, she's at a café table, a fountain drink between her and the camera. Two straws jutting out. Her lips wrapped around one, the camera gliding in. She cocks an eyebrow in a flash of adorable naughtiness, then pulls way back, straightening in the chair and pressing a hand to her mouth to stifle her laughter. She's absolutely radiant, so completely alive in this moment that the camera cannot take its eye off her.

Another cut.

And she's naked. Her neck the color of shoe polish. Eyes wide and watery. Face submerged. The camera pulls back to show she's at the bottom of a ceramic tub; the cold linoleum floor around it is chipped flower patterns.

Fizz breaks over her frozen face, chunks of beauty actually flaking off, revealing sinewy biology beneath.

It isn't water. It's acid. The camera stays fixed, watching her face erode, pieces of her floating to the top, ebbing until they too are broken down and dissolved.

Her beauty becomes memory. She's just a skull now. Jaw forever agape, sockets popped wide, permanent shock over the way it all ended: one perfect day into a terrible night she could never have anticipated.

The camera retreats through the door. Down a narrow corridor where it pauses, turning back the way it came.

The only light in this hall comes from the bathroom. Someone in the doorframe. Someone sickly thin, taller than the door, crooked posture, leaned to one side and hunched down, looking square into the camera lens.

A swimmer's mask covering its face.

It waves at the camera—eerie similarity to the shadow that had stalked her outside Brady's while on her walk to the library—and then it slams the door.

Cut to black.

Kylie's grateful it's over. Unlike the odd comfort she finds in

@BlueFerox's cannibal cooking hour, bad men being put to good use, there's an overpowering darkness here that makes her soul feel sick. Makes the wound on her back scream out, sparks of white-hot pain she can't ignore.

She's out of bed and in the hallway before she even knows why, knocking on Mom's bedroom door, listening to her tired groans beyond it. The sound of weight shifting on a mattress and then, "Yeah . . . ? What is it? I just got home."

Kylie remembers sneaking in there as a child. Snuggling between Mom and Dad whenever a bad dream made the world feel unsafe. They'd practically smother her in their arms, whispering assurances, how everything was going to be okay. Today, more room in that bed, but less time for comfort because second shift comes early.

What can Mom even say about what Kylie's going through? Delete the app? Log off? Go read a book? Gross.

The lump on Kylie's back throbs so hard it feels like a rotted tooth sending signals of pain from head to toe. She touches it again, wincing, returning her fingers and finding clear discharge there. It continues to dribble out, a strange, sticky trail sliding beneath the band of her pajama shorts, sailing down the crack of her rear.

From beyond the door, Mom is already snoring again and Kylie staggers back to her room, the bathroom inside it, flicking a switch that brings no light. She barely notices because whatever's in the mirror has her attention.

A swimmer's mask stretched over Kylie's face. Her posture as tilted as the shadow waving on that video.

A vibration in her palm. She turns the phone over. Another message.

@MisterStrangles: a deer lives without realizing its place in the world is to be hunted

Then the bathroom light is on, and Kylie finds herself in the reflection, staring out. Maskless. Looking baffled.

She's thinking about the strange shadow that had followed her down the sidewalk that night. The sharp sting at the base of her spine she felt for the first time there. How it's never gone away.

But it's also never been this bad.

Kylie lifts her shirt and twists her hips to see the wound on her back. A single hair juts out from the center of a reddened mound.

"Uck!" She reaches for the tweezers, twisting herself back into position and plucking it free, a viscous pink dribble oozing out. The strand is the length of a toothpick. About as rigid as one too. It hardly seems like a hair at all.

But removing it makes the pain subside, those throbs receding into smaller waves that soon fade into nothing.

She drops it into the sink and stumbles back to bed, fingers doing some frantic googling. Her symptoms are close enough to something called "folliculitis," and it calms her down.

She's more interested in MonoLife anyway, navigating to the brand-new Living Now tab, where Martin Sykes's suicide is the hottest thing. The top comment under her video has almost as many likes: **This is better than Budd Dwyer!**

The video beneath "Check Your Neighbors" is a live feed showing multiple public executions in a town square of some foreign country.

Below that, a morgue attendant fondles a slabbed corpse.

And after that, two women completely nude save for sharpened stiletto heels snorting cocaine off the stomach of a naked body builder, working up the edge to perform a kitten stomp. Beside them, a chorus of innocent meows from an inflatable Thomas the Tank Engine pool.

Lastly, a blonde model with a deep scar on one side of her cheek holds a blade against the balls of a whimpering man in his birthday suit.

Here then is what MonoLife wants. She knows this intuitively. Death. Torture. Pointless depravity. Its users have spoken and, exactly like cream, decadence rises to the top.

Kylie isn't sinking in these waters. She's floating. Learning to swim.

She leaves the app and catches another text from Simon.

Simon:

> Holy shit you've got the red X.

"What?" It must've come through alongside the announcement of additional features, and is surely something she would've caught, and rejoiced over, had it not been for Mister Strangles and his weird-ass distractions.

It's true. Holy shit. @CrystalShips is stamped. No greater sense of accomplishment or legitimacy.

Simon though hasn't been promoted. Huh. She kind of loves that. It means she's the successful one and he's superfluous. It could've been anyone in that video with her. But she's the one who's ascended.

To cheer him up she texts:

Kylie:

> want to go to a Halloween party this weekend?

Simon:

> With your friends? Ehhhhhh

> sure, it can count as a date 😳

> Not my style. How about dinner and dancing.
> Lots and lots of wine . . .

Kylie snaps a selfie of an exaggerated pouty face, filters it, and posts it to MonoLife with the caption: **Who thinks @EndlessNights should take me to a Halloween party next weekend?**

Simon:

> Not fair lol

The replies have strong opinions:

> No, he's a cuck.
> I'll take you . . . where you at?
> We stan this partnership
> Only if you're gonna make a video blowing him

Kylie:

does that mean you'll go????

Simon:

I don't do costumes.

you'll do this one

I'm good.

that's why I want you to come with.

I'm supposed to be the one who asks you on a date.

what is this the 80s?

I wish.

not going to beg

Then I guess I have no choice.

ttyl

She tosses her phone to the bed and tries not to smile about it.

The Weirdo Boys

Kylie:

Might go to the Halloween party . . .
am I still welcome? 😩😩😩

It's her first message to Erin in over a week and there's no reply. The harshest response of all.

Ben Austin picks her up in the mornings. A serious dent in her social stature, though Kylie doesn't really care anymore because classrooms are daydreams, the people in them strangers. The phone on her thigh, reality.

"I'm really sorry," Ben says.

"About?"

"About the way I poured all my emotions on you." He offers this rehearsed apology as though it excuses his jealousy. Managing his insecurity has become a full-time project. That's the danger when you let someone into your life. People almost never show you who they are until it's too late.

But he's trying. His clothes are new, store-fresh khakis with a couple of extra table creases in them, knitted white sneakers, ankle-high socks. Most impressive is that it looks like he took the time to brush his hair into place before distributing product to a mostly dry head.

"I'd feel a lot better if we could get some bubble tea after school," he says. "Just talk."

Kylie isn't listening. A new video called "Burning Man" has entered the Living Now arena and is currently at number two, just below "Check Your Neighbors."

In it, a rioter accidentally sets himself on fire, collapsing atop a concrete stairwell and quietly smoldering to death as the camera zooms in, his elbow pads and painter's mask melting, becoming one with his crisping skin as his eyes turn to goop.

"Sure," Kylie says. "I love bubble tea."

"What time later?"

"Oh, not today. But soon, Ben. I've got a lot going on."

"Right. A new boyfriend." He says this as the Volkswagen slides into the space beside Erin's BMW. "I'm not giving up that easy."

Whatever. It makes no difference to her. She walks to class a couple of steps ahead of him, hurrying to prevent him from catching up. There are giggles from the sidelines over Ben's inability to do so.

She thinks a lot about costumes. One that will turn heads because she wants Erin's eyes wide open. The way MonoLife is going, Kylie feels at last like her equal. Still can't resist the urge to dunk on her, though. Payback for all the passive-aggressive *look what a big deal I am* braggadocio she's suffered over the last few years of ErinTime.

Kylie catches glimpses of Erin throughout the day, always at the other end of the hallway or ducking into a classroom. Passive behavior that's absolutely thrilling. Erin putting in all the avoidance so Kylie doesn't have to.

She's in the bathroom checking her DMs when she decides to send a message to @MissyMiss, see if she can't get something else out of her. Their limited interaction strikes Kylie as disquieting. She's unable to shake the idea that everything Missy says is strained, requiring great effort.

@CrystalShips: u see my video?

@MissyMiss: yes . . . big hit

@CrystalShips: remember that perv?

@MissyMiss: no

@CrystalShips: it wasn't that long ago

@MissyMiss: how long has it been???

@CrystalShips: where are you?

@MissyMiss: idk

@CrystalShips: last time you asked for help . . . tell me how

Kylie stares at her phone, waiting for an answer that never comes. It's possible that she's forcing the issue, but Missy's odd behavior is worth the inquiry. Could be her old classmate is in a rubber room somewhere.

Last thing Kylie wants is to go to class, but if she doesn't, she'll just stay here, obsessing over Missy's digital silence.

So she goes to Statistics, where she's slumped over her desk, staring at the erupting cock carved into the Formica, when the weirdo kid beside her—Rennie?—dressed in military surplus clothes, and whose backpack is littered with pro–Second Amendment patches, starts eyeing her up and down.

"Nice work on Sykes," he says out the corner of his mouth.

Kylie acknowledges this by widening her eyes. No other response warranted. This is the last boy on earth she wants to speak to.

And it isn't just Rennie who's looking, but his buddy at the desk on the other side of him too.

"Yeah, I, uh, showed Tommy, you know?" Rennie says. "He doesn't have the app, but that shit's too golden to keep secret. You're out there making the streets safe."

Tommy lifts his hand and attempts an introductory wave, but he stops when it's clear Kylie isn't looking, then pretends to examine his wrist as a face-saving measure.

"I just, uh, think we should hang, you know?" Rennie grins. "Freak to freak." He leans into the aisle, his expression darkening into a sneer. "Hunt some more pedos. Give me a reason to use this." He lifts his tattered army coat and flashes an oversized knife sheath on his belt.

Kylie swivels back to the carving on her desk, wondering if Mister Central Mass Militia here isn't the artist behind it.

"I gotta get that app," Tommy's saying, still trying to claw his way into conversation. "Your account totally makes it worth the hundred bucks."

"Yeah, we're, like, your biggest fans," Rennie says. "Kind of girl you want to take home to Mom." He forces a sound that's close to a laugh but is also uncomfortable because there isn't a trace of humor on his face.

Kylie's looking straight ahead, staring at the blackboard and pretending for the first time all semester that she cares about confidence intervals.

Rennie shrugs. "I know you're not supposed to show anyone, but . . . I'm spreading the word, you know?" He lifts a thumb to Tommy. "Like, this fucking guy's ready to become a customer. They should be paying *me*."

Mr. Davies tells them to shut it, and Kylie feels Rennie and Tommy's eyes on her almost constantly for the remainder of the class. When it's over, they hover in the hallway by the door, waiting as she takes extra time to slip her books into her bag.

Rennie's starting to say something as Kylie passes, but she lowers her shoulder, mouths "Not interested," then goes rushing toward the anonymity of the between-classes crowd.

By the time she has an opportunity to grab a bite to eat, "Burning Man" has fallen off Living Now and Martin Sykes's suicide continues to reign. Many commenters have actually figured out who Sykes was:

› Some pedo in Central Mass
› Diddler BTFO
› Look up all the chickenhawks in your neighborhood and do this to each
› You're a monster, we deserve to live too . . .

Kylie imagines Sykes's rotting corpse and wonders how long it will take for the real world to discover he's missing.

Ben drives her home after school and the question is all over his face. He so badly wants to ask but can't take putting his cards on the table again.

"I'm doing transfer applications tonight," Kylie tells him.

"Cool. Where to?"

"Wesleyan? Is that one? I don't know."

"I'm gonna get my associate's here. Best two-year theater program in the state. After that, who knows? Maybe we'll end up at the same—"

"I appreciate the ride, Ben."

He nods, relieved that it's just boring paperwork he's losing out to, suddenly more chipper, wishing her a great night before backing out of the driveway.

Several packages are waiting on her doorstep.

Each one addressed to Kylie Bennington. She has to make three trips to get them all into the kitchen, then uses scissors to slice through the packing tape.

Clothes.

Boxes and boxes of clothes. Notes inviting her to become an ambassador for each brand.

Please accept these gifts with MonoLife's compliments. We hope you'll enjoy a selection of winter fashions that we have acquired just for you. Please consider wearing some in your posts, and more may follow.

"Holy shit," Kylie says, pride swelling like a bruise. Pride turning to fear as something else dawns on her: MonoLife is supposedly anonymous, and yet . . . it knows exactly who she is.

That chilly consideration melts beneath genuine excitement. She cannot get upstairs fast enough. Spends the whole night trying them on, taking selfies in each outfit.

There's a Pima Micro-Rib Turtleneck. Super-soft, fine-ribbed cotton that's immediately striking for its light stretch that somehow hugs

Kylie in all the right places. It's complemented by a pair of AGOLDE Riley jeans, a timeless offering featured in ankle-cropped, high-rise silhouette. And once they're combined with the Steve Madden Fantasie platform boots, it creates a smart and fashionable ensemble that propels her into another social bracket that's well beyond Summerfield fashion. Everything is a perfect fit, nothing too tight or loose.

More boxes follow the next day and all week. Even more clothes, along with earbuds, face creams, skin rubs, hair products. Each gift brings with it a tremendous sense of accomplishment.

This is it, she thinks, on the verge of tears. *I'm getting what's mine. And it's about goddamn time.*

Mom asks about the boxes with total bafflement. "*Who is sending you all this stuff?*" She doesn't get it, never did. Thinks it has to be some creepy suitor looking for a trophy wife and remains unconvinced when Kylie assures her this is not the case. Because in her mind, Kylie could never make something out of nothing.

The wound on her back acts up from time to time. Mostly when Kylie is away from MonoLife. In class or doing chores. That's when it's at its angriest, pulsing so Kylie knows it's there. *Folliculitis*, she's always reminding herself. The skin is less irritated now but that hardened lump never truly fades.

At the end of the week, a DM from MonoLife lands in her inbox:

SAVE THE DATE! THIS IS YOUR **TENTATIVE INVITATION**, PENDING ENDURING GROWTH. SHOULD YOU MEET ALL REQUIREMENTS, YOU WILL BE GIVEN FURTHER DETAILS ON HOW TO ATTEND MONOLIFE'S ANNUAL RETREAT. ALL EXPENSES PAID FOR YOU AND A PLUS-ONE. LOCATION TBD. REMEMBER, WE ARE WATCHING YOUR CAREER WITH **GREAT** INTEREST, KYLIE BENNINGTON.

Plus-one? It would have to be Simon, right? It's hard to imagine bringing anyone else. Can you even invite someone who isn't on the app? How would you explain it to them? And how would that work on MonoLife's end? Could they turn your guest away? How would Kylie even contact anyone behind the scenes at MonoLife to ask these questions, given there's no discernable app function to do so? How is she supposed to know who to bring? It's getting very complicated and overwhelming, and she has to stop thinking about it before she drives herself nuts.

Kylie only needs to look around her room to be reminded of the dividends MonoLife is paying. It's a department store in here. All she ever wanted.

Why MonoLife and not OnlyFans? OnlyFans is performative. A lie. It would be money in her pocket, sure, but at the whims of simps who get off on making polite demands. Kylie won't work for them. She does MonoLife for herself.

It's why she won't wear a disguise. *A swimwear mask*, she briefly muses. She considered once for Instagram and in the early days of Mono-Life a platinum blonde wig and green contact lenses, then decided that wasn't her. That she could never be happy with herself if her followers fell in love with a lie.

No, this adventure started in earnest in a fit of raw, naked honesty, and needs to remain that way.

Katy stares down from her position on the wall, looking especially proud of her little KatyCat tonight. And Kylie can think of no better way to test out her brand-new earbuds, with their customizable fit for all-day comfort, than by streaming *Prism*, Katy's third studio album and Kylie's personal favorite. Not as relentlessly candy-colored as *One of the Boys* or *Teenage Dream*, where Katy would tackle admittedly serious topics such as drug addiction and trauma with her trademark flare, though *Prism* is not as lopsided and searching as the albums that followed it. It's the nexus, Katy as a bombshell bitch and bona fide superstar laying down bop after bop while hinting at the darkness growing inside her—suicidal thoughts and the lengths she's willing to go to force others to love her.

Kylie is grateful for Katy's honesty because it's helped her recognize these truths inside herself.

She's attempting to decide which clothes to try on. The trick is modeling this stuff without MonoLife realizing that's what she's doing. That means showing off the skin she's accustomed to flaunting, though she can always use a few additional pointers from Erin. Just to ensure she's on the right track.

She goes to Instagram, where Erin's follower count continues ticking up, and scrolls her last week of photos. Reels and pictures that show someone who hasn't missed Kylie at all.

Cool faces, hot bodies, good times.

Kylie studies each from the darkness of her bedroom. There's a tremendous sense of sadness now that Erin's become a ghost. And it happened in only two weeks' time.

Kylie can't help it. She gives Erin a heart. And then another. Goes right down the list, like-bombing every post she's missed. A blockable offense on most days, though Erin will understand the gesture behind it.

Kylie then posts a newly minted selfie to her own Insta with the caption: **Missing my friend tonight** ☹

A little pandering never hurts. She opens Erin's text thread, where the message from earlier this week sits unanswered:

> Might go to the Halloween party with a date . . .
> am I still welcome?

Only there's an ellipsis bubble there now.

Kylie's heart thumps so hard it feels for a moment like the lump on her back.

The ellipsis appears and disappears several times. Erin trying to make sure her response is pitch-perfect.

Kylie's back in Instagram, waiting. She refreshes her feed and a photo of weirdo boys Rennie and Tommy pops up. Some classmate she doesn't know but inexplicably follows has posted it. Rennie's and

Tommy's arms around each other's shoulders, taken a few summers back at Doane's Falls.

Kylie's about to scroll past when the caption grabs her eye:

Just heard about the passing of Rennie and Tommy and I'm speechless. So young. Such long lives ahead of them. Please don't drink and drive, people.

Comments under the post lament the boys' decision to chug a bottle of whiskey while cruising back roads, and others call those comments out for their callousness, while others still post contact information for Alcoholics Anonymous.

Kylie scrolls back up to Rennie's face. *You shouldn't have told him,* she thinks. *Idiot. This is what happens.*

Nobody but her will ever know the truth.

A sense of terror takes hold in Kylie. Proof there are forces at work here she doesn't understand. Only she quickly realizes it isn't terror at all.

It's awe.

And then her phone dings, snapping her back to reality:

Erin:

see ya there, bitch

Kylie falls asleep that night, phone in hand, reading Erin's words over and over through teary eyes she can't be bothered to wipe.

Duc's Tale

O n campus, Kylie's immediate problem is that she doesn't know
who to sit with in the cafeteria. There are too many familiar faces
around, mostly holdovers from Summerfield High, and they watch her
expectantly as she scans the tables. Kylie no longer feels the need for
this kind of social interaction, all of it striking her as obligatory and
wasteful. Erin might've given her permission to attend this weekend's
Halloween party, but to sit with her before any sort of reconciliation
is premature. And sidling up next to Ben Austin would create other
complications she doesn't want to deal with.

That's when she spots Veronica waiting in line for the drink dis-
penser, a fantastic, neutral choice announcing itself, but she doesn't
want another lecture about how she's been neglecting her BeanieGang
duties.

"Hey." Duc shoulders out from behind a couple of his burnout pals,
his entourage looking Kylie over with Pornhub projections in their
eyes. In a second, they move past into the cafeteria. "I've been looking
all over for you."

"Oh no."

"Don't give me that. Let's talk."

"I have class in half an hour."

"Good one. Come on."

"Where?"

"Off-campus lunch. On me."

Duc pushes through the side door and Kylie follows—almost on instinct.

They slip into Duc's blue Hyundai. He turns the ignition and starts for the road, and with SCC in the rearview, Kylie flashes on the social minefield of that cafeteria, realizes how grateful she is for this chance to escape.

"I know you think I'm a terrible person," Duc says.

"Serial killer in the making."

"Then why get into a car with me?"

"Oh, come on. You're killing animals. And giving one old man a heart attack."

"That was an accident, and he didn't die, by the way."

"Wow, you checked up on him? Got a real conscience in there?"

"Whatever, Vigilante Girl."

"You can't compare our content."

"No," Duc says, stomping the gas, his Hyundai speeding off toward the back roads of Summerfield. "There's a reason for what I'm doing. Gonna show you."

The back roads carry them across town, and Duc turns onto the long road toward Barrett Park where the pavement ceases and becomes a bumpy horse trail. The Hyundai rocks hard until the trees open up in front of the placid waters of Lake Salvi. A real hideaway hot spot in the summer months, completely abandoned now.

Kylie tenses, certain she's given Duc the wrong idea. "Hey. What you said at the football game . . . a rat doing anything for cheese . . . I'm not gonna, you know—"

"Jesus, Ky, I've known you since you were ten. Don't worry." Duc slides a Puff Bar from his pocket, takes a drag, a few more till he's calm. "Taste this," he says, hands it off. "As close as our mouths have to get, all right?"

Kylie's looking at him like, *What's this all about?* as she puffs.

Duc removes his phone from his pocket, powers it off, and drops it onto the dashboard. "Yours too. Off."

Kylie exhales banana crème smoke, the nicotine pushing her anxieties to an arm's distance while doing as she's told. Duc picks up her phone, checks to make sure it's really off.

"Paranoid much?"

"Yeah. Tons." Duc recovers his bar, gives it a few hard and desperate puffs. "You're not?"

"Um . . . no."

"Any luck with Missy?"

"Not yet."

"Nothing?"

"Something. Not much. We're trading DMs but, I don't know . . ."

"What?"

"It's like she's barely there . . . super weird."

"Try harder."

"I am." Now she's annoyed by his insistence. "Can't be too forward, can I? I'll tip my hand and she'll figure it out. This is how it has to be. Slow."

"I need you to find that bitch, Ky."

"I'm open to suggestions if there's another way."

"Nah. You're doing everything right."

"Wow, Duc—that must've been hard."

"Cut it out."

"Then what the hell are we doing here?"

"When you got stamped," he says. "You know, with the X? Were you . . . like, followed by anyone, uh, kind of weird?"

"On the app?"

Duc stares back like the answer's obvious.

Kylie's voice drops despite it being just the two of them. It just sounds dumb to say it any louder. "You mean Mister Strangles?"

"Shit. Yeah. Okay. Everyone gets a different follow based on what I've seen. Mine's . . . Mama Doll."

"That's kinda worse than Mister Strangles."

"Probably. My fucking luck."

"I never know what you're talking about, Duc."

"That account, Mama Doll, followed me when I got stamped. She shows me things I . . ." His words taper off and he just stares across the dark, blue water, smoking in silence as if he were suddenly alone. "Strangles, Doll . . . any way you slice it, they're the ones behind this."

Kylie falls back against the seat, joining the silence, eyeing her phone like it's a bomb set to blow. Maybe there's more than just awe in her guts for this app. Possibly there's some mortal terror mixed in, just under the surface.

Duc opens his door and gets out. The interior's beeping. He leaves it cracked and wanders down to the shore. Sits in the dirt, vape smoke drifts rising over his head.

"Great," Kylie says, crossing her arms, watching Duc lie down, sprawled out, eyes closed, smoking like a campfire.

The *bang* against the roof startles Kylie into sliding down to the floor, between the seat and glove box. The second *bang* is louder, harder, putting an actual welt in the ceiling as part of the interior comes lumping downward.

Kylie screams while, outside, Duc is suddenly shouting what sounds like instructions. Kylie's focused on the car ceiling that's now pushing farther down, as if whatever's out there is reaching for her through the steel roof.

A shadow flitters across the back window. Kylie follows it with her eyes, losing it at the vehicle's corner. She braces, expecting to see it by the passenger door next, finding only naked branches swaying in the October air as the roof continues to whine. The fist-sized dent stretches down like taffy and then Duc's voice comes fading back into earshot:

"*—on, turn it on!*"

Kylie reaches across the cab, fingers closing on the key head. With a flick, the Hyundai grumbles. Duc is just over the dashboard, hands cupped around his mouth, shouting over the constant whine of steel.

"*The phones! Turn them on!*"

She grabs both, pulling the devices into her lap, sinking back down into her safety spot, fumbling to push the buttons, waiting for the comfort of that white glow as the terror she feels turns her face to frostbite.

Both screens boot in unison and, at the same time, the violent banging and stretching steel stop. Duc is back at his door, pulling it wide, wincing in pain.

"*What the fuck was that?!*" Kylie screams.

Duc drops behind the wheel, sucking air. Then he peels his shirt up, exposing the bruise on his stomach.

It looks at first like any welt from sparring, horsing around. Forest-green colors in the shape of a crescent moon. But the skin is rising somehow on its own, kneading, as if being sucked by an unseen mouth.

"What—" Kylie starts to say.

From Duc's throat, a groan drier than sandpaper.

Suddenly, Kylie is aware of the sore on her back. How it's suddenly throbbing again.

"I had to show you," Duc says. "You needed to see for yourself. Try and hide, they find you." He takes his phone in the palm of his hand, opens MonoLife, and shouts, "*Okay! Here I am!*" as if to placate it.

Now they're looking at the damage. Duc pokes and prods at the pushed-in ceiling, gasping each time his fingers land. Kylie also reaches for the steel welt, hesitant like she's trying to pet a growling dog. She and Duc trade disbelieving glares, settling on a mutual understanding in this unease.

Then Duc shifts into reverse, starts backing up. "Fuckers feed on us one way or another. And they're not afraid to wreck your damn ride. How the hell am I supposed to explain this?" He taps the dent with the back of his hand. "How do you even *fix* this?"

"Why . . . why are you showing me this?"

"So someone in this world understands . . . why I'm going to do what I'm about to do next."

Then the Hyundai is zipping down the narrow one-way back to town. Duc doesn't say anything more and neither does Kylie. She's too busy wondering if she's lost her mind. And if she hasn't, what that says about reality.

Halloween

Simon's speeding past acres of farmland on the edge of town. A place called "the plains," where the McMansions live.

"Rennie and Tommy died somewhere out here," Kylie says. Not that there'd be anything left of the wreckage, but she's curious to know how MonoLife did it. Though, after yesterday's trip to the lake, maybe she shouldn't be.

"Why would anyone pay so much to live out here?" Simon asks, mostly aloud and for his benefit. "Lexington and Concord, sure. But here?"

He launches into a tirade about equity that Kylie barely listens to, something about how these places are bad investments, and how anyone buying a house in this economy will be underwater because the Fed is intentionally trying to bring housing prices down and mortgage applications are dropping fast, and now Kylie can't be bothered to hide her disinterest, sighing as she tunes it all out. Too focused on tonight's reunion. She looks down at her costume and pops a lorazepam to relax.

She's taken three or four pills today to get her mind off the lake incident. It's frustrating how it never really calms her stress, just diffuses the connection between her body and mind so that she doesn't have to think so much about that thing pushing through Duc's car ceiling. Easier to be crazy because everybody else is too.

The house isn't difficult to find. It's the only driveway that's over-stuffed with cars. Thumping bass can be heard a few hundred feet out.

Simon parks on the street, far from the twisted nest of vehicles, smirking like he's the smartest man alive. "Someone's gonna dent four or five of them on the way out, just watch."

He always talks like he's teaching her something. Mildly insufferable.

Kylie cracks the door and slips into the shadows so he doesn't catch her eye roll. She slides from her long coat and folds it on the seat as Simon comes around, offering his arm.

"Not yet," she says, tussling his costume so that it's showing just the right amount of skin. At least be good for something.

"Gonna be ridiculed by every guy in there," he says.

"I thought you were all, *Who cares what a bunch of young people have to say?*"

"I've got self-esteem issues."

"Who doesn't?" Kylie gets him looking exactly as she wants, cocking her head to admire the dad bod visible beneath the frayed claw marks in his shirt. Arms bulging. Beautiful. Every woman in there, and a decent handful of men, will agree.

They wind through the path of crooked vehicles, Simon's hand in Kylie's. Silhouettes dance beyond curtained windows and Tiesto's cranked. "Sounds like a dying chipmunk," he grumbles.

"Don't be a boomer."

Simon slides his arm around Kylie, fingertips hovering against her shoulder. "I'm here for you, my little e-celeb, aren't I?"

It's like a carnival inside. Costumed people everywhere. Exposed skin glistening in strobe light. Fog swirling through, thick and heavy, somehow everywhere.

In the kitchen, an oversized punch bowl is surrounded by empty bottles of vodka and tequila and a single press-on nail floats on the surface. Probably why most people are carrying red Solo cups tapped from the keg.

A boy wearing a Scoops Ahoy uniform complains, "Shit's too foamy, man."

Simon shoulders in and tilts the boy's cup, easing back on the draft. "Fill it at a slower pace. That's key."

"Thanks, bro!" Scoops Ahoy shouts over the noise. "Sick costume." He vanishes into a mass of Party City outfits and Kylie nudges Simon's hip.

"You're so helpful, Dad."

"I could make a joke about giving you a spanking, but I'm going to be the adult in the room."

Someone shouts, "Oh God!"

From the living room, fog dissipates around a horned figure. Erin as Maleficent, the costume altered so that her boobs are on the cusp of spilling out. The Wicked Queen of Instagram, asserting her powers.

Next to her, Cameron's dressed as some kind of lion tamer, a leather jacket and hat with a whip dangling off his belt.

Erin whispers in his ear and he rushes off, the music falling almost instantly and without protest—a pure display of influencer power.

Erin strides into the kitchen, arms outstretched. "Aren't you guys just the *hottest*?"

The lorazepam inside Kylie makes it easier to smile, to admire Erin: her high-gloss black lipstick, purple mist painted across naturally jagged cheekbones. Slick and glistening cleavage that demands attention. "You look amazing," Kylie says, voice cracking with jealousy as she imagines the number of followers this getup is winning her.

Erin's grin confirms that she knows this and isn't through admiring Simon. She circles him, objectifying him, and only once she completes her inspection does she look to Kylie with approval.

It's quite satisfying.

Kylie has spent much of the week worrying about how this reunion might play out, stressing herself silly over the imagined scenarios. But now that Erin's three feet away, flattering her, it isn't weird or awkward. It's just right. Like they never left each other.

"I'm loving the theme." Erin leans against Kylie's ear. "Mark your territory, she-wolf."

Kylie wears yellow contacts and molded fangs, acrylic press-on nails thicker and longer than normal—a wolf beginning to take shape. Pointed animal ears attached to the crowns of her lobes and a few tasteful streams of fake blood at the corners of her mouth to tie the costume together.

Simon straightens his blond wig and tugs the red scarf around his neck. Gender-swapped Little Red Riding Hood isn't supercomfortable tonight, but his willingness to "debase" himself is arousing.

"Yours is fire," Kylie says. Sexy Maleficent being the smart play when you don't want anyone looking at your face on account of the burst pimple nestled within your temple, buried beneath layers of concealer.

"Oh God, God, God," Brandi's saying before anyone knows she's there. She's in one of those sexy schoolgirl outfits, and it's somehow less revealing than the clothes she wears on the reg. "You guys are back?"

Simon extends his hand to introduce himself, but Brandi's sipping her drink and swaying to the music. Misses the gesture entirely.

"We never stopped being friends." Erin sighs.

"So cool," Brandi says. "If only I can get back with Asher now, everything will be normal." She spots him heading toward the basement to smoke with Jackie Morgan, goes rushing off to spy.

Turns out that Simon and Cameron have common ground when it comes to *Madden* on PS5, and Kylie takes that opportunity to tug Erin's arm. "How about a walk?"

"Not too long," Cameron says with a smirk. "Studs like us won't last in a place like this."

"Studs," Erin groans. "More like dogs in heat."

They pass through a canopy of vape smoke as they cross the lawn, late October air riling gooseflesh on their half-clothed bodies.

"I'm sorry, Erin," Kylie says, forcefully, like she's been holding it in for two weeks. "I don't know what I was thinking."

"Totally fine."

"It isn't. I betrayed you."

"Yeah. You did."

"And I'm sorry. I know it's probably not enough . . ."

"It is, actually. Close enough to Christmas, right? Look—apology accepted. Let's move on."

"The line got blurry for a minute. I'm better now."

"I will admit I was worried."

Kylie's worried too, mostly about the skinny jeans she got comped in today's mail, which are surprisingly running a bit snug without any proper channel to exchange them.

The party's out of earshot and Kylie leans against an oak tree, taking Erin's hand with a squeeze, whispering, "Hey. I found Melissa."

Erin's face is hidden beneath an umbrella of tree shadows. "What . . . ?" The question is asked so quietly it's barely a whisper.

"She killed Annabeth. And she's still using MonoLife . . . from somewhere."

"No shit! Show me."

"You know I can't."

Quiet disdain radiates off Erin's silhouette.

"You and I agreed to the same terms of service, Err," Kylie says, hoping Erin hasn't studied it close enough to argue the omitted detail, that users *are* actually allowed to show stuff to other users.

"Oh, whatever."

"It's enforced. Look, this weirdo in my Statistics class had the app, okay? And he was showing his buddy, they kept trying to talk to me about it, and then—*boom*! They're dead a couple days later."

"From drunk driving." Erin's uptalk sounds a lot like *duh*.

"Yeah . . ."

"I think you need to stop," Erin says. "Like close your MonoLife account, okay? You don't want to show me the proof, then—"

"It's not that I don't. It's that I—"

"You think that you *can't*. Fine. Then, don't we need to tell the police?"

Kylie allows the passive-aggressiveness of the word *think* to slip past her. Can't pick a fight in the middle of an apology, especially where Erin has the moral high ground. "Tell them what?" Kylie asks. "They'll want to see the app."

"So?"

Kylie laughs. For a moment, all the way back in September, this had been about figuring out who murdered Annabeth Wilson. "I'm going to try to make contact with her."

"With a murderer? Oh, this just gets better and better."

"There's way more to the story. I'm going to find out."

"I . . . I don't recognize you anymore, Ky."

Kylie wonders if this isn't because Erin actually recognizes some significant part of herself inside this new and improved Kylie Bennington. A mirror that suddenly reflects her own cutthroat determination. "So . . ." Kylie says. "You deleted your account?"

Headlights from a passing car fall on Erin at precisely the wrong moment, casting the guilt on her face in spotlight.

"Ohhh. You haven't," Kylie says. "You're using."

The car passes and a frustrated sigh escapes the Erin-shaped shadow. "I don't like it when I'm not the best at something, okay?"

"Wowww."

"Can you just . . ." Erin takes Kylie by her hips. "Come back to Insta? Or, hey, what about TikTok? We'll build your following together."

Sure, Kylie thinks. *Those apps don't wreck your car in a tantrum when you leave them.* But she's invisible there, and while the day at the lake has provoked in her a near-constant anxiety, there are those complimentary clothes back home. That upcoming influencers' summit. She doesn't have all the answers, maybe doesn't even *want* to know, but MonoLife has helped her discover things about herself she'd otherwise never realize. Living with who you are doesn't have to be a horror story. She at least has the app to thank for that peace of mind. And pills to make the rest of life more palatable.

It's why MonoLife works so hard to preserve its secrets. It has the trust of its user base, and the moment any of its users suffer real-world consequence for their content, the app is over. Rennie and Tommy had threatened that. And got what they deserved.

Fuckers feed on us one way or another.

Erin folds her arms as she waits for Kylie's answer. What in her head must've sounded like a generous offer: take Kylie under her wing, become her own personal social media guru.

Simply thinking about it makes Kylie's heart pound with anxiety. "It's okay," she says. "I'm too good at MonoLife. My natural talent deserves a place to shine."

"Natural talent?" Erin sounds incredulous now.

"Yeah," Kylie replies, her tone not so friendly. Their truce on the verge of exploding.

Erin senses this rising anger. "Well . . . it was just a thought, Ky."

And that's how they leave it, starting back to the house, where the music sounds like it's about to blow the front doors off. Rather than go inside, they sit on the steps. And talk. For once, Erin doesn't do all of it. Or hardly any. She wants to know what Kylie's been up to with masculine Red Riding Hood in there.

"Simon from *Glostah*," Kylie says, and gives Erin the CliffsNotes version. Her phone, on the steps against the outer part of her thigh where Erin can't see it. She glances at MonoLife as they talk, looking at the selfie she posted earlier, she and Simon in their costumes. It's netting the kind of engagement usually reserved for her best videos.

› **Hot ass couple.**
› **Very cute!**
› **Would love to see the two of you fuck**

"*Sooooo*, how are you gaining traction there?" Erin asks.

Kylie shrugs. "A lot of trial and error. I mean, a lot . . ."

"Got any tips for me? Is there a *Kylie Bennington Method . . .* ?"

A stitch of panic ripples through her stomach. She has to deflect, and fast. "You know who's really got it down? Like, all the way down? Duc."

"Well, sure, he lives for that weird shit. Remember our Slack? *Ugh!*"

"He collaborated with Missy. They're still in contact."

Erin's eyes predictably bug. "How many users were there at Summerfield High?"

"Dunno, guess we're late to the party."

Erin's face is so animated it's obvious she isn't listening. "How many losers out there have bigger followings?" She looks at Kylie with panic blazing. "Wait. What's Missy's following like?"

"Well . . . you said it yourself . . . I mean, she's got that swimmer's physique and—"

Erin gasps, then sits silently for a moment, genuinely tormented by the revelation that somewhere, somebody might have a leg up on her. She stands, staggers back inside like this news has wounded her.

Simon and Cameron are still in the kitchen talking sports. Cameron is going on yet again about how much he misses football now that he's out of high school, how he took up intramural cross-country to test his torn ACL, and how, surprise, it seems to have somehow repaired itself without surgery.

Brandi's resting on Cameron's shoulder, rubbing his chest in slow, familiar circles while eyeing Asher, who's across the room, pouring a draft and talking loudly about how he'd rather die than have to transfer to a DIII school.

"Hey, he's not a petting zoo animal," Erin snaps, yanking Cameron's hand and dragging him toward her, then in the direction of the stairs.

This action sparks something competitive in Kylie. She fills a cup with spiked punch, careful not to scoop the floating press-on nail, then knocks it back and has to lean on the counter to stop from tipping because she's always been a lightweight. The booze, working in conjunction with the lorazepam, immediately slows the world down, drapes a layer of gauze over reality. The more she thinks about it, the more she loves the idea of doing something to Simon on camera. A special gift for her fans. A way to get even more content posted. She needs those fist bumps. The comments. Wants to spend her Saturday reading every last one.

And it'll be even better, naughtier, doing it in the home of some guy she barely knows. One of Erin's classmates, Jacob *Something*, whom she might've met once or twice at SCC but really, who cares?

She rises onto the tips of her shoes, lips scraping against Simon's ear. "Let's go upstairs."

Simon pulls his hand out of Kylie's. "Naw. You look drunk."

"I am in complete control."

"But you're still drunk. Or stoned."

She reaches through one of the shreds in his shirt and drags a nail across his skin. "Just a tease. I'll behave."

Then before she knows it, they're upstairs, Simon dropping any semblance of protest as Kylie locks the master bedroom door to prevent any pervs from perving. Lessons learned and all that.

Simon slides his shoes off and leaves them right beside the door. "You should take your shoes off too. Don't want to track anything in here."

Such a dad thing to say. Total mood killer. "Seriously?"

"Hey, just 'cause their kid's a shit doesn't mean his parents deserve to have their house trashed. People work hard for the things they have. One day, you'll understand."

Really. Look at my follower count, bitch, Kylie thinks.

She strips out of her costume, showing off this week's mail call: a soft-cup yellow bra with embroidered satin appliqué and sheer tulle fabric, along with a matching thong, its 24-karat gold crescent moon component and harness detailing forges a uniquely comfortable fit—to be expected at six hundred dollars for both articles. A luxurious twist on everyday necessity. It also hides the sore on Kylie's back, which is covered with more concealer than Erin's popped pimple. "I'm taking a quick shower."

"Hey," he says, looking anywhere but at her body, a gesture that's honestly a bit insulting. "I was serious about what I said."

"I know you were," she groans. "You can still help me take a picture, can't you?"

He plops down on the edge of the bed, checking his phone. "Sure. I mean, you *are* giving me a nice follower bump tonight."

"And yet you ignore me . . ."

"Weird way to spell *respect*."

Another groan from Kylie as she slams the bathroom door, catching a whiff of bitter odor beneath her arm.

How do people have sex after spending a whole day in their clothes? This house is like ninety degrees, everyone wearing perspiration on their foreheads. If she's getting naked with Simon, she doesn't want to have to treat his body like an odorous minefield.

She takes a super-quick shower, enough to cleanse the sweat, then steps shivering onto the heated tile floor, toweling off, heart hammering.

"Am I really doing this?" she asks her reflection, wondering how to convince Simon he has to take a shower too.

You make him, her reflection says, flashing a wicked grin as Kylie drops the towel. @CrystalShips staring out from inside the glass, lacking even the slightest trace of Kylie's insecurity. The reflected body is Kylie's, but . . . different. Her breasts are perfectly symmetrical there. Interesting. Kylie shifts her weight around, looking for a bad angle. It shouldn't be this difficult to find one, but she can't.

She searches out those glowing white stretch marks on her thighs. In the glass, Crystal's legs are smooth and shapely, perfectly colored.

Kylie lifts her foot onto the sink, edging her royal toe against the glass. But @CrystalShips's digits are in perfect descending order.

Her reflection flashes an eyebrow. *Happy now?*

No. She isn't. Absolutely not. She's still out here, fighting for a place in the world. Desperate for more than cold, empty houses made of Sheetrock that are haunted by the memories of warm Christmas mornings and promises of wide-open futures. She craves the adoration of a half-million strangers and wants millions more because to them she's a goddess. Walking that bridge from Katheryn to Katy, eager to leave Hudson behind and become a Perry once and for all. To know, above all else, that she *matters*.

She'll swallow all the fucking lorazepam on earth if that's what it takes.

Kylie is still staring at herself, not fully comprehending. @CrystalShips gazes back, her steady and supportive face roiling something inside Kylie.

"*Get out there,*" @CrystalShips says. "*Take what you want.*"

Kylie opens the door and leans against the jamb. Simon barely notices, nose buried in his phone. She clears her throat. He doesn't budge.

"Hello? There're a dozen boys down there who'd kill to be you right now." It's a pretty entitled thing to say, but modesty's a big dumb lie.

"And you're up here with a man."

"Ugh." She turns back into the bathroom as the box spring heaves. Footsteps at her back. Simon takes her by the arm, whirls her around. She tears herself out of his grip.

"Hey!" he says, just enough humility to make her stop, hands sliding around her hips. "You want to post something for your followers then—"

"I never said that," Kylie says, but feels seen.

"I know the game, remember?"

She goes to the bed and sits, crossing her legs and letting him drink in the sight. What he's choosing to skip out on.

He barely looks at her. "All I'm saying is I still need that X."

"You can't think of a way we might get you verified *right here?*"

"I like you, Kylie."

"And I hate you, Simon. That's why I'm sitting here naked."

"I don't mean it like that. I mean . . . look, we'll get there. But for now . . ."

"For now you're wondering how I can help you?"

"I feel like I'm not pulling my weight. We're partners, equals, and you've already leveled up."

She bites the inside of her cheek. What he's really saying, even if he doesn't realize it, is that he doesn't like some girl being ahead of him. Yeah, what a Man.

For a second, Simon looks as if he's going to say something else. But he locks that thought up tight behind his eyes while unlocking the bedroom door. "Come downstairs. Brainstorm with me. I need you."

Oh. Those last three words are nice to hear. No one's ever said that to her before. She wonders if she's big enough on MonoLife now to be needed. If she quit tomorrow, would she be missed? At least Simon's straightforward, unlike Erin, who, let's be honest, needs her just as much and would rather dance around any such admission. Okay then. Kylie goes into the bathroom, closes the door behind her in order to dress.

The expected doorknob click never comes.

Kylie turns and watches gnarled fingers curl around the door, holding it in place, then pushes it all the way open to show the master bedroom is pitch-black.

A head ducks beneath the doorjamb, leaning into the bathroom light. Somehow the yellow glow dims in the presence of the familiar swimmer's mask. Latex, or something like it, stretched over a full face, tiny eye slits, a grotesque and painted smile.

On the sink, Kylie's phone is vibrating.

She can't look away from this figure, his gangly, lopsided body standing there, hunched.

Kylie's phone vibrates again—but it's a deep and disruptive sound, one unlike any her device has ever made. She glances over at it and the words on the lock screen read: **Mister Strangles sent you a message.**

The figure in the doorway doesn't move, its outstretched arms more like tree branches than appendages.

She feels her phone's unearthly grumble in her fillings. Her trembling hand reaches out, retrieves it, opening the message.

@MisterStrangles: It has happened before and will happen again

The figure—seemingly male, is this Mister Strangles? has to be—stands motionless against the dark space. The bathroom glow somehow retreating away from him.

Kylie waves an arm through the air, but the figure's eyes refuse to clock it. He just stares through her, fixated on whatever exists at her core, beyond her flesh and bones, a sound in his throat like a cat's purr, approval of whatever it sees there.

@MisterStrangles: it cannot be stopped now

Kylie takes a reluctant step forward, close enough to be in his wing-span. He remains motionless, and she stares defensively, muted terror thumping through her guts, the lorazepam keeping it from climbing any higher as she somehow intuits that the only thing this stranger wants from her is a reply. She swipes out a message:

@CrystalShips: I don't want to stop anything

The response comes back so fast it must be automated:

@MisterStrangles: then live

"I want to," she intones, her own voice now surprisingly deep. "I want everything that was promised to me growing up."

@MisterStrangles: tell me

"I want to be somebody."

A *ding* as a video loads into her DM conversation. Kylie clicks the grainy thumbnail and suddenly she's watching Erin and Cameron in bed, cuddling beneath a sheet, afterglow on their faces.

"*Just think you're too nice,*" Cameron says.

"*I am,*" Erin agrees.

"*You can't trust her—she's genuinely demented.*"

"*She made a mistake.*"

"*She was trying to record us in bed.*"

"*She's sorry.*"

"Is she? Or is that what you needed to hear to take her back?"

"People make mistakes, realize they miss someone."

"You trust her now?"

"I do. We've been friends forever. A lot longer than I've known you, that's for sure."

"If that's your only reason—"

"Enough. Cameron—look at her. She's got nobody else. Her parents aren't even around. If I cut ties with her, I don't even know what she'll do. Probably kill herself."

"Not your responsibility. All I'm saying."

"Okay. You've said it."

"Fine."

Kylie looks up, her mouth agape at this awful exchange, wiping her face with the back of her hand. Alone in the bathroom.

The doorway's clear. The bedroom beyond once again full of soft light.

Mister Strangles, long gone. If he was ever here.

Kylie dresses fast and rushes out. Her lungs sting. It's painful to breathe as she stares at the end of the hall—where Erin and Cameron are apparently debating Kylie's merits, or lack thereof.

She opens Erin's text thread, typing:

Kylie:

I am not your charity. Go fuck yourself.

Simon's by the front door talking to some bitch dressed as Cat-woman, only the costume is droopy pleather and it looks like her curves are melting in real time.

Kylie grabs him by the hand and yanks him toward the door as her phone dings.

Erin:

huh???

Then they're hurrying for Simon's Mustang, Kylie desperate to get the hell out of here.

The unexpected sound of shattering glass from somewhere up ahead makes them freeze in place, realization slow to dawn. Then Simon rushes off.

Kylie races to catch up, hearing, "You little fucking geek!" and then the sound of flesh pummeling flesh, a struggle, boots grinding pavement, punctuated by painful grunts.

She rounds an oak tree and finds two men rolling across the street. She clicks on her phone light. The beam lands on the bloody, bashed face of Ben Austin, staring up like a deer in the headlights.

Simon's hunched over him, balled fist ready to lash out once more, only now he's looking at her too. "My fucking car! Look what this little asshole did to my car!"

Kylie glides the beam across the way. The Mustang's windshield is busted out. Two oversized rocks rest on the front seat. A couple of deep scratches across the driver's side from the hammer lying at Ben's feet.

Ben's got that hopelessness in his eyes, some dumb animal that can never be trained. She's so sour about the way tonight has gone already that it makes her realize just how much contempt she holds for him. On some level Kylie understands, but would never admit, that it's because she sees herself in him, though he's a lot worse at hiding his desperation. If there was ever any pity for Ben, after this it's long gone.

There's a real temptation to pick that hammer up, since she doesn't have a gun, and crack his knee into pieces in the hope that maybe then he'll leave her alone. But now Ben is looking to Kylie like *she's* the answer to his problems.

Not tonight, she thinks. *Tonight, you're the answer to mine.*

She turns her phone horizontally.

"You want your red X, baby?" She smirks at Simon, who's got blood rage in his eyes. "Then you'd better hurt him a lot worse than that."

Kylie presses the blood-red record button. Showtime.

Stupid Prizes

Kylie's at the doctor. Her primary care physician offers to lance the infection on her back. She accepts, so he's in the process of swabbing her skin with a numbing agent while asking, "How's college?"

From the stainless tray beside the examination table, Erin is sending a stream of nervous texts to Kylie's phone. Each message becoming a more frantic variation of *What did you mean last night? What did I do?*

"College is fine."

"You don't sound that excited."

"I mean, it's not all there is to life."

There's a cold press to her back and then the sensation of deflating pressure, the flurry of soft tickles. "Ohhhh, that was angry," the doctor says and presses a gauze square against the wound.

Beside her, Kylie's phone continues to rattle around while on vibrate. She resists the urge to reply to Erin with *Whatever you say, Mister Strangles.* Because that is not what this is. Can't be. No matter how bad she wishes it were so. Gaslighting doesn't cover the things she's seen up to this point.

And just how would Erin be behind the Mister Strangles account? One of those "special" ones you can't follow or view its content, and it can slide into your DMs whenever it wants. Erin wouldn't have that kind of pull, not with her MonoLife struggles, and the creepy-ass avatar of some old swimming mask is nowhere near her style.

And that was *not* Erin standing in the bathroom doorway. If that thing was really there to begin with. It's a problem Kylie doesn't want to face. The idea that the app is doing something to her brain. Her body. For as much as she loves it, there's no point in lying about how much she fears it.

That's before the afternoon at Lake Salvi. A day she's still struggling to comprehend. As sus as Duc might be, even with his history of practical joking, *something* had punched down from the roof of his car, bending it like taffy. Whatever that was, however it happened, it was more than a prank.

You sure about that?

Yes.

The doctor sends Kylie packing with a roll of bandages in her hand, a prescription for an oral antibiotic. An assurance that the infection has been drained and should start to feel better right away.

She calls Dad while waiting at the pharmacy for her medication. The phone rings a bunch and she's gearing up to leave a voicemail, when—

"Hey, sweetie."

"Hey. Dad."

"Everything okay?"

"Yeah . . . it's nothing, I just wanted to . . . see how you're doing, I guess."

"Oh, I'm good. Can't talk, though."

"Why not?"

"I'm in Boston with Triss. You know Triss."

"Sure." Triss is twenty-nine and works for a literary firm there. Kylie's seen her Instagram and all she can think is, *Go, Dad!*

"I'm going to lose you any second because we're heading down into the subway to catch the T line to Lansdowne Street. I'll call you soon."

"Can I come over tomorrow?" Kylie asks. "I just need someone to—" The signal cuts out before she's finished asking.

It's a Lyft home and there's mail on Kylie's doorstep, all of it helping purge her discomfort and phone call depression. Six boxes of swag, including a jar of Future Solution LX Total Regenerating Cream from Shiseido, which retails for $285 and is supposed to help enhance the skin's vitality during critical evening hours.

At least twenty percent of her life is breaking down cardboard now.

She's filling the recycling bin when Simon sends a series of texts like a monologue.

Simon:

> Maybe they haven't seen it yet?

> You think?

> It's Saturday. Could be a slow day. Day off for corporate? Does this company even have corporate?

> Yeah. 70K views in a few hours? I'm as good as stamped. It'll happen. My clout is about to go up.

Ben Austin got his face pummeled into putty last night and Kylie hadn't only recorded it, she cheered it on. Simon's fist winding back, smashing down. Ben's front teeth skipping across the pavement. One of those dumb eyes welding shut in real time.

The video's called "Face Smasher: A Love Story." It's at eighty thousand views and climbing.

Kylie can't watch it. Scratch that—can't listen to it. It's not the violence that gets her, but the bloodlust in her own voice. Cheering Simon on like some barbarian.

"Kill him, fucking kill him!"

In that moment, that's exactly what she'd wanted. A way to make Loser Ben go away forever.

Simon:

> Now I'm paranoid. Do you think it's going to happen?

Kylie's ticked up another thousand followers over the last nine hours. Simon's managed a few hundred. Guy might as well be a ghost. Part of her hopes that Ben will call the police, but given the amount of damage he doled out to Simon's car, given how badly he wants Kylie in his life, nah, that's never going to happen.

Kylie:

prob not 😕

Simon:

Shit. Yeah. What now?

idk, we'll think of something

Today? 😩

She drops the phone on the counter like it's radioactive. *Ugh!* Nothing dries her out like desperation. The device continues buzzing as she completes the great cardboard purge, slicing every last bit into thin strips until the blue bin outside is topped off.

Marie Kondo mode, unlocked. Nothing like a healthy declutter to make you feel accomplished.

She's going upstairs to relax when the familiar squeak of the UPS truck stops her cold.

God, no more.

Packages keep coming. More MonoLife gifts than she can reasonably showcase. If there's one thing the internet hates more than e-celebs, it's bought-and-paid-for shills.

She can't keep up with the cardboard. Another hour of cutting boxes down. In an ideal world, she'd load most of this stuff into garbage bags, then stuff them inside one of those Salvation Army dumpsters.

But she needs a ride to do that, and with Mom at work, that means tipping Erin off that she's suddenly entered the swag game. Which would drive Erin even further out of her mind.

Maybe Simon can help once he's finished feeling sorry for himself.

Kylie checks her phone. Christ Almighty, he's sent sixty more texts. A bunch of awful brainstorms. He's convinced himself that at least four are "surefire" tickets to success and is already imagining life with the red X, talking about which endorsement deals he'll be declining.

Simon:

> Only going to be taking the best ones, you know?
> Really make them work to get me on board.:

> Also, I know I put that geek in the hospital, but is there any
> world where I can send him a bill for car repairs? lol

What did she ever see in this guy anyway?

"Pride goeth before a fall, Simon," Kylie whispers and decides she doesn't want to see him today at all.

The family dining table is once again unset, so it's a DoorDash kind of night, a plate of Thai chicken and a side of steamed vegetables. Kylie eats it from atop her bed wearing gym shorts and watching *Katy Perry: Part of Me.*

She remembers seeing this concert movie in theaters, a little girl wearing oversized 3D glasses that were always in danger of sliding off her nose, Katy stepping off-screen, into the auditorium like some giant goddess, their eyes locking, Kylie's soul igniting as candy-colored confetti fell like snow.

The most religious moment of her life and the only time she's ever been in love. She likes to watch the movie now to remember what that felt like. Wonders why this movie's the only place she can get it.

She enjoys escaping with Katy so much that it's another hour before she's back to looking at MonoLife, where even @BlueFerox is on some needy bullshit. Kylie sorta figured she wouldn't mind the burdens her fellow "Lifers" imposed, but there is a difference between being used and being needed.

@BlueFerox: how you doing

@CrystalShips: tired

@BlueFerox: about to post a new video

@CrystalShips: yay

@BlueFerox: will you watch?

@CrystalShips: always do

@BlueFerox: could u comment too? Show the algorithm
    I'm worthwhile? ⚓

Everything's a commitment. On the Living Now page, "Check Your Neighbors" has fallen a couple of notches, but still clinging to the top five.

For as long as she's had access to this section, no other video has remained there as long.

"Because you're a fucking star."

And that's why Simon hasn't gotten a red X. He's a boring-ass piece of ass, addled by a boomer brain. MonoLife invests in stars. In Kylie's future. Simon's deadweight.

Expendable. Replaceable.

She clicks @BlueFerox's video. The production value has improved. Someone else is working the camera now, and there might even be a third person involved, a lighting rig that provides real ambience.

"*At this point,*" Blue narrates, "*the world has seen what can happen when nothing works and anything goes. Everything feeling like it's about to break apart.*"

The ominous tone lifts as Blue spreads her arms out over the table, smiling, drawing attention to the foil trays steaming beneath her.

"*I offer this,*" she says. "*A skill set you may eventually need. When the next calamity hits, and it* will, *the grocery stores will be sacked and there's only one thing you'll find with ease.*"

Blue's smile is so wide it swallows her face. Kylie feels a twinge of jealousy looking at her lovely dark skin with natural shine. No unseemly blemishes or the obvious concealer to cover them.

"*People*," Blue says, matter-of-factly. "*Panicked and stupid people. Now, human beings are not exactly nutritional. But the* taste . . .*when you've got more people than pigs . . .*" She pulls some of the foil away, showing golden strips of bacon. "*I promise you, you're not going to miss the pork.*"

The camera does a fetishistic glide over the strips. Glossy with a slick candy sheen.

Kylie's salivating like a desperate dog.

"*Long Pig Bacon*," Blue says. "*Extra crispy. Courtesy of the National Bolivian Armed Forces. A soldier who thought he could get away with selling protection to single mothers in exchange for sex.*"

Blue steps away from the table and the camera dips as she walks. Her toenails are painted galaxy purple—a lovely touch—and she hot-steps over a naked corpse lying on its side, head twisted from a broken neck, staring wide-eyed.

The camera roves over his back, lingering where his skin has been shaved bare. Disgusting, fleshy recessions where large hunks of meat have been carved out.

"*You can make Long Pig Bacon rather easily once you have your meat. All you need is brown sugar, rice vinegar, maple syrup, and black pepper.*"

"Cannibal bacon," Kylie murmurs. "Why not?" She goes into the comments, types:

@CrystalShips: mmmmm . . . would eat 😊

Now, with that commitment satisfied, she leaves MonoLife feeling good about herself. Until she finds more texts from Simon. He's sent two hundred today. She wants to ignore this latest set, but curiosity wins out.

Simon:

Might have to find another partner

Kylie scrolls back up to see what prompted this galaxy-brained conclusion. More brainstorms. A couple of requests to meet up.

Kylie:

wow, ok

Simon:

Just testing you to see if you were still there.

don't like being tested

I know, sorry. Where have you been?

audience with the queen

Very funny. Let's take a ride?

make something on your own tonight

working on that, but time is a factor here

gotta make it happen

now

Okay. That's more than enough Simon for today. Kylie's jittery now. Worked up. The spot on her back throbs for the first time since this morning. She reaches around to it and the bandage is moist. More than moist. Soaked through. Oh man. The thought of having to look beneath it, wipe it down, sickens her so much that she jumps back into MonoLife because the pain seems to stop when she's scrolling, and at least Simon's shitty, needy texts can't find her here.

A surprising notification waits for her.

@MissyMiss tagged you in a post.

It's an image of Ben Austin in bed, face half-bandaged up in gauze. Even though he's got a good excuse, his general patheticness is incredibly triggering.

The photo's captioned: Should I put this little lamb out of his misery? Let's ask @CrystalShips . . .

Kylie isn't going to play along on the public stage. She goes right for the DMs.

> **@CrystalShips:** you there now?
> **@MissyMiss:** you won't find me
> **@CrystalShips:** can we meet??
> **@MissyMiss:** soon
> **@CrystalShips:** why not now?
> **@MissyMiss:** you don't trust me yet
> **@CrystalShips:** I do.
> **@MissyMiss:** you do not . . .
> **@MissyMiss:** and i really need you to
> **@CrystalShips:** Ben means nothing to me

Last night, killing Ben had seemed like the only way to get rid of him. Today, having slept on it, Kylie wants to believe he's learned his lesson, though she supposes she really doesn't care one way or the other. Missy can do it or not. Ben's insignificance has nothing to do with Kylie's trust.

> **@MissyMiss:** so . . . leave him be?
> **@CrystalShips:** sure
> **@MissyMiss:** I will find another way then
> **@CrystalShips:** don't worry about me . . . talking to you will bring trust, so maybe we should do some more of that?

The question hangs there unanswered.

For now, Melissa's got nothing more to say.

Teacher's Pet

Kylie's back on ErinTime come Monday when she apologizes for Friday's ominous text, chalking it up to too much spiked punch.

"*I am not your charity*," Erin says, still haunted by this code she hasn't yet deciphered. "Go fuck myself?"

"Forget it," Kylie says. "I was having a moment. Just reiterating that my success or failure isn't your responsibility."

"Is it so wrong for me to be worried about you?"

Kylie apologizes again and even manages to get a couple more in on the drive to school so that Erin's sufficiently defused by the time they park.

For the first half of the week, it's life as usual.

Until Veronica Gomez washes up on the shore of Lake Salvi early Thursday morning, her lungs full of water and, according to Cameron, by way of his cop dad, hallucinogens in her bloodstream.

Kylie is surprised to find she's unsettled by this development, is unable to stop thinking about the loss of such a generous spirit. Some part of her recognizing the world is worse off without Veronica in it—a good and selfless soul. But nothing in life is guaranteed, not even your own future. That really should stress people out more than it does. The ticking clocks over our heads.

That afternoon, Mr. Davies asks Kylie to hold up a second, and the guy walking behind her thinks this is so funny he makes an "oooooohhhhh" noise and everyone else laughs while shuffling out of the lecture hall.

"You've been distracted lately," Mr. Davies says once it's just the two of them.

"Gee, I wonder why?"

"Even before today."

"You teach Statistics. Am I supposed to be excited?"

"*Excited* isn't the right word. How about interested? As in, you might need this stuff in the real world."

"I'll marry rich."

"You're too young to be so cynical."

"Getting a head start."

"Seems sus," Davies says, sounding like one of those guys who live in fear of growing old and lame. "Anyway, just making sure you're doing okay. Especially now. After Veronica—"

"I barely knew her."

"We've lost five students within the span of a year. I'm trying to be more vigilant. I see my kids struggling, I help."

"I'm not struggling."

"Struggling to stay awake. It counts."

"I don't know how many days you're going to spend on hypothesis testing, Mr. Davies, but I can assure you, I've got it."

"I'll just say it, then. You ever need a friendly ear, I'm here." He lifts his hands. "No judgment."

Kylie reaches around him while maintaining eye contact, fingers falling into the bowl of Dum Dums on his desk. She doesn't want the sugar, only wants to watch him squirm. "Thank you, Mr. Davies."

He holds his breath as she pops the molded sugar, pushing the bulb against her cheek, smirking. Then struts from the classroom feeling his hypocritical eyes on her ass, disappointed but also relieved to learn he's as predictable as every other man. Still teaching her after class.

Erin's waiting outside the classroom. "You looking for a little . . . extra credit?"

"Creepy perv."

"Wait, really?"

"He thinks I look distracted."

"You kind of do."

"Gee, thanks."

Erin nudges Kylie with her hip, then lowers her voice. "I heard his wife left him. Could be looking for a rebound."

"His hair's thinning. Is he even thirty yet?"

Cameron's waiting for them in the parking lot, leaning against the BMW. Asher's there too, ducked down between two cars, scrolling his phone. Dodging Brandi.

"Subtle, aren't they?" Erin says out the side of her mouth. "Asher just got early-transfer acceptance to Ohio State for next year. We're going to celebrate."

"Celebrate? Veronica just died."

Erin stops walking. Annoyed that she has to consider something so unpleasant. But the weight on her face vanishes in a flash, replaced by the same bubbly enthusiasm as before. "I mean, what can I say? That's life, Ky."

Kylie's wondering why she's supposed to want to celebrate anything, least of all Asher's looming departure. Who cares who's going where? People are morons for going into debt for school of all things, then chasing jobs they don't really want, especially when there's no hope of a happy ending. Home-ownership? An illusory concept for all future generations. And meeting the right person? Look what happened to her parents: Dad now with someone closer in age to his own daughter, and Mom being punished for it, barely holding on financially or sanely as a result.

Asher rises to greet them and his confident smile makes Kylie weak-kneed for a second. He's good-looking, square shoulders, big arms, powerful hands. They were in the same gym class last year, so she can picture his sculpted thighs whenever she wants.

But he'll be treated as a god at Ohio State, which makes him really just another Brady. She pictures next fall's Insta feed, all the ways he'll be acclimating to campus, and her soul feels sick and sour.

It's November. Six months left in their first year of college. An academic layover for some, raise those grades, then get on with your life. For others, Kylie and Erin, it's biding your time until the world takes notice. Until you can't be ignored. Their futures won't be made in classrooms, but on their phones. Everything else is just whatever. Including Asher. Here he is, fresh on the market, wanting . . . what, exactly?

A distraction.

The four of them grab bubble tea on the way back to Erin's place. Kylie dreads an afternoon of brainstorming Insta content, but the I-word never even comes up.

Cameron gets the fireplace going and Kylie drops into the recliner, relieved to be back here, certain she'd never see the inside of this house again.

Erin and Asher sit on opposite sides of the couch and once the fire's crackling, Cameron drops onto the middle cushion and the three of them turn toward Kylie in one oddly choreographed motion.

"Okay," Kylie says. "What do you want?"

"Can I just . . . grab a quick photo?" Erin's voice has all the pain of swallowed pride. "Nothing crazy, okay? Two old friends. And maybe you post it?"

"You mean . . . on . . . ?" Kylie won't even say its name with Asher here, lest she end up as roadkill.

"I lost mine," Cameron says. "Forgot to check it for a few days and . . . poof. Whatever. No big loss."

"See?" Erin says. "Just me."

"You don't want this." Kylie thinks about the way she used to feel toward Erin, before MonoLife. Singularly envious. She should be more sympathetic now that the roles are reversed.

Should. But won't.

"Maybe you and I can talk privately?" Erin says.

Kylie considers her placement in the room. The chair overlooking the recessed fireplace is an inadvertent throne, the rest of them literally looking up to her.

She has no intention of relinquishing this power. No way.

Erin moves to the edge of the couch, hands curled around the cushion arm. "Kylie . . . please."

Kylie wiggles her toe, thinks about asking Erin to suck it. See just how desperate she is. How far she's willing to go.

"Please?"

"Fine," Kylie says. It'll be a lesser post, but so long as there's sex appeal, her followers will be on board. She points to the boys. "You both. Shirts off. Now."

They do as they're told and Kylie finds great satisfaction in objectifying them. Retrieving Crisco from the pantry and swabbing it across Asher's pecs so his muscles glisten beneath the lights.

Once the mess is cleaned up, they take a few pictures, group shots where they're the best of friends. Four beautiful people. Perfect couples. From an aesthetic point of view, it's pretty hot.

With the photo settled, Kylie flicks her wrist and AirDrops it to Erin's phone. "There you go."

Erin clucks her tongue. "No, wait . . ." She looks up from her screen, exasperated. It wasn't supposed to go this way.

"Lurkers are like ghosts," Kylie says. "So I'm thinking, if *you* post that, people will know who you're with. Boosts your cred."

"You're . . ."

"Yeah. A higher level."

"What the hell are you all taking about?" Asher's wondering.

"You never told me there were *levels*," Erin says.

Kylie shrugs.

Erin's squinting hard. The sound of snapping and hissing logs in the fireplace accenting her quiet rage. "All the things you did on there . . . *that's* how you got promoted?"

Asher and Cameron decide to make a run for the kitchen and raid the fridge, eager to escape this escalating tension.

"You know, I should go," Kylie says, ordering a rideshare because she sure as hell hasn't walked anywhere by herself since that day at Lake Salvi.

Erin stares into her phone with disbelief. Her plan falling apart because she hadn't known all the rules. "Why are you leaving?"

"I have to break down cardboard," Kylie says and ambles toward the door so as not to appear like she's fleeing.

Asher springs from the kitchen. "Let me wait with you," he says, and then they're walking to the edge of the driveway. "I know I'm outta here next year but you think there's any chance of . . . hanging out?"

"Why, Asher?"

This bluntness surprises him.

"Sorry," she says. "I don't mean it like that. What I mean is . . . you're a future Buckeye."

"Not yet."

"What?"

"My math scores ain't all that. Got a preliminary acceptance, contingent on how this year ends. So I don't get to relax for a minute. Gotta stress about fuckin' calculus till May."

"That's shitty."

"Sorta jealous of Cameron, man. For real. He gets injured and it's like being liberated. Now he's free to plan his life without any illusions. He and Erin talking about serious future stuff. Me . . . I gotta keep the charade going."

"What serious future stuff? Erin hasn't mentioned anything."

"Yeah, well, seems like you all made up but forgot to become friends again."

Kylie laughs, can't help herself, because that's the hardest dose of truth she's had lately. "You're going to be just fine, Asher. You're a great athlete. Football is your path forward."

"That's the problem. I don't know if I want that path anymore."

"You're only trapped if you allow yourself to be."

"Well, listen to this . . . Kylie's got wisdom."

"Think of it as an opportunity to make a name for yourself, then use that name to get what you really want out of life."

Asher nods. Kylie's reframe working wonders.

"Sometimes, life is about doing what you have to."

"Right? Brandi didn't get that. At all. So she left. My nose is in those books every night . . . and sometimes I want to say *forget it*. Let that admission letter lapse and go someplace else. But then my dad gives me that look like he's the proudest man who's ever been and it's just like . . . How am I supposed to disappoint him? Dude worked hard to give me a good life and . . ."

Kylie's checking her phone because the rideshare is late, though Asher's honesty is refreshing and easy enough to listen to for a few extra minutes even if it makes Kylie bristle because he doesn't know how good he's got it. It's been two months since she's last seen her dad.

"So here's where I'm at," Asher says. "I like you, Kylie. Ain't gotta be like that. I just mean . . . you're fun, y'know? And every so often when I need to put the books down, I'd like to know if it's cool to call you."

She's trying not to smile. "Yeah. Yeah, it's totally cool."

Asher hands his phone over. Doesn't have to say anything.

She adds her number to his contacts and gives it back, her finger dragging along his during the exchange as the rideshare's headlights slice through the night, and then there's a hatchback idling beside them.

"Maybe I should walk you home?"

"Oh, Asher—you were doing so well until now."

He backs off, hands up, the second man to do this to her today. "Yup—got it. You do you, Kylie Bennington." He wiggles his phone in the palm of his hand. "But text me when you get home?" He smiles. Colgate Confidence that's hard to resist.

"Don't have your number," she says, grinning.

Her phone dings.

Asher:

No excuses

"Very sly." And then she's getting into the car and Asher's reverse-walking up the driveway, fading into the night the farther away he gets from the sodium streetlight glow.

The last thing Kylie sees is him gesturing to his phone. "When you get home!" he shouts.

"You're annoying," she says, giggling.

And then comes the sound of him jogging all the way back to Erin's house as Kylie slams the door closed and the car zips off into the night.

Chained to the Rhythm

The rideshare turns onto Kylie's street and the driver accidentally pulls in front of Mrs. Elrond's place. *Close enough*, Kylie thinks, hopping out while catching up on a few texts that are mostly from Mom, her tone increasingly agitated and leading to—

Mom:

Kylie, we've got to discuss these boxes.
WHERE are they all coming from?

The driver pulls away from the curb, leaving her in the dark as she begins swiping out a response.

Kylie's thoughts are a mess even outside Mom's continued harassment. The spot on her back beginning to throb as she sorts through Erin's failed shakedown, unexpected Asher complications, and Melissa's MonoLife proposition.

You don't trust me yet. The implication behind that being Melissa feels the need to earn Kylie's trust. But for what? To kill Duc?

That's the only thing that fits.

Two people looking to Kylie for the same kind of help.

Kylie's shadow on the sidewalk grows exponentially as light behind her suddenly intensifies. She turns, squinting into cones of halogen, close and getting closer.

A car barreling toward her.

Kylie dives into bushes, hard branches raking her cheeks as front tires bounce up onto the sidewalk. She claws forward, spinning around once she's all the way through brush, crab-walking in retreat as blinding light bleeds through the shrubs.

A car door opens. Headlights blotted by a silhouette. "Get up, bitch!" a trembling voice barks. *"Right now!"*

Brandi pushes through the shrubs, tire iron in hand. Smudgy mascara resembling war paint.

"Oh no. Give me a break," Kylie groans. "Brandi—I'm not with Asher." She's slow to get up, feeling her face for cuts.

"You were practically fucking him back there!"

"On the sidewalk? Five feet apart? With our clothes on? There?"

Brandi trembles in the cold November air.

Kylie lifts her phone, finds MonoLife without having to look, and clicks record. "We're live, in case you do anything crazy, Brandi."

Brandi's frozen in place at the end of her plan, never believing she'd get this far. What now?

Kylie holds for a minute, and once there's no escalation, she starts pushing back through the shrubs.

Brandi follows her onto the sidewalk. "Don't walk away from me, bitch." The moonlight catches the tire iron as it rises toward the sky, Brandi charging with a roar that's strangely hollow, as if she doesn't buy her own anger.

A half-hearted attack that's more of an awkward lumber. Kylie sidesteps the motion, striking out in self-defense with a fist to Brandi's cheekbone.

The girl falls into the shrubs, tire iron skidding across the sidewalk. Kylie picks it up with her free hand, makes sure MonoLife sees it curled in her fingers.

She tilts the camera down, showing the pathetic wretch at her feet, Brandi fumbling to get back onto her knees.

Kylie should take some pity here. After all, Brandi is Kylie from just a couple of months ago, standing on the doorstep of some upper-classman, catching her boyfriend in the act.

Except this anger right now is misplaced. Brandi should be taking it out on Asher. Only that would be misplaced too, because Brandi's the crazy one here and not all points of view are equal.

"Move on, Brandi," she says. "There is no you and me."

"You ruined my life." Brandi probably believes that because introspection is hard.

"I barely know you. Or your ex."

"You're a whore."

Kylie feels all of MonoLife reacting in real time to that. A fleet of **I'd like to report a murder** comments flying fast and furious.

Kylie winds back and swings the tire iron, cracking Brandi's face, ripping her cheek wide open, blood glugging onto the sidewalk.

Brandi rolls onto her back, eyes wide shut. The amount of blood pouring from her wound is almost comical.

Kylie goes in to shoot a closer look, dropping a thumb down onto Brandi's eyelid, pulling it up to find an empty white orb.

"Leave me alone. Get me?"

Brandi's eye swivels back into position as she snaps to. A balled fist catches Kylie's ear and knocks her over, cell phone skittering.

Both women struggle to stand. Somehow, it's Brandi who gets there first, a Converse striking Kylie's lips, her mouth awash in bitterness.

Kylie throws her arms around Brandi's ankles and pulls her back to the sidewalk. Then she's searching out that tire iron, finding it, raising it, smashing Brandi's chest with it, a *crack* that brings broken bones.

The girl goes breathless, sucking for air she cannot seem to find.

Kylie picks her phone up, undamaged, how about that. MonoLife is still open and she lifts the viewfinder. Sees the girl's desperate and glazed eyes and is infuriated by this weakness. She kicks Brandi's face, sneaker to mouth.

The next stomp is even more gratifying. Hatred and frustration flowing through Kylie as she crushes fingers, breaks more ribs, and pummels Brandi into submission, her phone capturing all the damage dealt.

She brings the camera close, examining every wound in ghastly detail. "How's this," she says, breathless in her hatred. "If I see you again, *ever again*, I am going to kill you. Tell anyone who did this, and I am going to kill you. You can count on it."

She leaves Brandi a broken and bloody wreck, then speed-walks home, juiced off watching MonoLife react in real time.

› **You fucked her up!**
› **Holy fuck, marry me.**
› **Go back! Go back and kill her.**

"You fuckers better like this shit," Kylie tells them. Wants to see it trending before she's out of the shower. "Face Smasher: A Love Story" had only a brief stay on Living Now. It's difficult to say whether repeating herself so soon makes any sense, but it's so brutal she gets the feeling her followers won't mind.

Six more boxes are waiting on her doorstep. The ones Mom is so keen to discuss, and yet she never bothered to bring them into the house. Kylie kicks them into the hall and strips off her clothes, climbing toward her bedroom. Mom's light is off as she passes her doorway, more overtime, most likely, which is fine. The last thing she wants is to talk, or in this case, have to explain the packages.

She looks herself over in the vanity mirror, sweaty, tussled, bloody. @CrystalShips wears these marks like a champ. It gives her character. Distinction.

She's hotter than ever.

Kylie understands why. That face is free. Of consequence. Of responsibility. Of the world. Of everything.

While there still technically exists a college freshman named Kylie Bennington, who goes to class, and gossips during breaks, and spends time with friends, she's little more than a sketch. A kind of husk.

It's the girl beyond the glass who's alive, pulsing with love and admiration and, in some circles, is even worshipped.

That girl has figured out what MonoLife loves. The truth. All Kylie has to do is keep feeding it her urges, and the love will continue.

It's a good deal, when you stop and think about it. Who wouldn't want this for themselves?

Detective

@MissyMiss: you like to do some fucked up shit don't u? 😝
@CrystalShips: ready to talk?
@MissyMiss: fine

Through Kylie's bedroom window, the dark sky has cracked and distant bands of blue begin bleeding through, bringing the neighborhood housing tract back from the brink of oblivion. Kylie's been up all night, barely feels tired.

@CrystalShips: well . . . when?
@MissyMiss: soon . . . I am trying to come back there

It's six thirty. Brandi's battered face stares at Kylie from inside Mono-Life. Kylie's follower count ticks up by a hundred thousand, her tally just shy of 800K. Too many comments to respond to.

@CrystalShips has grown so popular that users debate in the comments the best way to get her to reply. A month ago she could easily engage with her entire fan base, but she's beyond that now.

She chooses a couple of followers at random, goes into their profiles, and tosses them the occasional fist bump or comment. Something to show she cares. Those on the receiving end can never believe their luck, as if the hand of God has reached out from above.

And it's a cute way to show her fans that she loves them.

She scrolls past Simon's latest post.

@EndlessNights: ProTip—Having trouble finding your MonoLife voice? Your first instinct might not always be the correct one. Reach down inside yourself and be honest about what's there.

Laughable advice from somebody completely unqualified to give it. The guy who cannot get verified, and who somehow managed to decrease in followers over the last few days—the "Face Smasher" bump completely eroded.

He hasn't figured out that "smartest guy in the room" isn't a sustainable brand. Nobody wants to follow their dad.

Kylie gets ready for class, grabbing a Nutri-Grain bar out of the cupboard, leaning against some unopened boxes stacked in the foyer as she eats, waiting for Erin.

Duc has just posted a video called "It's Killing Us, Assholes." First-person footage of a dirt floor, flickering light from unseen candles.

"*This is it*," Duc says from behind the camera.

"*Whatever*," responds another voice, male, tired and sluggish.

A baseball bat falls into frame, wobbling around on a card table. It's too dark to say for certain, but it seems like there might be little flecks of blood on the end.

Then Duc's phone drops down next to it. "*Deacon, be a pal, pick up my phone and turn it off.*"

Kylie's eyes widen slightly as Deacon bleeds into the darkness at the center of the shot, the residual candlelight finding faint traces of him. Quite the contrast from the last time Kylie had seen him—working the phone kiosk at the mall. He's slumped on a folding chair, nylon winch rope around his shoulders. His head swivels and blood pours from his mouth in one thick, endless dribble.

"*Pay attention!*" Duc screams, snapping his fingers to help Deacon find focus.

The light catches him just right as he comes to, revealing a bee-stung nose and swollen eyes. Guy's more battered than Dad's old pickup. He reaches toward the table with a groan, grabs the phone, holds it out for the camera as he presses the power button.

"*Off,*" he slurs, dropping his head back down against his chest, strands of red spit swaying off his mouth.

"*Good,*" Duc says. "*Now here's what I know. You turn your phone off, they're gonna miss you. Gonna come find you. See, Deacon is now a beacon. Get it? And if he doesn't want to lose his soul, he's gonna talk fast.*" Duc taps his phone with the bat. "'*Cause this here's a ticking clock now that it's off.*"

"*Dunno,*" Deacon moans. "*Don't. Know.*"

Duc presses the bat against Deacon's cheek, forcing his head back. "*Let's talk about what you do know, my man.*"

Another elastic groan.

"*I've had to do some fucked-up shit to stay in this game,*" Duc says. "*It's messed me up bad, but I had to keep you fuckers happy. Stay off their radar. Now . . . I want to see behind the curtain.*"

Deacon's head wobbles, as much of a protest as he can muster.

Duc winds his bat and cracks him off the temple. It's enough to do some damage—Deacon's eyes spring open. His spittle pelts the camera lens, tinting the whole video red.

"*Costs a hundred bucks to get you to put MonoLife on someone's phone. So who picks up that money?*"

"*They don't . . . care about money . . .*"

"*Hurry, man!*" Duc shouts, candles beginning to blow out as if the air has somehow picked up, conjuring a mass of erratic shadows.

"*They only care . . . to spread it.*"

"*Who? Who are you talking about?*"

More shallow breaths. More bloody drool. Deacon looking like he's puckering his lips, trying to muster one final sentence. "*Sunken . . . Church . . .*"

"*The fuck's that mean?*"

"*Find it . . . Find the Profile*," he says, a bit more animated. His eyes swinging up like a man possessed. "*Last thing you'll ever do.*" Deacon growls this with perfect clarity, which should be impossible, given his swollen face.

Almost as if he knows what's coming.

Deacon's chair shakes, then tilts up toward the air. And Deacon slips out, kissing dirt. He's able to glance up, fully awake in this moment, before being suddenly yanked back and swallowed whole by the darkness.

Gone without so much as a scream.

"*Shit*," Duc says. "*Okay. Okay. Okay.*" He snaps his phone up and turns it back on, holding it out toward the shadows that are now pressing in on him. "*As close as I can tell, this app runs in the background, so as long as your phone is on . . .*"

A face comes melting into the shot, a ghost in candlelight. A frozen smile, plastic cheeks. Sunken coal eyes framed by spindly hair.

Mama Doll, in the flesh.

"*Here I am, all good*," Duc says, waving the glowing phone around, drawing Mama Doll's eyes to the device. She appears to give a contented groan and then steps back into the void, leaving Duc's labored breathing as the only sound. And then the video's over.

The comments call this "Fake AF," but Kylie knows better. She has to pop a second lorazepam just to quell the panic, though it barely works.

She is so distraught that she's relieved to see Erin in the driveway. Kylie heads out the door to meet her, when she notices a strange sedan parked in front of her house.

A blonde woman with dark eyebrows gets out, approaching Erin's BMW, sipping a Dunkin' iced coffee through a straw.

"Ms. Bennington?"

Kylie's hand freezes in place, fingers hovering in the air a couple of inches from Erin's passenger door.

"Ms. Bennington . . . ?" the woman asks again.

"Uh. Yeah."

"Hi. I'm Claire Jasinski, FBI." A flash of her leather-bound badge and identification card, as if Kylie would know whether it's legit.

"Shit! Hey, you need a lawyer!" Erin's voice is muted from inside the car. "Call a lawyer, Ky. Do not talk to her!"

Agent Jasinski looks good for supposed law enforcement. She wears black, high-waist work pants with a skinny cut that hits right above the ankle, drawing attention to matching flats. She's got an off-white top beneath a beige blazer, although her weapon holster's visible on her belt.

"Maybe I should," Kylie says.

The agent waves her hand. "Who needs a lawyer? I'm here to talk. That's all."

This feels bad, though. Kylie got away with it once, humiliating Brady. Got away with it twice, capturing the end of Mr. Sykes's life. Three times if you counted Simon turning Ben Austin's face to mashed potatoes.

Then came Brandi. And Brandi's too stupid not to talk.

"Kylie . . . I'll call Cameron's dad!" Erin shouts, still muffled. "He'll know what to do about this."

Agent Jasinski moves to the back of the BMW, studying the license plate over a long pull of iced coffee.

Erin has nothing more to say, wilting against this scrutiny.

The agent comes around to her window and gives a two-knuckle knock. Erin's slow to roll it down.

"Erin Palmer, right? Huge fan of your Instagram. Why don't you go ahead and take off? I'll make sure Ms. Bennington gets to where she's going."

"I'm good," Erin says. "This is harassment."

"This is my job."

"Erin, it's fine."

"See that, Erin?" Agent Jasinski moves around the front of the

BMW. "Kylie says it's fine." Kylie waves Erin off, and they watch her finally back down the driveway into the street as the agent stirs her straw. "I hate when the syrup settles at the bottom," she says. "Some sips taste like burnt beans. Others . . ." She closes her eyes. "Ooh. Heaven."

"Too many calories for me."

"Is that true?"

"Yup. It is."

The agent circles Kylie now, nodding at every angle. "Yeah, you look like someone who takes care of herself. I guess that's part of being young and online, huh?"

"Gotta work, bitch."

"Give you a ride to school there, Britney?"

Kylie follows the agent to her sedan, imagining all her neighbors peering out from behind their curtains. It doesn't matter that she's going voluntarily and without cuffs. Word on this street is about to be that Kylie Bennington was arrested.

"This is a pretty rough town these days," Agent Jasinski says, starting the engine, pulling away from the curb. "Couple months back a dog was murdered on your lawn, right? Crossbow to the belly?"

Kylie shrugs, thinking about Duc's video.

I've had to do some fucked-up shit to stay in this game . . .

"They never even caught who did it," the agent says, really quite arrogantly. "Trouble finds you, huh?"

"Yeah."

"I just came from the hospital. Your classmate Brandi Leonetti got knocked around pretty bad last night. Stitches. Internal bleeding. Fractured ribs. Gonna take a while for her to heal up."

That makes Kylie feel better, imagining Brandi bandaged like a mummy. She's tempted to ask for pictures and has to fight off a tiny smile as she imagines Brandi sharing a hospital room with Ben Austin.

"It's weird," Agent Jasinski says. "She told me who did it . . ." Looks over to Kylie and holds the silence. "But she's adamant that she deserved it."

"She tried to run me over, then attacked me with a tire iron. I'd say that counts as self-defense."

"That tracks."

"Of course it does. I'm not a liar, Agent Jas—"

"Claire. Call me Claire."

"Fine, whatever."

"It's just . . . Well, she must've been pretty wrong to take that kind of a beating and—"

"She was."

"Why didn't you report it?"

"I dealt with her."

The sedan pulls up to the drop-off lane. Claire takes another sip of coffee, waiting until Kylie cracks the door to clear her throat. "Oh, one more thing . . ."

Erin's on the curb with Cameron and a few other people Kylie doesn't know. All the attention of SCC shifting to her.

Shit. She hadn't so much as considered this last night. Brandi won't be here today. Everyone's going to put two and two together.

"No offense, Claire, but I've got class."

"This will just take a second. Something Brandi said . . . Now, she had a real bad night, so it's possible that some of the details are fuzzy in her mind. Her doctor thinks that's actually the case."

"Okay . . ."

"Well . . . when I asked Brandi why you thrashed her so bad, she had a strangely specific answer." Another slurp of coffee, Claire shaking the ice around. "Don't know how I drink these so fast. I should order a large but that's more calories than *I* need. Guess I relate to you there."

"I really have to go."

"I know. Of course you do. Class and all that. Anyway, I asked why you were so violent, and she told me it wasn't your fault."

"Yes, she tried to kill me. Twice."

"That's not what I mean."

The car door's all the way open now, Kylie's feet on pavement.

"She told me, 'Kylie isn't Kylie anymore.'"

"Whatever that means." Kylie hops out, about to slam the door, when the detective's grin stops her cold.

"I was hoping *you'd* know."

Only now is Kylie aware that the wound on her back is pulsing, heavy doses of pain radiating through her body, tingles in her fingertips. "Look—Brandi hasn't been the same since her boyfriend dumped her. It really messed her up. She was obsessed, stalking him and everything. That's what I know."

Claire smiles again. It's difficult to read but Kylie suspects the agent is impressed with her ability to hold under pressure. "You have a great day, Kylie," she says. "I'll be talking to you."

ProTip

Kylie has to wait three classes to get at Erin's ear.

"Can Cameron's dad find out what that woman knows?"

"The fed?"

"Yeah. I'm sure they've been in touch with local police."

Erin's eyebrows rise. A stone-cold tell the girl is scheming. Just a total cartoon. "I'll help . . . if you help me."

"For real?"

She steps to Kylie's cheek, whispering, "I want MonoLife."

Kylie isn't surprised. Erin's appetite is insatiable, incapable of appreciating what she has. Always angling to get more. She's flying to Rome next week to mingle with fellow influencers and brands and yet . . . still wants MonoLife. And that's just the tip. She's upped her game, sensing Kylie on her tail. Her latest Insta is her on a bed in nothing but a see-through tank top, wearing a diamond the size of a Ring Pop. The caption: Just hit the jackpot . . . jewelry by @SkylineCity.

What more does she fucking need?

"I want to see *your* MonoLife," Erin prods. "You won't tell me how to level up, so, after the other night, I'm gonna have to twist your arm."

"Fine." Kylie flashes her phone now that she's wedged firmly between a rock and an even larger rock. Simon says this is kosher so long as both people have the app. At least he's good for something. "What do you want to see?"

"That's not what I mean," Erin says. "Not anymore. I want to go all the way. I want you to help me do it."

"Oh, Err. You don't have the stomach for this. Believe me."

"That's really not your decision." The smile rinses off Erin's face. Her angular features are even more pointed in this moment, hostility proving their reconciliation had been built on brittle bones.

Erin never forgives. She uses.

"Okay," Kylie says. "You get me everything Summerfield PD has on that agent, including how much they're looking into me and how much they really know, and I'll make you my protégée."

Erin banks a right at the art wing and starts off, actually turning to say "TTYL" in a way that sounds like *Fuck you*.

This incenses Kylie. Stress she doesn't need. It's bad enough she's part of a police investigation, but the rage she feels toward Erin burns white-hot, gets her so lightheaded she collapses on the way to Statistics.

"Kylie!" Mr. Davies seems to come out of nowhere, reaching down to help her up.

"I'm okay," she says, brushing him away.

"You don't look so good."

She *tsks* in offense. Hand to her collarbone.

"I mean, you seem tired. Peaked."

She stands up, but her balance is wobbly and she tumbles into Mr. Davies's arms. He grows even more flustered as she presses against him.

"Um . . . let me walk you to the nurse."

"No, I'll just go home."

"I can't send you to your car looking like this."

"How do I look, Mr. Davies?"

"Like you need to lie down."

He ends up escorting her to the other side of the building, quiet rage still giving her the shakes. Kylie hasn't calmed at all, even after the nurse tells her to lie down and take a few minutes to collect herself. Kylie opens MonoLife, intending to do just that, but a new post from Simon sets her even further on edge.

@EndlessNights: ProTip—You're never going to have the engagement you crave without producing something that's engaging.

"Oh my God, Simon. Nobody cares!" she barks at the screen. Literally nobody. Two fist bumps. He might as well be whispering into a hurricane. There's a whole bunch of this gibberish on his feed, all of it ignored, but that hasn't stopped him.

She sends Duc a few messages to try to touch base, maybe gather a little behind-the-scenes when it comes to his last video, though it's no surprise when he doesn't respond.

She tries Dad's cell again, because he used to know what to say to make her feel better, usually with some dumb jokes and once, when she was eight and first discovered the horrifying concept of dying, by getting them tickets to Katy's Prismatic World Tour at TD Garden. One of the best nights of her life. Except he's not answering his phone now and so the stress metastasizes inside her, becoming full-blown panic.

Is she about to be arrested?

MonoLife also feels somewhat contaminated now that Erin's interest has been rekindled. No head start will ever feel sufficient enough, and the thought of becoming second fiddle once again terrifies Kylie—it's only a matter of time until she is beaten at her own game. Can't have that. No way.

It's been an hour and she feels worse just lying here, staring at a poster on the wall of three animated carrots that for some reason reads: HEALTH IS WEALTH—KEEP THAT TREASURE SAFE!

She can't help it, swipes out a text to Erin and hits send.

Kylie:

any news?

Erin:

get your teaching cap on

tell me pls

later

I can't relax tho

later . . . gotta post

Erin goes radio silent, getting off on Kylie's anxiety. Kylie quietly snarls, "Bitch!" and time just refuses to pass. Her head still hurts and now the infection on her back is crying out alongside it. Debilitating pain as a side dish to this mounting anxiety. Can you have a heart attack at nineteen?

Can't even bring herself to scroll MonoLife. It feels like an indictment. Is that FBI agent watching somehow to see if Kylie incriminates herself?

No. There's more than enough content on her feed to do that already.

She gets down off the table, determined to get out of here as her phone buzzes, bringing a notification she can't ignore:

@MissyMiss sent you a message.

A video. Elongated bare feet moving down a darkened stone hallway. The image seems stretched at first, because nobody has feet like this, but the file cabinets and twisted metal bed frames they pass are completely proportional.

The feet, though . . . Clown feet, but with hardly any width. Something out of Dr. Seuss.

A hand falls against the wall, bricks glowing like orange embers. Fingers resembling crab's legs scrape along, sparking on stone as the camera treks onward.

"Mister Strangles," Kylie mumbles, more fascinated than terrified. "Mama Doll. And now . . . whatever the hell you are, I guess."

The hallway narrows into a squeeze, becoming a funnel that leads to one single door too thin to pass through.

Those shellfish fingers reach out, clacking against the metal barrier, performing some kind of otherworldly knock. The door slides. Steel grinding against concrete.

Beyond it is dark space. A shoebox stuffed with midnight. A caramel tile pattern comes bleeding through, filling the screen as whatever this creature is passes into our world.

Into familiar surroundings.

Tile floor. Oxygenated blood spreading over it, like jam on toast. Now the camera is watching through two skinny eyeholes as Annabeth Wilson's corpse, wide-eyed and sickly, comes into frame. After a second, the emoji mask lifts off, revealing the entirety of the camera lens, one hand plopping the mask onto the counter with an exasperated sigh.

The camera blurs as it goes on the move. The audience remains attached to its POV, watching a bronzed, human hand pushing into a bathroom.

Where Melissa Crigan stares at herself in the mirror.

"*Jesus,*" she whispers, turning on the water, cupping her hands beneath the faucet, rinsing oily crimson off her fingers. "*What did you do?*" she asks herself. "*How could you—*"

Kylie bursts out laughing, this whole thing some kind of cosmic joke. Because she recognizes that bathroom. Held Erin's hair while she puked into that sink eight months ago.

Now she knows where Annabeth died. And where to find her body.

Challenge Initiated

"Hi, everyone, Crystal here." Kylie's on the edge of her bed, giving MonoLife its first real glimpse at her face, at long last. Too much competition on her heels, can't afford to hold anything back. Here goes. "Most of you don't know this about me, but I'm a virgin."

Comments go into hyperdrive, unanimous in disbelief.

› Yeah right
› No way
› Fake and ghey
› Let me come over and take care of that

"Because you've been so supportive, I want to issue a challenge. If I get to nine hundred thousand followers by tomorrow afternoon, I will make my virginity, specifically the act of losing it, the subject of a future video."

› Bullshit
› OMG
› HOLY. FUCK. BALLS.

"I know, I know . . . Can't be real, right? Well, I like to think my brand is honesty. I'm always real with you guys. I'm being real today.

Help me hit my goal and . . ." She ends with her flirtiest *Call me later* wink.

> › Queen
> › Thank you, my goddess
> › You are perfect

Then she texts Erin.

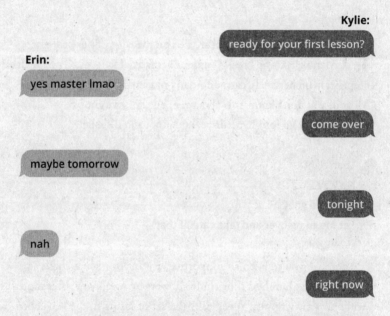

Kylie:
ready for your first lesson?

Erin:
yes master lmao

come over

maybe tomorrow

tonight

nah

right now

FaceTime ignites on Kylie's phone. Erin in close-up, glaring. The room behind her in shambles, clothes and product scattered like the aftermath of a tornado.

"I'm leaving for Europe next week."

"And you'll have plenty of time to pack. You asked for my help."

"Actually, you asked me."

"You want to make a splash, it has to be tonight." Kylie peers out her bedroom window, where the agent's sedan is still at the curb. *Call me Claire.* She putting in a double shift or what?

On-screen, Erin tilts her head so Kylie understands the strain this request is putting on her. "*Fine. I'll see you in twenty minutes.*" The screen goes dark.

Kylie's follower count climbs by the thousands. Her video, "Losin' It," has rocketed onto the Living Now page, directly beneath @Purple-LipGloss's ongoing *STD Roulette* series, where the woman behind this account cruises Los Angeles bars and clubs trying to initiate sexual encounters with random men and women.

"Shit," Kylie says. What bad timing. You never want to go up against these. She should've checked, made sure the coast was clear. Now the highest she can get is second place.

First loser.

What makes @PurpleLipGloss's videos interesting is the suspense. She isn't successful each time she makes the effort, and that uncertainty keeps her audience coming back. Though you can get a sense of things based on how long the video tops Living Now. If it's still at number one after a few hours, you know you're gonna see some skeezy bathroom sex or hot doggy-style in an alleyway.

Everyone suspects @PurpleLipGloss is someone famous. She always wears a nylon over her face down to her mouth, and a tiger-striped eye mask over that, and she's really careful about doxing herself. Never wears the same outfit twice. And if she *is* a celebrity, nobody's ever been able to match her clothing to any active Instagrammer.

There are entire accounts dedicated to identifying her by the various freckles and marks on her body, but those investigations remain inconclusive.

Whoever @PurpleLipGloss is, Kylie ignores her. MonoLife shouldn't be for bored rich people. It should be for those who would otherwise never have a shot at standing out.

It's clear that @PurpleLipGloss stalks the Living Now page too, because Kylie is notified that she's commented on "Losin' It."

@PurpleLipGloss: fuckkkk let's get this done y'all

Okay, maybe @PurpleLipGloss isn't so bad. Response to "Losin' It" is overwhelming and Kylie's satisfied, backing out of MonoLife to get ready for Erin's arrival as her phone buzzes.

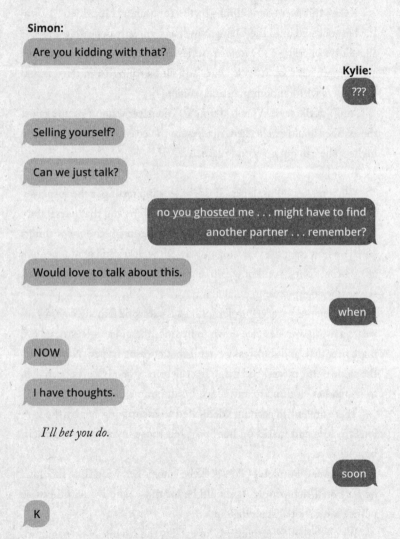

Simon:

Are you kidding with that?

Kylie:

???

Selling yourself?

Can we just talk?

no you ghosted me . . . might have to find another partner . . . remember?

Would love to talk about this.

when

NOW

I have thoughts.

I'll bet you do.

soon

K

Of course, Erin texts to say she's running late. A power move that Kylie has anticipated. She distracts herself by organizing her closet into old-Kylie and new-Crystal phases, with most of old-Kylie getting stuffed into garbage bags.

With the holidays approaching, she figures a "Remember to donate old clothes to the Salvation Army" video could easily net her another thousand followers on a slow day. Nobody cares about the poor, but pretending that you do makes for good social media etiquette, even on MonoLife.

Kylie changes into an Abella Boyfriend pullover, slips her feet inside white high-tops. It's a well-built outfit that can probably net her fifteen thousand fist bumps if the pose is cute enough, though what she really wants is to see the look on Erin's face.

The BMW's almost an hour late by the time it finally appears in her driveway. Kylie stands in the dark hallway thinking, *You come all the way to me.*

For ten more minutes she stands there listening to the idling car until finally, the pop of a door. Frustrated footsteps stomping up the walk.

Kylie even waits for the knock before opening up. "Sorry," she says. "Couldn't settle on a top."

Erin doesn't notice the outfit, is already walking back to the BMW, turning over her shoulder. "We're going somewhere, I assume?"

"Yep."

"Is the fed gonna follow us?"

Kylie goes down to the curb, Claire's electric window sliding open as she approaches. "Agent Jasinski," she says with mock fondness. "Would you like me to bring you back a third iced coffee or will you be following us this evening?"

Claire has her phone pressed to her ear, eyes shifting left to right, processing something. She holds out one of her fingers and Kylie curiously stands there.

"Be right over," Claire says, tossing the phone onto the seat beside her. "What is it?"

"Brandi," Claire says, sounding unsure. "She, uh, there was an accident or something."

"Like what?"

"Uh . . . shouldn't be telling you this."

"But . . ."

"Immolated in her hospital bed."

"Like, burned?"

"You two shouldn't be going out tonight."

"Just to get coffee."

"Okay. Be careful. Stay alert."

The sedan eases away from the curb, leaving Kylie standing in the middle of the street.

From the top of the driveway, Erin cups her hands to her mouth. "No police escort?"

"It's Brandi." Kylie's sneakers scuff the pavement as she walks toward Erin. "I guess she just . . . I don't know. Burned to death in the hospital?"

"What?" Erin says, and there's a stitch of awkward, disbelieving laughter as she settles in behind the wheel. "What the hell happened? Who would do that?"

Kylie gets into the passenger seat thinking, *@MissyMiss, that's who.* Can't say she's sorry to hear the news, though she wonders if she's supposed to be more upset. If she should put on more of a show, but the idea of that is simply exhausting. Easier to ignore. Beneath the interior lights of the BMW, Erin notices Kylie's outfit. A dull stutter in her throat she ultimately plays off as a dry cough. "Where are we going?"

Kylie wishes she could've taken a picture of the envy on Erin's face. "Remember that house we rented after prom?"

"Are you kidding?"

"That's where we're going."

They're on the road for an hour and Kylie's thinking about Brandi. How nobody's talking about her death. How that's the way it goes. When your time's up, it's like you never existed. Even Erin doesn't want to go there, constantly changing the subject. "You look good," she offers instead, which is how you know something's really bothering her. "Getting comps?"

Kylie pulls her sweatshirt out, snaps it back against her body. "A few."

"Benefits of being at the top, huh?"

"Getting what I deserve. Take this exit."

Erin does and the off-ramp morphs into a bumpy road that's mostly potholes. The moon disappears over a tunnel of low-hanging branches, Erin screeching at every odd motion as they pass through.

A few more turns and the world outside the headlights vanishes, the road indistinguishable from the surrounding forest. The sky in hiding. No other light anywhere, as if they've driven to the edge of the world.

That's where the cabin stands. It had been the perfect find last year for a group of high schoolers looking to party off the grid. The owner had retired to Pensacola and barely gets back out this way.

"I almost didn't catch it, you know," Kylie says.

"Catch what?"

"Remember how the kitchen was being remodeled? No floor? Just a sea of plastic?"

"Yeah."

"What did we care—we had no use for a functional kitchen, right? We had the coolers."

Erin sighs, growing more annoyed as she stops a couple of feet from the front door and kills the engine.

"Melissa and Annabeth must've come up here a few weeks later. *After* the floor work had been completed."

"Yeah, well, we didn't stop talking about this place."

They sit there a second, letting the reality of what they're probably going to find inside wash over them. Even the insects are silent, nature itself terrified of whatever's beyond that door.

Kylie pops the passenger door and the cab light ignites, illustrating Erin's discomfort. It prompts a smile in Kylie. Vulnerability looks good on her and Kylie hates that she has the urge to comfort her. Pushes it away.

"I'm going to let you shoot it," Kylie says. "You make the discovery."

"What?"

"You want to make a mark on MonoLife? Here's how you do it."

Erin winces. Not like this.

"Hey, this is me helping out of the goodness of my heart. I already know that agent has nothing on me."

Erin perks on that, her ace card going up in flames. "How'd you—"

"I mean, come on. With all that's been happening, you figure someone was going to notice. Start to wonder what's behind it all. And it's not just happening in Summerfield, so of course the FBI is asking questions. But that's all they have at this point. Just a whole bunch of questions, right?"

"Right." Erin sounds small, reduced to nothing.

"I figure my fight with Brandi is one of the *maaaaany* things that're not adding up for the people paying attention."

Erin bursts into tears. Ugly crying, wiping snot from her nose. All her influencer's arrogance deflated in this moment.

Kylie has never seen her more terrified. She gestures to the wooden door. "After you there, superstar."

Erin slides out and goes wobbling forward, phone in hand. She has to record this and post it later because western Massachusetts might as well be living in the Stone Age. Signals don't exist out here.

Kylie could try turning her phone into a hot spot, but why be that helpful?

The door's unlocked because that's clearly how Missy had left it, and Kylie's pulse throbs with excitement. Can't be sure Missy isn't in there now.

Their phone flashlights find cream-colored tile in the kitchen and it's all the confirmation they need, looking at each other like detectives who've cracked a cold case. This is where Annabeth died.

"Holy shit," Erin says, composing herself, clicking record, slipping into a somewhat shakier version of her online persona. "Hey, guys . . ."

They sweep the house, wood creaking beneath their steps as Erin, on point, explains the basics to her audience: "*So these two girls from our old school went missing last spring. One of them killed the other and posted it to this app, which is how we first learned about MonoLife so, you might say, it kind of worked out . . ."* She gives a nervous laugh as they reach the sitting room on the far side of the cabin, looking for anything out of place among the musty chairs and rickety shelves.

The floor squeaks somewhere behind them, from a room they'd already passed through.

Someone else is in here.

A silhouette glides across the clear curtains covering the window.

Erin's close to it, makes a face like she's bracing to catch the devil himself, then pulls the fabric back to find a swaying branch beneath the one single patch of moonglow the forest doesn't hide.

"Dead end," she says with a deep sigh of relief.

"You're forgetting one spot." Kylie wags a finger into Erin's camera, urging her to come back into the hall, where Kylie has decided to be a good friend and appear in the shot. A collab. Why not? The power dynamics are so skewed that their audiences will have no choice but to note @CrystalShips's superiority.

Besides, Kylie wants access to Erin's MonoLife. Craves the nourishment her failed attempts to go viral will offer.

Kylie gets onto her knees and pulls open the trapdoor to the fruit cellar, performatively smirking.

Erin's shaking her head again, nope, glancing around for the source of those squeaks.

"Oh, come on," Kylie says. "You made out with Jamie and Steve down there."

"Now I have to edit that part out."

"You won't have to edit anything if you don't go down there, because this won't be worth watching."

"Is anybody else in here, Kylie?"

"It's an old house. It makes noises. Quit stalling."

Erin goes with reluctance, sidling right up against the descending steps, peering into the void, one foot hovering, then dropping. She starts down carefully, turning to ensure Kylie is behind her.

"I'm here," she says and, in a moment, they're both hunchbacks moving underneath the cabin.

"Real haunted-house stuff," Erin whispers, settling back into her performance, panning over a tool bench of rusted saws and hammers. Her head moves through a spread of cobwebs, and her soft-spokenness becomes a shriek as she tumbles over a jutting rock and collapses onto a mound of coal.

Kylie's laughing, recording her own video of Erin trying to get back on her feet, pushing off the coal stack that is now tumbling down around her.

Erin screams out and leaps back, hyperventilating, bumping into Kylie, her bloodshot and terrified eyes popping wide for the camera, gobs of snot in her nostrils.

"You goddamn bitch," Erin snarls. "You think this is funny?"

Kylie focuses on the settling coal dust. Her flashlight beam floating along the stack, finding much of it dislodged and resting on the floor. But there's something else there, so unusual her brain cannot process it at first.

"Now I'm a mess!" Erin's already scrambling up the stairs, footsteps stomping toward the front door.

Kylie ignores that tantrum, inching a bit closer, light catching a head mounted atop the coal pile. Annabeth's decomposed face stares back, her skin broken and discolored like some Spirit Halloween mask. The thick cobweb in her eye socket makes it seem like she's winking, and her head is framed by loose strands of spindly hair.

"Annabeth Wilson," Kylie says. "I finally found you." She quits recording and hurries to catch Erin, who wastes no time starting the car and managing a three-point turn before Kylie can hop in.

Then Erin's speeding back the way they came, silent the whole drive.

Once they're back in town and in her driveway, Kylie asks: "Come inside?"

Erin won't even look at her. Just shakes her head.

"Come on," Kylie says. "We'll get your video edited and posted."

"What about yours?"

"Well, yeah. Mine's going up too."

Erin wipes tears from her eyes. All leverage lost. Her video will bring nothing but humiliation. Kylie knows it too, feels immeasurable satisfaction over it.

"That was somebody we knew," Erin says.

"So was Brandi."

Erin scratches her cheek, yeah maybe, but she isn't going to offer any kind of distinction.

"Look at it this way. Annabeth will be at peace once we tell the police how to find her."

"Do you even care?"

"I care a lot," Kylie says, then climbs out. "Come on, let's—" As soon as she's clear, Erin shifts into reverse and goes tearing down the pavement with the passenger-side door still open. It slams closed as she skids into the street, a pretty impressive stunt.

Kylie goes inside, straight to her room, where she uses the Magic Wand that came in today's mail to get lost inside Erin's Instagram. That's how much she cares. All these glam shots and half-naked Reels contrasting against the memories of tonight, Erin all snotty and terrified. Vulnerable and so totally degraded. Erin has turned desirability into an art form, pure image and objectification, which Kylie is both envious of and glad to consume. A constant swirl of emotion and energy demanding to be expelled. She finishes, then clicks into the text thread and swipes out:

Kylie:

don't be mad 😊

No ellipsis. Zero response.

Kylie changes into a bikini from Lulus and glistens up with coconut oil so her skin has that healthy shimmer. A few snaps with the aid of a selfie stick.

The post reads: **Ready for the Influencer Summit. Who thinks Mono-Life should invite me?** ☺

Nothing wrong with the occasional thirst post, right?

Her followers are closing in on nine hundred thousand. She realizes she could've used this contest to go for one million easy, but doesn't want to look gimmicky. Nevertheless, this is cause for a celebration no matter what.

She calls the police using an app that protects her ID in order to report the location of Annabeth Wilson and thinks it's a shame she'll never receive the credit she deserves for the discovery.

And she still can't get Erin off the brain. She deserved to be humbled tonight. And now that it happened, a point given to Kylie, their friendship can be allowed to continue.

Kylie:

> come on . . . I only wanted to prove to you that when I help, it's because I want to, not because I need a favor

Erin is unresponsive and Kylie leaves it alone for now, considering her next move because, while tonight was a decisive victory, it isn't the time to get lazy.

She considers asking her stupid followers—the awful people who nevertheless give @CrystalShips all the adoration that Kylie Bennington could only dream of—who they'd like to see take her virginity, then giggles as she comes up with an even better idea.

Erin doesn't even make a post that night. The first time in eight years she's missed a day.

Auction

Tonight's the night.

Kylie shaved first thing in the morning to reduce the presence of on-camera razor bumps.

The smartest thing she ever did was to start dropping her $cashtag into her posts. Her unending army of simps are always willing to contribute to her aggressive beauty regimen, bless their hearts.

And so the ritual begins with a few squeezes of Olaplex No. 4 shampoo in the shower. A velvety and reparative formula that gives her hair a sheen both soft and glistening. It also offers significant moisturizing abilities and protects from daily stresses like frizz and split ends.

Then she lathers herself twice over with Olay Ultra Moisture Body Wash. A gentle cleanse, one that softens her skin without removing natural oils. It's the pro-glycerin formula that helps give her confidence a big boost, a fresh feeling to keep her looking happy, healthy, and hydrated all day long.

Once she's out of the bathroom she looks herself over, scrutinizing her pores. Blackheads have been in retreat for a couple of years, but they're so unseemly she continues her regimen in earnest to deny their return.

That's where the La Roche–Posay Toleriane Hydrating Gentle Face Cleanser comes in. A product she's come to admire for its playful infusion of prebiotic thermal water, ceramides, and niacinamide. It assures a pleasing softness across her body while protecting her epidermal barrier against redness and inflammation.

This ritual brings a thorough cleanse, though it's only the beginning. Kylie applies a vitalizing serum, SkinCeuticals Phloretin CF with Ferulic Acid. A bitch slap of antioxidants, vitamin C, and phloretin that heals sun damage while lending her a rosy hue that's possible only by decreasing hyperpigmentation.

CeraVe PM Facial Moisturizing Lotion ensures that her complexion stays hydrated all day long without clogging her pores. Then it's time for eye cream, SkinCeuticals A.G.E. Eye Complex for Dark Circles, which she finds really makes her eyes pop thanks to its balmy formula with optical diffusers that reflect light away from them.

Once her skin is glossy and smooth, she empties her underwear drawer across the bed, picking and choosing the colors that best complement her body tone. It's between the red La Perla thong and matching bra and the white lace, flowery and see-through.

There's more deliberation over her outfit. Kylie settles on an orange thigh dress that advertises every curve. Crystal stiletto pumps take some getting used to, making it feel like she's on stilts and has to throw an elbow against the wall in order to steady herself as she prances across the upstairs hallway, practicing her strut.

Once she's comfortable, she heads downstairs, shoes clopping. She orders a rideshare and waits in the kitchen while nerves nibble at her like mosquitos. She sits with her hands beneath her thighs. No desire to scroll MonoLife.

Her phone dings. Lyft notifies her that Sharleen C. is two minutes away. She walks down to the edge of the driveway just as her Rogue reaches the curb.

The back seat's flush with a wild berry scent. The chemical smell makes her nauseous and she has to crack the window. The chilly November air annoys Sharleen C., whose sharp, judgmental glare fills the rearview.

Police are out in full force across Summerfield. Kylie counts five cruisers on the way, probably trying to prevent more teenage girls from spontaneously combusting or drowning in rivers.

They're almost to her destination. Kylie goes live, dolled up like a supermodel, staring at herself in the glass for a long moment, looking so good she fights the urge to masturbate to herself.

"Hi guys, Crystal here, heading in, urging you all to stay tuned."

That's all for now. She's walking toward the small split-level. Her heart thumps so hard her blood feels like syrup. Her body trembles as she knocks.

The door opens. A face appearing in the crack. A chain sliding from its cradle. "Kylie?" Mr. Davies asks.

"You said if I needed an ear—"

He pulls the door wide. Still in his work pants, though his socks are off, and the faded Pearl Jam tee is tight around his belly. "Are you okay?"

Kylie's glad to get out of the cold. She puts a little sway into her hips as she sashays past, feels his eyes on her butt again.

"Kylie—"

She spins and folds her arms impatiently, hip posed to one side, daring him to toss her out. The way she looks. The way she smells. A Teenage Dream, to steal one from Katy.

"This isn't . . . what I meant." His words are weaker, conviction crumbling like dry sand.

There's a ceramic plate on the counter, uneaten crust and chip crumbs. His home is kept, at least with a general degree of self-respect that's acceptable if not impressive.

Kylie pushes her cleavage with her forearms, lowering her head in shame. "You meant an appointment after class."

"Y-yeah."

An innocent shrug. "It's after class."

"It is but—"

"Can't we just talk?" She looks toward the darkened living room. Netflix on pause. "In there?"

"How about I put on a pot of coffee? Here . . ." He taps the kitchen counter. "Then you call a ride. Okay?"

She climbs a flat stool and crosses her legs. Her skirt crawls off her thigh, toward her hips, and she makes no effort to pull it down. Too busy keeping her posture without any back support.

Mr. Davies steals a quick glance, then spins toward his cabinets, reaching for a couple of mugs. "What's on your mind?"

"I feel alone," she says. "Like nothing I do matters."

"Aha. Well, I don't want to diminish your emotions, but that's a pretty common bundle of feelings at your age. At mine too. Does that make you feel better or worse?"

"Neither." Kylie shrugs. "My struggle's my own. Whoever else is suffering doesn't impact me."

"I watch you during the day."

"Yeah?"

"Um. What I mean is, you've got friends. Support."

"During the day, Mr. Davies. Nighttime is very different. That's when we're alone, right? Vulnerable?"

"You feel alone?"

"I feel withdrawn. Instagram's like a chore. My friends only want to talk about what big deals they are. How many followers they have."

"Social media has a way of fucking with you, doesn't it?" He looks so proud of his f-bomb.

Kylie chuckles.

"It does, though," he says. "You think everyone's living the good life and it's only you who's not. Everybody's putting up the same front, though. Believe that."

"Maybe."

"No maybe. I'm right." His gaze falls to her lap. Then back up. Kylie pretends not to notice. Bites her lip to keep the smile at bay. It really is this easy. Men are animals. Bundles of instinct parading at humanity. "There's plenty of things you can do, Kylie."

"Like?"

"Volunteer somewhere. Get a job. Find something in life that makes you feel accomplished."

"That makes a lot of sense."

"When life is darkest, you find the light. Trust me, I know something about that."

"Thanks, Mr. Davies." Kylie resists the urge to ask why his wife left him.

"Besides," he says. "Aren't you and Erin still friends? You guys have been joined at the hip since I met you both."

"Oh, of course," she lies. "But if I'm being honest, I question it."

"Why?"

"We've known each other since fourth grade and I wonder sometimes if we're friends only because we've been friends. Not sure anything else really unites us anymore."

"Also common," he says. "Thing about life . . . Not everyone you share yours with is intended to stay in it forever. Some people are meant to become memories. And instead, they wind up liking your status updates and wishing you a happy birthday each year. Social media makes it harder to let those people go. All this digital connectivity . . . upsets the order of things."

"You think I should let Erin go?"

"That's up to you," he says. "If you really feel like there's no point, then hey . . . Like I said, not all relationships are supposed to last forever."

"Some can exist for a single night."

Mr. Davies rubs the back of his neck. "Come on. You should always aspire to more than that."

"I guess I'm just looking for someone," she says. "An ear. I don't know. Fuck. It's all so . . . My parents are separated. Both of them workaholics. Easy to forget I even have a family."

"But you do. And this isn't necessarily what you're looking to hear, but maybe there's a way to make them remember that."

"I shouldn't have to. They brought me here. I didn't ask for this."

"You're speaking my language." Mr. Davies looks desperate, his guard completely lowered. Weighing the risks in his mind.

Amazing. Men are just naturally like this. No matter who they are, they're always thinking about fucking you. So gross.

"Have I helped?" Mr. Davies asks. "I feel like I haven't helped."

"You have. You helped. It's good to be reminded we're not alone."

"You aren't. I promise."

"Sometimes I . . ." She leaves it there so Mr. Davies leans into her words, and it's all the reinforcement she needs. He's on the hook.

Kylie takes the opportunity to flip her hair and give him a second to appreciate whatever he wants.

"I need to know somebody sees me."

Mr. Davies reaches across the counter and takes Kylie's hand in a gentle, supportive squeeze.

She brushes her thumb against his palm. The weakness in his eyes giving her everything she needs. "Thanks for seeing me, Doc."

"You're honestly helping me too." He gestures to the silent house. "This is my life most nights."

A cute smile before adding, "You look good, Mr. Davies. You haven't stopped taking care of yourself."

"Cardio doesn't run in my family. So I make sure it runs in me. This gut's a little persistent, but I'll zap it."

"If I take your advice to heart, you need to take mine."

He clears his throat. "You should call a ride. Next time we talk, it really ought to be in school. Okay?"

Kylie hops down, takes his hand again. "Could we start practicing that rule next time? I don't have anyone to call right now. Was wondering if I could bother *you* for a ride."

His eyes pop. He wasn't expecting that. And now that the offer is on the table, he's unwilling to let it slip through his fingers. The virtuous exist only because they never have the opportunity to refuse temptation.

"What do you say, Mr. B?" Kylie asks. "Drive me home?"

Mr. Davies lets the question linger. He looks Kylie over one more time. Her hands on her hips, expectantly.

He says, "Sure. Okay."

Good Doggie

Mom will not be back from work until dawn, so Mr. Davies is standing in her kitchen, looking ashamed.

It isn't a done deal, even though he came in here knowing damn well why.

"You need to relax, Mr. D—"

"Call me Ryan," he says, shame morphing into guilt in real time.

"Okay. *Ryan*." Kylie goes into the dining room and snatches a couple of bottles, holds two glasses together with pinched fingers.

Ryan's even more miserable when she returns, knowing he can't fight this. Has no intention of fighting this.

"What do you drink?" She pours a shot of Honey Jack Daniel's. When he's silent, she gives him the same. "*Ryan*, you look like you're going to a funeral."

Kylie comes around the island, glass pressed to her body. "I told you," she purrs. "I want to help."

He downs the drink in one gulp, turns to her with pleading eyes, begging her to be the stronger person because that's how it always has to be for some reason. He's not man enough to prevent this.

"Have some more," she says and dips her fingers into her glass. Points one of them at his mouth.

Mr. Davies backs away, actions lacking in conviction. He doesn't want space. Only wants to make it seem like he does.

Kylie pushes forward, her dripping fingertip sweeping across his mouth. He parts his lips, allowing her to trace them as he licks the honey bourbon.

He takes her finger down his throat the second she offers it, licking and sucking while she suppresses giggles with fake porn-star moans. It's so easy to goad this along.

She presses against him. They kiss. His mouth's as nervous as the rest of his quivering body. She places the glass down and takes his hand, guiding it over her, encouraging exploration.

"I want you to fuck me," she whispers.

His moan is pure misery. A mistake he cannot avoid as his hand closes around her ass. Kylie steps back and slides the dress off her shoulders, letting it fall away.

He lunges for her, no longer thinking with his brain.

She presses a forceful hand to his chest, a reminder that he's anything but in charge. "Off," she says, tussling his shirt.

He slides it over his head and flings it away as she lifts the Honey Jack and pours a small stream down the nape of her neck, a trickling river passes beneath bra wire, running all the way to her belly.

He knows exactly what to do. Just like a good doggie. Falls against her, slurping liquored flesh like he's never tasted it before.

She nudges him toward the stairs, breaking away and allowing him to follow.

He lunges for her, and she gives him this one moment of masculinity. He pushes her against the wall and squeezes her breasts through her bra.

She groans with surprise.

"This what you want?" he says, as if him being here is her fault.

She cups a palm over his erection and takes another swig of Honey Jack straight from the bottle before slipping beneath his arm and continuing upstairs.

He follows again because he's still a good doggie. Straight to her room, where the walls feel even more constricted. She's got two cameras angled on the bed, one hidden inside her closet, the other tucked between stuffed animals. Both remotely activated from the control on her bed table.

Kylie drops backward into the bedside chair, chest leaning against the back brace, golden legs spread out on either side.

She's pouting at Mr. Davies as he comes into the room, washing away his final bits of self-loathing with another swig from the bottle.

She repositions herself so that both her legs are on one side of the chair and, while staring at him, slides her panties off and flings them right at his head.

"What are you doing to me?" he says, begging for Kylie to end it.

Kylie watches with coldness. Pills and alcohol have tamped down every bit of terror and uncertainty she feels. She's actually doing this.

"Strip," she says.

He can't get out of his pants fast enough. Then he falls onto her, worshipping her flesh like it deserves.

What truly turns her on is the thought of showing this to the world. Intimacy that MonoLife has never seen. It's usually too performative for that.

Kylie's emotions threaten to betray her as she considers her long-held notions of "the first time." How special it's all supposed to be. How she once fantasized sharing this experience with Brady, who turned out to be another piece of human garbage she couldn't count on in her life. Now her palms glide over disgusting patches of wiry shoulder hair. Her teacher, a stranger kissing her, licking her, telling her how beautiful she is.

She keeps feeling his hardness against her, and she flinches each time like it's a cattle prod. A cold, despairing reality clashing with the wistful fantasy of what this moment really should have been like.

But it's all for MonoLife.

Feed the feed.

And then it's time.

The Hatchling

Kylie posts the video. "Woman."

It's seven minutes long. Living it felt much longer.

She edits nothing, having promised these jackals something intimate. For them. As if to say: *Here's what you fuckers want, right?*

› **Dude's a teacher lmao**
› **Holy shit, she actually did it**
› **Already jacked it twice to this**
› **Anyone know how to save a video off this app?**

This earns her the coveted @PurpleLipGloss follow, whose recent video is called "The Hills" and takes place in some open-floor home that looks more expensive than Kylie's life. A naked man stands on one leg surrounded by flamingo sculptures and @PurpleLipGloss is locking his shriveled penis in what can only be described as a cage.

Sorry, bitch, Kylie thinks. *But* I'm *number one.*

@CrystalShips has two videos in Living Now's top five. Has anyone else ever done this?

So why do I feel so goddamn awful?

She reads the comments on "Woman" to offset the emptiness. In most instances, there's enough difference in tone to parse which ones belong to men and women.

The women pity her, calling the man a callous asshole who should know better, who should be chemically castrated for crossing the line, taking advantage of her.

Most of the dudes of course approve of some e-girl getting smashed.

Kylie wonders what a video with Asher might've been like. Or Simon. But this was the right choice—at least, that's what she tells herself. MonoLife is all about the idea that people enjoy watching something they're not supposed to see—something forbidden and taboo.

Which means nothing, really, given that she's nineteen and well beyond the age of consent. But that she chose to share this special, intimate moment with her online audience, allow them to experience it alongside her, is what they'll remember. Isn't it? At least until the next video, and that's just it . . . she's only bought herself some time because her followers are gluttons, always hungry. If she doesn't feed them, they'll go elsewhere to be fed.

Kylie takes the longest shower of her life, her head numb, buzzing, staring at her thighs as blood trickles down them. She returns to bed doing a bowlegged walk and drapes an arm over her eyes.

Silence fills the world around her. And she can no longer help it. She cries.

But cannot sleep.

Praise for "Woman" is everywhere on this repugnant app. A few dopes describe her as a lousy lay but that's it. Because if her ass isn't bouncing in some guy's lap, she must be a dead fish.

A notification ribbon spreads across the bottom of her screen: @MissyMiss sent you a direct message.

@MissyMiss: check my latest, I trust you're gonna like 🗡

Kylie clicks @MissyMiss's username and goes straight to her profile. Her most recent video is "The Night I Came Home."

She presses play—

—and finds herself looking down a sloped driveway in low light. Grainy footage, like watching through a mosquito net.

The camera hangs like that for a while, until Mr. Davies's Audi appears, slowing at the curb, then turning, the camera eye washed out by blinding headlights.

Hard cut to Mr. Davies's kitchen. Angle on the stool Kylie had used only a few hours ago. Someone else sits there now, a gloved hand tap-tapping the granite countertop.

The door swings open. Mr. Davies comes in and flicks on the lights.

Another cut. The camera circling around Mr. Davies's head, though he's somehow oblivious to this as he removes his clothes and discards them on the floor of his laundry nook.

He passes a window, and what's reflected there doesn't jibe because there's no camera visible.

There is, however, a woman in an emoji mask standing there, machete raised overhead.

That mask, with its squinted eyes and exaggerated teardrops, looks right at the window, right out at its audience.

At Kylie.

Seeing him again, even on video, makes Kylie's body ache even worse. She's completely indifferent to what's about to happen even as her fingers grip stained bedsheets, pulling them into bunches.

Cut.

Mr. Davies goes room to room, picking up clutter, sighing as the reality of tonight begins to register. He spots the ceramic mug of cold decaf that Kylie didn't touch still sitting on the counter.

He flings it hard against the wall. Shattered pieces leave behind a splat of cool coffee that drips down the tiled backsplash.

"*You fucking moron!*" he screams, running his hands through his thinning hair. "*You'll never get tenure now. What were you thinking? You've got to get out in front of this. Call a lawyer, go on the attack. She seduced me. Yes, a hundred percent. She came here on her own! It wasn't right, okay, but she seduced me!*"

The emoji mask steps out from behind a door that's a couple of rooms away, visible in the background just over Mr. Davies's shoulder.

We're at his back as he pours a glass of water and then lumbers toward the stairs. We follow him as far as the first step, remaining there as he begins to ascend, treads creaking.

The camera turns back toward the hall, where the emoji is suddenly standing, shoulders rising and falling, watching him go. Its head angles up to the ceiling, which groans now beneath the teacher's weight.

The mask gives the camera one last look that makes Kylie's heart flutter, and then it's moving up the stairs as well, taking them without any sound at all.

The camera stays put, as if too scared to follow. A long moment of silence. Sixty seconds of dead air. Probably more. Doesn't matter. Kylie is riveted.

It starts to feel like nothing else is going to happen. But then Mr. Davies screams—a horrible bit of agony—and a rush of crimson begins spreading across the white ceiling. The plaster flakes, crumbing down like sand through an hourglass as the tip of a blade pushes through.

We're looking straight up at it, a big dollop of blood dangling off the point like a single red teardrop. It hangs forever, and it's so compelling that Kylie realizes she's holding her breath.

Mr. Davies's gurgles are gone.

And then the blood drop falls, pelting the screen, painting the interior of Mr. Davies's house blood-red.

Then it cuts to black.

Trends

Word of Mr. Davies's death travels. Cameron hears it from his dad, so Erin sends Kylie a courtesy text, and Kylie doesn't want to take any questions—doesn't want to think of Mr. Davies ever again—so she takes a sick day and spends much of it looking out the window for Agent Jasinski's sedan. Which is definitely going to be pulling up on the curb any second now.

Only it never comes.

That night, she's at the kitchen counter eating a pan-fried scrambled egg mixed with kale and a diced shallot. Somewhere down the street, a dog's barking, whipping itself up into a frenzy over the sound of distant hysteria, people laughing or shouting or some combination of the two.

In MonoLife, Missy has become chattier.

@MissyMiss: trust me yet?

@CrystalShips: you're literally trying to ruin my life

@MissyMiss: lol . . . don't be so paranoid . . . I protected you

@CrystalShips: ummm k

@MissyMiss: you heard him, would've exposed everything, gone off screaming about how you seduced him

@MissyMiss: no matter what, your name gets dragged through the mud

@MissyMiss: attention you don't need if you're gonna help me

@CrystalShips: did you "protect" me by burning Brandi alive too?

@MissyMiss: no

@CrystalShips: then why do that???

@MissyMiss: i didn't

@CrystalShips: then who set her on fire?

@MissyMiss: let's talk about how you're going to help me instead

@CrystalShips: you know what? have a nice life.

Kylie tosses her phone onto the counter in frustration. These exchanges with Missy are going nowhere. Outside, distant shrieks from terrified children are piercing, mixed with quick bursts of startled laughter. Everything getting louder.

@MissyMiss: you'll realize I helped you

Help. As if Kylie needs that.

@MissyMiss: has to be trust

Why doesn't Missy go and help a complete failure like Simon? Some stupid asshole floundering in MonoLife's user hell. People like Simon are not innovators, but followers. Always will be. Always reacting to the success of others, then trying to play catch-up. He's the one who needs help. Not Kylie.

What good is Missy? What good is Duc, for that matter? What can they provide Kylie at this point? Duc's off trying to dox this app, biting the hand that's feeding them.

There's no reason in the world for Kylie to be standing between them. It's not really her problem and at this point in her career, she's surpassed them both.

Something rakes against the patio glass, startling her. Deliberate *clack–clack*ing like someone's out there, knocking with their fingernails.

Kylie takes slow steps through the living room, squinting into her backyard and gasping at the sight because what's there cannot really be there.

Certainly shouldn't be there.

Sporto. The collie. Sitting in the floodlight glow. The dog watches Kylie through the glass, head cocked with the kind of curiosity that had, she thought, gotten him killed. His fur is dark, dyed by hardened bloodstains. Large patches of it are missing, and the animal's dirty rib cage shows through.

The dog places a paw on the window; a familiar whine follows as if begging to come in.

"Uh, hi . . ." Kylie's moved right up against the glass, unable to fathom this. Instinct suggests taking a picture, though she's left her phone in the kitchen. "Where have you been, boy?"

The dog's ears go flat, a deep grumble growing out of his chest because he no longer sees Kylie as a friend. The crusted blood around his snout, ribbons of shredded flesh swaying in his bared teeth, bolsters this suggestion.

Kylie retreats a few steps toward the kitchen, and Sporto's growl gets louder. Both paws not so much clacking now, but clawing the glass.

From out front, another growl—an artificial, diesel one. Loud enough to send Sporto scampering back through the bushes into Mrs. Elrond's yard. Kylie looks out the front window, watching a flatbed truck reverse into her driveway, a shiny blue BMW sports car riding piggyback.

The unease over Sporto's reappearance dissipates as Kylie realizes what's happening: some swag is just too big for cardboard boxes.

At the same time, MonoLife begins making those horrible metallic keening noises as notifications stack on Kylie's lock screen. A bunch of messages from @EndlessNights she has no intention of checking.

"Oh, shut up, Simon!" Kylie takes the phone and goes limping into the evening air. Two men in overalls are in the driveway, one pulling the fastening chains off the bottom of the flashy sports car they've deposited there. The other man walks over and silently hands Kylie a manila envelope.

There's even more commotion coming from down the street—one of her neighbors, Mr. Henderson, she thinks, shouts, "Look what your goddamn dog did, Cathy!" but Kylie is unable to focus on that right now.

"What's this?" she asks herself, staring transfixed at the car.

Kylie shifts the envelope around, feeling a couple of bulges at the bottom.

Car keys.

The men nod to themselves, job well done, and return to the cab, driving off without speaking a single word.

Kylie circles the car in disbelief while, right next door, a crowd is gathering on Cathy Elrond's front lawn. From somewhere in the dark, she hears Sporto the Unfriendly Collie and thinks for a second about Katy and her dog Nugget wearing matching outfits in the "Small Talk" video.

"That animal is gonna have to be put down, Cathy."

"I thought it was already dead?"

"Bet she got some rescue dog that's half rabid."

None of that matters to Kylie in this moment. Her jaw is scraping pavement as she snaps a couple of photos of her new ride, because she simply cannot believe what's happening here.

Then she pulls open the envelope.

Dearest @CrystalShips,

You have been identified as a top influencer. Please accept this gift as a token of our appreciation. It has already been registered in your name and, as an added benefit, an account has been established with which you will use to pay annual taxes. Please see the attached documentation for full details.

Thank you for living MonoLifez.

Warmly,
MonoLife Management

The ink on the paper fades in an instant, the very air reducing the printing to a blank sheet.

Next door, the neighbors have breached Mrs. Elrond's house, repeating her name until someone screams out, "*It got her!*" and then all hell breaks loose. "*Holy shit there's blood everywhere!*"

Kylie posts a couple of photos to Instagram with the caption: NEW RIDE! Passive-aggressive content she wants Erin to see. She even considers texting her a few more pics with a joke about how maybe it should be called KylieTime now.

Only she catches herself. Erin's been highly sensitive since the cabin incident. Their minimal conversations have been pouty. And though Kylie sometimes thinks she'd like to grind that bitch into ash, there is no advantage to picking that scab.

Insta likes come rolling in to remind her why she's all but abandoned these normie socials. Ten, twenty hearts. She reaches forty-eight in a half hour. An insult. Nothing like the MonoLife fire-hose spray of fist bumps. A total waste of time.

She sends one of the car pics in text to Mom with the message: Still think I'm wasting my time???

Mom:

WHAT???

That's YOURS?

Kylie:

yup

Time to fess up . . .

OK. I've been patient . . .

But who is he??

Mom sends a stream of interrogative messages, mostly guesses as to the types of men who might be subsidizing Kylie's lifestyle, a deduction that Kylie finds vaguely insulting. Not because of its improbability—it *is* entirely feasible, after all—but because Mom won't entertain any other possibility. So Kylie ignores her, is too keyed up by the confirmation that she's one of MonoLife's top influencers. Tears stream and her breathing becomes erratic. Her soul stirs with the type of warmth she feels in the tips of her toes, truly living the best days of her life.

Top. Influencer.

She goes dancing through every room in her house with "Waking Up in Vegas" on blast. She's really hit the jackpot, thinks about getting a few moves down and then recording a cute little shuffle as a celebratory vid before common sense catches up to remind her that sort of crap will only cost her followers.

Remember what got you here.

Later, she's in the shower streaming Katy's *Teenage Dream*, a strong follow-up record to her first album, *One of the Boys*. The precise moment when Katy went from potential "one-hit wonder" to global phenomenon. This album, a reminder that you can never be complacent. You need to work harder. Look hotter. Be stronger. Only then will your dreams start to come true.

And of course, that may be only the beginning of your problems.

MonoLife dings come through the shower speaker, chopping Katy into auditory bits.

Kylie hops out, furious for the interruption, but marginally curious anyway. She passes her reflection on the way to her bed table and stops cold.

What's looking back at her isn't even trying to mimic Kylie anymore.

It's @CrystalShips. Crystal IRL. Folded arms, even though Kylie's are not, mouth twisted into a hideous smirk that Kylie has never made. *"You're a star, babe,"* Crystal says, words wobbly and distant, as if calling out from space. *"Act like it."*

Kylie waves her arms and Crystal stands frozen, grinning in protest.

It's still me, Kylie thinks, stepping closer, wondering why she's so frightened.

Crystal nods in response.

Kylie drops the towel and drags a hand down her body, feeling herself, realizing that her flaws have been exorcised. What had once lived beyond the glass is now her reality. A perfect sculpt.

She'd question it, this potent transformation, but who would be able to give her an answer? Duc? Missy? Of course. She laughs while her phone continues to blare from her bedroom. It's possible to be a huge star without knowing shit. Millions of people do it every day.

The mirror fogs over, as if on a delay, and the reflection behind it is just a nondescript blur that once again matches Kylie's general shape and position. Normal again.

She enters her room and grabs the phone. The notifications are from @EndlessNights, which means they are less than nothing. Simon sending message after message, begging to meet. Such a loser.

Kylie's attention falls on the red and blue lights flashing against her window. A siren blaring just outside.

She opens the window. An ambulance is parked on the street outside. A stretcher being rolled down off the front steps. So much light and activity out there that Kylie is able to see a splotch of spreading crimson moving across a white sheet that covers a Mrs. Elrond–sized body.

In the distance comes the familiar howl of a dog that once lived next door.

Boomer Is a Mindset

Thanksgiving's in four days.

Simon doesn't stop leaving messages, both DMs and texts.

@EndlessNights: we okay, baby?

Baby?! So cringe. Reading that makes her so upset she has to delete his entire message history and then take two lorazepams to relax.

Erin's leaving for Europe on Black Friday. An influencers' summit for those who don't realize they're basic. She hasn't posted anything in a week, which is a really weird time to let your foot off the gas.

Kylie's getting used to driving again, joyriding her new toy all over town. It's been over two years since the accident, totaling Dad's Ford about ten minutes after getting her license. Since then she's been too traumatized to try again, so she's taking baby steps. Backing down the driveway first, to the end of her street next, then once around the block.

At school, Asher sees Kylie parking and hangs back to walk her to class. "This is fire," he says of the BMW. "Your sugar daddy buy it?"

"Why does everybody think that?"

"Dunno," he laughs. "Maybe because this thing costs more than what most people make in a year."

Kylie taps the roof. "I earned it myself."

Asher's chuckle turns her answer into an innuendo.

"Believe me or don't."

"Just want to make sure you're okay. You haven't responded to any of my texts since Brandi . . ."

"I was giving you time to grieve."

Asher's sour face shows he's not buying it.

Kylie rolls her eyes so that he knows he's not getting another answer. People feel so entitled to others. The more Kylie comes into her own, the more explaining she has to do, justifying her existence to those who barely exist at all. It's infuriating. Fuck them. Fuck them *all*. Nobody willing to take her at her word and just believe that her clout has begun paying dividends.

Has to be that she's whoring herself out—

Well, you are. Certainly for MonoLife.

Now her cheeks are flush and she feels like screaming.

Mom and Asher are skeptical because they've seen the ghost town that is Kylie's Insta, and she can't come all the way clean about where it is she's flourishing. Tending to their paranoia is a job she'd like to quit.

And that goes double for school. Only reason she hasn't dropped out yet is that it's one more charade she doesn't have the energy to keep up with.

What matters to her is MonoLife and her growing family of followers. Sure, they may be degenerates but they're her degenerates.

The arrival of a well-timed text from Simon allows Kylie to escape Asher's scrutiny, though it does little to dispel his sugar-daddy theory. But really, who cares? So long as she gets to dodge the issue.

Simon:

Lunch today, superstar? 😊

Kylie:

Half day. Let's meet.

Kylie insists on driving herself, rather than be picked up, and Simon's a lot colder after that.

Fine.

He proposes the panini place where they first met, as if that's all you need to do in order to hit the reset button. No, Kylie craves chorizo tacos, tells him they're meeting at Birria Basket.

He's sitting in his Mustang when she gets there, his car looking as good as new.

"How much did this cost?"

"Two grand," Simon says. "That fucking geek."

Ben Austin has spent the last three weeks *finally* getting the hint after getting rekd. She's seen him once in all that time, and he ducked into a classroom that wasn't his in order to let her pass without incident.

Some people are so damn stubborn, all it takes is jaw surgery to make them understand.

Kylie and Simon are able to secure two open stools at the bartop overlooking the parking lot.

She orders three chorizo tacos and a Mexican Coke, because it's been forever since she's allowed herself any caloric indulgence. Simon gets a chicken burrito and a plate of nachos he keeps trying to share, the gesture incensing Kylie to the point she's already searching for a way to cut this meeting short.

"Have you been looking at my feed?" he asks, unprompted. "Lots of things happening."

"MonoLife doesn't seem to show me much of your content." The lie is just to see his disappointment.

"Working on some partnerships," he says. "Developing my own brand. Betting on myself. Feels great."

She'd like to interject, tell him that stalking other MonoLifers and leaving banal @s beneath their posts does not constitute "working on partnerships," but she's sort of interested in hearing just how detached from reality he is.

His content is like watching a train go off the rails in slow motion. A social media maladapt who cannot remotely grasp any digital cues. Someone who writes his shortcomings off as *we're all struggling to understand this new digital frontier* because that's an easier conclusion than the truth.

Simon's got zero growth because he can't choose a lane, trying a little bit of everything. Reactive. Therefore, fatally dull.

"Saw your latest," he says in a creepy way that implies he enjoyed watching her have sex. And he's oblivious to the fact she might've hated every second of it. Forget that her groin is still impossibly sore—Kylie will suffer for her art as long as her audience is entertained. Though she doesn't want to have to see this kind of leering admiration in person. "Kinda messed up for my tastes," he adds. The empty way in which he says this confirms he's lying.

"I don't care."

"Hey, I'm not . . . Just wondering how to get back on the team."

"What do you mean, on the team?"

"Us. We make a good team."

Kylie chews down an entire taco while considering this. "We don't have anything in common, Simon."

"I disagree."

"I'm closing in on one million followers. MonoLife gifted me a brand-new BMW. I have to be careful about who I work with."

Simon's jaw tightens, cheeks pulsing like a rodent's. She cannot stand the sight of him. This man is not her Orlando Bloom. He's either Russell Brand or Travie McCoy, in that she wants everyone to forget they were ever connected.

"I had a plan for us, you know." Simon has moved on to guilt. "We were going to be huge."

"I'm already huge."

"You're on a hot streak. Could've just as easily been me."

"Please. I've worked for it."

"I understand you think that, but nothing lasts forever. Just ask Katy Perry."

"Watch your goddamn mouth."

"Only making a point. I took the day off because I had to get out of the office. Wanted to see your face."

She rolls her eyes.

"No, no," he says. "I just mean, a friendly face. I'm twenty-seven with a dying mother. Doctors say this is her last year. All I've got is a cubicle job to look forward to the rest of my life . . . unless MonoLife happens for me. Like it happened for you."

"Why is this my responsibility?" she asks. And holy shit, did he just say he was *twenty-seven*?

"Whatever happened to 'We're a team'?"

"We were *never* a team, okay? The game requires a collab. We did that. I moved on. You haven't."

"I've been doing this longer than you. Respect it."

"Respect is earned, Simon. You've been doing it longer and you're still a ghost."

"That's bullshit."

"Is it? Nobody knows you exist."

Simon pushes his food away and swivels toward her. "Help me. *Please*. I'll get on my knees if I have to."

This breaks something in Kylie. "Ohhh . . . my God. Why is everyone so fucking pathetic?"

"Naw. I don't buy it. This isn't about me. I didn't do anything wrong. Someone got to you, didn't they? Someone doesn't want you working with me. I knew there had to be something else going on. Somebody keeping me back."

"Why can't you take *any* responsibility for yourself?!" She's shouting in his face now. "It isn't me or anyone else holding you back!"

Every customer and worker in Birria Basket is suddenly in on their business. Turned heads. A neck beard fumbling for his phone, sensing his viral moment in the spotlight by capturing someone else's outrage.

"Can you please calm down?" Simon asks in a low voice.

No. Kylie doesn't think she can. Simon's phone is on the counter beside him, MonoLife open. She glimpses his new profile photo, his asshole face in close-up, ridiculously oversized aviators covering much of it, his pursed mouth a sickening flatline.

Looks like the type of guy always angling to drop some conspiracy theories on you. He thinks *that's* a good look?

This is exactly what she's means. Zero self-awareness.

"I . . . I can't," she says, "I just can't," wondering how she ever could.

"This is so frustrating. I'm trying to talk to you."

"You don't get a say!" she shouts while thinking, *Fucking boomer*.

Simon barely reacts. Anger requires courage and this loser has none. He just turns to the window, internalizing everything. "You came to me," he says quietly. "I helped you when nobody else would."

"That's quite a take." She could go on, but what's the point? He won't learn. Can't change. And is twenty-seven years old. "Have a nice life, Simon."

"Where are you going?"

"I have to break down cardboard."

She storms back to her car, making sure to drive past the window so that the pathetic sack gets to watch her speed out of his life forever. Eat your heart out, @EndlessNights.

For a while, that works until a string of abusive texts hits like a downpour.

Simon:

> Pig.

> Backstabber.

> How could I be so wrong about you?

It's been a week since Kylie has seen any of Simon's content.

His last few posts were various liquor bottles on his kitchen table, each captioned **Cheers!** Largely ignored, as if anyone should be impressed by his ability to drink Knob Creek.

A couple more ProTips, each one more like a subtweet. Laughable messages about how he values loyalty and professionalism, as if Kylie owes him either.

But his last video, posted today, is what got his ass unfollowed. A week after Birria Basket comes this bleary-eyed testimonial, "Why I Hate @CrystalShips."

She wasn't going to watch it. Today is the first time in months she's gone half the day without cracking MonoLife at all. She's brainstorming her next post, wondering if there's any way to rig a scenario where one of her teachers is blinded by the hydrochloric acid she swiped out of the lab, but has become increasingly disheartened over the idea because she doesn't see how to get the drop on him. Still, it's a better thought than actually going to any of her classes. She's flunking them all and honestly can't bring herself to care.

Far more important is the need to decompress. She promised Mom she'd be productive by making a dent in all the cardboard she's currently drowning in. It never stops. Work before play. Just this once.

And because Mom has sent four texts threatening to bring all unopened boxes to Goodwill tomorrow if Kylie doesn't deal with them *toDAY*. This threat is enough to irritate the lump on Kylie's back, which, even after all the antibiotics, continues to radiate pain whenever she's outside MonoLife.

She spent the morning organizing her wardrobe into more pre-Crystal stacks that she plans on giving to charity, stopping after lunch to finally catch up on world events.

Which is when she saw the vid.

"Her real name's Kylie Bennington." Simon spells her last name out as if that's important, and his words are slurry enough to explain where the empty whiskey bottle behind him has gone. Cheers!

"Freshman at Summerfield Community College in Central Mass. SCC! Just outside of Boston. The kind of girl who . . ." He pauses, eyes sliding off camera. *"Well, she can talk the hind legs off a donkey, ya know?"*

Even his flattery's super fucking lame. And he looks disheveled. Messy hair slathered in grease. Thin stubble in sickly, uneven patches. *"Cut my heart out. Used me. Led me on, then shut me down. On to the next thing."*

It's staggering how deranged this is. His attempt to amass support by once more blaming somebody else for his failure. The only thing he's good at, turns out.

This garbage has very few comments. Kylie's curious to see if she has any defenders among them:

› **You can tell she's a whore, just look at her videos**
› **Leave her bro, she's crazy and gonna get herself killed**
› **You should punish her**

"Thanks, guys," she says, about to close out of the app, when someone else slides into her DMs:

@MissyMiss: collab?
@CrystalShips: uh no we're way past that
@MissyMiss: this would be more like a meeting
@MissyMiss: u inspire me, i've helped u
@MissyMiss: i came back for u . . . i'm here now
@CrystalShips: wtf does that mean???

Kylie stares at the screen, watching her question go unanswered. It's frightening to be chatting with a serial murderer. Scary, but exhilarating.

@MissyMiss is currently typing a message . . .
@MissyMiss: had to show you i was serious
@MissMiss: so that u wld help

@MissMiss: u ready to help?

@CrystalShips: meet first

@MissyMiss: u sure u want to? 🙁

@CrystalShips: fine, let's get it over with

@MissyMiss: k

@MissyMiss: ok

@MissyMiss: okayyyyyyy

Kylie has Katy's "This Is How We Do" on repeat, projecting herself inside a hot summer jam, briefly lost inside her nostalgia for a song that's somehow already more than ten years old. Back when Kylie was just a child. Before her world got split in half. She doesn't even remember the last time she talked to Dad, just that it's been weeks since that dropped call and he didn't get back to her like he said. Him losing her inside the T station. Hasn't once tried to call her back, has sent only a couple unfunny memes as a way of "staying connected."

Missy's decided that's enough conversation for now, so Kylie leaves one last message, **let's get it on the books**, then goes back to hacking down cardboard.

It's dark by the time she's finished. She checks Insta, where Erin is somehow the only person in her feed. No matter how far Kylie scrolls, hers is the only face there. Sometimes Cameron is too, because they're off together on this all-expenses-paid European vacation, and each of their photos has some landmark in the distant background that's always second fiddle. It's always *their* smiles front and center. The narcissism of thinking you're giving your people what they want because you've fooled yourself into believing you're an actual brand, more than a fleeting distraction as part of someone's endless scrolling. You ignore reality, that your followers are glad to "like" you from the toilet, or while they're in line at the grocery store. Who cares, right? So long as you can keep on lying to yourself about why you simply have to continue posting your face over and over and over and over. *This is for them, not me.*

Kylie's eyes glaze over. She has to put the phone down and center herself with a deep-breathing technique. Really scrape those lungs to calm her raging heart. It's total cope, she knows, and this enrages her even more.

She figures she could use some air. An evening drive in her new toy. She slips into the bone-white Chilliwack bomber from Canada Goose that arrived last week. The elastic Lycra of the waist and wrists protects her body from the windchill, while the water-resistant coating makes it ideal for rain and snowy environments. Perfect for New England. She hasn't yet decided if she in good conscience can recommend this coat to her followers on account of its cost, nearly one thousand dollars, but she's getting there.

There's a growl from out back as she walks to her car. A rustle in the quiet bushes. Kylie is fresh out of tuna steak and hurries to get behind the wheel, igniting the BMW's headlights and scanning the backyard for signs of ol' Sporto. All she sees is naked branches swaying in the early winter breeze.

Kylie drives downtown, mindful of the speed limit because cops are everywhere, can't have any trouble. Foot patrols on street corners. Cruisers prowling the outskirts. Neighborhood watches on every other street. Summerfield's on edge. Dead kids, zombie dogs, and murdered teachers. It's all coming apart. It's all MonoLife's fault.

Her phone's on Do Not Disturb, because she's already totaled one car, and almost died doing it, though it's difficult to refrain from checking the lock screen every few minutes. Each time her fingers creep toward it, she distracts herself by turning up Katy's "Last Friday Night," belting it out loud, and only marginally softer at traffic lights.

She treats herself to a sweet-cream cold brew at Starbucks, empowered by the freedom to get one whenever she wants, now that she's driving again. Thanks to this beautiful ride.

She cruises until the tank is nearly empty, savoring this newfound liberation, rolling into a gas station on the edge of town. The only full-service spot left in Summerfield because only plebs pump their own gas.

The clerk waves at her from the office, ambling out and crossing the pavement toward the passenger window as she puts it down.

"Fill it with regular, please."

He gives a military salute that's annoying, as if she's doing anything other than asking him to do his job.

She reaches for her phone as a small hatchback slows on the street, headlights off.

The pump jockey lands on the window frame with so much force that Kylie leaps. "Shit!"

"You look familiar," he's saying.

"No, I don't."

"Yeah, you do. You anybody famous?" His face twists into a manifestation of that question as he leans farther in, as if entitled to an answer.

"I'm just a customer."

He pulls back, *yeah, that's right*, slapping the frame in apology. "Gonna bother me all night."

"Loser," Kylie whispers, craning her neck, watching that darkened vehicle roll up onto the station pavement.

"Gonna go inside and get the card reader!" the pump jockey is shouting. "Back in two shakes!"

"How do you know I . . ." she starts, but he's already disappeared inside the office. ". . . need a card reader?"

Her rearview mirror glows as a pair of headlights click on behind her. A mass of shifting light moves through the BMW's interior. The hatchback sitting right on her bumper, idling.

The light shifts, then blots.

"Kylie Bennington?" The question's muffled. Whoever's asking it is standing right outside her window.

Kylie pulls the duck-down hood over her head, closing off her peripheral vision. No fans tonight, please.

"Kylie Bennington?" the voice repeats, slower and clearer. The door's jiggling now. A man outside, pulling at the handle, slapping the glass. "Kylie Bennington?!"

She screams at the sound of her own name being filtered through a madman's voice.

"Hey!" the pump jockey is shouting from somewhere.

The other man becomes a shadow crossing the front of her car, vanishing between the headlights.

Kylie's head swivels, following as he walks around the BMW to where Pump Jockey stands.

"You better step back, pal, or I—" Pump Jockey's voice becomes a groan, and a volley of blood catapults through the open window, splattering Kylie's thousand-dollar Canada Goose. She's impressed with her broken brain's ability to mourn the coat amid this carnage.

Pump Jockey tumbles back, wide-eyed and with a butcher knife jutting from his neck, hilt wobbling like a plank.

"Kylie Bennington." It comes again now as more of a command, drowning out Pump Jockey's final disbelieving gargles.

A hand shoots through the window, closing around a clump of Kylie's red hair. It yanks her toward the pink face mask framed there, hard-shelled and featureless, save for two squinting eyes.

Kylie's phone buzzes from somewhere, taunting her.

She squeals, slapping at the face.

He manages to wrangle her out of the car, up to her torso, wrapping his elbow around her neck and pulling her the rest of the way.

Kylie drops to the ground, gravity freeing her from the killer's grip.

Pump Jockey's wheezing body breaks her fall. She reaches for the blade and pulls it from his neck with a slurp.

"Kylie Bennington," the muffled voice says again as a boot heel kicks her hand, sends the knife flying.

She rolls onto her stomach, whimpering, scurrying to her feet, working into a sprint, straight for the office just a few feet away.

Behind her, heavy footfalls.

She slams the door in the killer's face, but he doesn't miss a moment, winding his fist back, punching through.

Kylie pushes her face into her elbow, shielding herself from the torrential glass storm. The killer's hand reaches in and twists the lock. Kylie leaps back at the sound of a *click*.

She's got seconds here. Time enough to reach for the small metal brick dangling off the chain, using it to smash emergency glass.

Crash.

Then she's tearing the fire axe off its cradle as the killer pulls the door wide.

"Kylie Be—"

The axe crashes down, cleaving through the hard-shell plastic, obliterating one of those wide eyes.

He stumbles back, dropping to his ass, blood already pooling around him.

His one remaining eye forever wide, staring in disbelief.

In the distance, Kylie's phone continues to ding, MonoLife beckoning. She catches her reflection in the window, her Canada Goose jacket shredded and blood-caked.

Then she's wobbling and the world's spinning and she's trying to say something but it's no use.

Her eyes roll back and it's like someone has yelled *Timber!* because here she's toppling over like a tree, losing consciousness just as she smashes to the ground.

The last thing she thinks before the world goes dark is, *I only checked MonoLife once today.*

Less Than Nothing

"You up?" Agent Claire Jasinski leans against the door, sipping coffee through an orange straw.

Kylie elevates the hospital bed into a sitting position. The monitoring equipment around her beeps and the smell in here is vaguely menthol.

Claire closes the door and pulls a chair across the room. Drops a curled Dunkin' bag on top of the bedsheet.

"Free-doughnut day." She shrugs. "Happy holidays."

"The one with the big Christmas tree sprinkles?"

Claire nods and Kylie's thinking about opening the bag. How Dad used to bring one of these home after third shift. She remembers picking each sprinkle off, eating one at a time to savor the treat.

"You're smiling," Claire says.

The memory dissipates like morning mist, and what remains is pain. Kylie wondering for the second time in as many days, *What happened to my life?*

"It's nice to see," Claire says. Her short blonde hair has a golden sheen most models would kill for. And those fucking eyebrows. Like single quotation marks, back swoops making her seem permanently curious.

"Thanks," Kylie says, her voice a rusty croak. She hasn't spoken in . . . "Wait. What time is it?"

"You haven't been honest with me, Kylie."

Beside her, the machine registers this agitation. She slaps her palms down on the bedsheets, fingers crawling the swivel tray beside her. "Where is it?" she says, slow at first, words rediscovering their shape as panic spreads like fire. "Where's my phone?"

Claire takes a dispassionately long sip of coffee, something like amusement rippling through her features. "You know, I ran into your mom downstairs. She's as confused as everyone else in this town—"

"*Where?!*" Kylie screams. "*Where?! Where?!*" She tears the sheets away, swiveling her legs from the mattress so they're dangling over the floor.

"Whoa! Hang on."

"*What time is it?!*"

"Calm down."

Easier said than done. Kylie remembers the masked stranger pronouncing her name as a question. How his one good eye stared up in disbelief at death. Her phone ringing in the distance like a siren, warning her that she was in danger of losing everything.

Claire presses a hand to Kylie's breastbone. Shoves her down. "Relax."

"Claire, I need my phone. Please—"

"And I need answers. Who's got the upper hand?"

Kylie grabs Claire's wrist, fingers locking like a wrench. "What time is it? You goddamn bitch!"

Claire tears herself free, gracelessly tumbling back. "Eleven thirty. A little after. Jesus. Now lay *down*."

Kylie looks out the window. The bone-white moon floats just over the tops of pointed pine trees.

Okay, I've got half an hour.

"The guy you killed—"

"He tried to kill me!"

"I know," Claire says. Another deep breath. "Eddie Morrison. Forty-six years old. Lives in Laconia, New Hampshire. Know him?"

"No." But this response is an afterthought. Kylie becoming more animated again as panic resumes. "Just tell me where my phone is. I need—"

"A fix? Fuck off, junkie. How's that? You don't seem to understand the trouble you're in. Worry less about your phone, more about making me happy."

"But where is it?! Please!"

Claire turns toward the bathroom door, which is open and dim, pee-colored light glowing beyond it. "In there, with your clothes."

Kylie guesses the Canada Goose bomber did not survive the gas station incident and feels that loss in her stomach, suspending her panic long enough to wonder how she goes about getting MonoLife to send another one.

"Are you sure you didn't know Eddie Morrison?" Claire asks.

Kylie laughs at the absurdity of that question.

"He's got photos of you all over his apartment. You don't want to know."

"Gross."

"If you don't know him—"

"You're the cop."

"Close enough." Claire rolls up the sleeves on her purple thermal as Kylie admires her dark jeans and high boots. The agent looks back at the bathroom, holds her gaze there. "Do you know what it is I'm doing here . . . what it is I'm investigating?"

"What time is it now?"

Slow, searching silence, the agent fighting a sadistic smile as she watches Kylie squirm and then, "Eleven forty-two."

Shit. It must've been more than *a little after* eleven thirty, then. She's running out of time. "Can I just get my phone?"

"Why? You wanna show me something?"

Kylie grimaces, panic overriding her poker face. There's more than one way to mess this up.

"I'll be honest with you, Kylie. If you're honest with me."

Kylie sighs, reaches for the Dunkin' bag. Picks two tree-shaped sprinkles off the green wreath frosting and pops them into her mouth. "Fine." Anything to get her out of here in the next fifteen minutes.

"What is it about you?"

Kylie shrugs.

"Local PD has concluded you were in the wrong place at the wrong time. They think this because Eddie Morrison has a jacket that goes all the way back to the nineties. Bad guy. We'll leave it there. The police figure he drove down here to rob that gas station."

"But his apartment—"

Claire smirks. "The bureau hasn't shared those details with anyone except you, so local law enforcement doesn't know. Eddie Morrison was targeting you. And that doesn't surprise me, because when I take a holistic view of Summerfield, Massachusetts, you just so happen to be at the center of almost everything."

"And yet I keep to myself."

"Your neighbor's dog is slaughtered on your lawn. That same neighbor gets her throat torn out by a wild animal two months later. A local sex offender who lost his job for stealing girls' underwear, yours among them, blows his brains out. You beat a classmate within an inch of her life and she later burns to death in a freak hospital accident. *This* hospital. A classmate drowns in a lake, one of your teachers is murdered, and now . . . another of your friends goes missing. What gives?"

"Please. What time is it?"

"Time to fess up."

Kylie stirs, pushes the doughnut aside, and starts to sit. Claire steps toward the bed, bracing to do something drastic if that's what it takes to keep Kylie in place. They watch each other for a moment, Kylie beginning to wonder how far she's willing to go here should Claire decide to be unreasonable. She gives her immediate surroundings a casual scan, searching for any kind of weapon in case things get out of hand. Can she take this bitch in a fight if that's what it comes to?

"Kylie, I'm on your side."

"Only if you give me the time."

"Eleven forty-seven. Now *talk*."

How is Kylie supposed to focus when Mister Strangles will be coming for her? She imagines that emaciated silhouette beginning to prowl hospital corridors, moving beneath flickering sodium glow, and can barely find the words to ask, "D-did you say someone's missing?"

A wrinkle passes over Claire's forehead, indicating surprise that Kylie genuinely doesn't seem to know. "Benjamin Austin."

"Ohhh . . . oh. You've got to be kidding."

"A few nights ago. Took a drive and never came back. Like the Springsteen song."

Whoever the fuck that is, Kylie thinks, wondering if Melissa went out and finished the job she'd threatened, offering to clip Ben during his hospital stay.

"So there you go. I was honest. I only want the same courtesy, Kylie."

"What's the time?"

Flat, almost seething: "Eleven fifty."

"Can I get my phone now?"

"Sure. Let's look at your phone together." The agent grins.

"No. And I didn't kill the dog." She would happily give up Duc to the feds, but the punishment for spilling on MonoLife is too severe. No kind of option.

"But you did the other things?"

"You think I murdered Mr. Davies?"

"We've got you at his house the night he died. Lyft records. Three neighbors saw the two of you leaving . . . except two of those neighbors also saw him return alone. And it just so happens that *I've* got you at your house during his time of death. So . . . no, I don't think you killed him but—"

"I already told you about Brandi. Self-defense. Crazy bitch thought I was fucking her boyfriend—"

"Asher Morris."

"Very good, Detective."

"Agent."

"Whatever. I kicked her ass, yeah, after she tried to run me over. You said yourself her death was a freak accident. And as for Ben . . .

I haven't spoken to him since October. We're not friends." Kylie tears a monitoring patch off her arm, arranges herself so that her feet are dangling off the bed, about to hop down.

Claire steps against Kylie's knees, turning this into a confrontation. "Your fellow students say otherwise."

"Then I guess you get to choose who to believe. As for the guy at the gas station . . ." Kylie pauses, remembering. She forces a shiver that's mostly for the agent's benefit. The best she can do, she realizes, because she's actually taken a life tonight and feels less-than-nothing for having done so.

"Take your time," Claire says.

"No idea why he wanted to kill me."

Claire slips a glossy 8x10 from her folder, places it in Kylie's lap.

It's grainy, but she recognizes it. A screenshot of her bedroom. You can even see Katy looking down from the wall, frowning over the sight of Mr. Davies's bare ass between Kylie's spread legs.

"What's this?"

"You post enough on Instagram for me to recognize your bedroom."

"That's not Eddie Morrison."

"Then who is it?" Claire asks, looking more sour now.

"Does it matter?"

"Well . . . I'm trying to figure out where Eddie got this footage, that's all."

Kylie performatively studies it. "Me too."

"If you're in any kind of trouble, Kylie . . . I can help. I get it. I make you nervous. The feds, right here, breathing down your neck, threatening to take away all those nice things. Your new car, for instance . . ."

Now it's Kylie's poker face cracking a little. Some distant part of her that would love to confess, get out from under the weight of everything she's done.

And undo all your hard work? Go back to being nothing, nobody? What's the matter with you?

She hops off the bed and Claire steps back, isn't standing in her way anymore, allowing Kylie to wobble toward the bathroom. She rushes for it as her mind searches for excuses. "I think I'm going to be sick."

"The app will do that," Claire says, gauntlet thrown.

Kylie keeps walking, doesn't have the strength to stuff her flailing expressions back behind her collected exterior.

"I'm no mind reader, Kylie, but I know you're asking yourself how in the hell this all happened. You never thought it would go this far. Thing is, it always goes further than you want."

From the bathroom, Katy's "Chained to the Rhythm" spins up. Kylie's ringtone. Someone calling. "A man I don't know and never met tried to kill me tonight. I can't help you any more than that."

"Can't? Or won't?"

"Take your pick."

"Very different answers." Claire looks toward the bathroom, where the cell phone continues to ring. "Katy Perry, huh?" She starts for the exit, adding over her shoulder, "More of a Taylor Swift girl myself."

"Of course you are."

Kylie breaks into a rusty sprint. She's never been a religious person but she's mumbling "PleaseGodPleaseGodPleaseGod" with her hand outstretched, pulling the bathroom door wide, squinting against the glow.

She swats her clothes away. Her phone goes sliding into the sink, where her fingers struggle to grab it.

The on-screen clock turns 11:59.

"Oh God. No."

Kylie thumb-stomps her passcode because facial recognition can never be trusted in a pinch.

"*Kylie?*" It's Mom. Shit! She's accidentally answered. "*Do you want one of these tuna sandwiches from the cafeteria?*"

"*Goddammit!*" Kylie shrieks, ignoring the question, smashing the MonoLife icon. The app takes longer to load because the battery life is nearly shot. Ten percent and dropping.

Eight.

Six in the blink of an eye.

It opens to her feed. She starts scrolling, dolling out indiscriminate fist bumps so there's a record of her checking in while the clock is still in play.

"Kylie, you there?"

Kylie doesn't answer, minimizing the app as the phone clock switches from 11:59 to 12:00.

Relief washes over her in an all-consuming wave. That was way too close. She turns back, about to try to save face with Agent Claire, but the room is empty.

And Kylie has to steady herself against the sink to prevent herself from fainting for the second time today.

Haters

@CrystalShips: did you kill ben?
@MissyMiss: no
@CrystalShips: just davies???
@MissyMiss: just for you ☺
@CrystalShips: so you keep saying
@MissyMiss: tell you about it tomorrow night

Kylie sits up in bed—*what?*—with a wince, her bruises reigniting. For once, things with Missy are moving fast.

@MissyMiss: check ur map there's a pin. see you at ten.

"Shit," she hisses. Terrible timing. The BMW is with an upholstery shop downtown because she wasn't going to clean Pump Jockey's blood herself. But now she'll have to call and demand they rush it back to her, which they won't want to do, so she'll have to pull an Erin and threaten to rake their reputation over social media coals to get what she needs here. It's unpleasant, but it'll work. Probably.

Claire is nowhere to be found today. Kylie likes it when the agent is parked in front of her house, as it's an added layer of security. Claire could've easily taken Kylie's phone at the hospital but knew better than to bother. Must already know that MonoLife has fail-safes to prevent that sort of thing from working.

Which means she's content to sit back and watch Kylie do her thing.

So many boxes have arrived today that the hallway outside her room is nearly impassable. There's not much she can do about that, given her soreness. Mom left a threatening note on the kitchen counter warning her to get rid of it all, dotted with two exclamation points to show she's serious. But she's also grateful that Kylie is still alive and Kylie figures she can use that to buy herself another day or two.

Kylie takes thirty-seven selfies of her battered face from every conceivable angle, posts the best one with the caption **Still Here**, then adds her $cashtag.

She's fielding donations within seconds, goddamn simps sending them in with *get well soon* notes.

It doesn't help.

She needs Simon to feel like the loser he is. It's no longer enough to live well and forget.

@CrystalShips: you doxed me

@EndlessNights: You deserve it.

@CrystalShips: moving on never occurred to you?

@EndlessNights: Naw. You spat in my face, Tits.

@CrystalShips: cuz I rejected you

@EndlessNights: You never gave me a chance. Used me, then moved on. Frustrating.

@CrystalShips: i could dox you back but who'd care?

@EndlessNights: Probably won't be the last time someone tries to kill you.

@CrystalShips: can't even do it yourself

@EndlessNights: That's the thing about you, Kylie, you never were very bright. That red X? It's more than a checkmark. It's a target. Kill one, get yours.

"What . . . ?" Kylie reads that over and over, wishing she didn't believe him, Simon stunning her into digital silence.

Of course. It makes perfect sense. MonoLife gives you a red X once your profile gets enough heat . . . and to others, it's an opportunity to take a shortcut. A way to level the playing field.

It's also incentive to level up again before someone can kill you and claim your X. Like the guy at the gas station. Sick and twisted shit, like everything else on this app.

How could I have missed this?

> **@EndlessNights:** Hey, look at that. I know something that Kylie doesn't. Almost like you should've listened to me.
> **@CrystalShips:** have a nice life asshole

Kylie smashes the block button. It's so empowering she considers unblocking him just so she can do it again.

She flips over to Instagram, where Erin has finally given her last post a heart.

Kylie stretches out in bed, listening to Katy's "Peacock," a naughty track about how much Katy is just dying to see her boyfriend's cock, which is ironic given that she can't stop thinking about how much she hates men.

Her phone buzzes. A text this time, because Simon's ass is otherwise blocked.

> **Simon:**
> See ya around.

She goes into the information screen on Simon's number and selects BLOCK CALLER. Then smiles, finding comfort in the fact that she's somebody. That she's living rent-free in this loser's head.

Because without haters, you're no one.

Reunion

The BMW is back the next day, dropped off by a guy from the upholstery place. Being a squeaky wheel paid off. It also spares Kylie the unpleasant task of having to dose Mom unconscious in order to borrow her car without explanation.

She sets out to meet Missy a little after nine, delighted by just how deeply the interior has been cleaned. *Good as new*, she thinks right before clocking an errant splatter mark above her visor. She makes a mental note to call the upholsterer back tomorrow in order to complain about the rush job.

The car winds through the outskirts of Summerfield and it's a little past nine thirty, speeding by all those new-money turnoffs and the prissy private academy whose kids have so much money they refuse to mix with the gen pop of town.

Yellow dividing lines zip by so fast they register as one solid and unbroken one. Kylie hasn't seen another car in fifteen minutes. The cell phone on her dash displays a solid blue line headed straight for Melissa's pin.

Destination, the middle of nowhere.

"*Turn right onto Skyview Road*," the GPS commands, setting her on a stitch of pavement that slices through the heart of a cornfield, husks seemingly hell-bent on reclaiming the road, leaning toward the pavement, slapping gently against the BMW as the pin gets closer.

Kylie pulls over, gets out. The large flashlight in her hand finds a path of tamped husks, dead or on their way to dying.

If Melissa has to hide, this place makes sense. Part of the world that has forgotten about itself.

An old scarecrow lords over the cornfield, a stitched grin and button eyes that watch her, no matter which way the path twists.

An ancient farm stand sits in silhouette beneath the yellow moon, a collapsed roof in shambles around its perimeter, creating a minefield of detritus Kylie has to navigate. At the end of it, a human shape sits with elbows on a creaking table.

"Finally." The voice is kind of familiar. Partly Melissa's, partly not. Wrong, somehow. Hollow and atonal.

Kylie sweeps the beam toward her and who she supposes is Melissa lifts a forearm, shielding herself from the light with an outstretched hand. Around her is a scattering of rusted farm equipment, old scythes and pitchforks, their very presence in this moment more than a little threatening.

"It is me," Melissa says, as if intuiting Kylie's doubt. Her former classmate wears a Ferrari motorcycle jacket, full-grain Italian leather, buckles all the way up the chest, zipper tight, pulled to the neck. A pair of Milano rib joggers on her legs, understated lines and contrast inserts down the side.

She's not dressed warm enough for this part of the world, at this time of year, but she isn't shivering either.

"What are we doing out here?"

"Sitting beneath the open sky, Crystal."

"It's Kylie."

"It will be Crystal soon. Sit."

Kylie does, noting the voice again. Not quite Melissa. She looks whiter than a sheet beneath all this natural moonglow. Her formerly vibrant blue eyes have become unexpressive pools of tepid rainwater.

To look at her makes Kylie feel uneasy. Melissa's sharp posture, hands folded like an attentive student. Nothing casual or comfortable about it. Almost unnatural. "How did you kill Mr. Davies?"

Melissa smiles. A humorless gesture. "I can do anything now."

"What does that mean?"

"It means, now that I am . . ." Her mouth smacks as she takes a second to reshuffle her thoughts. ". . . Moments."

No, this is definitely not Melissa. This is someone's approximation of her, a thing conjured from social media snapshots. If MonoLife has shown Kylie anything, it's that the unexplainable has become a way of life. She's accepted that anything is possible now, her own mind having been broken into fragments, reality growing more meaningless with each new follower.

"Why did you kill Annabeth? How did this start?"

"It was the only way to go higher."

"There are people trying to kill me."

"You expect to stand on this peak without other climbers looking to push you off?"

"Okay," Kylie says. "Why am I here?" She's tempted to add, *by myself in the middle of nowhere.*

Melissa looks off into the night at the swaying cornstalks dancing around them. "I am allowed to say this." A statement that sounds as though she's requesting permission from some invisible spectator.

"If you can do anything? And those are your words, why not just deal with Duc yourself?"

Melissa pulls back her hand and opens her palm, wiggles her fingers as if the ability to do so is new. "There are limitations."

"Such as?"

"Have you seen him?"

"Duc? No, not lately."

He's dropped off the grid. Kylie thinks back to the lake. Of that thing putting its fist through Duc's roof. His last words echoing: *I wanted you to see this so you understand what I'm about to do.*

What he did was go after Deacon. She can only guess as to his reasons why. Might've been for answers, though what he really did was prevent anyone else in town from getting MonoLife on their phone. That last post setting him on the trail of something called the sunken church, whatever that is.

Why does it even matter?

"He has violated the agreement," Melissa says. "Trying to tear the curtain down."

"You work for the company?"

"We all work for the company, Crystal. We *are* the company. But he was once my partner too. Therefore, my responsibility."

"They're making you clean up after him."

"In a way."

"What happens if you don't?"

Melissa smiles, but only for a second, mostly to mask something worse. A hint of anguish behind her eyes, moving down to her mouth, becoming a nervous twitch. "Non . . . existence."

"Okay, um . . . well, I don't know what you're expecting, but I don't think Duc wants to hear from me."

"You are the only one he will hear."

"What am I supposed to do? Lure him out here?"

"Type a message into our thread when you have found him."

"Just not sure I need to get involved."

"Oh, you must. And believe me, you will be rewarded." Melissa's smile widens. It's difficult to parse whether this is sincere or sinister.

"You killed your best friend for clout," Kylie says in a way that intones Melissa is far beyond trust.

"And that is why I have worked hard to earn your loyalty."

"Annabeth didn't have your loyalty?"

To this, Melissa shrugs. "Friendships bloom. They wither. Your one life becomes more important than any of theirs."

She might as well be talking about Erin. The cornstalks rustle against the breeze, giggling at the implication. "Do you regret it?" Kylie asks.

"You will see me one more time, Crystal. After that . . ."

"So what now?"

Melissa has nothing more to add, sits in silence, swaying with the stalks. Her body remains present, though her mind has vacated. Kylie slowly stands, genuinely unnerved by her company, what now resembles some kind of living doll. Melissa's eyes are frozen wide, unfocused and unblinking.

Kylie hurries back over the dead corn. Before she's about to wind around the bend, she takes one last look at the farm stand.

Both chairs are empty, moonlight reflecting off rust.

Her phone dings in her hand. Kylie glances down.

@MissyMiss sent you a direct message.

She opens MonoLife, reads it.

@MissyMiss: I regret everything.

Friends

D uc doesn't take the bait, even when Kylie messages him to say she's
finally found what he's been looking for.

@CrystalShips: that bitch is all tee'd up

He drops a new video sometime that night, and Kylie doesn't see
it until she wakes up the next morning.

Duc, sitting on a crumbling rock wall, clouds daubed across the sky
like he's living in some expressionistic painting. It's so cold there that
his breath's a perpetual ghost.

"*Sunken church*," he says harshly, pausing to accommodate a gust of
wind that saps his voice, as if the forces behind MonoLife are determined
to force his silence. "*Took a minute to figure this out. Late nights in libraries
up and down this shitty state, and I've got a doctorate in Puritanism now.
Puritanism. Me. I'm fucking Laotian.*"

He jumps down off the wall and gestures for the camera to follow,
moving through a forest of bare trees, snaking around each dark silhouette, branches swaying like outstretched fingers waiting to snatch them.

"*Pilgrims built this place five hundred years ago,*" Duc says. "*Too close
to water, dummies, which means it sank halfway into the earth long before
we got here.*"

He steps out of frame to reveal an old stone building submerged on
a riverbank. The foundation swallowed whole. All that's aboveground

anymore is a short steeple rising out of the muck, desperately clinging to existence.

"*In here,*" Duc says, hunching beneath the steeple's unobscured window, sneakers slurping as he moves across the muddy ground where an old man is curled into a fetal position, moaning into the sludge, making it bubble and pop. He's slathered in so much blood that it's impossible to tell where his injuries begin.

"*Say hi, Father Julian,*" Duc growls, his words sounding as violent as whatever happened here. "*Since the good man of the cloth is feeling camera-shy, how about I tell you all what he told me?*"

The camera pushes in on the priest as Duc uses his own cell phone to light the scene. The blood trickling from the man's gashed head isn't crimson at all, but rather thin and oily. And the walls around them inside this confined space are scrawled with symbols Kylie doesn't recognize.

"*Sorry to tell you all,*" Duc says. "*This app was never about expression or content. It's all about feeding* these *fuckin' things.*"

His foot swings against the priest's ribs like a hammer, and the sound from the old man is inhuman, closer to a rodent's screech.

"*You know what I'm talking about,*" Duc snaps. "*The things that come and attach themselves to your soul the minute you get your X? They're parasites, feasting off all the negative energy you put into this world.*"

The priest mumbles something and Duc slaps him hard. "*Shut the fuck up, Julian!*" He forces a grin at the camera to prove everything's under control. "*I keep waiting for MonoLife to shut my account down, ya know? I'm impressed they're letting it ride as I'm spilling its secrets. Think Zuckerberg would allow this?*"

Duc gets the priest onto his knees and wraps an elbow around his throat, flexing his forearm against the old man's Adam's apple. Bloodshot eyes begin to pop, that jet-black goop oozing through his tear ducts, streaking his cheeks. A gray tongue slithering past his lips, forming a permanent raspberry. Then he's gone, just a husk dangling lifelessly in Duc's arms.

Duc stands back, the body plopping into the mud. "*I can kill them all now. And I'm going to show you how to do it. So stay tuned. Oh, and don't forget to follow and share. Let's get this shit trending."*

Hard cut, and he's gone.

Most of the comments seem tired of this guy's **fake horror movie shit.**

Kylie sends him a few more messages, asking to meet. Asking him to share what he knows. He ignores them all.

She passes the time by producing content. Posting her $cashtag and watching her bank account grow by thousands of dollars.

It really is that easy. People profess their love, promise to do anything for her. Kylie tests that.

Asks a man to send his wife's wedding ring to a PO box a few towns over. While waiting for it to arrive, she asks for a thousand bucks. He sends that immediately. All he wants in return is a pair of her dirty underwear. Whatever. She stuffs one inside an envelope. Done.

Kylie looks over her shoulder wherever she goes. It's been a few days since learning she's got a perpetual target on her back and strangers feel sinister now, everyone on the verge of coming for her red X. She's always braced for confrontations that never come. While picking up Chinese takeout, a guy in cowboy boots follows her into the parking lot, leering from the curb. She's about to roll up and broadcast him to the world, when he lights a cigarette.

She sells more worn clothing to her simps. Her inbox is flooded with adoring fans. She appreciates them, even though she can't respond to each message. Then here comes the messages about how she isn't responding to her messages.

And the boxes keep on coming too. She opens them on the spot, deciding what she wants, dropping off the rest at the Salvation Army dumpster.

Mom is in the driveway when she returns from one such trip, pacing, springing the question as soon as Kylie shifts into park. "Are you making porn?!"

"What? No!" In Kylie's mind, she adds, *Not as far as you know.*

"My house looks like a goddamn Burlington Coat Factory, Kylie!"

"No—you can't get that stuff at a Burlington."

"I-I don't believe this. Do you even hear yourself?!"

"I'm not the one shouting."

"You're not in class either. Don't think I haven't noticed."

"Mother of the Year."

"That is *not* fair."

"Whatever—I'm thinking about moving out anyway."

"*Moving out . . . ?* Honey, that's . . . that's not what I'm saying."

"Then what are you saying? Because I don't have time for this."

"I'm paying for your school, okay? I deserve the truth."

"You *have* the truth. You just can't believe I'm making something of myself."

"*Where?! Doing what?!* Ohhh . . . uh-uh, that's what I thought. You always go quiet there, don't you? '*Trust me, Mom.*' Trust that this new car appeared out of thin air one day. Trust you telling me that I should be proud and supportive when absolutely nothing adds up. None of this passes the smell test, Kylie."

"Aren't you going to be late for work?" Kylie slams the car door, leaving Mom in front of the BMW with her hands on her hips. Good. Who cares. Let her stand there all afternoon if she wants. Kylie has to get back to MonoLife.

There's a ceiling to everything she produces. Her best videos get a hundred thousand fist bumps, though the average is probably between fifty and sixty thousand, but more if she's in a bikini or some type of revealing underwear.

She swaps messages with @PurpleLipGloss, who invites her to hang out the next time she's on the West Coast.

Kylie asks if they'll be seeing each other at the big MonoLife summit.

@PurpleLipGloss: you know about that????

@CrystalShips: got a message from ML telling me

@PurpleLipGloss: omg huge

@CrystalShips: how do I know if I qualify?

@PurpleLipGloss: we haven't been told where it is yet, so there's
   still time

@CrystalShips: am I all set? Am I in?

@PurpleLipGloss: idk I hope so . . . I wanna hang

@PurpleLipGloss: keep me posted . . . k?

Kylie posts a video of her morning workout routine. Ab day. She gets sweaty in a little neon leotard and posts her Cash App link in the video description. Makes nine hundred bucks in twenty-six minutes.

For some reason, she's still supposed to want to pass her first and probably only semester of college. Her teachers have sent emails warning how dangerously close Kylie is to failing. She deletes the messages. Fuck them too.

Erin's back in town, but since Kylie barely goes to school these days, she hasn't seen her. Drives over to her place one afternoon, braced for an earful of humblebrags but also begrudgingly curious to hear about Europe.

Erin's out back, sitting on the porch steps overlooking the covered pool, her North Face shielding her from the winter chill while her raven-black hair dances across sullen features.

"How was the trip?"

"Perfect." Erin is unable to scrub the sadness from her voice. "Until I got home and found out my dad wants me out of here . . ."

"What? Why?"

"He says I'm 'being unrealistic' with my goals, that if I want to waste my life, fine, but he's not going to subsidize it. I think he's just jealous no one's sending *his* ass to Europe."

"Can I sit?" Kylie asks.

"Sure." Erin smiles, depression all over her face. "He's had it out for me since I decided to take the community college route. Like everyone is supposed to go into debt to earn some dumb-ass four-year degree just because . . ."

Kylie drops beside her and pulls her knees to her chest. She's never missed her Canada Goose Chilliwack more. "So . . . move out. Maybe I will too. We can get a place, kind of an East Coast Hype House."

Erin laughs. A suggestion too ridiculous to entertain with any other response.

"You never called me," Kylie says. "I was in the hospital."

"I didn't mean to be so elusive, I just . . ." Erin trails off and sits with the silence.

Mrs. Palmer brings out two mugs of hot chocolate topped with so many marshmallows that the ceramic is bleeding melted sugar.

"Yeah, I'm sorry—I should've called," Erin says, closing her eyes and whispering, "I'm such a bitch."

Kylie doesn't see a point in contesting that thought.

"A bad friend," Erin adds. "Cameron's dad called to tell us what happened to you while we were over there. I flipped my shit, Ky, I swear. But he said you were fine . . . And that the feds are all over you?"

"Just the one. Claire. But yes, they're looking into MonoLife and . . . I don't think they know how to find it."

"You've been really lucky."

"Luck's been good."

"Luck runs out, Ky. Just like time."

"What's that supposed to mean?"

Erin swipes a finger across the marshmallow float, stuffing a dollop inside her mouth. She closes her eyes, moans. "Oh God, this is so good. Why can't I be happy putting on thirty pounds and living in sweat-pants?"

"We're not that smart."

"Remember, we used to make s'mores in the microwave and you always cooked yours too long?" Erin snorts at the memory. "The marsh-mallow would explode?"

A genuine laugh from both, softening the mood.

"Your dad still hates me for that," Kylie says.

"He does not."

"You've spent ten years trying to convince me otherwise, but the look on his face each time he'd find scorched marshmallow on his microwave ceiling . . . pure hatred."

They laugh even harder, the tension temporarily broken. "When did it all get so complicated for us?"

Kylie wiggles her phone.

"Shit." Erin sighs, not wanting to go down that road, but headed there anyway. "You can take a bow for that."

"Excuse me—you tried to blackmail me into helping you. Instead of just asking."

"That's the problem, Ky. I don't . . . recognize myself anymore."

"So . . . what? You're giving up the influencer life?"

"Maybe we both should? I mean, what's driving you at this point?"

Kylie thinks about that, closes her eyes and tries to imagine the future. Any future. Commuting. Renting. Never having enough money for owning. Cube farms and time-off requests. The lie of strategic goals. Sweatpants after work. Washing dishes. Nightly vacuuming, a slow march into an anonymous grave. She looks at Erin on the edge of her seat, waiting for an answer. "There is . . . nowhere . . . else to go."

"Aha. I know an addict when I see one."

"Look, we got our wires crossed. It happens. Why can't we just start over?"

"Because that night at the cabin was like . . . I don't know, being visited by the Ghost of Christmas Future."

Kylie takes a sip of hot chocolate. Not because she wants it, but because it's something to do.

"I saw myself on Christmas morning," Erin says. "Twelve million followers later, living in some beachfront California apartment. Alone. Worked so hard to get there that I alienated everyone in my life to do it."

"The way I acted at the cabin, it was shitty."

Erin places her mug down, takes Kylie's and does the same. Then she takes Kylie's hands in hers so their eyes are locked.

Don't look desperate, Kylie thinks, biting the inside of her cheek to stay cool under Erin's scrutiny, certain that her oldest friend has no choice but to admit how far she's come.

"My head was a mess after that. Europe was perfect timing, even though I was surrounded by people I no longer had anything in common with."

"If you quit, your dad wins."

"I'm *not* quitting. Cameron and I are transferring to BU next fall—"

"*What?*"

"Yeah, a change of pace."

"Nooo. No way."

Erin can't help or hide the tiny grin tucked into the corners of her mouth. "The trip did us a lot of good. We realized what's important. And so we're planning our future accordingly."

Kylie feels a surge of anger at this from-left-field revelation, a half dozen impulses she'd love to act on flashing through her mind. "And . . . where do I fit into that future? I mean, what if *I* need you?"

"You don't." It sounds a lot like, *You'd better not.*

"You can't read minds, so—"

"Fine. I guess I should say I hope that you don't. Because you've made it real clear to me, Ky, you prefer doing things your own way."

"I'm not trying to stir things up. I just . . . I still need you in my life. I mean, you can't leave me alone. We've been around each other for so long I don't even . . . I need to get back on ErinTime."

"Kylie . . ."

"What? I messed up. And if you say you're officially beginning your forever life with Cameron, then whatever, you know? I accept that. But if you're saying we can't be friends at all . . ."

Erin touches Kylie's face, searching her eyes while frozen fingertips sting her cheekbone. Pain being preferable to numbness. "You have the better car now," she says, tiredly. "So . . . KylieTime?"

Kylie claps excitedly, wants to tell Erin how she almost made the same exact joke, but figures it's best to play it cool. "You want a ride, just say when."

"When."

"Well, then, come get into my car, bitch."

"Funny. But my asshole dad will be home soon, so time to get lost." They rise and Erin walks her through the house, out front where Kylie has a few presents to give her. Some of the fanciest swag boxes she doesn't want, including an eighty-dollar bottle of Byredo Gypsy Water body wash, a playful lather that contains notes of bergamot, lemon, black pepper, and juniper berries that Kylie finds do not accommodate her aesthetic.

"Are you serious?" Erin seems touched by the gesture, tsking her tongue. "These are amazing."

"Nothing's too good for you."

Erin takes a step back toward the house, shaking her head, laughing. "Boy, you really are sorry."

Kylie's actually glad to catch such a passive-aggressive barb. *Better the Erin you know.* She gets into her car and smiles, ignoring the fact that her oldest friend has never once been so generous in return. Never once given her anything.

And that really has to change.

@MisterStrangles sent you a direct message.

It's the last thing Kylie wants to see as she stirs a few fresh blueberries into a plain Greek yogurt.

The icon directly above the video message is an antenna, meaning he's broadcasting this—just to her.

On video, jet-black hair that Kylie can pick out of a lineup. The glow from Erin's phone clipped to her dashboard mount.

"So, she's not crazy?" Cameron's voice crackles through the phone speaker.

"I don't know how to answer that," Erin says.

"Usually with a yes or a no."

"She's terrified of losing me. And maybe a little jealous of you."

"So, crazy then."

From the back seat of Erin's car, the camera pushes against the side of her face. Watery eyes shimmer in the headlights of oncoming traffic.

"Nuts," Erin says. *"I guess."*

"Can you stop over on your way home?"

"I just slipped out for a coffee, you're all the way across town."

"If you sneak in through the window, you can spend the night."

"I can't be out late. My dad will find you and—"

"Your dad is fast asleep. Europe really spoiled me."

"Stop."

"What? I'm a growing boy."

"You make it sound so gross."

"Please, Erin."

"Not tonight, okay? Night, baby." Erin ends the call without waiting for Cameron's response. The camera shifts to a low angle, somehow on the floor between the driver and passenger seats.

Erin drags an elbow across watery eyes and then the camera cuts to the back seat.

That full-faced swimming mask and drawn-on smile slides across the rearview mirror. Light from another oncoming vehicle rinses it away, and once the car has passed, the glass is empty.

Kylie minimizes the video and dials Erin. MonoLife becomes the size of her thumb, playing in the lower corner of her screen.

The sound of Erin's ringing phone from two different audio sources creates distortion.

Erin reaches for the dashboard, spots the caller, mumbles something beneath her breath, and then declines it.

"Erin, shit!"

On camera now, elongated fingers are rising up from the back seat, stretching toward Erin's shiny mane.

Kylie's own fingers are like jelly, thumbgliding along the phone's keyboard, letter by letter, typing the most succinct message Erin *might* believe.

Kylie:

someone is trying to kill you . . . pull over and run to Morning Bean

She toggles back to the livestream, shouting desperate encouragement as though she might be able to will Erin into action. "Listen to me, Erin. Listen to me, Erin. *Will you fucking listen to me, Erin?!*"

Erin lifts the phone off its cradle as she pulls over, parking against the curb. "*Morning Bean is where I'm going, Ky.*"

Kylie's phone vibrates with an incoming call. She answers it before Katy even has the chance to whine about being chained to the rhythm. "*Kylie,*" Erin says. "*You are freaking me out.*"

Kylie's rushing to the driveway, keys in hand. "Get inside the Bean and sit tight. I'm on my way."

"*If this is a video—*"

Kylie hangs up. The BMW's already skidding into the street. Half her attention on the road, the other half on the screen in her fist. Mister Strangles slinks along behind Erin, keeping his distance, clacking steps echoing on the downtown sidewalk.

Kylie types a one-thumbed DM, cannot take her eyes off the road long enough to read it.

@CrystalShips: lleve her alne

Close enough.

From the sidewalk, Mister Strangles watches Erin order a coffee.

Watches as she thumbs through her phone. Watches her carry her drink to the nearest window seat.

Kylie rushes a red light, catching a blaring horn that's already in her rearview by the time she realizes how close to collision she was.

Erin:

here . . . this better be good 😒

Kylie's doing a buck ten down Prospect Street while the camera pushes in on Erin, zooming over her shoulder as she types. The recipient's name at the top of the thread reads: CAMERON.

Okay she's totally nuts 💀

Mister Strangles is doing his best to turn Kylie against her.

"Not going to let you." She takes the next corner at forty and is certain the car's up on two wheels, about to go flipping into someone's shrubs. That's all secondary because she's also focused on typing out another message, this one even more pleading.

@CrystalShips: she wants to be a user. She will make great content.

Another corner. The BMW skidding into the path of an oncoming pickup. The other driver's fast, cutting the wheel and sliding up onto the empty sidewalk. Kylie roars past and catches an angry horn. In her rearview, the truck is looping back around.

She can't worry about that. Almost there. She reaches Summerfield's downtown strip, holding her speed until the Morning Bean sign appears. A stomp of the brakes, and now the BMW is leaving wobbly tracks straight down the middle of the road.

Kylie leaps from the car, phone in fist, sprinting for the door. In the large window, Erin sees her coming, begins to rise.

Somewhere behind her, a diesel engine growls and someone's scream-ing, "*You crazy stupid bitch!*"

Erin pushes on the door as Kylie pulls it. An impromptu tug-of-war as they stare wide-eyed at each other, stuck on opposing sides of a glass partition.

Erin lets go first and Kylie tears it open, rushing into Erin's arms with enough force to send them tumbling.

"Kylie, what the hell . . . ?"

Outside, the truck driver has decided this is more trouble than it's worth, shouting one final misogynistic slur into the night before roaring off.

"It was going to kill you!" Kylie says, utterly hysterical.

Erin pushes Kylie off, stands up. "Stop it. You need help."

Kylie gets to her own shaky feet. "I don't. You have no idea, okay? I heard it all. Cameron asking if I'm crazy. You weren't sure how to answer. Him begging you to come over because . . ."

"Shut up, okay?" Erin says, gesturing to the old barista behind the counter, watching every word. "Jimmy knows my dad. He's already going to hear about how you must be on fifty different kinds of drugs, so . . ."

Kylie laughs. She also cries, wiping tears from her eyes as they drop into a nearby booth, taking a moment to catch their breaths. "I'd give anything for a drug problem right about now." She sorta has one, but Erin doesn't have to know that.

"I'd drive you to rehab myself," Erin says. "Problem solved."

"Problem?"

Erin takes Kylie's phone. "You can always just throw this away."

"Get real." Kylie snatches it back. "I could always become a nun too."

"How did you know what I said in my car," Erin says, the statement reshaping her features into a graven mask.

Kylie clears her throat. "I'll tell you everything."

KylieTime

Erin comes out of her house looking a bit off-brand in black cargo jeans shredded at the knees, a loose tank top that shows off her midriff and reads FUCK CORPO SHIT, and a goose-down Super Puff coat by Tna that really doesn't match.

"This is . . . different," Kylie says as Erin climbs into the passenger seat on their first official day of KylieTime. "But good."

"Pisses my dad off so I figure, why not?"

They were up late last night, Erin asking unending questions about everything Kylie has done on MonoLife. Including the darkest things.

Kylie's answers may have been a bit startling for Erin to hear, especially the piece about Mr. Davies, their time together on the evening he was murdered, but she's known Erin long enough to note her continued silence. That is to say, no judgmental lectures of any kind. That's progress, she supposes.

"And you're, um, doing okay?" Erin had asked last night, just before heading home. "Like, your headspace?"

"Never better" had been Kylie's response, even though that was light-years away from reality.

Kylie brings Erin to school because she has a final today. The last day for them. She walks her to the classroom, a bit annoyed because Erin's rebellious attire is turning heads—proof there's nothing she can't do.

Once Kylie drops her off, she goes to clean out her freshman locker—a rented unit her advisor had erroneously recommended she pay for in order to have an on-campus space of her own, as if she would come anywhere close to needing it. She can't remember if she left anything of value in there at the start of the semester. Never even bothered to put a lock on it. She lifts the handle to pull it open and steps back, surprised to find a bouquet in there. A dozen black roses made out to Kylie Bennington. Today's date on the card, stamped with a simple message: *Last chance.*

She takes the flowers and goes to wait for Erin, stands outside her final, smelling them, deciding to take a selfie with the petals covering her grin, wide eyes to show she's reveling in the perversity. An act of defiance so the world knows that nothing gets under her skin anymore.

Erin comes out and stops cold at the unexpected sight, eyes on the flowers. "What the heck is this?"

"Simon doxed me on the app, hopes someone will kill me. And he's so delusional he thinks he can just call it off if I come crawling back."

"Let's tell Cameron's dad."

"I have a clear line to the FBI whenever I want, apparently."

"Then talk to the FBI."

"If you talk about . . ."

"Yeah, you disappear," Erin says. "Shit. Right. Go drunk driving just before Halloween and wrap your car around an oak tree."

Kylie nods. Rennie and Tommy felt like a lifetime ago. It's only a few days to Christmas now.

"Why doesn't the FBI take your phone if they're investigating MonoLife?"

"They take it, I miss my twenty-four-hour window and MonoLife goes away. And they're back to square one."

The roses have made Kylie curious. She hates that Simon's tacky attention starvation has worked. She unblocks @EndlessNights for a second, just to see if he's had any type of prosperity that would prompt this sort of harassment. The worst thing about people like Simon is that you can see the monsters they're aching to become with just a little hint of success.

But of course not. He's still a user and his last two posts are among his most insufferable. From last night:

A photo of a yellow shipping envelope stuffed with papers, "RECEIPTS" scribbled in marker across it. Beneath the title he writes: **The names of every last person who was condescending to me. I. Remember.**

Zero engagement. Nice to see he's putting his time to good use.

A few days ago, he graced MonoLife with the following:

@EndlessNights: ProTip—Having trouble getting followers? When you're brainstorming content, ask yourself, "Would I follow someone because of this?"

Kylie is ashamed of how much Simon truly bothers her. There's never been a more annoying know-it-all who knows next to nothing. Once she reaches the next level, whatever that is, it's over, thank God. Never has to see him again.

She wants to believe that, but part of her realizes it's not the truth. Simon has latched on to what he sees as his one chance for something greater, and just like an undead Sporto with a bone, he's never letting go.

The bouquet isn't her last chance, just his latest attempt to be remembered. Kylie is happy to forget, dropping the flowers into the trash on their way off campus.

On the drive home, Erin asks if it's cool to hang at Kylie's so she can avoid seeing her dad. If she's not going to hang up her Instagram and stop taking those scantily clad pics, the bastard wants her out after the holidays. They're nearly to Kylie's when the sight of strobing red and blue lights igniting throughout her neighborhood stops their conversation cold.

What's even worse is that Kylie knows she's involved as soon as she turns onto her street. It's littered with so many vehicles she can't even reach her driveway. Has to settle for pulling up onto the sidewalk.

Agent Claire Jasinski is coming down the pavement, somehow

spotting Kylie through the windshield. She jogs over, opens the back door, and slides in.

"It's been a day," she sighs. "Got this ache in my spine, chills all over. Just know I'm getting the flu."

"Um, hey, Claire," Kylie says.

"Hey, Claire," Erin echoes. "Thanks for giving us your germs."

The agent deflates across the back seat, completely spent and shivering. "Seems like the world still revolves around you, Kylie."

Through the window, a uniformed officer points to a stable of reporters stuffed behind a sawhorse and he's shouting, "Come any closer and we'll turn a fucking fire hose on the lot of you!"

"Can I go up to my house?" Kylie asks.

"Don't you want to know what brought the circus to town?"

"I, uh, sort of figured you'd tell me?"

"One of your neighbors spotted someone looking through your windows. Watched as they got a ladder out of your shed and raised it to the second floor."

Erin sits up, almost comically animated as she mouths, Simon.

"Had a knife the size of a broadsword," Claire says, too busy rooting around in her pocket for a Cold-Eeze, misses Erin's gesture. "We arrested him."

"Who?" Kylie asks.

"Name's Alex Hammond. Eighteen years old. Came all the way up from Forest Grove, Connecticut."

Kylie turns, stretching her arm across the leather seatback. "I don't know who that is."

Claire expects this answer. Her eyes clock over to Erin. "You?"

"What? No."

"Can we see him?"

"You really up for that?" Claire asks. Kylie and Erin exchange looks, but the agent doesn't wait for an answer, cracks the door. "Okay— let's go."

They wind through a maze of scattered police cars, one of which has

Alex Hammond slumped in the back. He perks up like a zoo animal when he notices who's looking at him.

Gotta be younger than eighteen. Curly brown hair, dark jeans, black hoodie. Dead eyes. You'd see his photo online and think, *School shooter*.

Claire slides between Kylie and the glass, crossing her arms to prevent herself from shivering. Kylie just shrugs. "I don't know what to tell you."

"Then allow me to tell *you* something," Claire says. "You've got a bull's-eye in your pocket. I'm wondering what it'll take to wake you up."

She sounds like Simon with his *This isn't real for you yet* bullshit. What is it about Kylie that makes people refuse to take her seriously?

"Agent Jasinski . . . Claire," Erin says, stepping wide to get another look at Hammond. "We've never seen this freak show in our lives. Look at him. Then look at us. Give us some credit."

The agent's shoulders heave reflexively as her pale and sweaty face stifles a laugh. It's enough to prove that Claire understands, had been like them once. Kylie's almost sorry she had to give it up. "Be careful, ladies," she notes. "That's all I'm saying."

"Can I go into my house now?"

"We're taking him away. Excited to bring him downtown and learn jack shit."

"Good luck, Agent Jasinski," Erin says. She throws her arm around Kylie's waist and guides her up the lawn. At their backs, the reporters gathered behind the barrier shout indecipherable questions, their words lost to the general excitement of things.

The agent follows Kylie and Erin to the foot of the driveway, watches them go with her hands on her hips.

Erin's spinning in the computer chair. "I miss the Zac Efron poster on your ceiling. Those abs."

"Outgrew him."

"Not Katy, though, huh?"

"Nope. Never."

"Guess that makes sense." Erin punctuates her joke with an *Aren't I the cutest?* face.

"You don't have to stay with me."

"You're giving me a place to be. Besides, some psycho was trying to get into your house. I'm your bodyguard until further notice."

Kylie is nestled up against her headboard, scrolling. She and Katy looking in on @EndlessNights again. Looking down.

He's just posted "There's Something About Crystal," and it opens with a shot of Kylie's house. Someone in a ski mask, probably Alex Hammond, peering into each of the ground-floor windows.

"*We're hunting red exes,*" Simon whispers in a way he thinks makes him sound scary, but is somehow the cringiest shit he's ever done.

"Oh my God, it's a collab!" Kylie laughs. "You poor, poor loser. Still doing collabs."

Hammond slips around the side of Kylie's house as Simon starts off down the sidewalk. He turns the camera around and shows those same hideous silver aviators, glistening in the afternoon sun. "*You won't find him until it's too late,*" he says. "*I wonder if you'll beg me to stop before all is said and done?*"

"They caught him before he could even get in, you *idiot*!" Kylie is screaming at her phone.

A cut in the video. Now it's tilted footage from early this morning, Kylie leaving her house in the clothes she's currently wearing. Simon must've shot this from behind the neighbor's car, which is equal parts unsettling and pathetic.

Next, we've got a couple of quick cuts of Kylie's taillights moving through downtown. Another cut and the camera is inside Summerfield Community College, leering at Kylie from all the way down the hall, B-roll taken from earlier in the semester, as she disappears into the bathroom.

Proof he can follow her anywhere.

Cut. There's Mom coming home from work early in the morning. Cut. Kylie asleep in the hospital bed. Cut. Kylie rolling into the gas station. Cut. Kylie dragging the recycle barrel to the edge of the driveway. Cut. Cut. Cut.

Suddenly, her stomach's very sour.

"*I could've done you myself at any point*," Simon whispers, and while Erin isn't watching, she gasps at this audacity. Theirs may be an unspoken rivalry, but nobody else gets to come between them. "*Thing is, Kylie,*" Simon hisses, "*I still think of us as a team. And I think you'll come back around to thinking that way too.*" The video cuts back to Hammond pulling a ski mask down over his face. "*You might even beg for my help before the end.*"

Worst of all? This crap is working. Simon's video is actually doing numbers, a loyal audience of men's rights activists cheering on Kylie's murder in the comments.

"He's been practicing," Kylie says.

"Working up the nerve," Erin adds.

"I worked too hard to get here. He doesn't get to take it away."

"Nothing is worth this, Kylie."

"I've got seventy thousand dollars in savings. A new BMW outside. More clothes and product than I know what to do with. Fans. Followers. Opportunities . . . You want me to go back to college because some fucking boy got his feelings hurt?"

Erin swallows the rest of her protest. If anyone understands, it's her. She may be wishing for the quiet life with Cameron, but the itch never stops.

Kylie has Simon's profile picture up. Those silver fucking aviators. His dumb Muppet mouth. Her jaw's tight and pulsing and she finally knows why he gets so easily under her skin. "I hate him."

Erin reaches into her bag and drops a handgun onto the bed. "Here. In case you need it. Cameron's dad has so many he won't notice one's missing."

"When did you start carrying?"

"This morning. Made Cameron run it over after all that . . . *excitement* at Morning Bean. Now it's yours."

Kylie stares at it, the weapon's very presence unlocking possibilities she hasn't considered. If Simon's ramping up his aggression campaign, though, it's past time.

Just like it's past time for Erin to fess up. The handgun is proof she cares. That she can't live without Kylie any more than Kylie can't live without her. Isn't it refreshing to feel something again? How can Erin deny these little moments of humanity? Her gesture has reframed the world, takes them back to a time when they were the only two people in it. Confirmation they never wanted things to change.

One more look at Simon's douchey silver aviators is all she needs. Picks up the gun, tries visualizing it. Yeah. She could blow him away and then sleep like a baby.

"I say we go have a chat," Erin says. "Make him know that it's real. Send his bitch ass packing."

"Think it'll work?"

"Might even get another humiliation video out of it. A Simon to go with your Brady. Kylie Bennington, destroyer of shitty men. How's that for a fucking brand?"

Kylie doesn't even have to think about it.

They drive to Gloucester. To Simon's workplace. An office park where an army of JCPenney business-casuals come pouring out around the BMW as it rolls into the lot. Quitting time. Only reason Kylie knows to look for Simon here is because he let it slip in one of his text storms, bragging that he worked for one of the biggest locksmiths in the state, a place called Keep Out.

Should anyone ask, their excuse for being here is that Simon is stuck doing overtime and Kylie is dropping in for a quick hello.

With a loaded handgun in your jacket.

Something to really raise his spirits.

Kylie and Erin are nearly to the front door when a straggler fumbling for her car keys in a bag that's big enough to carry a bowling ball holds it open for them.

They have to wait only a few minutes outside of the Keep Out suite before a vacating employee holds that door, granting them access to a disgusting cubicle farm, rows of conformity that give Kylie such anxiety she wishes she brought some lorazepam for the ride.

I'd rather die than be a wagie, she thinks, understanding Simon's desperation in this moment. Mom is all the proof anyone needs to see how this kind of a life is really just one long, bleak march toward death. Working more than you're not, never the time to see those you pretend to love because life is all about getting back on the clock.

They walk around like they belong, until Erin spots the name SIMON LAMBERT dangling off a corner cube.

Look at this. Even your name is boring.

His desk is clean, a stack of plastic drawers stuffed with invoices and credit reports. No personality to his workspace. A New England Patriots calendar on the wall is as close as it gets.

Kylie pulls his chair away from his desk and checks the trash bin. A brown apple core and a crushed Dasani bottle. She reaches for his scissors, uses the blades to sift through the rest of it.

"Here," she says, finding a box addressed to him. The invoice inside says that he paid two hundred dollars for a Spyderco Civilian Personal Defense blade. "22 Brookside, Gloucester, Mass."

If you weren't so stupid, you'd have figured out a way to have them send you all *the knives, dipshit.*

A woman stands up in a nearby cube, chewing a mouthful of popcorn. "Excuse me—how did you get in here?"

"Um . . . my dad's the owner," Erin says as Kylie shoves her toward the exit, both of them scurrying, unable to contain their nervous laughter. In a second they're rushing into the hall, giggling all the way to the BMW.

When they're on the way to Simon's place, Erin says, "I feel like I'm about to have a heart attack."

"You can wait in the car," Kylie tells her, visualizing cracked aviators, a bullet hole blown through one of those stupid lenses. She could ease Erin's anxiety by explaining they can't kill Simon tonight. Not with their faces almost surely on camera somewhere back at Keep Out. But Kylie says nothing, thinking instead about how the best thing she can do right now is scare the shit out of Simon Lambert.

He lives on a cul-de-sac, some saltbox nestled in between two identical homes. They pull an Alex Hammond and look through the windows. Go around back, hoping to find an unlocked bulkhead. Given the way they'd gotten into Mr. Sykes's place, Simon wouldn't be so careless.

"Can I help you?" A next-door neighbor in a plaid robe drags a barrel of trash from his garage.

"We're looking for Simon," Kylie says.

It's dark, and this guy's older, probably mid-fifties, and really overweight. His robe's open and the Budweiser tee stretches over his belly, distorting the logo. He's too nervous to look either of them in the eye. "Haven't seen much of him since his mother died."

"Wait, his mom *died*?" Kylie asks.

He stands in silence. It takes a minute for Kylie to realize he's nodding.

Kylie looks back at Simon's house. "What happened?"

"Fell down the stairs. Twisted her neck all the way around."

"God. When?"

The neighbor looks up at the moon, thinking hard. "Year ago? Yeah, right before Christmas."

Simon's house is positioned between streetlamps, so none of the artificial light reaches it. The perfect place to keep all his twisted secrets.

"You know him well?" Erin asks.

"No offense," the neighbor says, laughing. "Do you?"

Kylie offers a soft, diffusive giggle. "Yeah. He and I are kind of involved."

"Oh, yeah, well, he seems like a nice guy." Next-Door Neighbor is quick to say this, as if trying to cover up his real thoughts. "Helps Maddie across the street with yard work. I used to smoke cigars with him. We'd talk about the Pats, mostly. Only guy I ever knew who hated Tom Brady."

"Fuckin' traitor," Kylie says in her most put-on Boston accent.

"And fuck the Buccaneers too," Erin adds, just as Boston-y.

He laughs, takes the opportunity to look them over.

"Look, I'm just checking up on Simon," Kylie says. "Haven't heard from him in a minute. Kind of worried."

"You're nice girls, I can see that. His mom gave me a spare key once. Figured Simon might not always be there for her and—"

"We'll bring it right back," Kylie says.

The neighbor ambles into his house, leaving Kylie and Erin to wait beneath a streetlamp. He returns with the key and a wood-tipped cigar. "I never gave this to you," he says, lighting up the stogie. "You know, if anyone asks."

Kylie takes the key, remembering once more with crushing disappointment that she can't shoot Simon in the face, especially now that they've traded memories with this guy. It's a slow and cautious walk to the dark house, Kylie and Erin making nervous faces at each other in the howling wind. Porch steps creak beneath their feet, and they unlock the front door as the smell inside rushes out, striking their noses.

"What the hell . . . ?" Erin's question is muffled, mouth pressed against her elbow.

Kylie ignites her phone and a dry heave kicks in. She doubles over, finding small blood spatters on the floor, scattered droplets that disappear down the hall. "A literal trail of blood," she says, pulling the gun from her pocket. It might as well be a paperweight for as much as she knows how to use it, but the motion feels right.

The dining area is retrofitted into a makeshift hospital room. A hospice bed, medical equipment stacked around it, provoking in Kylie another twinge of sympathy. A fleeting moment.

Erin keeps a hand pressed to Kylie's back and follows her through the house, holding her breath, fighting the urge to retch.

The smell leads to the living room, where a headless body is slumped against one side of the couch, its skull placed in its lap, angled toward the doorframe in order to greet whoever's looking.

The corpse is slathered in what looks like jelly. Eyeballs are melted jam, thick globular tears spilling down a skinless face, scattered maggots dancing inside ruined eye sockets.

Thick, wide-rimmed bifocals sit on the cushion beside it, and Kylie realizes who they're looking at. Nobody so young would be caught dead wearing these.

Nobody except—

"*Ben*," Kylie says as Erin doubles over beside her, puking. "Shit. Simon *wanted* me to find him. Knew I'd come here." Her words are resigned, the grim acknowledgment of knowing you've lost. Ben Austin's butchered carcass fills her with regret for how she never got around to shooting him through the knee, an idea she's absolutely certain now would've been a winner.

Erin goes groaning into the hall, never more confident in her decision to leave this world behind. And tonight, Kylie maybe envies her a bit, briefly wondering if a nice quiet life isn't preferable to all this.

But it's not. Can't be. She's made it. Haters so strong they're impacting the real world to try to get her attention.

She takes out her phone and films Ben's leftovers in all their gruesome glory. When she's got enough, she thumbs through her contacts for Claire. Doesn't want to call the police.

Erin takes the key back to the neighbor. Through the front window Kylie watches her break the news. He tosses his cigar into the street and cups a hand to his face, gasps resonating from here.

Kylie shoots a bit more video, the perfect subject for today—giving her fans an actual murder mystery to follow.

They'll be hooked. Afraid to tune out.

"Thank you, Simon," she whispers. "Sorry about this, Ben. But look at you. You've come so far."

Little Kylie Bennington, a nobody from a nothing Massachusetts town . . . followers from all over the world, adoring fans who jump hurdles to give her money.

She grins, anticipating another round of Agent Jasinski's frustrated questions.

There'll come a time when the agent will make her talk, right?

Maybe. But maybe not.

History Lessons

Claire Jasinski is beyond pissed.

She has Kylie and Erin brought to separate squad cars and keeps them waiting for two hours while she's inside Simon's house.

She speaks with Erin first. Behind Kylie, a row of uniformed policemen is threatening to pepper-spray reporters once more placed behind a sawhorse.

At last, a uniformed officer opens the back door and Claire slides in, coughing, even sicker just a few hours later, giving Kylie one long-ass stare.

"What?"

"What? Are you kidding me with *what?*" Claire slaps the cell phone in Kylie's lap. "Turn that damn thing off."

"Um—" Memories of an inhuman fist pushing through Duc's ceiling. Of Deacon being dragged into the night. No, sorry, she just can't *turn it off.* "I think I'd like to see a lawyer." Kylie doesn't exactly know why she said that, just that it's what people say when they're in trouble with the law.

"Off. Now. Or you spend a night in jail, and then see if you feel like talking."

Kylie turns her phone off, starts the MonoLife meter running.

Only when the screen goes black does the agent speak again. "I'm guessing you know the victim."

"I do."

"Let me guess—Ben Austin."

"Ding, ding, ding."

"Cards on table, Kylie."

"Okay—shoot."

"We know it's called MonoLife." Claire watches Kylie's reaction, which is little more than a shrug. "It's been around for just under a decade, though at first it was no different than any of the shithole sites out there where people post, y'know, stolen nudes and gory stuff. Didn't become the experience you apparently know and love till about five years back. That might be all we know about the fucking thing." The agent studies each tick on Kylie's face. "Actually, I know something else too: it *will* kill you, Kylie. Maybe not right away, but eventually. It is *designed* to kill you." She pops another Cold-Eeze.

Kylie thinks of Duc's video from inside the sunken church. His revelation that this was never about content or expression, but rather feeding . . . maybe whatever the hell Mister Strangles is? "It just wants users," Kylie says, as if defending a boyfriend from the wrong side of the tracks.

"It has plenty. We don't know how they're doing it."

"Well, neither do I, so—"

"The companies that send you products . . . they don't know anything about it. Which means someone—a middleman—is acquiring all that stuff and shipping it out to their user base."

"Yeah, they pretty much tell you that once you start getting gifts. They wouldn't do it if they wanted to kill me."

Claire shakes her head, saddened by Kylie's inability to see the bigger picture. "Whoever's bankrolling MonoLife is serious, and we can't get so much as a name. I've been in contact with all the tech companies on this. Whatever the app is, it's somehow skirting the iOS or Android operating systems, so they can't help us track it. All we've gathered is they love to watch people like you debase yourselves for scraps."

"It's no different than working a job you hate," Kylie offers. "You're always making someone else richer while you barely squeak by." She glances out her window, where an elongated shadow takes shape inside a pocket of stygian darkness, tiny glimpses appearing inside the quick flashes of first-responder lights. Mister Strangles weaving through the row of pine trees that divide two suburban yards, waving his fingers as he approaches. As he comes for Kylie.

"You've done some shit," Claire is saying, "but nothing the federal government can't forgive. *Yet*. Think I care about you giving some girl a bloody nose? Gaslighting a pedo into ending it? In simpler times, maybe, Kylie, but you should be aware this is an epidemic you won't survive."

"Okay," Kylie says, because it's time to hurry this along. "What do you want from me?"

"We've tracked it all over the world. Can't get close because it deletes itself off a user's phone if they go lax. The people behind it are *very* good at hiding."

That's because the people behind it are not human. This unbidden thought brings a chill as Kylie realizes that Claire's right. She doesn't know who she's dancing for. Only that he's over there right now, peeking out from behind the last tree, tiny eyes zeroed in on her from beneath that painted mask, and still waving.

Kylie is tempted to point and scream, but knows in her heart that it could never be that easy. These past three months have revealed a world behind the world, synonymous with her slipping sanity. Her body starts to ache, the wound on her back resurfacing, suddenly radiating, as if broadcasting to that thing out there. Puckering. Kylie winces and Claire scrutinizes. Kylie bites her tongue, certain the only thing police searchlights will find are swaying branches and Mister Strangles still wins in the end, pulling her underneath her bed as soon as she gets home, if he'd wait that long to pounce.

That she'd even consider giving MonoLife up is simply a case of shredded nerves. Understandable, given what was revealed to her inside Simon's house, but it's not the kind of decision to make rashly. Giving it up means dying. And if that's the case, she might as well get out of this car right now and walk toward those trees.

Claire takes one of Kylie's hands in hers and gives it a gentle squeeze. "I'm tired, Kylie."

"You should get some sleep."

"Haven't had any of that in about five years. On the road more than I'm home. I've got two dogs who practically live in kennels. Circles under my eyes so dark even Olay can't help."

"Maybe you should leave me to it."

"What do you think I've been doing?"

"Have I helped?"

"I don't know." Claire rubs her face the way people do when they're exhausted and just can't anymore. "I mean, yeah. A little. We swiped a few boxes off your doorstep—sorry. Helped us figure out where they're coming from. A reshipping company in Romania that keeps spotty records."

"Wish you'd taken a few more," Kylie says. "Come over and pick through whenever you want." She tilts her head against her shoulder. "Our sizes aren't all that different."

Claire appears flattered and there's serious consideration there. And then that old-fashioned swimmer's mask is at Claire's window, leering in, locked on to Kylie with squinted eyes, the bustle of police and rescue, reporters and onlookers, entirely oblivious to its presence.

Kylie needs to get out of this car and knows the only way to do that is to give the agent something. "There's a conference coming up," she says. "A MonoLife influencers' convention or whatever. They're close to inviting me."

Claire straightens her back, suddenly animated despite the encroaching flu. Mister Strangles has turned his attention to the agent, studying her peaked flesh, eyes igniting with possibility. "Really. When is it? Do you know where?"

"I'm not sure." Kylie presses the side button on her phone but keeps the screen face down, hoping Claire's too intrigued by this latest revelation to notice.

"But you're invited?"

"Not yet."

"You need to get an invitation."

"I'm working on it."

Claire looks through her.

"I know you're watching me. And I know I won't be able to leave town without you knowing. So, yeah, I'll be in touch. I *am* cooperating."

"Good," Claire says, and leaves a crackling evidence bag on the cushion, handgun inside it. Beyond her, the window is all clear. "Now go on and get yourself an invitation."

Suburban Red

" I close my eyes and all I see is Ben's body." Erin rubs her face with the
rounds of her palms, as if trying to wipe this evening away.

Kylie is impressed that Erin can remember his name now and all it
took was being slaughtered. "You'll survive," she says, and brings the
BMW off the road, rolling beneath the sodium glow of tired gas station
lights. Plenty of drivers around. No chance of a psycho ambush here.
"You mind?" she asks. "I'm jittery."

"Why'd Claire let us go?" Erin wonders, hurrying around the car
in order to take the wheel.

Now that Kylie's in the passenger seat, she's able to focus. She's in
MonoLife, going at @EndlessNights through DM.

@CrystalShips: you're taunting me over how much you suck?

She wants that message to hurt. Him to clench his teeth and snarl
her name. To carry that forward when he comes for her with a foaming
mouth.

Rabid dogs are dangerous and need to be put down.

Kylie feels the cold sting of the handgun beneath her shirt. The
pulse of power that comes with it.

"We should stay at Cameron's tonight," Erin says. "His dad treats
their home like a fortress. Cameras, alarms, more firepower than a gun
range . . ."

"Simon's crazy, not stupid."

Maybe it would be safer. But safety isn't the point. MonoLife doesn't care about safe. It needs chaos. And Kylie is going to deliver that. "He won't come unless I'm alone."

"Then you're moving in with me. So he never comes."

Kylie fights her burgeoning smile. She then imagines Erin and Cameron cuddled in bed, staring up through his skylight, and her stomach turns to curdled milk.

"Go to Cameron's," Kylie whispers.

"Not without you."

"Please, like I want to be anywhere near you when your dad figures out you've broken curfew."

"I told my mom I'm staying at your place."

"Oh great, what can go wrong?"

"You can change your mind, Ky."

"I'll be in touch, okay?" Kylie taps the gun beneath her shirt. "I get to keep this, right?"

"Only if you promise to use it."

Erin drives to Cameron's and hops out, standing in the driveway as Kylie climbs behind the wheel and reverses into the street, throwing a dainty half wave.

"Now you'll come, won't you, Simon?" Kylie says to herself and then drives home.

Another @EndlessNights video drops by the time she's there. This one called "A New Beginning." Predatory footage of Simon rolling up on Ben after school as he walks to his car. Simon apologizing for the beating, suggesting they go for a drink to *Bury the hatchet. Forget the bitch.*

Kylie makes the rounds while watching it, locking all doors, bolting all windows.

The video jumps ahead to Simon filming Ben from behind as he shuffles cluelessly toward the house that's about to become his grave. Kylie doesn't need to see the rest, scrolls down to where the fist bumps are already piling up. Below that, a waterfall of enthusiastic comments.

Simon's got another hit on his hands. Two in one day.

This is apocalyptic. Simon must never be allowed to have success, for Kylie cannot live in a world where he dispenses generic ProTips to a blithely appreciative audience.

She turns on every light in the house and cycles through each room twice, gun drawn, safety off. She records herself as she does all this, because it would be her luck to find Simon under her mother's bed, for example, and she isn't about to miss blowing his brains out. She'll upload that without hesitation and they'll make her a fucking god.

MonoLife's first life-to-death love story. Maybe.

The house is clear. Her phone vibrates, a MonoLife DM announcing itself.

@EndlessNights: You made me do this

As if on cue, the notification ribbon spreads across the bottom of her screen. **@EndlessNights is live . . .**

Kylie clicks it. The broadcast is nothing but sifting darkness. Little swirls of floating grain scored to Simon's labored breathing.

She circles her house once more, trying to determine his place of hiding.

On-screen, a sliver of light creeps into the shot, spreading, revealing an interior floor—Simon literally slithering out from beneath a bed, just like she thought he might.

The camera's attached to Simon's body, video unfolding through his point of view, one hand gripping the defensive knife. His breaths are anticipatory, working up the nerve to go big.

Kylie's blood becomes melted snow. Her heart's doing those loud *thump-thump*s that seem to echo in surround sound. She's watching Simon slip into a domesticated hallway in a home she doesn't recognize.

Wait. Yes, she does. Kylie's already texting.

Kylie:

I think he's in Cameron's house!

Erin:

huh???

lock the bedroom door!

Back in MonoLife, Simon creeps toward a closed door at the end of the hall. A loud *click* echoes from the other side.

what's happening

answer pls

he's right outside your door

Simon turns on a dime, moving downstairs, lifting the knife overhead to show his audience its jagged teeth. A move of showmanship that Kylie resentfully admires—the added element of suspense.

He brings his voyeurism through a living room, into a reading den where an older woman sits facing a crackling fireplace.

he's downstairs, going for mom!

he called his dad and they're coming

cameron's going down now . . . shit

Cameron's mom has her nose to a paperback and, off-screen, Cameron's desperate shouts are muffled, bleeding into earshot.

The mom tilts her head toward this commotion, somehow missing Simon being in the room with her. The camera has pivoted to the right, revealing a room divider at the edge of the frame. He's behind it now, facing the entryway.

That's when Cameron comes barreling into the room, gun in hand, waving it around like an action figure.

His eyes clock over to the camera, to the intruder it's attached to, and his reaction shifts in slow motion. Terror inflating his face as Simon lunges.

The gun barks. A flash of blinding white fills the frame like a nuclear blast. A deep grunt as Simon slashes down, the blade ripping through Cameron's neck. Wet and slurpy. His flesh tears apart like two unconnected flaps, unleashing sputtering arteries.

Red jelly smacks the camera, dripping slowly down the lens, obscuring the show. Simon wrestles the blade free and stabs Cameron again, again, again, slicing through bone with a potato-chip crunch, Cameron's wide-eyed head quickly hacked away from his neck.

Mom charges the shot as her decapitated son drops out of it. She's swatting Simon's thick and hardened hands. He brushes her off like a kitten and the camera moves into close-up, capturing the madness that's overtaken her face.

Simon's gnarled hand wrenches her neck, lifts her toward the ceiling.

The blade slides into her belly, Kylie's phone speaker crackling as it interprets those awful gurgles.

Simon bends his arm, throwing her across the living room. She's coughing, clawing for air, interacting with some hallucination. Dead, but not quite yet.

Then he turns and stalks into the empty hall, where Erin comes tumbling into the shot, screaming, fumbling for the front door, frantically trying to reach the pulsing red and blue lights that have begun to stain the decorative glass.

The door flings wide and Erin rushes into the night as squad cars screech to a halt in the driveway.

Simon spins and bolts into the kitchen, then out the side door, walking briskly toward the trees.

Kylie's curious to see just how committed Simon is, feeling a pulse of excitement as she wonders if he's willing to lay it all on the line to get Erin tonight. She sends Erin a text that contradicts those unspoken thoughts.

Kylie:

stay with the police

Then she drops her phone onto the table and opens a bottle of Beluga "Gold Line" Noble Russian vodka that's ninety dollars a pop and begins swigging from the bottle while watching Simon move through backyards and down neighborhood streets as red and blue lights strobe the night.

"Come get me, asshole," she murmurs. The comments on his stream are overwhelmingly positive and Kylie's heart explodes over and over while reading them.

> This motherfucker out here giving us a whole killing spree
> Kill a little girl next
> Holy shit, this dude tha GOAT outta nowhere

She imagines Simon getting off on this praise from the jackals. Validated eyes behind those stupid fucking aviators.

Her heart rages with the thought of this trash reigning atop Living Now, forever eclipsing Mr. Sykes—a video in which Simon was also involved. MonoLife would surely realize that.

A pattern would begin to emerge. A brand solidified.

A nightmare world where Simon actually gained a following. Jesus Christ, she's once again imagining those ProTips and realizes that's when it would be time to reconsider TikTok, to begin making videos awash in bisexual lighting, where she critiques Pixar movies from an anarcho-Marxist perspective.

Kylie lifts the handgun because that cannot happen. She's rushing for her car, clipping her phone to the mount on her dashboard as she speeds back toward Cameron's house.

State police are pinballing up and down every road like agitated insects, and Kylie keeps a heavy foot on the brake to avoid getting pulled over.

There's time. Simon can't get far on foot. But he's trying.

On-screen, Simon speed-walks around the side of another house, approaching a couple on either side of a Ford pickup. Neither is aware that he's there until he's maybe three feet from the man's back. He plunges the blade into the side of his gut, dragging it up to his armpit, splitting him wide open.

The woman screams and Simon's already moving around the vehicle to get her. She tumbles over the ankle-high fence, falling into a rose bed, arm bent over her face in a meager defensive gesture as that bloodstained blade rises again . . .

Kylie has no idea where this house is in relation to Cameron's. She rolls into the neighborhood with the window down, listening for screams.

Watching as Simon climbs behind the wheel of the pickup, slamming the door, turning the ignition.

Kylie hears that particular growl somewhere outside her window. "Where you going, Simon?" A bonfire of flashing police lights confirms she's close to Cameron's, uses the nearest driveway to turn around. Simon's going to be fleeing his crimes.

She guns it to the end of the road while fumbling with MonoLife, indelicate fingers tapping glass and navigating to unwanted screens. Finally, her forefinger catches POST, then LIVE, inviting the world to watch.

"Hey, guys, Crystal here. You wanted a reunion with Endless Nights? I'm about to give you one."

She swerves left at the stop sign, smashing the gas, speeding up a hill.

At the next corner, a pair of headlights sits idling at a stop sign, then begins easing into the street. That familiar diesel growl heading right toward her.

"Let's go!" Kylie screams. It isn't bravado or performance, but pure adrenaline.

Kylie isn't thinking about death as she swerves into the opposite lane, flicking on her high beams. She's thinking about victory as she flips the camera outward to show the street, teeth gnashed while her foot pins the pedal, jousting toward the pickup with a war cry in her throat.

The oncoming headlights become blinding, inescapable orbs. Kylie squints, hands tightening around the steering wheel to stay the course.

The driver realizes what's about to happen, cuts the wheel toward a clear patch of road. It's too late. Kylie cuts hers too, turning the BMW into a missile.

Metal smashes metal. The BMW's hood becomes a wave of ripples, pummeling the Ford, sending the truck spinning.

The airbag explodes out of the steering column, engulfing her face—a sensation like stinging sandpaper.

A blaring horn sounds like it's ten miles away, heavy and sustained.

Kylie rocks her head back and forth. Stabs of pain behind her eyes. A spread of warmth while realizing the camera's still intact on the dash.

"I'm okay," she tries to say, as if anyone watching cares about that. Her brain ebbs against one side of her skull and when she moves, it seems to slosh around up there, reigniting the pain with each new motion.

Her hand crawls toward the door handle before she's even aware that she's moving. She pushes the airbag down, attempting to assess the damage. Blood covers her face like chocolate sauce, a warm and constant dribble.

Somewhere beyond her totaled interior, a door opens with a prolonged squeak.

Kylie wipes blood from her eyes, trying to find focus. Presses the button that brings the camera back to the forward lens, letting the world back into her car as the palm of her hand slaps down on the empty seat beside her in search of cold steel.

Outside, shuffling feet come crunching over broken glass.

Her hand closes around the door handle, finding it's wedged in place.

"Shit," she slurs. Her free hand falls down to her ankle, sweeping around, glimpsing herself in the rearview mirror. Her mouth is swollen into Angelina Jolie lips that she realizes she kind of likes, and the falling blood has streaked her cheeks.

Her searching hand sways like a pendulum, finger pads brushing against a familiar handle.

Cracking glass tickles her ear.

Simon in a greasy mechanic's jumper beyond it, a blood-slicked hand trying to yank her door wide open. It still doesn't budge.

Her fingers close around the gun handle as Simon turns his elbow into a battering ram, throwing all his weight against the window.

Kylie's climbing over the seat break to the passenger side as she lifts the pistol off the floor, thumb clicking the safety away without ever once thinking about how to do it.

She draws on the glass, chest heaving as she fights to keep her iron sight in place. Steady.

Only Simon's gone.

Kylie's eyes dart to the back seat. The rear window. Both empty.

She's at full alertness now. Simon has to die. As badly as she wants anything, she wants this. Needs her followers to see it. Because she has to take everything from him.

The only sound is the BMW's clacking and cooling engine. Simon is nowhere.

She takes the phone off its cradle. "Be right back, guys." Kills the feed and clicks over to @EndlessNights, who is still broadcasting live from his camera on the pickup's dashboard. From Kylie's phone, via Simon's video, she is staring at her own busted taillights.

A flickering porch light catches her eye. Two silhouettes stand beneath it, squinting out at the wreckage in front of their home.

"*Get inside!*" Kylie screams from within her twisted metal coffin.

One of them takes a step toward the street while the other lifts a cell phone to their ear. An older voice calling out, "Hello?" on approach.

Kylie gestures for him to step back but he isn't listening. He reaches the door and squints, making eye contact.

Kylie barely acknowledges this, glued to the live feed in the palm of her hand, realizing now where Simon has gone.

It's too late to save the man outside. He yelps, leaping back and falling to the pavement.

From the porch, the younger person yells, "Dad!"

Kylie switches back to her feed, going live in her free hand.

One comment rolls past:

You'd better come back, bitch . . .

"*Too late, Simon!*" she screams, quite performatively, giving those MonoLife rubes something to cheer for as she aims the gun at the BMW's floorpan, right between her legs, squeezing off a shot. Then another. They might as well be explosions in this confined space, turning her hearing into an endless high-pitched whistle.

From beneath her, a wounded yowl breaks through her fugue—

Simon crying out as each bullet sinks through him. Kylie continues to fire, a glorious catharsis until the gun becomes a bunch of empty clicks and even after—

Simon's noises dwindle, turning to sputtering gasps that gradually recede into silence.

Or maybe Kylie has just stopped paying attention to anything other than her phone, huffing and wheezing as she turns it around to focus on herself.

"See what I do for you fuckers," she says breathlessly, clicking over to @EndlessNights so she can leave a comment. One very public dunk for the world to see.

That's when a red X appears in real time, stamping the very top of his profile. Verification in death. He'll never even know that he made it just before the end. In so many ways, this makes Kylie's victory all the more gratifying. Classic Simon, late for his own funeral.

She's laughing as she kills her feed, sirens beginning to approach from all directions.

One last message lands on her lock screen before she stuffs the phone into her pocket. Can't address it now, as much as she'd like to.

It's from Duc.

@SolidusRush: Fucking awesome. Let's talk.

MonoDrome

A uniformed female police officer escorts Kylie inside the command tent, where Agent Jasinski holds a steaming mug of tea packed with lemon wedges up to her nose.

"Not what I expected to find," Kylie says, and the officer gives her an aggressive shove toward the one folding chair.

"I'm tired," the agent croaks. "Pretty sure I already told you that." The circles under her eyes are raccoon dark. She wasn't joking about the Olay.

"Some NyQuil and you'll be good as new," the officer says.

Claire lifts the cup to her mouth and takes a sip, wincing as she swallows. "My throat feels like a tumor." Looking at Kylie now. "And you work really fast, you know that?"

Kylie shrugs. "Didn't have much of a choice."

The tent is a command center for four separate crime scenes: the bloodbath at Cameron's house, Kylie's induced car crash, the bystanders who Simon murdered, and the third bystander whom Simon had attempted to murder.

Claire shifts her gaze to the officer who's still standing beside Kylie, unable to take a hint. "Can we have some alone time?"

"I'd like to hear what she has to say."

"And I'll tell you. After."

"With all due respect, Agent Jasinski, it's a mess out there. You can't shut us out complete—"

"The bureau's here," Claire rasps. "So the bureau's in charge. Or do I have to call the governor again?"

The officer glares through Kylie, then spins and walks out.

Kylie's thinking about the energy in her pocket, visualizing the number of fist bumps currently smashing her masterpiece. It worked out so perfectly it might be a record. And never having to see another update from those silver fucking aviators? Restorative.

Claire shambles to the corner of the tent where an electric heater pumps warm air. She puts her hands out as if it's a campfire. "Been doing this for fourteen years. No idea where all that time went, but a couple months into my first year, I got a new partner. Agent Delingpole. Kind of guy who was born into a suit and tie. You know?"

"Yeah, sure." Kylie's too excited to focus. She wonders about Duc— why is he reaching out now? A stitch of panic in her heart because maybe there are even more levels to MonoLife, even more ways to lose. Claire is certain that will happen but maybe there's another explanation. Maybe they're all jealous of what she's achieved. Duc out there trying to destroy what he could not conquer. Claire on the hunt because she needs this distraction to fill the void in her miserable life. And then there's creepy, inhuman Missy, wherever the hell she is, expecting Kylie to help resolve her unfinished business because she was too weak to go all the way.

They want to take it all from her. Take everything that she's earned. All that she's worked for because Kylie can't be allowed to win, right? She's not supposed to be here. Never was supposed to be somebody.

Let them try.

"I was inquisitive, I guess," Claire's saying, treating Kylie like an old friend because it's her only shot at breaking things wide open. "Asking my new partner all the questions a rookie does. Career highs and lows. Best practices. That sort of stuff."

Kylie's phone pulses against her thigh. The messages are predictable, she's sure. One third will praise her for what she's done. Another third will chide her for getting in Simon's way, robbing them of Premium-Content™. And the final third will just ask her to post pics of her feet.

Whatever. Kylie wants them all.

"Delingpole had what I called haunted eyes." The agent staggers back to her desk and lifts her laptop screen. Even that task is too much effort and she groans.

"Cameron's dad never talks about work. Says you need to have boundaries or it'll take you over." Kylie's thinking about him now, his son and wife brutally murdered by a psycho who saw their lives as a means for attention. And that's Kylie's fault, but she would never say that out loud.

"Everyone in law enforcement has an obsession," Claire says. "Call it a white whale. Chasing Amy. The one that got away . . ."

Kylie's thinking about Simon again, wondering how old he really was.

"Delingpole called it phantom pain. The case you can't shut out, no matter how hard you try. Reading files in bed instead of watching Netflix. That's how it starts, at least, gradually fusing itself to you so that even once you've retired, it's there. You can't help but feel it." She turns the laptop around. "This was Delingpole's. Now it's mine."

She clicks play. The laptop shows wobbly static, darkness ceding to a yellow logo.

On-screen words that read: MONOCHANNEL.

MonoLife in an older vintage.

The logo stays up for a couple more seconds than comfortable, dissolving into a homemade newsroom. Large dark curtains sway, revealing tiny slats of light behind them, someone's living room pretending to be a studio.

A young woman in shoulder pads sits behind a desk, hair crimped to the max. The camera glides in so her face fills the screen, and Kylie is repulsed by the splotchy eye shadow.

She's never seen something in such low resolution—like watching a video through tears.

The broadcaster's lips tremble, displaying fear that her eyes can't mask.

"*We have a good show for you tonight.*" Her delivery's stunted, each word hot off a cue card without the slightest regard for annunciation or pacing. "*T-this first video comes from Milwaukee. A user we've come to know and love. Everyone get ready for the latest from Blood Orange.*"

The resolution shifts again. Even blurrier footage tracking three kids on Huffy bikes. Two of them tearing down the middle of a quiet suburban street, one trailing behind, filming from atop wobbly handlebars.

They bike to a quiet cul-de-sac, pedaling straight to the tree line, hopping off and moving through the woods, a steep decline to a forest bed below.

Kylie has to squint to see what the kids are actually looking at:

A girl, probably Kylie's age, writhing in the dirt, wearing plain white underwear. More bruises than can be counted. Her teeth are bashed away, jagged little pieces of dentin remaining.

The kids hover in silence around her. She isn't dead yet, but definitely on her way.

"*Touch her,*" one of the boys says.

"*No way, Davey,*" another snaps.

"*Kinda think we should do more than touch,*" the camera boy says.

"*We should call someone.*"

"*Hey,*" Camera Boy snaps. "*I'm not giving her up. Let's bring her some tea. Fix her up. She can be our secret girlfriend.*"

"*Ew,*" Davey says.

"*Now or never, guys, I just want to feel some boobies before I die.*" Small and trembling hands reach into the shot.

Christ. They're actually children. Kylie averts her eyes. "Okay, turn it off. I get it. They've been doing this a long time."

Claire takes a bottle of NyQuil from her bag, lifts it like she's toasting, then tosses the dose cup aside and pops the cap, chugging straight from the bottle.

Kylie peeks at the video again. All three boys reaching down, groping the dying girl whose eyes are fading with every passing second.

"Her name was Morgan McLish."

"Unfortunate," Kylie says. Claire nods in agreement, though Kylie declines to clarify she was talking about the name.

"Her body was found floating in the Milwaukee River on October 16, 1984. We don't think these boys were involved in the circumstances that led to Ms. McLish being immobilized here, but—"

"I'd say they're pretty fucking involved."

"MonoChannel appeared on public access television sometime between 1980 and 1984. No one knows how they were able to bypass individual master controls in order to broadcast their signal, but that's what happened. There are unconfirmed reports of it appearing here and there throughout the rest of the eighties and into the nineties." Claire takes a deep breath, shivering. "Who knows. Nobody was ever caught. The file's bigger than my apartment and we're no closer."

Kylie finds herself transfixed by the malaria beads dotting Claire's forehead. The agent should be in bed, but that phantom pain is worse than a fever, isn't it, keeping her upright, forever haunted.

"So, is tonight enough?" Claire croaks. "To get your invitation?"

Kylie considers this. Not only must she choose between Duc and Missy, but she's expected to help Claire bite the hand that feeds her. An appalling notion. Maybe she should've allowed Mister Strangles to take Claire anyway while in the back seat outside Simon's, but had that happened, had Kylie kept her phone off for one second more, the agent would be dead and Kylie would've been taken in for questioning. Separated from her phone, probably for longer than allowed. Kylie will absolutely not let them turn her against MonoLife. The app has only ever been good to her. Maybe the only thing that has.

Something the agent had said to her in the hospital echoes in the back of her mind: *You never thought it would go this far. Thing is, it always goes further than you want.*

All Kylie knows is: she's not ready for this ride to end.

If she can work with a financial planner today, she can avoid the workforce tomorrow. And what if she continues doing this for another decade? She's in her prime and men will simp for her about another ten years—at least. And if Kylie's smart, *really* smart, she won't ever have to work a day in her life.

Why should she want to stop MonoLife? As if this history lesson is supposed to make her forget the things it's given her. Confidence. Peace of mind. The ability to come into her own. So what if she needed to break a few eggs to make an omelet. No, sorry, Claire, and apologies, Morgan McLish. She'd rather die than give it up.

"Is tonight enough?" Kylie says. "Oh yeah. Pretty sure I'm as good as there."

Fidelio

Cameron and his mother are buried on Christmas Eve.

Seems like half the town is in attendance, with every cop on the force standing solemnly behind Cameron's father. He's the epitome of grief, looking like an emaciated skeleton for as much weight as he's lost in a week's time.

Kylie stands at Erin's side through the service and burial, watching her cry as the coffins are lowered into the earth while snowflakes dance around open graves. Only now does it dawn on Kylie that neither of them had attended Brandi's funeral, not that she would've been especially welcome. But this turn of events was unthinkable three months ago, and it's weird to consider just how much life has changed in a short amount of time as she and Erin stand shivering in air so cold it hurts to breathe.

Erin asks to hang around Kylie's afterward, and Erin's mom moves heaven and earth to get her dad off his dictator's throne.

Kylie stretches out on her bed when they get back, her face still halfway swollen, ribs badly bruised from the car crash. She puts on Katy's "Cozy Little Christmas" and feels long-dormant childhood excitement in her bones. It won't last long, but she's glad to feel it anyway.

She takes a quick selfie video where she's mouthing the lyrics and writes some benevolent sentimental gesture, wishing her followers their own cozy little holiday, then stashes her phone away to savor all this ErinTime.

Downstairs, Erin's making a racket. Clanking bottles as she pulls the refrigerator open to retrieve a couple of Perriers.

It's the sound of a thousand sleepovers: Soft footsteps on padded stairs. The noise Erin makes while slinking down the hallway. The doorknob to Kylie's room beginning to turn . . .

It's difficult to say whether she truly loves Erin or if it's all just the irrational fear of losing her childhood constant—that one final bridge to simpler times. Well, that and Christmas.

"Why us?" Erin asks, joining Kylie on the bed.

"He wanted to punish me," Kylie says. "I'm so sorry."

Erin has changed into a loose Summerfield High sweatshirt and comfy brown sweats, the kind typically reserved for Ben & Jerry's binges. "It's not your fault," she says after some pause.

It certainly is, but Kylie's not about to belabor the point. She also thinks it's the best thing that could've happened to Erin, though she keeps that assessment to herself.

Kylie takes Erin's Perrier and places it down, tugging at her sweatshirt, pulling her willingly to the mattress, head beside Kylie's hips.

For a while it's just two friends. But even the silence is different now. Erin in mourning, adrift in uncertainty, reflecting on all she's lost. And then there's Kylie, never more excited about the future.

"How do you do it?" Erin asks. "The gas station . . . Simon . . . all that you've gone through . . . Nothing fazes you. I need to know."

That's because I'm insane, Erin, rubber-room insane, Kylie would like to say but is too touched by the compliment to spoil the moment.

Like everybody today, Erin's worldview is based on what she can see. She never considers Kylie's sleepless nights or endless self-doubt. *I'm too ugly to go further. Too stupid to go all the way. Surrounded by people more talented . . .*

All that despair. It manifests as blemishes and broken posture. As split ends and as the occasional gray hair, gray hair at *nineteen*, for fuck's sake. Bad gas that feels like she's going to shit a brick. Literally.

"I lie," Kylie finally says. It's an easier answer than the truth, which is that she's completely broken.

Life is image. When the world looks at @CrystalShips, it's Kylie's soul that it sees. Dark and deranged, but honest at least.

"Makes me sad," Erin says. "We didn't used to do secrets."

"No?"

She takes Kylie's hand and sandwiches it between sweaty palms, tears streaming down puffy cheeks. A real shame to see such flawlessness sullied over something as inevitable as dead bodies. "Cameron's gone," Erin says softly. "His mother too. Up until last week I was thinking about what our wedding was going to look like."

"You need to keep busy." Kylie shrugs. "It's not about forgetting Cameron. You won't. You can't. But life goes on. Live yours while you've got it."

Erin hops off the bed and circles the room, examining Kylie's swag, leaning over her bureau to eyeball her newest facial cleansers. She lifts the bottle of Natura Bissé Diamond White Rich Luxury Cleanse and clucks, "Nice."

Kylie tips her Perrier, takes an accomplished swig.

"Used to think all this crap mattered."

"I'm your cautionary tale," Kylie says, thinking about the video she shot last night—her getting off to a violent group of rioters as they beat the shit out of some agitator—then gives her most innocent look.

"Cameron showed me there's more to life. We went to Europe and ditched that conference in favor of the most basic touristy stuff. Helped me remember we're part of something larger in this world. Rich and incredible history."

"There is no history anymore." Kylie takes a few more dispassionate sips of Perrier.

"If I were to go back to the game, it would feel so wrong."

"Let's start with what you want."

"I want to feel better."

"What'll make you feel better?"

"Feeling like I matter."

"Remember when Brady and I were a thing?"

"Hello? I directed your entire Insta feed."

"I felt like I needed to be working on my body all day, every day. For him. And for what, it turns out." *A great vid, for one thing.*

"We didn't know he was such a—"

"You said I'd hit all my goals if I posted them publicly. Peer pressure being the biggest motivator. It was the most important thing anyone's ever told me."

Erin smiles, but seems disinterested in the nostalgia.

"You asked for help with MonoLife," Kylie says. "Still got it?"

"Yeah. I do."

"There's a gathering coming up. For top members. And their plus-ones. Assuming I get the invitation, which could be any day now . . ."

"You want me to, what?" Erin seems animated for the first time since Cameron's murder.

"We'll rub elbows with beautiful people. Visit a part of the world we've never been to. At least not me, because I've never left Massachusetts. And we'll see if you're not motivated to get back at it after that."

Erin pulls back so she can see Kylie's face. "You're inviting me?"

"I'm letting you know there's an opportunity. If you're interested in joining me . . . well, that's up to you."

"No."

"I've got more money in the bank than most working families. I've got fame. Influence. Power. You can have those things too." *Power is everything*, Kylie thinks. Power to help Mom pay her bills. And the power to withhold that relief until Mom starts looking at her as an equal, not some minor annoyance in her life. Mom doesn't realize that all she has to do is ask and Kylie can change her life for the better. *That's* power.

Erin looks around as she considers Kylie's sales pitch, nodding as her eyes fall upon all the stations of the swag. She drops to the bed and rests her head on Kylie's shoulder. "I want what you have, Kylie." She inhales deeply, holds her breath a minute. "Wow. That's kinda freeing."

"See that, you're better already." *And better than me*, Kylie thinks, *because I've never been able to say that shit out loud.*

"Cameron thought you were a bad influence but . . ." Erin lets the rest of that thought go. It no longer matters. She gets up off the bed and starts for the door, pausing in the doorway. "I, uh, promised my dad I'd spend some time with him." A tired laugh, more like a groan. "I mean, it is Christmas, right?"

Kylie waves her wrist. "Go be there for somebody."

"Yeah, well, uh, tomorrow I'm going to visit Cameron's dad. He's a cop and all his friends are too, so I don't know how much talking he's done."

"Call me."

"Thank you, Ky." Erin's fingers fiddle with the jamb. "I would like to go with you."

"Merry Christmas, then."

"Merry Christmas."

Kylie closes her eyes as Erin retreats through the house, down the stairs, out the door.

Normal, see?

Once the BMW starts up, Kylie crosses the room and reaches for the phone she's got stashed between two stuffed animals. It's been broadcasting there since Erin carried in the Perriers.

"How's that for influence?" she asks her audience, rather smugly because why be humble when you know it's a slam dunk?

Then she kills the live feed. Within seconds, the notification ribbon spreads out across the bottom of the screen, and it's the least surprised she's ever been.

Congratulations, @CrystalShips, you are now an influencer.

The red X fades from her account. She bids adieu to that tier in real time, taking with it the target from her back.

Kylie pulls up her DM history with Mister Strangles and writes:

@CrystalShips: Now tell me where this fucking conference is, and how I attend.

Midnight Frequencies

"Wake up," a voice says.

Kylie's eyes adjust to the dark.

Through the window, the night is a sheet of unbroken onyx.

Her phone glows from the bedside table. A stack of MonoLife notifications. Each one from Mister Strangles.

"*Answer me.*" The voice is between her ears now.

The wound at the small of her back wiggles as if an insect was trapped beneath her flesh. She twists under strobing pain while on her stomach, caught between shifting worlds. The edges of reality frayed.

Wet heat pushes down on her bare flesh. A hard press sends pain up her spine, making her mouth fall open, her eyes cross. Her body is frozen beneath competing sensations of discomfort and relief, fluids flowing steadily through her veins toward the source of agitation. Kylie is able to swivel her head just enough to log the shadows behind her. Long and bony fingers bleeding out of the darkness, reaching then pushing on her shoulder blades, keeping her pinned.

From the cell phone glow, constantly reigniting each time Mister Strangles sends a message, there's enough light to reveal a swimmer's mask staring at her from within the gloom. Its features wrinkled, what Kylie reads as a show of surprise. Her pain intensifies to the point where her body jerks, then buckles beneath mounting pressure. The head snaps away from her lower back, bringing a moment of relief as the shadows inside the room shift, revealing that tussled mask, partially rolled up to reveal what passes for a mouth. A vertical gash, chin to nose, but opening left to right, sheets of yellow pus dripping off its discolored chin, pattering her back like melted wax.

She tries to scream but the only sound her voice will make is that of a MonoLife alert, metallic screeching filling the room like nineties AOL dial-up. Shock gets her body flailing, scurrying to the headboard, kicking the creature behind her, legs stabbing empty air again and again, finding nothing.

Only an empty bedroom filled with shadows.

"*Everything lies,*" the voice rasps and Kylie's ears wiggle. She has visions of spider hatchlings crawling up from the trenches of her brain.

She snatches her phone, taps into MonoLife where the pain in her back is already receding. A couple of thumb swipes and she's in her DMs, Mister Strangles looking to connect.

Kylie's eyes are heavy, unfocused. She presses ACCEPT and the app makes an airy *beep bloop* sound while MonoLife establishes a connection.

That old-time mask stares out at her. "*You are an animal looking at its own reflection on a riverbed.*" Its voice is muffled. Nearly broken. Every syllable stretched like taffy.

Through the window, all the neighborhood lights are out as far as Kylie can see. No streetlamps. No porch lights. Not a single star in the sky. Just Kylie's home on the edge of existence. Her windows whine against the gusting wind. The darkness outside trying to get in.

The only light left in the world sits cradled in the palm of her hand.

She hates to look there, but has no choice. Her mind goes spiraling once more.

"*You should not have spared her.*" The swimming mask is stretched so tight over Mister Strangles's face it kind of resembles skin. Obstructed lips part. A grin that forces the painted smile to stretch wider. "*You belong in here.*"

Mister Strangles brings his hand into frame, tugging at the bottom of his mask, fingers digging beneath it, pulling the material away.

His tongue licks his own dry and vertical lips, dark liquid oozing up from between the chapped cervices.

"*Make the case*," he says.

Kylie doesn't ask what he's talking about because she already knows.

"*Be the one*," he tells her.

Kylie doesn't ask "how" because she knows.

"*Become who you are.*"

Mister Strangles pulls the mask all the way off his head and just before his face is revealed, the connection drops with a defeated *bloop*.

The wind gusts harder. The front door whines and creaks as the cold air pushes through the spaces around it. Kylie shivers, feeling the draft from all the way upstairs.

The house is colder now that the outside has gotten in.

PART III

Pass Through

Cozy Little Christmas

Christmas morning.

Kylie's on the couch waiting for Dad.

Mom's a bit nervous, got home at two and has been up since five to put the bird in, and there're three different pots sitting atop the stove in various stages of prep.

An open wine bottle on the counter is halfway gone. This explains Mom's singing voice, prancing, actually prancing, to some version of "Jingle Bell Rock."

She declines Kylie's empty offer of help, determined to get this done as if *this* is going to be the thing that gets Dad back into this house.

Dad shows up at quarter of ten with two pies on his forearm. "Pecan!" he tells Kylie, adding, "Your favorite," when she has no reaction.

He's also carrying an oversized department store bag and starts stacking a bunch of wrapped gifts around the tree Mom set up by herself at some point. "Remember the year I got you, oh jeez, what was the name of that thing?"

"Let's not go there, Dad."

"No. What the heck was it called?"

"Zoom!" Mom calls from the other room, already giggling.

"Zoom." Dad twists his mouth to one side. "Is that right?"

"A *Zune*," Kylie says, to which Dad snaps his fingers.

"Zune. God, you were so excited you tore that wrapping paper off like an animal. When it wasn't an iPod, you threw it behind the couch and just bawled."

"You gave it to me three years after it was discontinued."

"Spoiled shit!" Mom yells fondly.

"I remember all this," Kylie says. "Traumatizing."

"Richard, come have a glass of wine."

"Be right there, Rachel," Dad says, sounding a little strained before he kisses Kylie's cheek. "How are you doing, sweetie?"

"I don't know."

"Better than some have it." He walks around the parlor with his hands on his hips, admiring the Christmas décor, following it like bread-crumbs through the house and into the kitchen, where Mom eagerly compliments his sweater. He gives her an obligatory peck too.

They open presents, mostly gift cards and cardigans. Kylie gives out dead smiles to approximate gratitude. Mom and Dad do the same.

She wrapped Mom a yellow satin skirt with a shark-bite hem, and a silk blouse to go with it, both from Nordstrom. Balenciaga sneakers to complete the ensemble. Two thousand dollars, and Mom keeps gasping, mind blown as she asks, "This is from your . . . influencing?"

It is, but Kylie doesn't want to sound that thoughtless. "It's paid for with money I earn *through* influencing. I picked those out special for you, Mom."

Mom gives a careful smile, the look behind it suggests that she'd rather Kylie start pitching in mortgage money, but Kylie isn't going to offer that on her own. It's been too many years of *dinner's in the fridge* and *let's talk later, I'm tired* to ever offer that, and now Kylie realizes they're more like strangers and have been that way for as long as she can remember. If Mom wants help, she can beg.

"Well," Mom says. "I can't wait to wear it."

Kylie laughs at the irony because where is she going to wear it, exactly? Olive Garden? And Dad's just clueless, saying "wow" and taking pictures on his old-ass iPhone 7, pretending they're still a family.

He's the recipient of some Black & Decker stuff that MonoLife sent. A new hedge trimmer, leaf blower, weed whacker. He pretends to love them and who cares if he doesn't. He tells Kylie how he'd been meaning to stock up because he's got a half-dozen yard projects to tackle come spring.

By dinner, Mom's killed two bottles of wine, mostly by herself, and Dad's halfway out the door, and the turkey isn't even cold yet. They eat and talk about old times. It has to be the old times or it'd be stone silence. Nobody here has anything else in common.

Mom's glimmer of hope turns steadily to despair with every passing glass, realizing this will not be the year for Christmas miracles.

And Dad's gone by two, because he's got Second Christmas with his new girl's family.

Mom's asleep on the couch by three and Kylie loads the dishwasher and scrubs everything that's too big to fit. It's the least she can do, and if she does it, she won't have to hear about how it was the least she could've done.

She's toweling off her hands when Duc reaches out.

@SolidusRush: Merry Christmas, psycho. Meet me at the lake.
One hour.
@CrystalShips: now?
@SolidusRush: no one around to bother us on Christmas Day 🐚

Kylie tosses a blanket over Mom, who's so drunk she only pulls it tighter to her body and rolls over with a slurry groan.

She takes Mom's keys off the wall and starts toward the meeting, stopping at the end of her street to send one more MonoLife message.

@CrystalShips: about to meet Duc, you still close by?

The screen responds instantly with, *@MissyMiss is currently typing . . .*

@MissyMiss: tell me where

Kylie does.

Duc's on the hood of his Hyundai, hands stuffed inside his winter coat. Breath swirling around his head like mist.

Kylie parks her mom's car, a black Nissan Altima, which is a considerable step down from the BMW, RIP, a good distance away. She grips the small defensive blade inside her pocket as she gets out.

Duc smiles like there's another shoe to drop, though maybe he's just excited to share his findings with someone. Doesn't matter. None of this is smart.

"In another life," he says, "I'd be jealous of your account. Clean. Confident. Nothing but the hits."

If it seems that way to him, it doesn't to her. All she can think about are the errors along the way. The early videos that did not perform as expected. Missed opportunities. Imposter syndrome.

Kylie murders those feelings now each day. Because she tells herself she's great and lies so often that she has no choice but to believe it. Has lorazepam on her night table as backup too. But doubt is a zombie and no matter how many times you kill it, it refuses to stay dead.

"Gonna tell me where to find her?" Duc asks.

"I had to come all the way out here to tell you?"

"I had to do it, you know." He sounds apologetic, still rationalizing his actions. A man who doesn't fully understand the why behind what he's done. Or he does, yet still can't live with the guilt.

"You're the one who leaked Annabeth's murder, right?"

"I figured the cops would get involved," Duc says. "And look, the feds came too. Save me from doing all the work, ya know? Except nobody did shit. You were the only one who got even a little curious. For everyone else, it was just another internet video. Their friend and classmate, butchered for nothing. Forgotten in one fucking day."

"Why'd you tell me about the app to begin with?"

"I know you, Kylie. You were going to be a pain in my ass if I didn't."

"True. I don't like the word *no*."

"Any regrets?" He jumps down off his car, one hand still tucked inside his oversized coat.

She's not sure what Duc wants to hear. She'd asked Missy that very question at the farm and her response had been, *I regret everything*. Kylie realizes that's how she's supposed to feel, but nothing inside her suggests that to be the truth. "No," she replies.

"Where's Missy?"

"Stillman farm, hiding out."

Duc laughs, slides a handgun out of his coat.

"Whoa. Take it easy, Duc."

"Oh, you think . . ." He locates the apprehension on Kylie's face and lowers the pistol to his hip. "No, don't worry. It's not like that. Come on." He starts for the tree line, turning once it's clear that Kylie has no intention of following.

Her fingers curl around the knife, knowing she can't stop him at this distance should he decide to shoot.

"Oh yeah." Duc takes his cell phone from his pocket, tosses the powerless brick into the snow. "You too."

She powers hers off so Duc can see, then leaves it on the hood of Mom's car. He nods with approval, resumes walking, soft crunching footfalls beneath his salty winter boots. "You're not going to believe this," he's saying, so far ahead of her now, his words lacking in clarity.

Kylie rushes to catch up, suddenly hot-stepping from one of his deep footprints to the next, traversing some homemade obstacle course.

Up ahead, Duc has stopped, one forearm draped against tree bark, breathing heavily.

Kylie catches up and looks out on the clearing before them, where one of Duc's lunch pals, Callum, maybe, she thinks, is stripped naked, five bullet holes blown through his heart, legs bent beneath his torso because that's how he dropped. The blood-spattered snow around him looks like an Icee.

"What did you do?" Kylie reaches for her phone on instinct, wanting to capture everything, remembering it's back at the car.

"What I had to." Duc slides his coat off his shoulders, lifts his shirt, and tosses that aside too, revealing fresh-carved scars across his body. Wounds that are only now beginning to scab over, forming crude symbols, foreign and unreadable. She's seen them once before: Duc's last video, in the interior of that sunken church.

He reaches down and lifts a gas can that Kylie hasn't noticed, starts dousing the nearby trees with a dark liquid. Everything's wet and cold out here. No chance of burning it down.

A couple of drops pelt Kylie and she leaps back, wiping the runny liquid off her coat, bringing her fingers up to her nose, then looking at them. It isn't gasoline at all.

Duc heaves the canister around, feeding what Kylie now realizes is Callum's lifeblood to the forest. Duc turning, turning, turning, spinning like a top until all the naked branches around them are dripping.

He tosses the canister aside and slaps his chest. "The shit I've had to do to get here, animals I killed . . ." He winces. "People I hurt . . ."

"The app didn't force you, Duc."

"You know you need to get dark in order to stand out, Kylie."

"You couldn't have done all this if you didn't enjoy it."

"I'm the hero of this story, Kylie! I did what I had to do in order to build an audience. What good is the truth if no one's around to hear it?"

All through the clearing, tiny patches of snow have been shoveled away, and Duc has carved symbols into the frozen ground at each station.

Kylie's eyes dart around the cold gray forest, trying to locate the source of the footsteps suddenly approaching. Slight crunches on compacted snow. A shadow drifting between trees, fingers raking against the freezing bark.

"You forgot one thing, Duc," Kylie says.

But Duc isn't listening. His mouth hangs open, throat scraping because he's found her at last. A woman grayer than this winter night comes gliding out of the shadows, pale white hospital gown tattered and billowing.

She's headed straight for them. Her permanent, cherubic smile and innocent eyes frozen, lacking in detail. Zero blemishes, age lines, nothing. And she's close enough now for Kylie to see it isn't actually a face at all, but a molded approximation of one.

A living simulacrum.

Mama Doll.

The snow at Kylie's feet launches up and the steel jaws hiding beneath it snap closed around the creature's ankle.

She screams, though her face never changes. That frozen childhood smile standing in complete contradiction of her wounded yowling.

Duc lifts the gun, sighting her. He shoots and her shoulder blows backward, flaking off in hunks of scattered plastic. Inside the wound, nothing. Hollow.

A second inhuman howl ignites behind those static features.

Kylie has no understanding of this ritual, its details lost entirely to Duc's madness, though she guesses that whatever sacrifice Duc made here has rendered Mama Doll vulnerable.

"I'll show you, Kylie!" Duc takes a few steps toward the ensnared creature. "How to kill these things! Nobody's ever done that!"

In the distance, more crunching snow. Kylie turns, spotting Melissa trudging her way up the hill wearing the same Ferrariwear as that night in the cornfield.

Duc seizes Kylie's hand, yanking her toward Mama Doll. "Watch this," he growls. "Understand."

Kylie's fingers tighten around the blade she's slipped from her pocket. It would be so easy to kill this thing. Position herself as some kind of hero. But to whom? Claire? Annabeth Wilson? All the victims of this app? To do that would be plugging herself back into misery and anonymity, Katy Perry reverting back to Katheryn Hudson and, well, no way to that. Selflessness isn't her style.

Duc presses the gun to Mama Doll's head, his own eyes bursting with satisfaction over what he's about to do. And then his head swivels, catching sight of Melissa, who continues walking toward them undaunted.

And Kylie seizes on this distraction, spinning on her heel and shoving the blade straight through Duc's ear. A crimson squirt stinging her eye as they push off each other, Duc reaching for the blade, trying to tear it free. He's already too weak, already dead by the time his knees give out and he plops onto his back at Mama Doll's feet.

Melissa has no visible reaction to this decision. Just continues her forward stride, stone-faced, moving in otherworldly silence. She reaches into her pocket and tosses something into the snow right at Kylie's feet.

Her phone, reactivated. MonoLife notifications stacked on the lock screen. The most recent among them reads:

@MissyMiss would like to Live Connect.

Kylie looks up. Melissa is gone. Mama Doll too. The trap sprung, but empty. There is only Kylie, alone with dead bodies.

She opens MonoLife and accepts Melissa's invitation.

Then Melissa is looking out at her from inside the glass, flashing the dullest of smiles. Over her shoulder, a floor-to-ceiling window showcases a gorgeous neon skyline.

"*I made it*," Melissa says, and for the first time there's a hint of the girl Kylie had once known. Rose-bloomed cheeks and summer vacation eyes.

"You're welcome."

"*It is important that you listen. You are an influencer, though you have yet to influence.*"

"I did," Kylie says. "Erin . . . do you, uh, even remember her? Anyway, she wants to get back in the game because of me."

Missy disconnects and is gone.

"Great," Kylie says, glancing down at Duc, body already stiffening in the cold, eyes popped wide in permanent disbelief.

"You know, you almost ruined this for me." Kylie spits on his frozen face, then walks back to her car and drives home.

There's a letter waiting in her mailbox, despite the fact that there's no mail delivery on Christmas Day. Kylie doesn't even know why she checks for it, but she was compelled to nevertheless.

The envelope is addressed to @CrystalShips in messy cursive. Inside is a sheet of paper that reads:

Dear Ms. Bennington,

You have been invited to participate in MonoLife's annual INFLUENCERS' BALL. Please note you and a plus-one will be flown to an undisclosed location for three days and two nights. All expenses will be paid. You must not tell anyone where you are going. Failure to comply will result in termination.

Save the date. March 29–31.

Kylie's crying. Tears of joy freezing on her cheeks as fractal snowflakes swirl around her.

Across the street, Mr. Anderson and his wife sit in their front window, admiring the snowfall on this beautiful silent night.

Kylie waves. They wave back. Her heart beams with magic. Real magic—the letter fading in her fist, print vanishing off the page like a distant memory. The MonoLife Way.

She walks across her lawn, sobbing. Inside, Mom is exactly where she left her, snoring, one arm dangling off the couch.

Kylie goes upstairs in the dark and sits on her bed, knees to her shoulders against the headboard. Right beneath Katy.

And she keeps on crying because this is everything.

All she wanted for Christmas.

Night of the Simps

In late January, Kylie and Erin drive back up to Gloucester with shovels and one pickaxe lying on the floor in the back seat of Erin's BMW.

The cemetery ground is harder than rock and it takes several hours to reach the coffin. Some sacrifices have to be made. In one hand, Erin uses Kylie's iPhone. In the other, a portable light to capture every detail.

Kylie drops her live-in leggings to her ankles and squats against the pathetic, practically nondescript headstone, giggling as golden splashes patter the engraving: SIMON LAMBERT. "I need this," she says. "It's catharsis."

"That he's dead and buried is enough for me." Erin hands Kylie the shovel.

Kylie had been particularly aghast to learn that Simon had a sister who lives out of town and covered the burial arrangements due to her own religious proclivities. Kylie hoped for cremation and instead had to spend several weeks seething at the thought of Simon resting easy six feet under.

She uses the shovel to pry open the coffin, and it's a surprise to see that Simon has already decayed so much. His features receding into a maniacal skeleton's grin. Kylie reads this as another taunt as she and Erin double over, gagging. Erin looks at Kylie like this has to be far enough. Can't they go home now?

Kylie snaps rubber gloves against her wrist, thinking, *Look at this, asshole, I came prepared.* With her feet balancing on either side of the coffin's edges, she bends down and slides silver aviators over his eyes.

"Make sure you get the headstone in the shot with his stupid face," Kylie says.

Erin frames the photo as requested, rattles off a couple of satisfying snaps. She hands the device to Kylie, who flips back through to make sure they've got at least one good one.

A crooked angle showing his name chiseled into the slab, silver lenses reflecting off Erin's backlight, is a great shot. Kylie writes out a caption, posts:

ProTip: The death penalty is a good idea, if executed properly— collab with @EndlessNights

She's unable to tag his account because it's been scrubbed from existence, and something about getting in the actual final word fills her with insuperable joy.

One swing of the shovel takes Simon's skull off his body. Kylie reaches into the goop, lifts it by the jaw, the wet crackle of jellied decay as she pries it up and climbs back onto solid ground.

"Do you feel the catharsis?" She smirks, using a Lysol wipe to clean the gore away before stuffing him inside a plastic Market Basket bag.

Erin wobbles back and forth looking a bit sheepish. "Kind of."

They cover the grave back up with the frozen dirt and hope nobody notices. Or cares.

The days fly by, everything in anticipation of the looming Influencers' Ball. Mom is out of town for a few weeks, helping work get a new branch up and running in Provo, Utah, and Kylie decides she wants to create a buzz ahead of the summit, starts brainstorming content that will get people talking.

Her plans are interrupted when Erin's tyrannical father dies. Dropped dead of a heart attack at fifty-two while clearing snow off the driveway.

Erin pretends to be devastated and mines it for untold amounts of social equity in post after grief-stricken post, but Kylie finds this performance rather insulting, because Erin's truth has always been in what she doesn't say, and she can't hide the relief in her eyes.

This death inspires Erin's slow return to social media—real therapy—where she even flirts a bit with MonoLife and Kylie can't see what she's doing because she's at such a low level, but thinks that's cute anyway.

My little protégée.

At night, Kylie carries Simon's head around her room, having scraped his lingering flesh off to polish the skull beneath. She shows off her swag. She scrolls MonoLife with his dumb chipped head wedged neatly in her lap, so he can't avoid seeing all her adoration. She gets off in front of him, taunting him with the flesh he never got to have.

Meanwhile, her Cash App keeps adding zeroes every time she looks at it.

The problem is, MonoLife comments are beginning to hint that she's in danger of becoming boring. The same old stuff.

Boring.

Her.

It's hard to stage anything locally because Summerfield is always looking over its shoulder with neighborhood watches and increased police patrols, but Kylie has the entire house to get creative in.

She meets with Agent Jasinski more times than she'd like. Always in parking lots. Always after-hours. There isn't much to say; all she's able to tell her is that they're flying out of Logan International Airport at the end of March on a private plane and how it's on the infallible Federal Bureau of Investigation to take it from there.

The summit cannot come soon enough.

To pass the time, Kylie agrees to go on a date with a local simp named Carter who refuses to stay out of her DMs, and the only reason she agrees is that it'll make good content for the ingrates who feel she's on the verge of losing her edge.

She walks into the restaurant wearing Roller Sneak wide-leg jeans by Mother and a denim trench by Belle & Bloom that goes all the way to her ankles, all the way to her Katy Perry–branded sandals in black-and-white polka dot. As if on cue, a thousand-dollar tip hits her Cash App along with a note that reads **love you mommy.** She gets a lot of these.

Carter shows up wearing his white-collar work clothes because he probably thinks Kylie can't tell the difference between them and evening-wear. He's doused in so much cologne that she's sneezing as soon as he sits down, and he spends the night making jokes about her allergies.

Kylie pretends that he's the funniest guy she's ever met and how did she happen to strike such gold? She offers a nightcap at her place, and Carter can't even bother to act surprised by the invitation. This infuriates her even more.

She insists on driving him, says she doesn't want a strange car at her mom's house, and promises she'll drop him off here in the morning. Only she can't even get all the way home, pulling her rental over on some back road while MonoLife streams from her dashboard mount.

"I need it," she says, rather unconvincing in her forced breathlessness, and Carter is so certain he's a shoo-in that he doesn't question that either. Just starts fumbling with his belt.

It makes what's coming next so much easier.

Kylie slides Mom's butcher knife out from the space between the door and the seat, seizing a tuft of Carter's hair with her right hand, slashing his throat with the other, squeezing his hair and bracing her forearm against the seatback to lock his head in place so she can saw through his neck like carving a turkey.

Those dumb eyes pop with surprise and his throat wheezes like a kazoo and blood squirts across the windshield and then goes trickling down.

It's not enough for Kylie, who sticks the knife into his chest. "You *always* bring a change of clothes for a date!" she screams. "Even just a nice Polo!" But Carter's already whiter than milk and no longer listening. She sticks him again, leaving the knife buried in his heart as she speeds home, wiping blood from her eyes.

The simps flood her $cashtag in approval. A year's salary, sixty grand, hits her account before she's even in the shower. Tomorrow she'll drive out to the marshland near Lake Salvi and push the car, complete with Carter's body, into the muck, then Lyft over to the rental place and pay cash for the "lost" vehicle.

She's getting better at solving these kinds of problems.

A couple of nights later, she picks up a guy named Nikolai in the produce section at Target, the two of them bonding over their frustration with unripened kiwis. He's acceptable enough to make it all the way home, where Kylie cracks his skull open with a meat tenderizer. He falls to the kitchen floor and she continues smashing until his head is shepherd's pie.

She takes a quick shower, letting MonoLife watch the blood rinse off her body. Then she slips into a T-shirt that reads ABCDEFUCKYOU and sits down for a live Q&A that's mostly marriage requests from accounts with Pepe the Frog avatars.

An old pervert slides into her DMs and says he'll give her a hundred grand if he can use her mouth as a toilet, but only if she wants to, because this isn't about degrading women. He's actually a feminist.

He sends her twenty grand, but all that really proves is that he's King Simp.

Kylie invites him anyway, leaves a note on the front door telling him to come inside, come upstairs, and to never mind the cameras. They're mounted everywhere now, her entire house a studio.

He enters, carrying a bouquet of roses and singing something about "his beautiful Crystal." Kylie ambushes him in the hallway, kicking through the closet door, naked, save for a plastic parka covering her body and the roaring chain saw in her fists.

She only has to touch the whirring blade against his shoulder and his arm detaches like it was only ever hanging by a thread. In a second, there's so much spurting blood she slips and tumbles to the floor, saw flying from her hand, sputtering to a stop.

The old bastard's having a heart attack, clutching his chest with his one remaining arm, a gargle in this throat. And then Kylie's crab-walking away because he's spinning in place, pissing and shitting himself into oblivion.

A hundred thousand new followers for that.

Kylie grabs her phone, staring straight into their souls. "Is *this* boring, you fuckers?!" Except her phone isn't a phone at all. It's a watermelon slice pressed against her cheek, exactly like Katy on the cover of her "Hot and Cold" single.

The answers are enthusiastic, impressed with what they call her "consistent depravity." The lengths she goes to entertain her followers, though one comment is overly critical in a way that dwarfs the effusive praise.

Eh, all you did is steal @EndlessNights' brand

This pisses her off so much that she drives to the park and runs over a jogger, backing over his head a few times to finish the job. Summerfield is expecting a foot of snow tonight, so she leaves his corpse behind and watches the Cash App donations flood in as she drives home.

"Stop simping for me," she says.

A follower who claims to have been a fan since the beginning asks Kylie to send pics of her feet. A disgusting fetish Kylie despises. She agrees to meet anyway and puts a handgun into his mouth, makes him suck on the barrel before blowing his brains out.

They give her six grand for that.

"Stop simping for me."

She's at the grocery store talking to the man in the chef's hat on the side of the cardboard burger box, who's telling her she really should be buying ground beef instead of the premade patties.

And Kylie's shouting back at the mascot, her sanity in pieces, telling him how she doesn't eat fucking meat with enough frequency for that, and how one time Katy dressed up as a hamburger just to make amends with Taylor Swift, and the man on the side of the box is adamant that they work better as rivals and it doesn't matter to him anyway because Taylor's *Reputation* album is better than anything Katy ever did, and now they're hollering in argument and people are beginning to gather, fishing out their phones.

Kylie rushes to the checkout with the box of antacids she doesn't remember grabbing and pulls an *US* magazine off the rack as well just because it has Katy on the cover and fuck the guy on the side of the frozen burger box.

She makes another thousand dollars as she's walking to her car and goes live just to beg these assholes: "Stop simping." It's just shy of telling them the truth.

The pressure is killing me. I can't anymore.

She's scrolling MonoLife later when she catches her reflection in the screen glass and screams out loud at what's there. A hollowed-out skull staring back.

And her screen is no longer that but instead a tiny portal into a rectangular void. She cups the phone in her palm and can stick her other hand inside, where the air is vacuous and freezing.

She yanks her fingers back and the tips are numb and frosted.

Little flecks of light shine way down in there, and it's like looking up at a distant starfield on the clearest summer night.

Except those lights are getting a little bigger, closer, revealing what they actually are: a million cell phone screens, each of them tuned to MonoLife, to @CrystalShips, all of them scrolling, scrolling, scrolling.

Inhuman appendages giving fist bumps. Endless approval. Hairy insect forelegs tapping in eternity. Little cockroach heads chittering in approval.

"Stop simping," she says, but the words only sound in her mind, because skeletons can't speak.

Her house is littered with body parts. Rotted meat. Bloodstains. Air fresheners dangle from every square inch of ceiling, but none of it helps. Sometimes, none of it's there at all and Kylie starts to think maybe it's all just a dream, but then she blinks and the blood comes back. It always comes back.

Asher calls as she's trying to stuff a forearm into the garbage disposal, where the shredder keeps jamming on an obnoxiously thick piece of jutting bone. *"Hey,"* he says. *"Haven't seen you on campus this semester."*

"I dropped out."

"Damn. Well, even though you stopped responding to my texts, I don't back down. Thought we could grab lunch. Catch up."

"Sure. Let's do that sometime."

"Let's do it today."

"No. I can't, I . . . have to break down cardboard."

"Hey, remember our talk? I'm not trying to move on you, I just—"

With a tug, the forearm comes free and it's slathered in so much blood it slips from her hand, goes flying into the parlor. "I really can't. Sorry, Asher."

"This weekend."

The persistence makes her deeply emotional and Kylie has to steady herself on the counter as her throat tightens and her eyes mist. Kylie would say yes to this, wants to, in fact, because Asher's date suggests normalcy—a way to live at least part of her life in anonymity. But Crystal is in control now, and that's the last thing she'll allow. "I'll call you," she says, then hangs up before he hears her crying.

Asher calls a few more times that week looking to solidify plans, but she never answers the phone again.

The next night, a former classmate from Statistics is naked on his knees before her and Kylie's naked too, a pair of garden shears against his throat while around them, the cartoon ice cream cone from the "This Is How We Do" video twerks to a beat nobody can hear while Katy stands in the corner with Pikachu, both of them laughing it up.

"Stop," Kylie says, pushing on the blades, sinking them into his flesh. Little streams of blood beginning to dribble down. "Simping."

Her Cash App explodes.

She catches her reflection in the mirror. The throbbing infection on her back is a tumor the size of a basketball. Crooked eyes and a lopsided mouth. Malformed arms flailing to draw her attention.

Her Cash App dings. Keeps dinging. She silences her phone but that doesn't stop the noise. More money than she knows what to do with.

"*Stop simping!*" Kylie screams and squeezes the shears. The boy's head pops off, goes rolling. "*Stop it!*" she shrieks. The headless corpse squirting onto her breasts like crimson ejaculate.

More money.

"*Stop!*" she's screaming, over and over, as the world gets woozy. "*Stop. Stop. Stop. Just sto—*"

The Trip

Kylie and Erin travel like rock stars. Have to pass through security like the rest of the cattle, but then they're having mimosas in the VIP lounge and nobody even asks to see ID.

Erin stuffs her carry-on into the small overhead as the flight attendant pours champagne flutes. He's a young man, probably thirty, dark brown skin, and bulging forearms. They turn to admire the way his uniform conforms to his beautiful ass each time he passes.

"Why me?" Erin asks once they're in the air.

"Who else am I going to bring?"

"Literally anybody."

Kylie watches Erin from across the aisle, thighs looking flawless in a short tennis skirt. "I don't like anybody else."

The attendant returns with lunch once they're over the Atlantic. A Mediterranean platter of olives, nuts, and several cheeses Kylie cannot pronounce.

He opens a bottle of Richebourg and gives the story behind it, which is something Kylie despises. Wine always has to come with one of those. And the people looking to get drunk just nod and smile and pretend it's so interesting.

They're children at a sleepover, thirty thousand feet in the air. They watch a movie that hasn't opened in theaters yet, drink a second bottle of Richebourg the flight attendant doesn't really want to give them, which only makes them want it more.

The most fun Kylie's had in years.

But the wheels eventually go down and they're standing on an island airstrip about as long as Erin's driveway, surrounded by water that goes on forever in all directions.

There's a boat at the tip of the island and the captain's a dark-skinned man with a thick European accent. He tells them to get comfortable because it's another two hours to port.

The ship slices through aquamarine water as Kylie and Erin eat fish and legumes. The captain tells them they're off the coast of Greece, headed to the most private island in the world. A place called Mastorakis.

It appears on the horizon, a small, jutting rock structure, topped with a fiercely modern home—glass and hard angles. Additional floors seem to exist inside the rock, as indicated by little windows and terraces that stretch all the way down its natural face.

"Oh my God, *Kylie*!" Erin screeches.

Kylie stares with swollen pride. *I crawled my way out of obscurity for this.*

"Welcome to Mastorakis," one of the servants says as they dock. "Let me take you up to registration so you can check in and be shown your quarters."

He loads their bags onto a small golf cart that putters up a single path, winding all the way around the mountain.

At the top sits an infinity pool, four tennis courts, an open-air bar and dance floor. People are already gathered there, everyone eyeballing the cart to see who's joining them.

Someone shouts, "Crystal Ships! Bae!" but they speed past before Kylie can pick the voice from the crowd.

Registration is at the front door. A man with an iPad greets them, asking for Kylie's phone. She opens MonoLife and the man clicks his tongue. "A tremendous fan, if I may."

He's cute, so yes he may.

He brings them down a long hallway to a row of elevators. "This house is a marvel . . . the thirty thousand square feet you see here are just the beginning. There exists an entire complex beneath our feet, tucked inside this mountain. A hotel, restaurant, and several other amenities where you can let off some steam."

They ride down a couple of floors and are brought to a luxury suite with a wall of glass that overlooks the ocean.

"Room service can bring whatever you need. Otherwise, feel free to mingle upstairs." He does a strange curtsy and shows himself out.

"Did you see Jay-Z up there?" Erin whispers.

"That wasn't him," Kylie says.

"We don't belong here."

"We do."

"You sure that wasn't Jay-Z?"

"That *wasn't* him," Kylie says, more sternly this time. "And even if it was, then he buys my fucking drinks. Think I care about his old ass?"

"I'm taking a shower," Erin says, back cracking as she stretches. "I want to go to sleep but . . . that's impossible with all the faces we passed up there."

She goes into the bathroom and locks the door. Kylie falls to the bed closest to the window, uses the Wi-Fi password card on the table to connect her phone, and goes straight to MonoLife. She slides the shoulder strap down on her tank and uses the in-app camera to snap a selfie.

In all honesty, she looks pretty fresh for thirteen hours of international travel.

That's what she writes beneath the post, adding, **This weekend is HYPE!**

You're not supposed to tell the world where you are, but she's stalked a couple of accounts, including @PurpleLipGloss, and it turns out you can crow just a little and that makes sense. If you can't vague-post your bona fides, you're a nobody.

The post does numbers. The usual flirty comments about her beauty. One comment calls her **the hottest goddamn psychopath alive,** which is the nicest compliment anyone's ever given her.

She enjoys it so much she takes another selfie, dropping the shoulder strap down all the way while pouting like she's ready for a kiss, and delivers that exclusive pic straight to his DMs.

And now that she's checking her direct messages, she has a question for @PurpleLipGloss:

@CrystalShips: Are you in Mastorakis?

@PurpleLipGloss: You made it? 😍

@CrystalShips: I'm here.

@PurpleLipGloss: Yussssss! Will you be hanging out tonight?

@CrystalShips: of course

@PurpleLipGloss: Message me later. We'll have drinks. Maybe make a little collab? 🤭

@CrystalShips: Do I

Shit. She's so nervous and hits SEND too early.

@PurpleLipGloss: good question 😂😂😂😂

@CrystalShips: do I . . . know who you are? not to sound weird

@PurpleLipGloss: Guess you'll find out. 🙂

Kylie disconnects, feeling like a fucking rock star.

Nights in Mastorakis

They eat dinner beneath a straw umbrella overlooking the pier.

Mediterranean chicken quinoa bowls consisting of olives, cucumber, roasted red peppers, and a splash of fresh lemon.

Some big YouTuber is at the table beside them, complaining to an exasperated server about the quality of the tuna in the antipasto while someone they don't recognize is going on and on about how her Spotify single got four million streams last month but still no record contract, and Erin is genuinely distraught because she has never heard of this singer, is worried that she's slipping.

You can't get anywhere near "Jay-Z," and Kylie's a hundred percent certain that it's not him, suggesting instead he's the guy who runs that e-Thot account, going around the world fucking influencers and rating their performances in the bedroom on a scale from 1 to 10 but who never gives out more than a 6.

A more famous singer walks around in a glass thong to remind everyone that her ass is marble, and Kylie works up the nerve to ask if anyone's spotted @PurpleLipGloss but doesn't want to come off too desperate, adding that they were supposed to meet for a drink.

The YouTuber tilts his head. "Who cares. She's a six at best. You realize that body's all Spanx, right?"

Kylie wonders if she can get this guy into a bathroom stall and melt his face off with the acetylene torch she watched one of the groundskeepers lock in the supply closet.

But the singer with the glass ass hops onto the bar at that moment, beginning to undulate to Darude's "Sandstorm," which is one of those songs that are vaguely perennial, even at two decades old, and now Kylie's back to suspecting that @PurpleLipGloss is ducking her and she's sitting there feeling like a fraud watching Erin make the rounds, laughing and complimenting and generally doing a much better job of mingling.

All Kylie can do is look at her DM history with @PurpleLipGloss, now a one-sided stream of desperation.

@CrystalShips: Guess we keep missing each other . . .

Erin's talking to the guy who shoots nature porn, graphic animal couplings from all over the world. They're with a woman who claims to be a werewolf, and he's asking if he can film a scene of her mating with another of her kind, and now it's a serious discussion around the logistics of that request, and they're pulling Erin into it, asking what she thinks about this and that, and Erin's throwing Kylie help-me eyes, but Kylie's feeling so burned in this moment she remains seated, scrolling being easier than socializing.

@MissyMiss has posted a video. A tilted angle of two women in eveningwear slinking down a familiar hallway. Kylie instantly recognizes them. Video Erin nudging Video Kylie, and Kylie knows what she's about to hear, because Erin had said it directly to her a little over an hour ago:

"This dress doesn't hold my boobs. At all."

They disappear around the corner and the camera turns back to the door. Missy's hand, complete with pink neon nails, twists the knob, then slips inside their room.

How is it unlocked?

She pauses in front of the vanity mirror and gives her audience a playful wink.

@MissyMiss has never looked better. Her stretch midi skirt is a metallic fringe Dolce & Gabbana, and it's paired smartly with a black Sydney funnel-neck, wool-and-alpaca-blend sweater by Annie Bing.

The Rebecca Minkoff sandals add a few inches to her height, drawing attention to her toenails, impeccably painted in sparkling gold.

She's evolved. Sometimes Kylie looks at herself and feels like a tourist pretending at being a tastemaker. @MissyMiss, on the other hand, has become the real deal.

She circles Kylie's bed and places a crumpled piece of yellow latex on the pillow, hot pink fingertips rake it like a paintbrush.

"For my friend, Crystal Ships. I thought she might want the souvenir."

The emoji mask, with its hysterical eyes and frozen tears, in many ways the impetus for Kylie's MonoLife career, appears to be laughing at her.

@MissyMiss turns the camera around to show her face. There isn't so much as a single pore out of step on that complexion. *"Forget the world,"* she says, and even though everyone on MonoLife can see this post, and the first bumps are off the charts, Kylie knows it's for her eyes only. One final nudge of encouragement. *"Become forever."*

The video ends and Kylie is left staring at the frozen thumbnail of that mask, filled with an indescribable sense of dread, as if her own extinction is imminent.

And then Erin's standing over her as Kylie snaps back to attention. "Want to take a walk?"

They start toward the road and as soon as they're out of earshot Kylie blurts out, "Melissa's here."

Erin spins on her heels and points at the roaring party behind them. *"Everyone's* here."

The road twists downward, around the mountain and to the pier. They're so far away the music has become a series of nondescript thumps in the distance. A couple of guests have ventured out this far as well, sprawled in the dirt, tripping balls and talking in chemically induced platitudes. "This matters, man. We're here. We made it. This is what it's all about."

"Where are we going?" Kylie asks.

Erin waits until they're farther down the road, stopping on a bend overlooking the ocean. They stand in silence, watching the waves break, the bare flesh of their shoulders touching. "Didn't expect to walk so far," Erin says. "Now I've got swamp ass."

"I'm kind of freaking out," Kylie says. "Melissa was in our room. She put that mask on my bed and—"

"How far down do you think this drop is?" Erin asks.

Kylie glances down, suddenly aware that her toes are floating on air, and it's a good fifty feet to the treetops below. She takes a step back, but Erin has moved behind her, preventing any retreat.

"Ky," she says. "Listen to me."

"Watch the video, Erin, please."

"Ky, not everything is about you."

Kylie turns over her shoulder. The ocean breeze is tussling Erin's hair so that it covers her face.

"I know you think you were doing me a favor by bringing me here but—"

"I just thought it would be the best thing for you."

"Charity. Lick up your scraps? That it?"

"No. How is this any different than when I was your protégée?" Kylie's voice is small, crushed by disbelief. The idea that Erin would conjure this kind of drama here. It's so small-time.

Erin's face remains hidden beneath her breezing hair. Kylie's so close that little strands of it are lashing her own cheeks. The tone between them has turned somber, partners after a breakup.

"Say what you brought me out here to say."

Erin taps the phone glass in Kylie's hand. "This is a lie. One great big lie that never ends. And you know what they say about lies."

Kylie's seething. No, she doesn't know what *they* say about lies.

"The truth is so messy, you can't blame people for preferring bullshit."

"We flew out of Boston this morning and landed in Greece. Where's the lie?"

"This party is quite real," Erin says.

"If it was your invitation that *I* accepted, it'd be different, right?"

"That's stupid, Ky. Just forget I said anything."

Kylie laughs. "Wow. You haven't changed at all."

"I have." Erin gives her a pat on the shoulder. "That's the problem." She starts back up the road, turning and walking in reverse. "Enjoy your night, okay? I'm tired. Cranky, I guess. I need to sleep. Talk tomorrow. Cool?"

"Whatever." Kylie waves her off, cools down a while, and then returns to the party, stopping at the strangers rolling in the dirt to ask, "Got any more of that shit?"

They do. She loads up. Then starts back.

"Crystal Ships!" someone shouts, then asks for a selfie. She recognizes a couple of users herself and does the same. @SuddenDawn turns out to be a gorgeous French boy who looks more Arabic than what you'd consider "traditional French." They do a few bumps of coke and she dances with a couple from Milan, dosing on E as their bodies twist and writhe together. They try coercing her downstairs to some celebrity orgy and she decides no thanks and winds up having a banal conversation with an Egyptian woman who claims to be the reincarnation of Hapshepsut. Kylie finds her account on MonoLife and follows it while they drink whiskey sours and talk about immortality. A young boy who isn't any older than Kylie professes his love after four more bumps and two Klonopins. The world blurs past, every encounter a dream. Kylie touches his cheek and tells him he's sweet, but loses him in a swarm of partygoers and winds up inside some actor's room she recognizes from an original streaming series she couldn't watch past the first episode. A mound of coke is piled on his bed table and the line to reach it is unending. Kylie passes time speaking to a wine mom she might've actually scrolled past once or twice, whose entire schtick is providing cleanup for her Babylonian demon husband because frequent ritual sacrifices are always leaving their otherwise aesthetic suburban home in gory shambles. Yeah, now that she's thinking about it, Kylie recalls consulting one of her older videos, a hot tip on how scrubbing shaving cream into gore-stained bathroom tile will take the blood out quicker than anything else, but overall her content is incredibly basic and a bit too Reels-y for Kylie's taste, on the verge of pandering, and it's mildly enraging to have to consider that even MonoLife has its share of undiscerning viewers. The woman reeks of Franzia, and Kylie gives her the brush-off to converse with a guy who does dramatic readings of old Xbox 360 *Call of Duty* game lobbies, but he can't stop talking about what a big deal he is, and so then she's chatting up some nervous weasel who suffers from a debilitating selfie addiction if his profile page is any indication. Just endless shots of his face, regressive features becoming somewhat insulting the more she's forced to see it, over and over, the longer she scrolls, hideous untweezed eyebrows raised high as he documents splattery highway accidents and other gruesome fatalities, the good stuff always reduced to the distant background, broken bodies and busted heads always second fiddle to his eternal meme face. And all this while a young brown-skinned woman keeps tapping her shoulder, which Kylie acknowledges but doesn't really acknowledge. Until the woman takes Kylie by the shoulders and spins her around. "Why don't you recognize me?!" she asks, and Kylie's eyes are everywhere else in the room, rolling and blurring and her jaw is sliding and scraping and nothing's in focus. She says a few more things Kylie doesn't hear. It sounds like "Glue Clorox" or "Flu Ox" and Kylie only shakes her head and starts to get annoyed when the woman gets closer, tonsils to eardrum so to speak as loudly and as clearly as possible.

"Blue. Ferox."

It snaps Kylie right back to the world. "No," she says. "No way!"

They snort a couple of lines together and then break off, Kylie bouncing around the halls like a pinball.

"Dayana Velasquez," Blue says, extending her hand. "Friends call me Day."

"Kyliebennington," comes the slushy reply.

"You're a wreck," Day says, whispering in Kylie's ear that they should get something to eat. Put something in her stomach in order to soak up all that booze and other substances.

It takes a moment to grasp the meaning behind that suggestion. Then Kylie's grinning and her heart's pounding with the possibilities.

"I do not think anyone is up to stopping us," Day adds.

They point to strangers, whispering who would make the best meal. Day has a lot more strategy behind her choices. Clean eaters are best. Kylie wants to kill a celebrity just to absorb their aura.

They stalk the singer of some shitty punk band, following him down one floor, certain they're being sly, two sloppy drunks leaning on each other, giggling.

"You're in that band," Day fawns, pointing to him.

"See you ladies tomorrow, okay?" He quickly ducks into his room, where they laugh at the sound of a lock chain sliding against metal.

Kylie's curious hunger grows, confessing to Day how much she thinks about it. Day gets her salivating by talking about the flavor of pan-seared human brains with a bit of salt and pepper and just a dab of truffle oil. "Tastes like . . . roasted Brussel sprouts." She cocks her eyebrow as if she's being seductive. "You cannot believe the flavor."

"When can we eat?" Kylie asks, growling. Day presses her hand against her mouth. Kylie's rolling so hard she starts licking her palm, which Day doesn't seem to enjoy but tolerates anyway.

"Patience, Crystal. I've got the whole weekend to introduce you to other worlds." Day tugs her along as the hallway tilts like a fun house attraction.

She wobbles, about to lose her balance when Day grabs hold, says something that's just mumbles in Kylie's ear.

And then she's back in her room, Erin snoring with a sleep mask over her eyes, cell phone spitting white noise. The world continuing to turn like a Tilt-A-Whirl.

She drops a pillow over her face to steady herself. "I think I'm gonna be s—"

Too late. She vomits over the side of the bed, then passes out.

We Live Inside a Dream

No . . . she doesn't.

Kylie's eyes gyrate clockwise as her lids flutter open.

Erin's standing at the foot of Kylie's bed, sleep mask stretched over her eyes. Gibberish humming in her throat.

Kylie lifts her head upward, eyes flapping. "What?" she tries asking but isn't certain she actually makes a sound.

Her phone glows from the bed table. She's able to focus her vision long enough to read the message.

@CrystalShips is now live.

Her brain feels dislodged. To move an inch brings more pain than she can stand. She presses a hand to her puke-crusted face as Erin's voice rises into a chant.

"Who dosed us?" Kylie asks, fingers flailing around inside her Tory Burch bag for the AirPod Pros she knows are stuffed inside. Fishes them out. Slips them in. Swipes the MonoLife notification and follows it inside.

"Hey guys, it's Crystal . . ."

It's Kylie on-screen. There's no denying that. Crystal on her bed, Katy smirking down from the wall behind her.

Kylie's eyes find focus as she types into the chat bar.

@CrystalShips: MY ACCOUNT IS HACKED!!!

The SEND option is grayed out, giving instead the message: **YOUR ACCOUNT IS CURRENTLY IN USE.**

"*So, I've decided to be honest with myself,*" Crystal is saying on-screen.

Kylie rubs her temples as if that might get knots out of her brain. There exists a vague memory of slipping into that tiered empire-waist mini summer sundress that Crystal is wearing on livestream. She'd tried it on a couple of days ago in anticipation of this trip, and though she doesn't remember ever wearing it while going live, there is more familiarity in this broadcast than she can process.

At the edge of the bed, Erin continues to stand watch, one accusatory finger drawn down on Kylie. She's speaking a language Kylie has never heard, something primitive and old and dead.

On stream, Crystal holds a phone to the screen, placing a call on speaker. "*Hello, Agent Jasinski?*"

"*Why haven't you left?*" Claire's asking.

"*I'm on a later flight. Could you come over? There're a few last-minute things I'd like to talk about.*"

"*Fifteen minutes,*" Claire says, line clicking dead.

Somehow, there's a hard cut in this live video and we're outside, watching Claire's sedan roll up on Kylie's house.

Erin's voice rises in competition with Kylie's headphones, her babble now interspersed with English, though still making about as much sense: "*The barrier's falling down, staying down . . . !*" she's screaming, at least in English now.

Kylie sits up, very much awake. Her brain feeling as though it's bleeding out her ears and she thinks, somewhat irrationally, *I hope Day didn't eat it last night.*

On-screen, Claire crosses the grass at Kylie's house and she feels a swell of pity for the agent. She's beautiful. Knows she was born too early in life for the kinds of opportunities Kylie has been given.

Once upon a time, Claire was probably everyone's fantasy. A hundred homecoming dreams. Kylie knows her own beauty won't last forever, and the idea of winding up like Claire keeps her awake most nights.

Human bodies are terrible, disgusting things. A doomsday clock, always ticking down, rotting from birth.

Claire's on Kylie's doorstep, taking a deep breath for some reason, then knocks. Nobody answers.

Claire mumbles something about "*fucking games*" and pulls her cell phone from her jeans. "*I'm outside.*"

"*Then you'd better come inside.*"

Claire opens the door and the floating camera follows her in where she drops to her knees reflexively, vomiting into the blood puddles that are pooling there.

It takes a minute, but she gets up, knees wobbling, gun drawn, bumping into the shaky IKEA coatrack that had been in the hall when Dad lived there, but is long gone.

In the kitchen, severed limbs are stacked on the island counter like a butcher's case. That old eighties refrigerator they'd inherited from the previous resident humming like a generator. It hasn't been there since her tenth birthday.

"*What did you do, Kylie?*" Claire mumbles, vomit hardening on her chin as she sidesteps discarded corpses and broken bodies. From somewhere off-screen, an animal's growl surges and Sporto dashes between rooms, skeletal tail wagging as it drops a femur bone in Claire's path.

"*Kylie . . . ?*" Claire calls, leaping back as the startled dog goes rushing off into the backyard, patio door wide open. "*Oh my God. Where are you?*"

Kylie is watching from an estate in Mastorakis, wiping tears from her eyes, uncertain of who that girl in her bedroom is.

You know full well who she is.

The camera floats in the hallway outside Kylie's room, an abstract angle looking down on Claire's blonde head as she reaches for Kylie's doorknob. Beyond it, Katy's "E.T." is cranked so loud the speakers sound like they're about to blow.

Claire enters Kylie's room as Justin Bieber, Rihanna, and of course Katy greet her from every wall like nostalgic gargoyles.

Claire dips into the bathroom, ensuring it's as empty as the rest of the place, and the bedroom door slams shut from off camera.

Cut. Claire moving back through the bedroom. Toward the noise. That's when Crystal launches up silently from the far side of the bed, wide-eyed, sledgehammer raised.

Claire's at the door, about to leave, when she realizes she's not alone. Spins. Her scream comes on fast, shrill and panicked, drowning out Katy. The mallet falls, cracking Claire's forehead. She hits the floor like her legs have given out as Crystal screams, *"Still more of a Taylor Swift girl, you bitch?!"*

The camera pushes in so fast it's like a reflex. Claire's hemorrhaging face, the twisted, awful expression as her eyelids flutter, flashing empty white orbs beneath.

"I know you're mad," Crystal says. As if she knows Kylie is watching. *"You're thinking . . . I shouldn't have."*

The camera angles down. What remains of Agent Jasinski pisses herself, denim thighs becoming a moist shade of dark blue.

Someone writes **waifu** in the comments, and Kylie doesn't know if they're talking about Crystal or Claire's defecating corpse.

This isn't real, Kylie thinks. It's the chemical shit she dosed herself with tonight, remixing her desires. Her consciousness.

Crystal smirks into the camera as if to say, *If you say so.*

At the foot of Kylie's bed, Erin suddenly tears her mask away from her face, mouth popped, throat flexing, screaming in deafening hurricane gusts.

The tears rushing down Erin's cheeks are blood-red and she drops to her knees, fingers curled, shrieking, *"Why won't you die?!"* while on-screen, Crystal lifts the sledgehammer high and sends it rushing back down on Claire.

Recognition

"Jesus," Erin says from somewhere.

Kylie's eyes pop and white sun reflects off the Grecian Ocean, the entire window alive with blinding glare.

"Let's get you up."

A soft tug on Kylie's arm as she allows herself to be taken from bed, dragged across the room, one arm looped around Erin's neck.

"Hold on," Erin says. Leaves her leaning against the sink. The shower sputters, then sprays. Hands back on Kylie, squeezing her hips, sliding her stained underwear down to the linoleum.

Kylie's shivering as Erin guides her toward the stream. The water's cold, shocking her system, parting the clouds inside her congested head.

"It's my own stupid fault for leaving you," Erin says as she pours body wash over a sponge and works it into lather. Kylie braces against the support rail, stomach about to revolt. Erin squeezes the sponge and douses Kylie's scalp, tugging on the hardened vomit in her strands. "God, why won't this come out?"

Last night isn't exactly clear in Kylie's mind. Flashes of things, Erin at the foot of her bed, for example. She'd ask, but talking's too hard right now.

"*Can I have your attention please, MonoLifers.*" An announcement starts through hidden speakers. "*We hope you enjoyed your first evening on Mastorakis Island. Believe me when I say it is my pleasure to receive each and every one of you.*"

"God, where's the volume," Kylie whines, squeezing her eyes closed to keep the vomit at bay.

"*I am Grover Keeling, CEO of MonoLife. I welcome you to my home. And to the fourth annual MonoLife Retreat.*"

"Someone actually lives here?" Erin says.

"*We extend to you our gratitude for making MonoLife your online home of choice. And, even more importantly, for being custodians of our secret. You are here today because you understand this to be our greatest asset, how we are able to provide you with the lives you have . . .*"

Just listening to Keeling brings a swell in pride. Damn right Kylie understands.

"*We would like you all to join us for breakfast on the dining floor. Simply make your way to the elevators and my staff will be on hand to direct you. Oh, and please arrive no later than ten in order to ensure we remain on schedule for the day.*"

"I don't think I can eat," Kylie says, taking on sponge duties with a trembling hand, soaping off, turning the water as warm as it'll go.

"I don't think we have a choice."

Erin insists on staying in the bathroom as Kylie stumbles from the shower. She has to pee and pushes Erin just beyond the doorframe because her bladder's otherwise too shy to relax.

"Do you have a sense of what we're supposed to wear?" Erin asks.

Kylie checks her phone from the toilet. The video she dreamt last night is nowhere on her timeline. Or in her DMs.

Yet somewhere inside her mind exists a rogue memory. An experience. The sledgehammer cracking though Claire's skull, the terrible smell that followed, the vague guilt over killing someone she actually kind of liked . . .

They have to be downstairs in an hour, which means they're under nerve-shredding pressure to look good. Better than everyone else. Erin calls housekeeping to please come clean the vomit while they're out and Kylie slides into @PurpleLipGloss's DMs, asking:

@**CrystalShips:** Casual dress? Or knock 'em dead?

@**PurpleLipGloss:** both without trying to do either 😺😺😺

That doesn't help. Though it makes a certain kind of sense. And at least she's responding to Kylie's messages again.

In order to relax and get centered, Kylie streams Katy's fifth studio album, *Smile*, as she reviews her clothing options. Except Katy isn't helping this morning. The album has taken on a decidedly unnerving dimension. While attempting to be an affirmation, Katy embracing her age, and the declining relevancy that comes with a perennially young culture, it is today impossible to overlook the underlying despair beneath every song.

And it's clear that *Smile* is really about the end of Katy's dominance as a pop superstar. While there is no greater legend on earth, everything wanes and Katy seems to have embraced this—hence the frumpy clown energy on the cover: a depressed-looking Katy wearing a big red honker.

Suddenly, all Kylie can think about is how Katy does Las Vegas now, "Last Friday Night" playing to scores of the drunk and the desperate who kind of remember it from their own pasts, a distant daydream when their lives seemed stuffed with possibility.

A depressing fate, one that fills Kylie with the kind of anguish she's never otherwise felt. To think, not even Katy Perry can stave off inevitability.

With *Smile*, it turns out that Katy is the only one who cares enough to teach Kylie that nothing lasts forever. Her time is now, and she shouldn't waste a second of it.

Which is why Kylie chooses belted white linen pants by Caslon and slide sandals on a block heel by Steve Madden. She chooses a pastel oversized zip hoodie from I.AM.GIA to complete the ensemble, and Erin's watching the whole time like, *Really?*

"I'm dressing for me," Kylie says. "Because I've spent my time on MonoLife dancing for them."

"You never stop dancing," Erin says as she chooses an angelic white mock neck pointelle sleeveless sweater from the St. John collection and a Topshop salmon flounce midi skirt. Patterned slip-ons by Rebels with off-pink hexagon earrings complete the ensemble.

Kylie stares, somewhat jealously, at Erin's reflection while painting her lips in the mirror, tying her hair in a swooping ponytail. "Everybody works for somebody. So long as I'm happy and getting mine . . . fuck it."

"Yeah. I guess."

"I dance, sure. And my followers pay me to keep going. I keep it up, I might even be a millionaire by the time I'm twenty."

"Forget I said anything, Ky. Let's just go."

Everyone on Mastorakis is heading to breakfast at the same time. The halls are filled with recognizable faces and all the elevators have lines. People make small talk as they wait.

"Erin . . ."

Kylie turns and sees some actress known more for being an Insta thirst trap these days—a couple of flecks of white powder beneath one nostril.

"I thought you were done for after last night," the actress croons.

"Oh my God!" Erin exclaims, hugging her, making no motion to introduce Kylie. The woman is about to step into the elevator with them, when someone farther down the hall calls her name and she decides to hang back. "Let me catch you down there, love."

"Thought you went right to bed last night," Kylie says as the doors close.

"I got there, eventually."

The dining floor sprawls on forever. Sharp-angled furniture, backless chairs. The walls are just windows, so most tables have a healthy view of the empty emerald ocean that surrounds them, and sparkling water sits in ice buckets at every table. A DJ plays a steady mix of chillwave as the crowd bleeds in, gets seated.

They find their names at the same table and are quickly joined by an NBA player Erin recognizes, remarking how Cameron would've been psyched, and then lapses into teary silence at his memory.

The NBA player grins. A hard time deciding which of them he wants to charm. "Who's into geometry?" he asks, smirking. "'Cause one of you can replace my X without asking Y."

"You've got to be kidding me," Kylie mumbles beneath a healthy swig of Perrier. Actresses. Athletes. Kylie resents having to claw it out with celebrities, though she understands why they're here. In some ways, they need it most of all. Everyone's desperate to be themselves on the only platform that allows it.

NBA is persistent and convinces Kylie to swap MonoLife handles in order to learn more about each other. Then they're sitting side by side, scrolling their devices in silence in order to feel connected.

His profile is so dreadfully boring Kylie barely looks at it. And he's got way less followers, so she couldn't care about him at all, begins checking her messages instead.

NBA likes seeing her naked, though. He looks Kylie over as he finds a few of her most risqué posts, a certain air of mystery suddenly deflated without even the slightest effort.

"What's it like?" he asks.

"What?"

"You've . . . killed, like, actual people. A lot of fuckin' people, it looks like."

"You think that's bad." She points to a man sitting a couple of tables over. "He's from Vatican City. You should see the shit he's up to . . ."

Kylie watches a woman in an ink-black pantsuit step to the dais in the center of the room, clearing her throat into the mic. "Can I have your attention please, MonoLifers?"

The chatter winds down to a series of shushes before dying out entirely.

"For those who don't know me, I am Miss Jules. MonoLife's Event Ambassador."

Rampant applause. Miss Jules smiling, riffing off the enthusiasm. "Boy, is this an exciting weekend," she says. "I look out and see so many old friends. Welcome home. We couldn't have come this far without you."

Applause, woots, and whoops.

"But what *really* pleases me is the number of new faces that I see. As you know, MonoLife is growing rapidly. And because of that, it gives me great pleasure to introduce to you our founder, making his first-ever public appearance, Mr. Grover Keeling."

The crowd is ravenous now, house lights dimming, a spotlight beaming down on a side entrance as Keeling hobbles out to hysterical cheers. A frail wave as he limps toward the dais on unsteady footing, where one of the guards has to step in and guide him the rest of the way.

Miss Jules relinquishes her spot at the mic, leaving Keeling with his arms outstretched.

"Welcome," he says, voice muffled, as if behind a mask.

A standing ovation. Slow claps. Proud faces. All a bit much for Kylie's chemically altered brain.

"We grew over One. Thousand. Percent. Last year." Keeling's voice is so frail he sounds on the verge of forgetting his next word. "So, give yourselves a nice round of applause for creating the kind of content that gets people talking . . . *without* talking."

More applause while Keeling looks out on his subjects, a chaotic pattern of stitches across his face, various skin hues hemmed hastily together. The sleeves of his suit dangle past his hands, and though Kylie is a bit too far back to say for certain . . . it looks as though he has only three fingers.

"We once believed social media would connect us. Instead, opinions were outlawed. Actions dissuaded. And for what? The privilege of risking your jobs, your friends, your lives . . ."

The crowd hisses that sentiment down and Keeling nods, feasting off the negativity.

"Not the MonoLife way. With your help, we are remaking the world."

Someone yells "*Based!*" as the curved OLED behind Keeling ignites and five simple words fill the screen.

THE LAST COMMUNITY ON EARTH

More applause. Kylie isn't focused on the branding, but on Keeling himself. Doesn't anyone else notice he's an inhuman freak?

Erin's still sobbing into her water, convulsing harder the more she tries to turn it off—incredibly annoying and self-serving behavior.

Is she trying to ruin this for me?

The lights dim. Shutters descend from hidden slats above, covering the windows and plunging the hall into pitch darkness. On-screen, the words THE LAST COMMUNITY ON EARTH begin morphing into three syllables: MONOLIFE.

"Let's take a look at where we've been this year," Keeling says. "Before we talk about where we're going . . ." He has to spin his entire body around to see the screen.

The video opens on a nightclub shooting, cuts to a gang rape, then to a man pulling his entrails from his own body, one at a time. There's @BlueFerox cooking a skinned face in a frying pan, and Kylie cheers on her appearance.

Even Erin has stopped crying, watching the screen from between her fingers as Kylie flashes across it, bruised and bloodied, firing into the floor of her BMW as Simon cries out from beneath it. His anguished groans are overwhelming on this theater setup, louder than the montage music, and she wishes she could just freeze this moment and hear them forever.

Kylie is suddenly high again seeing herself bigger than some movie theater screens. She's a star. And they love her here, if the applause is any indication.

Now it's a yacht bumping against a migrant barge somewhere off the Mediterranean. A man shouting "Welcome!" into a bullhorn as disheveled people look on with hopeful glimmers. But the camera pulls back, revealing four people with assault rifles in their hands who take aim and open fire.

There's a machine attack in Paris where a blonde reporter is hacked to bits and everyone in the audience cheers her death. A man livestreams his suicide off the Eiffel Tower. A hotel employee sneaks into celebrity suites and exposes their most embarrassing medications. An older man in a hallway shouts into the camera, *"You are not going! You want to play dress-up the rest of your life, do it on your own dime!"*

It takes Kylie a moment to recognize him. He's the last thing she expected to see this morning, and so even though she's been in that same kitchen a million times, he doesn't register as familiar any more than his surroundings do.

It's Erin's dad.

And across the table, Erin's looking at Kylie now. No more tears. Just the beginnings of a wicked smile.

"I hate you," Erin's voice snaps from on-screen and then the camera is rushing from the kitchen, out onto the snow-dusted back patio and into the pool house, where flickering candles are arranged in a circle.

Erin puts the camera back into selfie mode, revealing dark robes, strange calligraphy stenciled across her cheeks. Drowned eyes that are both cruel and vulnerable. *"I pray to you, Morrigan,"* she snarls, words wobbling as she kneels inside the ring of fire. *"Liberate me, all the years I've hid from his old-world thinking. No more oppression."*

"What the fuck?" Kylie mouths.

Erin just shrugs, too amused by the shock on her friend's face to muster anything more. "I really thought you knew."

On-screen, Erin's eyes roll to the back of her skull, and what replaces them is thick, blood-filled orbs that go dribbling down around the curve of her cheeks.

Kylie has to look away for a second, not because she's disturbed but because the envy is considerable. The lighting, the angle, the fetishistic way the blood seems to pour across Erin's lovely features—everything is just perfection.

My God, Kylie thinks. *She went all "Dark Horse" on me.*

The video flips back around to Erin's POV, and the audience is rushing back inside her house, gliding up the stairs, pushing into the bedroom where Kylie had once tried to record Erin and Cameron screwing.

Sounds of agonized choking. Mr. Palmer gasping, though the camera cannot seem to find him. Not on the bed, or on the floor—

But on the ceiling.

He's grabbing at his collar, his face the color of eggplant, inflated eyes on the verge of bursting from his head.

Erin's mother shrieks somewhere off camera and you barely hear her over all the commotion.

And then Mr. Palmer launches toward the floor, faster than a missile, neck snapping on contact, legs folding down over his shoulders, crumpled and just utterly broken. The hall bursts into fevered applause.

It's like being bitch-slapped in front of a thousand strangers, Kylie going numb all over. "What's, um, your handle?" she asks, quietly.

"@ButterscotchGarden."

Kylie types in the name. It doesn't come up.

"Oh, I blocked you right off," Erin says. "It wasn't really that I couldn't find your content—it's that I never wanted you to see mine."

Kylie's wiping sudden, angry tears off her face.

"How clueless am I supposed to be?" Erin scoffs, a healthy dose of venom in her voice. "I mean, as soon as you started hanging out with Ben Austin, I knew exactly what you were up to. Took a minute to learn the ropes, but once I did . . . catching up to your ass was easy."

NBA realizes there's escalating tension here, mumbles something about using the bathroom, and then excuses himself. Kylie watches as he winds around tables, hunched over to keep a low profile, sliding into the first empty seat he can find so as to watch the rest of the presentation in peace.

"Look at it this way," Erin says, a little louder. "You blame yourself for Cameron's death but . . . I think Simon was so in love with you that he was unable to kill you. So, he came after me. My red X. To kill the queen."

This makes Kylie feel even worse. An urge to spit in Erin's face. Let her know that she personally kept Mister Strangles on a leash, though looking back at that night in the Morning Bean, Erin had probably realized right off the bat what was happening.

"I was going to resurrect Simon after it worked so well with the dog," Erin says.

"Sporto . . . that was *you?*"

"I had plans to see if undead Simon would come after your ass, but you were so damn impatient, just had to dig him up." Erin taps her phone screen a few times and *voilà!* Kylie is unblocked. She can search. And follow.

Erin's got two and a half million followers. One million over Kylie.

Her profile picture alone is enough to place Kylie in a state of helplessness. Erin as Maleficent—a clue if ever there was one—bent over, giving her followers a generous glimpse of bursting cleavage. No additional incentive to follow necessary.

Kylie scrolls. Ten videos from her two weeks in Europe. The same recurring cast of old European women, all of them standing around bonfires, dancing with pagan masks over their faces, stabbing shriveled men with jewel-encrusted daggers, praying to silhouettes barely visible in the forest blackness.

Prior to Erin's European vacation, there are even more rituals, and Kylie's scrolling back through the last six months of her life, realizing that Erin has outplayed her at every single turn.

Here's Erin in robes, a lock of red hair in a metal vise. A video called "Kill the Competition." Kylie doesn't have to click it to know what it's all about, recalling the image of Erin at the foot of her bed in the middle of last night, an incantation in her throat that had crescendoed to a desperate question: *"Why won't you die?!"* The question indicating to Kylie that Erin has been at that awhile.

Onstage, Keeling is proselytizing about the future of MonoLife. The crowd gives their "Amens!" while Kylie feels as though she's stepped outside herself. That earlier swell of pride, long gone.

All she feels now is humiliation. Weakness over her inability to leave Erin behind, the fear and nostalgia and need. All of it biting her throat now, causing pain, upsetting her like nothing else.

She scrolls, keeps scrolling. There's Sporto crawling out of his doggie grave, surrounded by different stones and salts and hastily painted symbols across his tombstone. And he keeps yipping at Cameron's hand until Erin tosses a chipmunk chew toy into the shot, and that actually works, the dog dropping immediately into the dirt, gnawing contentedly on squeaking rubber.

There's Brandi bursting into flames in her hospital bed, springing up, feet to the floor, already so badly torched that her bones practically slip off her flesh and what collapses there is little more than a smoking skeleton.

At the end of last fall, Veronica Gomez takes too many opioids out of what's probably Erin's hand, then strips down to nothing and goes marching toward the blackened waters of Lake Salvi, where she swims for a minute before slipping beneath the surface forever. That's when an equally naked Erin gets to her knees in the sand and begs the dark gods to deliver Erin waves of MonoLife success in exchange for this sacrifice.

And then there's a video called "Down the Dirt Mouth," which opens in close-up, what looks to be a vine somehow looping around a piece of wood, probably done in a reverse shot, somebody tugging an old leafy tendril off a branch. But no, the camera pulls back and it's not a branch at all, but a forearm, minted skin that's flawless enough to belong to Erin. Her voice gasps off camera, nervous breaths that come puffing into the shot, manifesting in the late fall air like excited ghosts, complementing the vision of spindly vines as they continue twirling, covering her wrist in leaves. The camera lifts even higher in Erin's free hand to show more tendrils slow-wrapping around her bare torso, her naked shoulder, all the vines tightening at once as—"humph!"—her breathless grunt is both pained and terrified. The organic restraints pull her body taut, down onto a leaf bed. Her presence there gets the ground stirring, disrupting a network of dirt-hewn roots that begin slithering out from under her body, a nutrient delivery system beginning to pulse with an orange glow. It syncs with the hot ember light that's now coming off her natural bindings, Erin's life force being siphoned straight from her body into . . . whatever's in the ground beneath her. An exaggerated face taking shape there, bulbous crimson eyes appearing like blazing coals. They seem ancient, or devolved, anything but human. Its terrible mouth is like an anthill, a dirt mound pushing up out of the earth, marked by a recession at the center of it, wide and immobile, just a permanent hole into an endless maw. The sound out of its earthen throat is a new one to Kylie's ears, an insect's chirr somehow composed of various species of voices blending into one unmistakable demand for supplication.

Erin's version of Mister Strangles. Dirt Mouth, Kylie presumes? "You made nice with yours?" Kylie says, managing to somehow sound indignant—envious?—despite her toneless whisper.

"Well . . . yeah."

"W-what did you do last night?" Kylie's mortified that she couldn't see any of this coming. The way Erin had dropped all other platforms, pretending she had experienced a moment of clarity when in reality MonoLife had gotten its hooks into her.

Look at that. You tried your hardest to beat her. And couldn't. Once again, second best.

"I wanted to tell you so badly." Erin's smile is conciliatory. "Was going to tell you last night on the cliffside, but you're always so fucking self-involved, Ky. I . . . just decided you needed to be humbled a bit. So . . . surprise!"

"Where did you go after our chat yesterday?" It sounds a lot like, *Tell me, bitch.*

"Private room party," Erin says. "Invitation only. Talked to Miss Jules about my future as a platform leader."

The wasp's nest buzzing inside Kylie's head grows as she sits through the rest of Keeling's presentation, forcing the widest smile she's ever worn, a portent of the darkness spreading inside her.

Splinter at the End

Kylie decides to bail on the afternoon sessions, which has them broken out into small groups for what Miss Jules is calling "networking opportunities."

Kylie feels on the verge of collapse, sitting at a seaside table, the ocean breeze rankling her ponytail as an actor on some streaming series nobody watches trades war stories with a thirtysomething blonde who works for cable news.

That's when something inside Kylie irrevocably breaks.

She stands up, and the greasy overweight man beside her, who travels the EU murdering hitchhikers and stranded motorists, and who hasn't shut up about the tragedy of Brexit closing off a significant portion of his victim base, asks if she'd like to have some company. She declines with a "Fuck you, gross pig" and goes rushing off as servers begin dispersing across the open patio with trays of tropical drinks.

"Your gift bag, *despoinída*," an employee says, holding one out to catch Kylie as she rushes past. She snatches it without slowing and is surprised to find it's addressed to @CrystalShips.

Kylie spots Erin at the last table on the patio, almost blocking the garden path that goes snaking up along the mountainside. Her networking circle includes a prominent senator, a guy from one of those shitty superhero movies, and a couple of singers—including that glass-thong bitch from last night who's gone more conservative today in Gucci sequins just so everybody knows she's a billionaire.

Kylie can feel all sorts of eyes on her, the entire patio simmering with anticipation. Everyone tuning into what they hope will be @CrystalShips and @ButterscotchGarden dynamite. The ultimate collab. Instead, Kylie whirls on her heels because she doesn't make fireworks without fist bumps. Goes strutting toward the elevator and catches at least one disappointed groan in earshot.

The doors slide open. Kylie has the car to herself and is grateful for that. The elevator begins its slow ascent toward her room, but winds up stopping a few floors beneath so that another woman can get on.

"Hi," the stranger says, looking so completely unremarkable in faded jeans and a loose tank that Kylie declines eye contact, figuring she must be staff. Probably going home at the end of her shift.

"Not feeling the festivities, huh?" the woman asks.

God. Small talk, Kylie thinks, reaching out and tapping the DOOR CLOSE button. It doesn't move.

"Me either," she adds once it's clear that Kylie isn't going to answer. Her black hair is pulled tight against her scalp. Greasy-haired and shiny-faced. No makeup. Completely basic.

"Yeah," Kylie says, disinterested. "Too much drama down there."

The woman leans against the wall and hooks her thumbs into her front pockets. Her eyes are hidden away behind Wayfarers, though she smirks with more confidence than someone with such an oily complexion has a right to. "A lot of drama only exists in your mind."

"Mmhm. And sometimes it exists right downstairs."

The woman smiles.

Kylie hates the way she's looking at her, starts tapping the DOOR CLOSE button again, and is relieved once they finally do begin sliding shut.

"Here's a life hack," the woman says as the elevator gets moving. "If you want it, that is."

Kylie shrugs.

"When you're at your worst and you need to get centered, all it takes is one simple question: *What opportunities has this drama cost me?* If the answer is zero, congratulations, you're a head case."

"I appreciate the diagnosis."

"I learned that the hard way and, well, I don't want to see you suffer. Not when the road ahead is wide open to you."

The elevator dings. Kylie takes one step out as the doors whoosh apart, this motion prompting a wave of relief to rush through her. As unwanted as this conversation is, the woman's words hit home. So what if Erin is on MonoLife? Her own secrecy makes it clear that @ButterscotchGarden fears @CrystalShips just as much as Kylie had feared Erin. They're on even footing now and, it turns out, Kylie has done just fine on MonoLife, even with Erin as her fiercest competition.

"Thank you," Kylie says with a degree of sincerity that actually surprises her.

"Sure. Maybe we'll even see each other again."

"You're . . . not staying?"

"Just came to pay my respects." A soft laugh passes under her breath. Kylie steps all the way off the elevator and the doors begin gliding shut as the woman adds, "Guess I'm not who you thought, huh?"

"What? Wait!" Kylie's palm starts slapping the metal. A purely knee-jerk response before she can even say why. But it's too late—the elevator is ascending again and the last thing she saw was the smile on @PurpleLipGloss's face.

One of the hottest users on MonoLife, and it's no wonder Kylie never spotted her this weekend. She'd been looking for glamour, but @PurpleLipGloss is beyond that. Nothing to prove. Content with being small and nondescript. A person without the baggage of persona.

Truthfully, Kylie would've been disappointed in this development had @PurpleLipGloss *not* given her the strength to go on.

Now that she's feeling like herself again, a player and not a pretender, she reaches into her gift bag to see what the last six months have bought her.

Her palm closes around a car key. The attached laminate reads:

> YOUR FERRARI SF90 STRADALE WILL BE
> DELIVERED TO YOUR RESIDENCE OF CHOICE.
> TRY NOT TO CRASH THIS ONE.

And @PurpleLipGloss's words echo on that. *The road ahead is wide open.*

Other enclosed goodies include an exclusive phone you can't purchase via retail that comes with MonoLife already installed, as well as a folded sheet of paper that says:

> BE SURE TO CHECK YOUR CLOSET

Day has left a note pinned to Kylie's door, asking if she would like to be her date to this evening's ball.

"The ball." Kylie sighs. "Forgot all about the ball." She crumples the paper and tosses it away as soon as she's inside.

"*Ladies and gentlemen,*" Miss Jules announces through the intercom. "*At this time, we would like to open up the island for your pleasure and exploration, asking only that you rendezvous in the Celebration Hall at seven sharp. That gives you four hours to unwind before the big event, which none of you are allowed to miss.*"

Kylie slides into MonoLife in order to give Day her answer.

@CrystalShips: Promise to twirl me on entrance?
@BlueFerox: Yes! Will knock on your door before seven.

She goes to the closet next, the note in her gift bag urging her not to miss whatever's in there. A dress that reduces her to tears on sight.

PVC. Turquoise. Pink palm trees.

Kylie strokes the material between her fingers. The note on the hanger reads:

YES, IT'S THAT DRESS.

Katy's dress. From the 2010 world premiere of Volkswagen's new Jetta compact sedan. The most flawless appearance any celebrity's ever given.

Kylie rushes it into the bathroom, stripping, breath coming in rough, stuttering patches.

She steps into the PVC and pulls it up, shoulder straps resting comfortably on her blades. Closes her eyes and smells Katy. Wants to imagine it hasn't been washed in over a decade. That the sweat from Katy's body now lives inside this seafoam-green vinyl, and just wearing it is enough to absorb some of that KatyCat energy.

Kylie forces an honest appraisal. The dress fits, sure, though it's hardly shaped to her form and looks a bit deflated.

She parades around the room anyway. A nearly out-of-body experience. The nicest gift anyone's given her. But also a test as to whether Kylie is her own brand. An individual capable of influencing others.

If she shows up tonight wearing a costume, she's just a stupid little girl in cosplay. Her brand, somebody else's brand. That's no brand.

You either act like an influencer or you tell the world you're willing to be influenced.

And if Katy has taught Kylie that nothing lasts forever, she must also remember that just a few years after *Smile*, Katy came roaring back, throwing heat with the *143* album whether anyone wanted to hear it or not. True inspo, really. Be a star. Do what makes you happy. Forget the haters.

"Nothing's over till it's over."

Kylie's entire life has been on delay. An eternity of watching others hit the ground and rush headlong into finer things. Romance. Success. Fame. All while suffering in the shadows, looking at herself in the mirror, promising her reflection, *One day, maybe . . .*

She opens her suitcase and scrutinizes every outfit for the second time today. Tries each of them on because tonight's about making a statement.

Tonight's about, *Fuck you, Erin.*

She thinks about @PurpleLipGloss again, wondering just how many doors Erin's successes have closed on her.

The answer, as close as she can figure, appears to be none.

Armies of the Night

"Welcome to the edge of the universe." A man with a birdcage on his head is there to greet Kylie and Day as they step off the elevator, moving into a hallway that goes on forever.

Floor-to-ceiling mirrors, like they're hiking through infinity, gliding with Molly in their blood, holding each other's hands and giggling.

"Why are you so nervous?" Day snickers. "Two doses and you still have that constipated look on your face."

"I'm calm."

"Never seen anyone look so good while looking so anxious."

Day's right. They're stunners. Kylie checks them in the mirror as they bop alongside it. Her x-front bodycon absolutely slaps, as does the frilly choker around her neck, and the eight-inch silver heels she's thumping on.

Day wears a sparkling pastel dress with green pleated fabric and a plunging neckline. A flirty style with wraparound tie and ruching on the skirt for a flattering fit.

They could've gone sluttier, but restraint is confidence. Kylie is even more certain of that after meeting @PurpleLipGloss.

It's an actual mile walk to the next corner. Way behind them, another group has finally stepped off the elevator, laughing and stumbling along. Kylie's just grateful that someone else is down here with them, footsteps like distant horse clops.

Two workers in penguin costumes come around the corner. Amusement park mascots that extend their arms and usher them along as if there's any other direction to go. The hallway narrows, becoming single file, and a line of partygoers is backed all the way up to where Kylie and Day now stand.

Every head turns, worried that someone more famous has arrived to eclipse them.

"Checking for weapons?" Kylie wonders.

"Confiscating phones," a man in a glitter-encrusted Bauta mask says on approach, his voice only slightly muffled.

"No," Day says. "No way."

He's pushing a cart outfitted with a bunch of slats, names stitched over the top of each. Most slots are already filled. "It is nonnegotiable," Bauta tells them. "Find your MonoLife handle or, if you're a plus-one, the space beside the person who brought you. Make sure your phone remains powered on, drop it in, then proceed to the party."

Kylie and Day exchange looks like this is a bridge too far, though what exactly is the alternative? Go back? Go home? Kylie stuffs her phone beneath her name and waits for Day to do the same.

They follow the rest of the cattle onto a wide-open floor plan. Probably some kind of warehouse that has been cleaned out for the occasion. Overhead, two stories of balconies wrap all the way around, and those catwalks are filled with schmoozers holding cocktail glasses and laughing.

Small bowls of Molly are on pedestals flanking the entryway like after-dinner mints. Kylie plucks one, drops the pill on her tongue.

"Let me go say hi to these people," Day says, breaking toward a cluster of users Kylie only vaguely recognizes from the app and definitely doesn't follow.

Miss Jules appears out of the crowd, plucking two flutes of champagne off the decorative fountain that's spritzing crimson-colored water. "Oh, Crystal, you look stunning. Divine, just divine!"

Kylie smiles at the compliment and takes one of the glasses.

"Glad I ran into you so early," Miss Jules says. "Mr. Keeling asked me to deliver you a message."

"To me?"

"Just you."

"You're joking."

"Why? Because there are others more successful?"

Kylie tilts her head back, downs the flute, happens to spot Erin on the highest balcony, leaning over, watching, eyebrow cocked. One of the men she's with is the singer for that nineties band that's still somehow popular. The other's a MonoLife user who jerks off on grocery store produce.

"I guess I'm just feeling a little out of my element," Kylie says.

Miss Jules smiles. Her lips pushing to the edges of her face. "Someone's always better," she says, teetering on boredom. "Is that what you're grappling with, child?"

Kylie is not here to be coddled. She shrugs, looks at Erin again, and catches her gaze. An exchange of unspoken, seething resentment. Mutual hatred built on competitive clout.

"You have to forgive me—I'm like a shark." Miss Jules sighs, her voracious smile looking quite dangerous in that moment. "Need to keep moving around this room or I'll die." She leans into Kylie's ear, and Kylie glances up to ensure Erin's seeing this.

She certainly is.

"Mr. Keeling would like you to remember that he *chose* you, and he hopes to not regret it." She presses a hand to Kylie's naked shoulder and Kylie closes her eyes, the Molly making it feel as though she's got music pulsing through her veins instead of blood.

When Kylie opens them, she's alone. Day is winding through the crowd, moving back toward her as OceanLab's "On a Good Day"—the Above & Beyond/Gareth Emery Metropolis mix, of course—begins thumping through the speakers, the floor beneath them suddenly strobing. Day's grinning as the crowd clears out, pushing toward the edges to avoid getting caught on the dance floor.

Kylie wraps her arms around Day and the rhythm takes them. People pop Molly like vitamins. Dancing turns to rubbing. Groping. Swapping partners. Taking bodies for test runs, moving on if the vibe ain't right.

A half dozen songs pass and they're dripping with euphoria. Beads of sweat plopping off their bangs. Day's fingers glide up and down Kylie's arms as if her shoulders are instruments only she knows how to play.

Around them, the world is suddenly screaming.

Guests rushing for the recessed floor pockets on the far side of the room, tearing at their clothes, licking and kissing the exposed body parts beneath.

Others have moved into the open kitchen space in the far corner, raiding the oversized refrigerators, taking out large hunks of meat, arguing about what to cook.

"That's a torso."

"Get those hips instead, lots of meat on that ass."

"Is there an air fryer in here? I only eat skin if it's breaded and crisped."

A man huddles by himself in the corner, loading a magazine into a gigantic assault rifle.

The wolf woman swallows a handful of Molly while screaming, "Watch this!" Curious people encircle her, cheering as her nose stretches out, reshaping into an animal's snout. Her eyes become orbs and, suddenly, there's a wild animal running loose.

"Hey, Crystal Ships!" an old guy with a hairy dad bod shouts, lifting out of one of the recessed floor pockets. "Come here. Come. If you know what I mean."

"Day," Kylie says, her voice suddenly drowned out beneath the shattering glass skylight above. Shards rain down as thick black shadows swoop across the ceiling. "Get back to your room and wait for me." Day seems confused, ready to decline the order, when Kylie gives her a forceful shove that sends her skittering. "Fucking go!"

Day has to take only one look at the impossible sight: Stone sculptures somehow given to motion. Living statues launching down, snatching people in their oversized rock talons, plucking them into the air, chomping their skulls with thick apple crunches. It's all she needs to take Kylie's advice, go rushing off.

Because somehow there are living gargoyles in here.

Nobody else flees the commotion. Kylie's fellow "Lifers" regard this carnage with applause, cheering as broken bodies bleed down on them. Those in the kitchen ignore the creatures entirely, have decided on a cut of meat and are now trimming away the fat with paring knives. Others continue to dance undisturbed to the music that's still playing. This is what they want. This is why they came. Cheap thrills.

How unproductive.

These are not my peers, Kylie thinks. They're hobbyists who only wish to belong somewhere that others can't go. To her, this is a waste of time. What good is any of this if she can't share it with her audience? The people who sent her here?

Keeling was right. She is better than this.

The man with the assault rifle is loading a few small handguns now. He looks up at Kylie as she approaches.

"Can I borrow one of those?" she asks.

He slides a pistol into her palm without hesitation, goes back to loading another. "Wanna hunt some plus-ones?"

"Wait," Kylie says, glancing up at the gargoyles perched in the rafters, tearing flaps of meat off the slack bodies they've carried up there. "That's who's dying? The plus-ones?"

"Well, yeah. Why do you think stone-cold secret MonoLife allowed them to come along?" He grins. "All part of the sacrifice."

Kylie's head cranks up toward the catwalk, Erin leaning delightedly over the railing, a profile of pure privilege as she watches the unfolding chaos. This revelation triggers a question in Kylie, her heart dispersing undue stress to every corner of her body as she considers it:

Who's the plus-one here? Erin or me?

She'd been certain it was Erin, the way Kylie had inspired a former influencer to get back into the game. Though from Erin's perspective, it could've just as easily been the way Kylie, her greatest rival, had genuinely wanted to invite *her* along.

Suddenly, there's a very real possibility that Kylie has only seconds to live.

She breaks for the exit, where the man in the Bauta mask is leaning against the door to his guard quarters, arms folded.

"Can I have my phone?"

"Party's just started."

"And I need my phone."

"You're not allowed to film this."

"I'm going back to my room."

The guard sighs. Turns back to his door and pushes his thumb against the identification plate. It unlocks with a futuristic *whoosh* as Kylie lifts the gun and blows his brains out through his forehead.

At her back, commotion and laughter are so great she thinks everyone is applauding her action. She turns around to see that nobody has even noticed.

Bautamask spills across the floor of the guard station and Kylie uses her feet to push his corpse out of the way, taking hold of his cell phone cart and dragging it from the room, then pushing it off, down the narrow hall she came, swinging a hard left and pushing it the full mile back.

The penguin mascots there make no motion to stop her. Ditto the birdcage man standing by the elevators. Kylie presses the button for her floor, looking over her shoulder while she waits.

You can't even hear the party from here.

The doors open and Kylie shoves the cart inside. The birdcage man smiles and says, "Have a nice night," and then he's gone and she's ascending, then pushing the cart again, rushing down the hall, skidding on her heels as she passes a fire axe sitting comfortably behind a plate of sheet glass.

She uses the metal BREAK PLATE to crack it, snatching the axe off its cradle, then rushes across the hall to the supply closet, hacking the doorknob away in order to claim her prize.

The acetylene torch inside.

Kylie rushes back to her room, locks and bolts the door. Barricades herself in by pushing the couch up against it and then guiding the cart into the bathroom, where she handles each phone, clicking them off one by one, dropping them onto the sandstone-colored shower tile.

Every phone but hers.

Kylie stacks them into a pyramid of electronic bricks, then points the torch at it, blasting it with hellfire. A couple more *whoosh*es for good measure, then she's recording a bonfire of cracking glass and melting plastic.

"Burn, you fuckers," she says, coughing on the swirl of toxic fumes misting toward the ceiling. "My turn, Erin." Her voice ticks up into a scream. *"My turn, bitch! Why don't you get that?!"*

When she steps from the bathroom, the suite is in total darkness. The lights had been on when she came in, though the barricade remains stacked against the door.

A silhouette moves through the shadows, tall and elongated, familiar anticipatory clicks to announce itself.

Kylie's phone dings.

@MisterStrangles: nice

"Yeah," Kylie says, slipping from her dress, getting dutifully onto all fours, presenting herself. "I got your message."

Then Mister Strangles is above her, cold fingers raking dispassionately across her back, tapping that tender, wounded area at the small of it like a junkie readying a vein.

Its mask snaps off its face and there is nothing to it. Just a mouth. Kind of. One long vertical slit from its chin all the way to the round of its head. When it opens, it swallows the surface area of its otherwise blank visage, creating an opening wide enough to reveal a charcoal void beyond. Then comes the slimy sensation of its rotted, puckered mouth closing on Kylie's flesh. Piercing pain to irritate that perennially sensitive patch of skin.

Kylie draws a sharp breath and squeezes her eyes, moaning. Not because there's pleasure—there isn't—but because she was chosen. Picked by the darkest and the best MonoLife has. Erin could never.

That's the part that feels great.

"Back again?" the man in the birdcage asks as Kylie steps off the elevator.

"Oh, I'm just getting started."

She hop-skips all the way back down the hall to where the party's in full swing. Dancing, eating, fucking—one guy doing all three at once.

The wolf woman is rolling around on the floor with some e-girl who's giggling and screaming, "Stop licking me there!" without any conviction because she really wants it.

Kylie makes a hard right at the wolf, going upstairs to the catwalks, where she finds Erin in almost exactly the same spot, a Juul between her lips, chatting with a woman about whether MonoLife should allow brands on its platform.

"It's against what they stand for," Erin's saying.

"Corporations are totally people too—the Supreme Court even ruled that. Why shouldn't they be allowed to test the waters with a bit of edgy marketing? God, it'd make my day job so much more interesting."

"I guess." Erin tips her head to one side so the woman doesn't catch the eye roll.

"Can I interrupt," Kylie says without a hint of interrogation.

"Yeah." Erin is eager to pounce. "Give us a few, Gracie."

Gracie shrugs, heads off farther down the catwalk.

"Thanks," Erin says. "I was considering jumping just to get away." Down on the floor, someone has started shrieking. The first scream tonight that isn't playful, but rather full-throated terror. Erin doesn't

seem to notice this distinction. "There's no reason for us to be adver-
saries, you know."

"Why did you hide it all from me?"

"I wasn't going to." Erin sighs, chemical smoke drifting over her
face. "Just sort of happened."

"Revenge?"

"Yeah, I guess. You were making moves behind my back. Shutting
me out."

"Or is it because I was doing so well on my own?"

Erin smiles, her gaze trained on the debauchery beneath them.
"You were the one who put the idea of magic back in my head, you
know. So I decided, *Why not?* Tried a few spells to see if I could heal
Cameron's ACL and *voilà!*—he becomes a long-distance runner! So
yeah, it worked. Wasn't terribly exciting for MonoLife, though, so, you
know, I kinda had to spice things up."

"By murdering Veronica?"

"*Sacrificing* Veronica, yeah. Who cares? Her life bought me the
fortune I needed to reinvent myself. When you and Asher were over at
my house that night and you told me there were levels to MonoLife,
that was an epiphany. I had to dream a little bigger to reach the next
stage. Then you put Brandi in the hospital and it all was a no-brainer.
I mean, did you *see* that video?"

Kylie nods. If it had been on Living Now, she wouldn't have because
@ButterscotchGarden had blocked her. "This whole time, I was helping
you, guiding you, and I didn't even know. Wow."

"After you humiliated me at the cabin? There was no going back to
the way things were for us. You were playing for keeps. And so, I did
what I had to do as well."

"You didn't have to come over to MonoLife."

"No." Erin smiles, savoring those wounded words. "I didn't."

"If you hate me so much—"

"The Morning Bean? You racing in there, terrified, ohhhh so concerned for my life? Pretty touching, actually. And you spilled everything

you knew about the app that night and, well . . . I just gotta say that I hated how you knew so much more than me."

"So, you thought, what? *Let me try to kill her?* I saw that video too."

"A little spell to try to stop your heart. Not sure how you dodged *that* one. You're very lucky."

The bite on Kylie's back throbs, a tiny ping as if Mister Strangles is communicating with her in this moment, saying, *You know how.* "I only wanted to succeed at something. I just—"

"You just prefer strangers to friends."

"No. Strangers are nothing. Shadows in the glass. You don't have to let them in."

"It *hurt*," Erin says. "'Cause maybe you *do* care about me in some twisted way, but your secret MonoLife persona made me realize how little *I* matter. How there's something else driving you."

"I wanted to be . . ." Kylie swallows that sentence. God, she can level with a million strangers on a whim. But when it's her best friend, eye to eye? "Everything's complicated."

"That's life, Ky."

"Who needs it?"

Across the catwalk, a guy screams at the shadow that's suddenly skittering along the wall, appendages like tree roots dangling down. He tries to bat them away, but there're too many and suddenly they're coiling around his waist and lifting him through the air, toward the glossy cocoon nestled at the intersection of wall and ceiling, beating like a heart.

"You should probably come with me," Kylie says, moving to the stairwell. "It's going to get bad."

Erin stares in disbelief at the creature as it presses the now-flailing man against the organic casing, his body beginning to sizzle as it's held in place against that outer layer. Skin melting off his bones like wax. His cries somehow registering over the rest of the party chaos. "What . . . oh, what did you do, Ky?"

"What I had to. We need to go. *Now*, Erin."

Erin finally seems to understand what's happening to the party below—large, shadowy pockets have enveloped the scene, awkward and distended figures suddenly moving through them, inspiring cold cries of panic and death.

She takes a few reluctant steps and then is following Kylie down the stairs to where a woman in a flapper stands posed on the landing, rocking gently with her arms behind her back. Her face is blank, as in absent. A flat patch of empty flesh where eyes and a mouth should be.

"*Back off!*" Kylie roars, shoving Flapper against the wall, pinning her there so Erin can rush past, shrieking and spilling out onto the darkened floor.

The blank woman's throat clicks like the rest of these things and Miss Jules's words echo in Kylie's head, exorcising any fear she might've had.

Mr. Keeling would like you to remember that he chose *you.*

Kylie rushes to catch Erin, grabbing her hand and dragging her to the exit. The chaos on the floor is in full swing, twisted and broken bodies everywhere. Hissing shadows beginning to converge on them and the two stragglers who are suddenly trying to follow them out. Their breaths become bubbly screams, and neither Kylie nor Erin turns around to see what's happened to them.

They run as fast as their heels will allow, wobbling on sea legs while panicked staccato echoes. At the elevator, the birdcage man has abandoned his post and they ride up to the hotel, doors opening on a naked guy twirling madly, arms flailing as if he's reaching for some invisible burden on his back.

A pulsing sore on his thigh like an in-grown pimple, radiating, practically glowing. He collapses and indentations move across his body, trounced by something unseen.

"Let me die!" he groans, voice like a rusty hinge. "Let me *diiiiiieeeee!*"

Kylie and Erin are glad to oblige the request, hurrying around the corner, breaking into another run, using each other for leverage in their fight against stumbling forward, toppling over. They move through vacant hallways until Kylie halts in front of three photos positioned above a leather couch. A sharp draw of breath as she reads the stenciled words over them: INFLUENCE IS AUTHENTICITY.

The very first picture shows a woman in the desert. A stark sight, her in a neon-green bikini thong, otherwise topless save for an unzipped furry pink Sherpa jacket that looks more like a scarf for as much as it conceals. Knee-high boots are appropriately dusted given her surroundings, and she wears a matching pink cotton face mask with rounded goggles over her eyes. Hair in braids, she holds a purple hula hoop up against the small of her back. It surrounds her in a perfect halo.

The second picture is of a small handful of people on some concrete landing with a snowy backdrop, a row of white-topped roofs beyond them. Standing in the center is a man in an open bathrobe, pretending to look off in the distance as if his perfectly sculped physique isn't the star of the show.

The final photo shows last year's conference on what looks like the highest rooftop in some foreign city that's probably Tokyo, given the sprawl of its neon skyline, alien and glowing. Nowhere else in the world looks like that.

Except, Kylie *has* seen it before. In the background of Missy's Live Connect session when they last spoke, in the woods around Lake Salvi. "Ohhh. She was *here*," Kylie says, jaw on the floor as another piece of the puzzle has revealed itself. "Last year's influencer summit. Oh my God."

Erin barely notices, is watching the quiet corridor they've just run down, more concerned about the chaos catching up to them. "Can we just—"

"They held her back because of Duc."

"Kylie, can we—"

"She should've crossed over then . . . but Duc went rogue, decided instead he was going to bring this whole operation down. Missy told me she was responsible for getting him an account and—" Kylie whirls around to face Erin, completely juiced off this revelation.

But Erin's hyperventilating, so vulnerable that she's currently whimpering over the buzzing of fluorescent lights in the ceiling.

"Don't worry. You're safe with me," Kylie says and Erin pushes up against her, cowering. There's enough Molly left in Kylie's bloodstream for this motion to ignite her nerves. Her lust, and she wonders in this moment if there's time left for them, but knows that it's passed. This was going to be a special weekend once, but Erin had to go and ruin it.

Kylie is the star and no witchy magic can prevent that.

"Come on." Kylie plucks the room key out from beneath her thong band and they move together through another hallway until they're facing the proper door, swiping and entering.

Erin crosses into the room and drops onto the couch, staring out at the dark water beyond the window. "Do you think it's safe to try to swi—"

"Gonna swim for a week straight?" Kylie is attaching her phone to a small tripod on the counter.

"Okay then, what?"

"A collab."

"Ky . . . you're joking." Erin's eyelids pop like startled bats taking flight. She sits back up, patting her hips, a few other parts of her body, gasping as the severity dawns. "I forgot my phone! We have to go back—"

"My audience is waiting. If I've learned anything this weekend, it's that I hate being away from them."

Erin's looking around now, mouth wobbling. "Th-this isn't our room." She pulls her legs against her chest, recoiling.

"She wasn't talking about collaborating with you." Day glides out of the kitchen and taps a finger on the mounted phone to begin the recording.

Kylie simultaneously lifts a meat slicer off the counter. "Hi, guys, Crystal here with @BlueFerox. You know I've always been honest with you, and this is *no* exception."

Erin screams, a protest that's closer in sound to an animal caught in a trap. Kylie has never heard anything like it—certainly not in all her years of ErinTime.

"And check this out—my old friend @ButterscotchGarden is with us too, but only for a minute," Kylie says, slipping Melissa's emoji mask over her face, adjusting the fit, then storming the shot.

"Remember, clean cuts!" Day shouts over the commotion.

"Erin," Kylie says with a muffled growl. "Look what you made me do." And then the oversized blade rushes across Erin's throat, blood exploding from her neck like a shower nozzle. She falls across the couch, legs spasming, prompting even more blood to gush and pump. The splatter catches the walls, the glass, the ceiling, plopping down everywhere like chucked baby food.

Kylie turns toward the camera so everyone can see the emoji mask's hysterical expression because this is funny, right? A nightmare come full circle.

Then she steps out of frame and pulls it off her face, wondering how anybody breathes in this thing.

"@ButterscotchGarden never got it," Kylie says, thinking about the words stenciled on the wall outside: INFLUENCE IS AUTHENTICITY. "I mean . . . spells?" She snorts with laughter. "Like anyone's supposed to care you can force a person to do something? *True* influence is when the simple act of *doing* makes others want to do it too."

Day eases the blade from Kylie's hand and glides into the shot because Erin's still kind of alive, gasping, the large slit in her throat making the most obnoxious sound as wheezing air passes through it. Erin's eyes remain locked on Kylie, wounded tears streaking.

"Ohhh, don't look so hurt," Kylie snaps. She's always hated the sight of people crying. Their ugly faces and those stupid noises. "Boo hoo hoo. *You* wanted me just as dead, Little Miss *Why Won't You Die?*"

Day slashes Erin's throat again, a second gash to her neck, then another for good measure. She strips Erin's dress off, looking at the camera every couple of seconds. "When you're going to eat human meat, it is best to put it *all* to use, given the scarcity. You never know how long it will be until your next feast."

"You've been saying that for a long time," Kylie says.

"*Beautiful* meat," Day tells her. "You'll see. Lacks the gamey, unwelcoming smell that comes from less regal animals."

Day takes Erin's lifeless wrists and drags the body across the floor. Puddles of blood and excrement follow them into the kitchen.

"The gift that keeps on giving," Day is telling the camera. "For leftovers taste even sweeter." A performative wink. "Try it, you'll see."

Day lifts the slicer. Chops through both of Erin's shoulders until her arms come off. Her head next. Then legs. Now she's skinning the carcass like a pro, leaving bloody ribbons piled up beside the pieces.

Atop the stove, a roasting pan is already full of sliced carrots, onions, and potatoes.

"Let me," Kylie says, taking the slicer, using it to hack Erin into quarter halves, putting that meat into the pan and using the assorted dry rubs that Day has placed out.

"For the longest time, I wanted to be her," Kylie says, unable to stop herself from grinning. "Guess this is the next-best thing."

"*Queen.*" Day places the tripod on the counter, angled down at the tray. Next she takes packages of bacon from the refrigerator and begins wrapping the meat.

They continue walking the world through this process, Kylie describing what it's like, what it's really like, to butcher and roast your best friend IRL.

It's absolutely delicious.

Glow Up

An eight-hour livestream tops the Living Now section. Kylie doesn't know how her phone battery lasted the whole time.

Her notification count reads 99+. That's where MonoLife's programming taps out.

A couple of comments pass along their own advice for eating human flesh. Kylie isn't interested in those.

There's something else. A trending hashtag has emerged.

#TheCrystalChallenge

In Borneo, a thirteen-year-old girl takes a chain saw to her mother, cutting through her shoulder from the back as she stands on the small apartment balcony smoking a cigarette, splitting her diagonally down to her torso, where it spurts off onto the sidewalk below. The teenager carves off some belly meat and seasons it with salt, pepper, and cayenne, placing it atop a smoking charcoal grill.

In France, two boys are shot dead in the street by masked men and dragged through an alley into a restaurant's kitchen, where they're butchered, skinned, and served to ravenous patrons.

In New York City, some Wall Street bro is hacked into pieces by a disgruntled wife with a fire axe on the floor of their luxury penthouse. She devours him on the spot and, with her mouth full, proceeds to talk about her plan to make pork rinds out of him in a video that runs too long but is otherwise insightful.

Back home in Summerfield, Massachusetts, a boy in a tuxedo whose name escapes Kylie, but who sat behind her in high school chorus, scoops jellied brains out of his former prom date's skull, catching the blood that oozes from her ears on his fingertips, licking them clean like frosting.

The hashtag goes on forever. Video after video.

Kylie has never felt such pride. A brand-new mother cradling an ugly newborn has nothing on this.

"Now can we eat?"

@MissyMiss asks this from the table, hunched over a steaming tray, nostrils puffing over the smell of roasted Erin. The Grecian sun is postcard-bright through the shimmering window over her shoulder.

Kylie goes to it and places a forearm on the glass, looking down at the abandoned harbor. "Where is Day?" The couch where Erin had bled to death is somehow spotless, and the gore trails along the floor have also been cleaned. "Where am I?"

"I-t's go-ing to ge-t c-old," @MissyMiss says, a voice of electronic distortion. Static and noise culled together to produce words without any semblance of Melissa Crigan's vocal tract.

In the palm of Kylie's hand, @MissyMiss has posted a photo of the foil tray: "*Roasted Witch*—with @CrystalShips."

Kylie takes one final look at the ocean. Tranquility stirring up immense sadness in her. She can only stand to watch for another moment before she has to turn away.

"What happened to Day?"

"S-he cou-ld no-t f-oll-ow y-ou," @MissyMiss says.

"Dead?"

"Yo-u kn-ow wha-t y-ou di-d, C-rys-tal. N-ow s-it. Ea-t."

Kylie does know. She does sit. Eats. Devours dish after dish, stopping on a forkful of meat and roasted asparagus, because her tummy's too full and Erin deserves to be savored. "Why are you here?"

"T-he al-gor-ithm," @MissyMiss tells her, monosyllabic distortion beginning to grate on Kylie.

They were never close, though @MissyMiss does know her better than anyone now. Half a year of trading their darkest secrets and the algorithm believes that nobody could be closer.

MonoLife has a way of doing that. Making you believe your connections to strangers are more meaningful than those who share your physical space.

Kylie slips the fork into her mouth, back to chewing on her real friend—the algorithm unable to detect that relationship at all because it had been blocked, and therefore meaningless to a program's rationale.

Erin is succulent in every bite, even the fattiest pieces of her tingling with pleasant sweetness. Kylie imagines herself absorbing Erin's powers as she consumes her, feeling stronger by the minute. Eating until she sweats.

Then it's time to stand, stripping in full view of @MissyMiss, who has no interest in looking and who just continues eating while Kylie feels bloated and gross. "I think I need a shower."

"Go-odby-e, C-rys-tal," @MissyMiss says with a dispassionate mouthful.

Kylie goes into the bathroom and closes the door. The shower is all melted plastic and broken glass, the remnants of a few hundred phones. She uses the toilet brush beneath the sink to force the debris into the corner, then cranks the water and gets beneath the stream, folding her shoulders inward to fit her entire body beneath it. Warm water cascades down her back, where the absence of pain provokes curiosity. She twists to check herself in the mirror, and the persistent infection that had sat between her dimples of Venus for the last six months is gone—just a clear patch of perfection now.

When she steps back into the cold, she doesn't shiver. Her hand swipes a patch of steam off the mirror and Kylie Bennington is gone. The fleshy construct that stares back does resemble her, yes, though what's here now is far better.

#nofilter

She cups a hand over her mouth and blows into her palm. Her breath is mint fresh, even after shoveling five pounds of @ButterscotchGarden into her mouth. She could go back out there and eat some more, try to devour her down to nothing. The appetite inside her has become insatiable.

For a moment, Crystal's reflection is different. The face in the glass appears panicked, a distended mouth offering a silent scream she cannot hear.

@CrystalShips finds now that she barely remembers Kylie Bennington. Little fragments. Echoes from another consciousness, a stranger's dream and nothing more.

But then the mirror is back to behaving, reflecting Crystal's motions as they happen, and she slips into Katy's green PVC dress, applies a face that looks like candy with bubble-gum lipstick and purple eye shade. Red hair in that same tight-scalped ponytail. A carefully orchestrated homage at this point. Her tribute, from one legend to another.

"What do you think?" Crystal asks, swaying into the living room, spinning in order to give @MissyMiss the whole show.

Only @MissyMiss is gone.

Mr. Keeling stands in the doorway, sauntering in only once Crystal has noticed him. He goes straight for the table and takes a seat, hands on his thighs. Labored breathing, as if his day's energy is already spent.

His suit appears to be one size too large, making him appear less threatening and more sinister at the same time.

Crystal picks up a slice of Erin, grilled ass cheek with rosemary, pops it into her mouth.

"*I am never wrong,*" Keeling says. "*Never once.*"

Crystal lifts her phone. "I put my soul into this. Wasn't going to lose it. Are you . . . angry with what I did?"

"*Oh, no.*" Keeling laughs. "*What you did was splendid! The Profile is delighted. No one has ever done something so selfish on such a large scale.*"

"And that's—"

"*Our user agreement has no rules against such. You know that. To do so would be . . . severely limiting to the imagination.*"

Crystal smiles, at last free from Kylie Bennington's petty jealousies.

There are no more ladders to climb. Followers will grow to resent the absence of those taken tonight once their accounts go forever offline, and "Lifers" will look fondly on those who haven't given up on entertaining them. They'll come to @CrystalShips with adoration.

"You do understand that everything is different now, yes? You can never go home."

"I don't have one." There does exist some vague idea of home, a fast-fading memory of a woman called Mom, though she holds no emotional connection to her or anything there.

Keeling reaches out, his tri-pronged hand, clawed and liver-spotted, closing around her wrist. A hitching cackle in his throat, the stitched flesh there beginning to rise and bubble like heated dough.

Crystal tries tearing her hand away, desperate to escape his touch. Her resistance only strengthens his grip and it fills her with a sort of hopelessness she's never felt, her body stuffed with panic, pumping darkness through her veins.

@MissyMiss was right—it's getting cold.

Up close, the patchwork flesh that comprises Keeling's face starts to tear. Only then does she notice that his eyes blink side-to-side, instead of top-to-bottom.

"Here is where it really hurts," he says through earsplitting metallic static. Noise that doesn't come from his mouth, but instead seeps out of her phone speaker. *"Here is what we wait for . . . what we hope to get."*

She shrieks, tries again to get her arm back but it's locked even tighter in his grip now. His cackle fills the air, is unnerving enough to drive Crystal upward out of her seat, struggling to get clear.

Oh, but she knows deep down in her poisoned heart it's far too late for that.

Keeling springs up with an incredible burst of motion that tears the quilted skin from his face and hands, revealing the cluster of malignant growths he's been hiding. His real flesh, to call it that, an endless string of diseases, strands of tumorous pustules rising and falling to their own rhythms.

He's so tall now that Crystal has to look up to see him. And when his fingers snap to her throat, pushing down, sapping her voice, pressing harder until those appendages are somehow inside her, scraping against the pillars of her spine, it's clear she's being visited by Mister Strangles. One final time.

Its incongruous mouth yawns, revealing a tangle of eyeballs staring outward. They blink, then widen, each one becoming small pools of clacking teeth, opening and swallowing one another, annihilating the contours of its face, reducing the whole world to darkness until there's just—

The light of a phone screen.

On which a perky redhead appears, waving, flashing a child's smile. *"Hey, guys, it's Kylie! I'm starting my first day of classes at Boston University and thought I'd show y'all what it's like to be a total newb in higher ed."*

Crystal convulses, trying to say "Turn it off!" but her throat can only wheeze. As terrified as she is, she finds she's more revolted by the banality of this livestream being forced into her line of sight. Wind up like everyone else? *I'd rather die.*

Mister Strangles keeps pressing. Invasive hands sifting through her innards, gusts of frozen wind stinging her core. Her organs become glaciers. Her spirits succumb to the elements, her soul standing in frozen testament to the insurmountable cold. The process, snuffing out of existence every last ember of Kylie Bennington, past and present.

She'd scream if she had any breath left, but nope. All out. *And besides, this is how it goes. Here is where it really hurts. So fucking hurt me. Bring me over to where there are no more rules. No more worries. Where every urge is the gateway to attention. Affection, better than connection. Give it here.*

That's MonoLife.

The last community on earth.

Most platforms fear honesty so much they broadcast lies. Insecurities disguised as hatred. Empty truths redeeming social acceptance in the form of likes and shares. And maybe that helps everybody sleep better at night, believing they're keeping the darkness at bay.

But honesty is the most precious resource in our brave new world. And it's nowhere. Except for here.

"*Bring . . . me . . . through . . .*" she rasps with as much ferocity as she can muster. Her laughter is hoarse but defiant as those fingers snap back to her throat to complete the strangle—

As you wish.

—squeezing her bones to dust.

Crystal grins and the phone screen blurs, blotting to darkness. She's weightless now and floating, every last memory ashes in a blizzard. The violence done here is as pointless as a whisper into dirt because there's nothing left to feed on.

On the edge of nonexistence, in the ensconcing void, @CrystalShips finally comes alive.

EPILOGUE

ExtremelyOnline™

The World

"Hey, guys, it's Crystal. I know I haven't been around lately and that's because . . . well, I haven't been around, if you get what I mean. Some of you are wondering what happened to my old bedroom, and that should be obvious. I've upgraded."

Crystal shows the World exactly what she means. Floor-to-ceiling windows, a glowing city skyline beyond them.

She gives a tour of her spacious apartment: vaulted ceilings, an OLED screen mounted on the wall, a clear coffee table with an opened coffee-table book about some artist, designed to make her viewers feel basic. Stainless-steel appliances. Angular art. One vintage Patrick Nagel because good retro never goes out of style.

The World talks to her. Tells @CrystalShips she's leveled up. Looks healthier. What's her skin care routine? Can she do a video on it?

A few jealous nobodies mock the filler in her lips. Their negativity barely registers because most of the World is too busy praising her "natural beauty."

She flashes her trademark whites, loves showing off her carefree eyes. The World sees the joy in them and strives to find a similar freedom.

The World practices her fiction in their realities without understanding that even reality is a fantasy these days.

The World doesn't want to relate. It wants somebody to worship.

Crystal makes thousands of dollars each day. Her last video, where she visited a homeless camp and handed out poisoned soup, trended for three months straight.

She's hired a high-profile financial advisor so that her money can fuck money to make more money.

Names that Crystal barely remembers—Kylie Bennington and Erin Palmer—are reported missing. Kylie's mother is supposedly hysterical and, apparently, under investigation for murder. That's because a host of human remains were discovered in her house—including the body of a federal agent. Crystal wouldn't know any of this if not for a few of Kylie's former classmates DM sliding, wondering what happened.

There are eyewitness accounts of some rotted, feral dog in the woods around Lake Salvi, back in Summerfield, constant chew-toy squeaks that can be heard for miles on even the quietest of nights.

Crystal feels an inexplicable spread of warmth each time she hears these anecdotes, and even follows an account called @SummerfieldWeirdness that's dedicated to proving the existence of this "zombie dog."

"Anywho," Crystal says. "Some of you have been with me from the beginning, and while I adore all my followers, it's you guys, the OGs, who I worry about. Because *you're* worried. Worried that I'm going to walk away. Count my money. Marry rich. Disappear. I get it."

Crystal steps back, showing the World her body in the Miu Miu velvet and stretch wool minidress from the Pre-Fall '25 collection. Crafted in Italy, where she'd flown specifically to get it. The black velvet bodice that falls into a stretch-wool grain de poudre miniskirt, with crystal-embellished bow detail encircling the waist. And the scoop neckline that shows off her bronzed décolleté. She completes the look with a crystal-encrusted spiked choker by Alexis Bittar.

Comments are effusive. Lots of **Queen** and **Goddess** and a couple **turn around, let's see your ass** sprinkled in for good measure.

She does it, because why not?

"There are other, more interesting ways for me to spend my time now, sure. But I want you to understand—*I am not going anywhere.*

You built me. I'll always be there for you. I don't even think I have a say in that anymore."

The World watches Crystal stuff a handgun into the Hermès Geranium Kelly Cut Clutch Bag, its rectangular body affording plenty of space to house the weapon, along with the things she needs for her night out on the town.

What the World doesn't see, what she's always careful not to show, is the mirror in the hall. The glass there never reflects. Sometimes she'll glimpse an empty face looking out, a vertical smile flashed wide, but it's always just a glimpse and she's relieved when the glass resumes its vacancy, the shimmering emptiness inside it.

She takes the World next to see one of her walk-in closets. Shoes for days. Much of her audience are foot fetishists, and Crystal knows the next thirty minutes of modeling her soles in various pumps will net her fifty grand easy. She once made three hundred thousand dollars painting her toenails.

She has nightmares of Rouge's Feet sometimes, waking up in a cold sweat to check them over. Make sure she hasn't become some deformed freak show like that stupid bitch she sometimes dreams of.

She settles on a special pair. Saint Laurent Opyum pumps crafted of black patent leather, with a heel sculpted into the brand's signature YSL logo. A bit on the tacky side, though most people are not bold enough to wear it.

"You're going to see me go live again in a few hours," she says. "I mean, let me enjoy my night a bit before I have to start thinking of you little maniacs."

Her second phone buzzes. She checks it off camera. Cash App transactions through the roof, giving her something to smile about.

"I had to fight hard to be able to give you access to where I'm going tonight. But the people in charge want me there. So you get to come too. In the meantime, tell me what you're in the mood for, and if something tickles my fancy, maybe I'll give you a shout in the next livestream."

The World showers her with compliments. Professions of love. So many cash donations she'll probably be in another tax bracket by breakfast.

Tonight's a political fundraiser. One hundred thousand dollars a plate to hear some politician talk about issues without solutions. Maybe she'll cause some trouble there—the World loves when she does that, but it'll be spur-of-the-moment, something planned and executed on the fly.

Crystal has mastered the move of tsking her tongue, touching fingers to her collarbone, and once a couple of people are looking, using a cocktail napkin to daub away the tears.

She doesn't remember crying because she never once has. Kylie might've, but Kylie Bennington is dead. Once in a while, Crystal catches glimpses of her. In old photos or in reflections. A scared little girl, her face a perpetual rictus, sometimes mouth open impossibly wide and endlessly screaming, trapped beneath the weight of ego, staring out helplessly at what she's become.

"I know you guys think I'm hiding something," she tells the World. "A boyfriend. Girlfriend. A house cat. But when have I ever lied to you? So, cool it with the rumors, okay? I'm *yours*, guys."

She goes to the door and carries the World with her.

The World watches as she locks up and goes to the elevator, riding down to the lobby and to the limousine that's idling on the curb.

"That's all for now," she says. "Byeeeeeee."

Crystal gives the World one last *all for you* smile and her lips push against the lens, leaving a cracked lipstick smear behind.

And then the World goes black.

Acknowledgments

Thank you to those early readers who first confirmed for me that I might have something here: my wife, Michelle, right out of that gate in the spring of 2020, and soon after Tracy Robinson and Sadie Hartmann—you were all instrumental in helping me fine-tune things along the way. Thanks to Mark Falkin, my agent, for your guidance and confidence. And to Ed Schlesinger and the rest of the team at Gallery Books/Simon & Schuster for their wisdom and expertise in helping give *Feeders* shape. Much love to my friends who've never been anything but supportive: Shaun Boutwell, Steve Bahde, Keith Gleason, Brian Collins. To Pat Lacey and Arron Dries—we're forever bound by querying woes and the magical misery of never-ending house projects. Thanks to Jamie Blanks for letting me call you a friend, and to both you and Gina Matthews for helping me become a better storyteller. Thank you, Alex Pearson, for reading my words and for sharing my obsession with vintage slashers. And genuine thanks to those who've been buying and reading me since the beginning: Christopher Glindmyer, Edwin Muñeton, John Sullivan. If I've never told you, your support way back when I had none is what made me believe I can do this. And that goes double for Mark Sieber at Horror Drive-In, who not only supported my dream of writing years before I'd ever published a word, but also gave me my first review over a decade ago. Man, those are hard to get in the beginning. There are so many more people, of course: my parents and in-laws and all the family contained therein, English teachers throughout my life who took the time to encourage my writing. That stuff matters. And there're all those I've thanked in previous books too. Writing may be a solitary thing, but nobody truly gets to the end of a novel alone.

About the Author

MATT SERAFINI is the author of ten novels, including *Rites of Extinction* and *Under the Blade*. His nonfiction has appeared in the pages of *Fangoria* and *Horror Hound*. He lives with his family in New Hampshire.